GOD
OF
FURY

RINA KENT

To the ones who scream in silence

AUTHOR NOTE

Hello reader friend,

Nikolai and Brandon's story is my first MM book, and one of the fewest stories that consumed me, heart, body, and soul. They live in me, and for a moment in time, I lived for them. Days turned into weeks and weeks turned into months, but I reveled in every lick of their intensity, every lash of their passion, and every sting of their angst.

I poured my heart onto the page to tell their story and I hope you enjoy their special, entirely explosive dynamic as I did.

If you haven't read my books before, you might not know this, but I write darker stories that can be upsetting and disturbing. My books and main characters aren't for the faint of heart.

This book isn't as dark as my other books relationship-wise, but it contains sensitive subjects. I'll list them below for your safety, but if you don't have any triggers, please skip the following paragraph as it will provide major spoilers for the plot.

God of Fury contains mental health issues, including depression, borderline personality disorder, suicidal thoughts and self-harm. There are on-page descriptions of a minor's sexual assault, suicide attempt, and violence. I trust you know your triggers before you proceed.

God of Fury is a complete STANDALONE.

For more things Rina Kent, visit www.rinakent.com

LEGACY OF GODS TREE

ROYAL ELITE UNIVERSITY

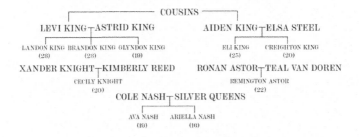

┌─────── COUSINS ───────┐

LEVI KING┬ASTRID KING   AIDEN KING┬ELSA STEEL

LANDON KING BRANDON KING GLYNDON KING   ELI KING   CREIGHTON KING
(23)   (23)   (19)   (25)   (20)

XANDER KNIGHT┬KIMBERLY REED   RONAN ASTOR┬TEAL VAN DOREN

CECILY KNIGHT   REMINGTON ASTOR
(20)   (22)

COLE NASH┬SILVER QUEENS

AVA NASH   ARIELLA NASH
(19)   (16)

THE KING'S U'S COLLEGE

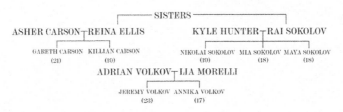

┌─────── SISTERS ───────┐

ASHER CARSON┬REINA ELLIS   KYLE HUNTER┬RAI SOKOLOV

GARETH CARSON KILLIAN CARSON   NIKOLAI SOKOLOV MIA SOKOLOV MAYA SOKOLOV
(21)   (19)   (19)   (18)   (18)

ADRIAN VOLKOV┬LIA MORELLI

JEREMY VOLKOV ANNIKA VOLKOV
(23)   (17)

I'm not attracted to men.

Or so I thought before I slammed into Nikolai Sokolov.

A mafia heir, a notorious bastard, and a violent monster.

An ill-fated meeting puts me in his path.

And just like that, he has his sights set on me.

A quiet artist, a golden boy, and his enemy's twin brother.

He doesn't seem to care that the odds are stacked against us.

In fact, he sets out to break my steel-like control and blur my limits.

I thought my biggest worry was being noticed by Nikolai.

I'm learning the hard way that being wanted by this beautiful nightmare is much worse.

PLAYLIST

Yellow—Coldplay

Do I Wanna Know—Arctic Monkeys

I Wanna Be Yours—Arctic Monkeys

Your Blood—Nothing But Thieves

Impossible—Nothing But Thieves

Demons—MISSIO

Maniacs—Conan Gray

Run Into Trouble—Bastille & Alok

Somebody Else—The 1975

Someone Else—Loveless

Losing Control—Villain of the Story

Yours—Conan Gray

Sorry I'm Yours—Circa Wales

Half-Life—Essenger

Dear Reader—Taylor Swift

Half of My Heart—Josh Makazo

Silence—Marshmello & Khalid

You can find the complete playlist on Spotify.

GOD

OF

FURY

ONE

Brandon

WHAT AM I DOING HERE?
Deep in the hollow corner of my heart, I know the answer. I know it so well that I can taste the nausea that slithered down my throat and hooked onto my bones the moment I got that godforsaken text.

A text I should've very well ignored, deleted, and then blocked the number.

A text I shouldn't have dignified with a look, let alone given it enough weight to intervene with my decision-making.

I did.

And that's the reason I'm here.

I did.

And now, I've put myself in an irreversible position.

I did.

And I'm not sure I can shove this lapse of judgment on to the possibility of having no choice.

In reality, I do.

I've just never been good with choices. Don't appreciate them. Don't care for them. Would rather not be presented with one.

The text was an obligation or, more accurately, a pertinent piece of information.

It was *not* a choice and certainly *not* a situation I could've escaped.

The reason I'm here is sorely due to my sense of responsibility that I've carried like excess baggage since I started learning what life is all about.

I'm at what looks like an indoctrination center. Other students stand on either side of me, forming parallel lines and wearing white rabbit masks that cover their features.

We're facing a huge three-story mansion with old-looking stone walls and an ancient tower on the far right.

The longer I remain unmoving, the more unsteady my breathing becomes.

My inhales and exhales flow in a fast, fractured rhythm, forming condensation on the plastic and forcing me to breathe my own air.

Tick.

The sound is low, but it slams into my brain like a fatal crash. My mouth starts to fill with saliva and I gulp it down, forcing my stomach to settle.

Tick.

I lift my hand, about to pull at my skull. Sometimes, I wish I could smash it against the nearest wall and watch as everything spills and shatters. Once and for fucking all.

Tick.

My fingers curl in midair, but I lower my hand and force it to hang limp at my side.

It's fine. I can do this.

Breathe.

You're in control.

My soothing words of affirmation splinter and crack as the scene around me comes back into focus.

No matter how much I attempt to delude myself, the reality is that I'm in the last place I should be.

And I'm not one to challenge fate or go places I'm not supposed to.

In my twenty-three years of life, I've always been the type of man who follows the rules. I've never deviated from what's expected of me and I'm creeped out at the notion of being different.

In any sense.

For whatever reason.

And yet here I am at the Heathens' mansion because I received a text and made the conscious decision *not* to ignore it.

I made the decision to attend the initiation of the most notorious club on Brighton Island—a secluded place near the UK's southwest coast.

For a university I'm not even enrolled in.

The Heathens are the leading club of The King's U college. A uni that reeks of mafia money and *la nouveau bourgeoisie*, where all American students flock like birds of a feather.

We have our own malicious club at Royal Elite University—or REU—where I'm working on my master's degree in art. It's called the Elites and is led by none other than my headache of a twin brother, Landon.

However, The King's U's clubs—the Heathens and the Serpents—are much more nefarious since they come from real mafia families and are using the uni experience to sharpen their fangs for the leading roles awaiting them back in the States.

If a week ago someone had told me I'd be standing here wearing a creepy rabbit mask and waiting for the entitled, violence-thirsty Americans to make their appearance, I would've laughed.

I'm certainly not laughing now. A lot of variables have changed in the span of a week and I find myself under the obligation to be here.

As part of the herd.

And it has everything to do with that headache of a brother I mentioned earlier.

Though they took my phone at the entrance, I can still recall the text I received yesterday word for word.

Heathens: Congratulations! You are invited to the Heathens' initiation ceremony. Please show the attached QR code upon arrival at the club's compound at four p.m. sharp.

While I'd heard of their nefarious initiations, I had absolutely no interest in them or the clubs. If I did, I would've joined the Elites since Lan has been asking for years.

So I ignored that text and was about to block the number, but then I got another one.

Unknown Number: If you want to see your twin brother breathing instead of being shoved in a casket and showcased to all participants, be at the initiation.

That's the reason I came here, even though every fiber of my being revolted against the idea of taking part in this madness. I called and texted Lan, but he didn't reply, so I had to save him from himself as usual.

My brother has always been the reason I've deviated from the core of my existence, though he'd argue this is my true character, and what I consider normal is a product of repressing.

Hiding.

Shackling my real self.

A sudden movement comes from my side and I tighten my muscles, ready to run away, move from the center of danger and pretend none of this has taken place.

The girl beside me—judging by her breasts and frame—laughs as she hits her companion's shoulder.

A general murmur of excitement bubbles in the air.

I don't understand people's obsession with these types of events. Is it the feeling of grandiosity? The opportunity to walk amongst gods?

But then again, it's impossible for me to understand some people due to how drastically different my personality is compared to the rest of my peers.

Don't get me wrong. I get along with almost everyone and I'm often described as extremely polite and a good sport, but my close friends are only a few. The only reason we're tight is because we grew up together and I spent several years familiarizing myself with their personalities.

Maybe my inability to form close connections after my childhood is due to being completely detached from most people's source of happiness. A glaring example is my complete bafflement at these people's sense of a thrill. They talk about the Heathens as if they're the personification of everything they aspire to be.

Wealth, influence, and, most importantly, morbid power.

I, Brandon King, belong to one of the most influential families in the UK, if not *the* most influential, but I still don't get people's obsession with selected elites.

Is it the illusion? The unknown? Something entirely different?

The girl's chatter comes to a halt and she looks up as everyone else grows silent. I follow her field of vision and pause when the balcony doors on the second floor open and five men stroll outside, all of them wearing neon-stitch Halloween-esque masks.

The one in the middle has an orange mask and carries a metal club. He's tall and broad, but the guy by his side who's wearing a yellow mask is taller and buffer, and he reeks of hostility, even from this distance.

He stands out because he's the only one without a weapon, but he still emanates a nefarious energy. The rest of them, however, seem to have their thoughts and tempers under control.

Red Mask's fingers wrap around a bat, letting it rest nonchalantly on his shoulder.

A recurve bow is nestled in Green Mask's hand and there's a quiver attached to his back, and White Mask strokes a heavy-looking chain that's hanging around his neck.

They're all dressed in black T-shirts and trousers like a conformist unit of destruction.

Fortunately, I've never crossed the Heathens' paths or interacted with them, which can't be said about my prick of a brother. Is he with them? Perhaps he's playing a sick game to be part of their inner circle?

Or is he maybe somewhere in front of me or behind me? Maybe next to me?

The problem is, I can never imagine Lan being a participant in another group's glory or a mere follower in someone else's mayhem. He's too narcissistic for that. Besides, how could he possibly get an invitation?

The same way I got invited?

Probably.

Maybe.

I watch the five Heathens closely. The one in orange, standing tall in the middle, is most likely Jeremy Volkov, the leader of the Heathens and a Russian mafia prince. If my friends' gossip can be trusted, he's ruthless to a fault and is rumored to kill everyone in his wake.

Green and Red Masks are possibly Gareth and Killian Carson. The siblings are affiliated with the mafia but are more American royalty instead of mafia princes. However, I'm not sure which is which. White Mask seems like the leanest of the bunch, so he can't be any of the three previously mentioned.

Yellow Mask can only be Nikolai Sokolov. Another Russian mafia prince, Killian and Gareth's cousin, and the craziest twat who ever walked the earth.

If rumors are anything to go by—and in Nikolai's case, they probably are—he's capable of punching someone to death just because they had the audacity to piss him off. I've only stood close to him once, a week ago when—*again*—my twin brother was fighting him in an underground fight club.

I honest to God thought he'd pummel Lan to death.

He didn't, because my brother is a cat with nine lives.

My concern about Lan shifted to disturbing unease when Nikolai looked at me with a manic expression while wearing my brother's blood on his bandaged hands.

I had this inherent need to get the hell out of there. And I did— after dragging my brother along, of course.

I've never gotten that feeling from someone younger than me, and Nikolai is *way* younger. Nineteen, I think. A kid right out of secondary school—high school for Americans.

Only, he looks *nothing* like a kid.

Even now, while wearing black clothes, his build stands out as if he's sculpted from pure muscle and malicious intent.

Good thing I don't run in these people's circle and never will.

Today is an exception. The sooner I locate Lan, the faster I can leave this immoral place.

Static rings in the air before a distorted voice speaks from all around us.

"Congratulations on making it to the Heathens' highly competitive initiation. You are the selected elite the leaders of the club think are worthy of joining their world of power and connections. The price to pay for such privileges is higher than money, status, or name. The reason everyone wears a mask is because you are all the same in the eyes of the club's founders. The price of becoming a Heathen is handing over your life. In the literal sense of the word. If you aren't willing to pay that, please exit through the small door to your left. Once you leave, you'll lose any chance to join us again."

A door beside the big gate opens, and about a dozen or less people exit. I contemplate joining them and putting an end to this madness, but I'd never, in good conscience, abandon my brother.

Never.

The distorted voice returns. "Congratulations again, ladies and gentlemen. We shall now begin our initiation."

I lift my head to the five Heathens, who remain unmoving. Completely grounded, absolutely apathetic about the promise of violence they're unleashing on the world.

All except for one.

The anomaly.

Violence on steroids.

Yellow Mask clenches and unclenches his fists at a rhythmic pace as if he's performing a ritual. That guy needs to be locked up instead of being allowed to be part of this nonsensical initiation.

"Tonight's game is predator and prey," the voice continues. "You'll be hunted down by the club's founding members. That will be five to ninety, so you have the upper hand. If you manage to reach the edge of the property before they hunt you down, you'll be a Heathen. If not, you'll be eliminated and escorted out. The founding members have the right to use any methods available to hunt you down—including violence. If their weapon of choice touches you, you'll be automatically eliminated. Bodily harm can and will happen. You are also allowed to inflict violence on the founding members—if you can. The only rule is not taking a life. Not intentionally, at least. No questions are allowed and no mercy shall be granted. We don't want any weaklings in our ranks."

Barbarians. The lot of them. Hopeless, outrageous savages with no grace whatsoever.

But then again, what to expect from mafia people?

"You have a ten-minute head start. I suggest you run. The initiation has officially begun."

The girl beside me and her companions sprint so fast, the pebbles crunch beneath their trainers. Everyone else rushes in the direction of the forest and I'm left with the option of following or remaining here like easy prey.

Cursing under my breath, I run as fast as possible. My heart rate remains the same—unperturbed, calm, and completely unaffected by the lick of danger and the lust for the thrill that hangs in the air like splashes of magenta on turquoise blue.

I guess that's the upside of having an abnormal brain. This type of nonsense doesn't affect it.

Despite going late, I manage to run faster and farther than the other participants. I might not be into these types of events, but I'm an athlete, pretty much a professional runner and also the captain of the lacrosse team at REU.

I take my physical activities seriously and never miss a day of training and running, whether for the team or for myself.

It's important to keep order and discipline, and I'm nothing short of perfection in creating stability and habits.

Besides, if I don't maintain a routine, I'll only slither down that rabbit hole of nothingness and eventually skid into an unfortunate freak accident.

No thanks.

In no time, I manage to reach what looks like the middle of the forest after losing the rest of the students. Late afternoon light casts ominous patches of orange on the dirt and between the huge trees.

But soon enough, the gray clouds strangle the beams of hope and swallow them into darkness.

I crouch behind a large bush that covers my entire frame and wait.

That's all I can do at this point.

Stay low. Wait. Observe. And never *ever* draw attention to my presence.

An activity I excel at.

If Lan shows up, whether as one of the Heathens—which is highly unlikely—or one of the participants, I'll get a gut feeling thanks to the useless twin hunch.

A few people run by like a pack of wolves, squeals of excitement falling from their lips and painting the sky in blotches of brick red on midnight black.

The stench of mindless violence lingers in the air and forms sinister halos around the participants' heads.

Their thrill is short-lived, though. Orange Mask stalks right after them, carrying his vicious club. I silently cringe when he hits one of them so hard, their face swings to the side, and blood explodes on his mask, which cracks in two.

I catch a glimpse of someone walking around dazed with an arrow stuck in his shoulder and a limp arm glued to his side.

Eliminated students' numbers are announced by that disturbing robotic voice, sometimes one after the other. I think the process is automatic, because whenever I catch a glimpse of someone getting hit by an arrow or Orange Mask's club, their number is immediately announced.

Throughout the whole freak show, I don't move, and when I do, it's only to adjust my position.

Where are you, Lan?

While I take pride in my stamina, I probably can't keep this up for an extended period of time.

Maybe I should strategically move to another nook of this extravagant forest in case my brother is on the other side—

A sudden chill scrapes the back of my neck, followed by scorching hot heat as a deep, rumbling voice whispers in my ear, "Why aren't you running?"

My senses saturate in a rush of overwhelming external stimuli and my brain is unable to keep up with the overload. I lose balance and fall on my arse, hitting the ground with an impact that reverberates in my bones.

I stare up, my eyes clashing with the yellow-stitch mask that's marred with splashes of dark red.

Blood.

It's everywhere—clinging to his mask, staining his dark shirt, forming rivulets on his neck, covering the tattoos on the backs of his hands like gloves, and sticking to strands of his jet-black hair that falls in waves to his shoulder blades.

Nausea floods my mouth and shoots straight to my fucked-up brain.

Tick.

Tick.

Tick tick tick tick—

"You didn't answer the question." Yellow Mask's gruff tone ripples down my throat and drowns the nausea, only to substitute it with dread.

Harsh and poignant.

What's worse is that I can't breathe.

The wanker is crouching close. So close that my nostrils fill with the metallic stench of blood and the smell of cigarettes, alcohol, and a hint of mint and bergamot.

The overwhelming mixture flows and floods my senses like a chaotic swirl of colors that blend and throttle each pigment until they settle on unassuming gray.

Faultless. Timeless. *Empty.*

Yellow Mask, who can only be Nikolai, pokes my forehead with a bloody finger. And although he's only touching the mask and not my skin, my stomach cramps, choking out rampant nausea that's ready to lurch forward and leave me heaving.

"Oy. You listening?" He's only using a forefinger, yet so much power emanates off the single action that I crack under the pressure. I've never been good with direct confrontations and prefer not to engage in them. Besides, if what I've heard of his infamous reputation is true, I could never take on Nikolai Sokolov, even if I were reincarnated a few times in the spirit of a warrior.

He's notorious for his savage behavior, unhinged tendencies, and penchant for breathing violence instead of oxygen. The evidence is splattered in red all over his person.

Definitely the last person I'd want to get in a disagreement with.

He clucks his tongue, the sound exceptionally loud despite the constant announcements of eliminated numbers.

I don't hear mine, eighty-nine, but Nikolai doesn't have a weapon like the rest, so maybe he has to do it himself.

Meaning, if I escape, I can resume my hiding game and look for my brother. I swear I'm going to be so cross with him about this mess—

Nikolai circles his forefinger against my forehead, but then he seems to wipe something. His movements come to a halt and his body remains so completely still, I cease to breathe.

The hostility and thirst for blood that emanated off him subside. Or more like, they lessen in intensity, no longer tightening his outrageously ludicrous muscles and bulging biceps.

Although he's crouching, his height and broadness are unmistakable. At six-foot-three, I'm not short by any stretch of the imagination, but Nikolai has an inch or two on me, and he's ridiculously pumped with more muscles than anyone needs.

But then again, he seems like the archetype of a sadist who gets off on inflicting pain.

However, that doesn't seem to be the case right now.

The flood of violence that he exuded in threatening waves a few seconds ago has been replaced by something a lot more morbid.

Amusement.

No, curiosity?

Interest?

His finger falls from the mask, but before I can release a breath, he suddenly wraps his hand around my nape, near the hairs I constantly assault.

Maybe it's because that area is particularly battered and sensitive, but the moment his rough skin touches mine, a flood of what I assume is nausea threatens to spill from my gut.

Only, it's not nausea.

It's—

Nikolai barks out laughter that echoes around us in a swell of burgundy and hot red-orange. "There you are. I've been looking everywhere for you, eighty-nine."

TWO

Brandon

"Y**OU KNOW WHO I AM?**"

I have no clue how the words tumble out of my mouth—in a sickeningly unsteady voice, I might add.

Tick.

A crack appears in my outer walls and extends to the ground beneath me.

Tick.

The black hole widens, and muddy black ink swallows my feet until I can't feel them.

Tick—

"Hmm. Should I?" The rumbling gruff of Nikolai's voice sounds sinister, reinforced by the splashes of blood on his neon mask.

I've been in a constant state of hyperawareness ever since he crowded my space, but that's not right.

This isn't how it's supposed to be.

A puff of breath heaves out of my constricted chest and, with it, my inhales and exhales return to normal.

I'm thinking too much—as usual.

I need to get back to working out or painting my calming nature scenes so I'll stop this vicious cycle of red on black.

Or, more accurately, black on dead gray.

I *can't* think. Thinking leads to fucked-up images that I'd rather leave in the unremarkable shed of my barely beating heart.

Nikolai sinks his fingers into my nape, digging into the skin until I *feel* him instead of *see* him.

"The answer is yes, preppy boy. I should know who you are, shouldn't I?"

A wave of rage tightens my muscles and I let it wash over me as I fall into it.

Rage is better than nausea.

Rage is certainly much more welcome than the doomsday ticking my brain practices like an orthodox religion.

How dare he talk to me in that mocking tone? I'm Brandon King and that last name means something in this world.

But you don't. Without your papa's last name, you're nothing.

The voice rolls in like sandpaper on glass, leaving a dry, scratchy feeling at the back of my throat.

I swallow the sudden rotten taste and force myself to calm down as I slap Nikolai's arm.

He doesn't move, not even one inch, as if his brute fingers are now an extension of my nape.

"Let go," I say or, more accurately, order. I'm nice and pleasant until someone oversteps, which Nikolai has been doing with flying colors since he surprised the shit out of me.

"In a hurry to go somewhere?"

"More like, I don't appreciate being touched, especially if the hands are filthy."

He stares at his free palm under the slowly setting sun that casts an orange glow on his haphazard jet-black hair. He glances at the dried blood as if he forgot it was there and lifts a casual shoulder. "You'll get used to it."

Get used to what?

Is this freak high or something?

I wouldn't be surprised if he snorted coke like a nineties rock star and smoked more weed than Bob Marley's fan club before this damned initiation.

"Let. Go," I repeat in a firm voice and push at his arm with all my strength.

He loosens his grip but doesn't release me.

An appreciative hum falls from somewhere in his throat. "Bossy. I like it. But you know what I like more? Your posh little accent. Question. Does it sound the same when you say crude things?"

I narrow my eyes. What on earth is wrong with this twat? Did someone hit him upside the head?

"This is the third and final time I'm telling you this. Let. Go."

"Why?" He strokes his fingers near my hairline and that wave of something that's not nausea courses through my veins in flashes of bright yellow. "I rather like it here."

"I don't." I tighten my muscles against the morbid unease flooding my bloodstream. "You disgust me."

"Yeah?" His eyes, the color of midnight-blue sky, twinkle with pure sadism as he leans closer and murmurs, "Even better."

His warm breaths skim the side of my neck. My jaw clenches and it takes everything in me to ward off the discomfort that's still *not* nausea.

Not in the least.

The sensation spreads from where his fingers glide over my nape and ends at my earlobe, where he whispered.

I need out of here. *Now.*

I reach to the ground behind me and grab the first object I find and then haul it square against his face.

He loses his hold on my neck and I don't wait to see his reaction as I jump up and sprint behind the bushes.

Fast.

Not looking behind.

I run as if we're in overtime during a game and the team depends on me passing the ball to the attackers.

It's me against the screwed-up notion of time. It's always been that way.

The sense of apprehension is replaced by a shot of adrenaline and the inherent need to escape.

Far.

So far.

A dark figure nearly slams into me and we both skid to a halt right before we crash into one another.

Red Mask.

He's carrying his bloody baseball bat and watches me as if I'm an insect that crossed his path.

The rush of adrenaline slowly dissipates and a tremor spreads in my limbs like wildfire.

Stop shaking.

Stop shaking, you damn weakling.

Stop!

I nearly manage to crack the sudden sporadic emotions, but disgust lurches from my stomach to my throat faster than I can blink.

The distinctive smell of alcohol, cigarettes, bergamot, and the stench of metallic blood envelops me.

No.

No.

No.

I glance behind me and my eyes clash with Nikolai's darker ones. They're more unhinged than a witch during a pagan funeral, bloodshot and filled with a promise of drawing blood.

My blood.

Not allowing myself to think about it, I walk in Red Mask's direction. He can hit me with that bat, for all I care. Maybe I'll be lucky and will lose consciousness and, therefore, can remove my brain from this situation.

"Look, I caught a stray cat." Nikolai's rough voice sounds like the trigger for nightmares. "He just wouldn't stop running, you know, and has a temper. Threw a whole fucking branch at my face and nearly knocked me out. Gotta love the motherfucking feisty ones. They're so fun to break into pieces."

I stride to Red Mask, who studies me up and down and then lifts the bat.

Finally.

It's done.

It's *over*.

I'll go back to a world where I don't cross paths with these wastes of human—

A heavy weight lands on my back, and I flinch as a strong arm wraps around my neck and nearly crushes my windpipe.

I can't breathe.

I can't—

Survival instinct kicks in and I elbow Nikolai with every ounce of energy I have left. He might as well be a wall because not only does he not release me, but he also tightens his grip.

Panic stiffens my muscles and I push with feral strength and bite him at some point, but Nikolai doesn't flinch. He drags me behind the trees, my feet scraping the ground, and I open my mouth to call for help, even if it's from another damned Heathen.

Nikolai slams another hand on my mouth, digging the mask against my lips. "Shhh. I'm going to need you to shut the fuck up."

My words come in mumbled, haunted sounds, like in those creepy horror movies where the nerd dies first.

That's me. I'm the nerd.

In a last-ditch attempt, I throw the entirety of my weight back. My muscle mass doesn't compare to his, but I work out a lot.

I run, too. More than should be humanly allowed.

Nikolai loses his footing and I dart to my right, but the world is pulled from beneath my feet. He tackles me to the ground, and I land on my stomach.

A massive weight slams against my back, and Nikolai is on top of me like a brick wall.

I cough, straining, and my deep inhale forces me to breathe in tiny particles of dirt. My lungs burn and I realize it's because he still has me in a chokehold.

"A fucking fighter. Jackpot." His voice echoes like the dark ink from my fucked-up nightmares. "Fight me more. Do it harder. Stronger. Faster. I want the fight!"

I tap his arm twice, wheezing and gasping for breath.

I get lightheaded and spots of yellow and orange spark behind my heavy lids.

"No fight?" He sounds disappointed. "Fine, guess you can't if you're being choked. If I release you, will you behave?"

My short nails scratch the long sleeves of his shirt, and he hums. "Though I'm fine with the status quo. I rather like this position."

Humiliation rushes through my bloodstream like poison as the feel of his body crushing mine registers faster than the lack of oxygen. His chest covers my back and his knee is jammed between my thighs. His entire weight spreads over me and he's so damn heavy.

I press myself against the dirt as if that will help me escape him. A dark chuckle erupts in my ear as he loosens his grip enough for me to breathe.

He makes no move to release me or push the hell off me, though.

I inhale cracked breaths and cough at the sudden rush of air.

"Anyone ever tell you how fucking hot you feel when struggling for control? I could swallow you alive and leave no crumbs." The last sentence is whispered against my earlobe and I nearly retch.

Out of my skin.

Out of my fucked-up brain.

I don't know where I get the strength, but I elbow him and crawl from beneath him faster than he can blink.

Once I'm on my feet, I start to run—

"I take it you're not worried about your brother?"

I come to a halt and slowly turn around. Nikolai is on his feet, arms crossed and head tilted to the side as he watches me nonchalantly.

Only, there's nothing nonchalant about him. The twat could only be described as mental.

"Heard he's into a lot of shit," he continues. "Landon, I mean. He's the reason you're here, right?"

My eyes widen behind the mask. "Are you the one who sent me the invitation?"

"And you didn't disappoint. Brother love for the win."

I storm toward him and grab him by the collar of his shirt, hauling him so close, his chest collides with mine. "Where is he?"

His hand shoots up to my hair and he grabs a handful, pulling at the roots until my head snaps back, then he peers down at me. "Where do you think?"

My grip doesn't loosen on his collar. I don't care if he's crazy or downright insane. If he messes with my loved ones, I'll be his worst enemy.

"Don't make me repeat myself," I grind out.

"Why? What will happen if you repeat yourself? I'm kinda curious, and by kinda, I mean I have to know. Now."

"You—" I cut myself off because his mask scrapes against mine. His breath bathes the plastic and my lips.

"Hmm? What? What am I?" he asks with an edge of lunacy, like a child ghost in a haunted castle who keeps repeating himself in a distorted voice.

I shove him away and he stumbles back, letting go of my hair, but like an elastic band, he bounces right back, invading my space and crowding me.

He's much more looming and intimidating in person. And I don't even get intimidated.

"Stop!" I place both hands up and the bastard bumps right against them, his muscles flexing beneath my fingers.

"You still didn't tell me what I am. Go on. Don't leave me hanging." He grins, the motion looking savage behind the bloodied mask. "Is it something good? Or bad? Either? Neither? Both?"

"Just *stop*." I have to keep all my strength in my hands as he pushes and wiggles against them like a damn bull.

The sound of his tut echoes in the air as he finally quits trying to glue his chest to mine.

I still keep my hands up, not trusting him to discontinue his frantic movements. I can't help noticing how taut he is, like a wall.

His pectoral muscles twitch beneath my fingers and I drop my arms to either side of me, chasing away the haze and the strange taste of adrenaline.

When I speak, my voice is calm. Collected. In control. "Landon. Where is he?"

"Fucking dull preppy kids," he mutters under his breath, then turns on his heel and marches in the opposite direction.

I stand there for a few seconds, my breathing condensing on the interior of the mask. Then I follow after, my legs feeling weightless and completely foreign, as if they're no longer an extension of my body.

"Are you taking me to him?" I ask when I fall in step beside Nikolai.

He whips his head in my direction and I have to suppress a cringe at the sight of blood. It's not a view I'll ever get used to, no matter how long I try.

"If I do that, what will you do for me?" he asks with that glint that I swear was muted not two minutes ago.

"Not report you to the police for your illegal activities. Though you should consider a change of hobbies to something less violent."

"But where's the fun in that?"

"Being normal for once?"

"Is that spelled boring?" He gets close and I step to the side, narrowly escaping his shoulder bumping into mine.

"Back off."

"Ah, fuck. I want to defrost that layer of control you're wrapped in and see what lurks inside the preppy boy."

My teeth clench and I release them slowly so as not to trigger the sensation I've been coexisting with for most of my life. "I'm not a boy."

"Whatever you say, posh kid."

"What the hell is your problem?"

"Me?" He points a thumb at himself. "You seem to be the one crowded with issues, boy."

My nostrils flare and my hand balls into a fist.

You have issues.

Lots of them.

You don't want to be a disappointment.

Nikolai tilts his gaze to my hand, bouncing off his heels as if he's waiting for a Christmas present. "What you gonna do with that? Punch me? Just so you know, you might get disgusting blood on your pretty hands."

The urge to hit him snaps my muscles into a tight knot, but I force my fingers to uncurl.

I don't do violence. *Ever.*

This crazy wanker won't be changing that.

"No? Bummer." As fast as they sparkled, his eyes become muted again, turning into two orbs of black.

Black on black.

Black on—

I briefly close my eyes to chase away the clouded thoughts. When I open them, I catch a glimpse of Nikolai stalking into what looks like an annexed house.

I didn't notice it earlier during our walk, too focused on the bastard and his unpredictable behavior to watch where the hell we were going.

Against my better judgment, I slip in behind him. Not that I have a choice. Nikolai knows where Landon is and I need to make sure my twin brother is safe.

The interior looks far simpler than the outside—clean and clinical—but the white walls are smudged with dirt in places. The decor consists of a leather sofa and a table against the wall, and there's a door to what appears to be a storage closet.

I stand at the entrance as Nikolai throws his weight on the sofa, arms flung on the back and legs wide apart like one of those macho guys who think they own the world.

He beckons me over with a forefinger and I snarl behind my mask. And I don't even snarl.

I don't run away or elbow or scream for help, either, and I've done all of the above this evening. Thanks to this bastard.

"Do that again and I'll break your finger," I deliver the threat with calmness and a smile. He probably can't see it, but fuck it.

"Get your ass over here if you want to see your brother breathe another day."

My shoulders tense and I take careful steps toward him, each one echoing a louder-than-necessary sound.

It isn't until I'm within arm's reach that I realize he's crowding the sofa that should fit at least three people.

I'm still contemplating his sheer size when a noise spills from my lips. A startled, funny noise that feels foreign as it scratches out of my throat.

But I don't focus on that, more concerned with the reason behind said noise.

Nikolai grabs me by the wrist and hauls me over so fast, I land on him, my chest crashing against his and our masks bumping.

The assault on my senses is much more prominent this time as that stupid glint rushes to his previously muted eyes. "Well, hello there. Lovely of you to finally join the party."

I bite back a curse as I attempt to get up. Nikolai lets me, but then I make the mistake of turning my back.

Brutish hands land on my hips and I stifle whatever noise that's trying to escape. A curse. It was definitely another curse.

And it doesn't matter that I actually don't curse.

Nikolai drags me down and my arse meets a hard surface. His thighs.

What the—

Panic dashes in my veins and I start to get up, but he pushes with enough force to knock my bones against his. "Stay fucking still unless you're in the mood to take care of the boner you're giving me."

My face falls, figuratively, of course. I'd pay money for it to disappear literally. Indefinitely.

I try again, needing to escape the wanker. But before I can move, he wraps his arm around my waist and spreads his palm over my stomach. "Someone has nice abs."

"Stop touching me and throwing out sexual innuendos," I hiss under my breath, sinking my fingers into his arm and pushing. "I'm straight and have no interest in your weird nonsense."

He chuckles, the sound reverberating like a symphony gone wrong. "You don't say."

"What the hell is that supposed to mean?"

"I don't know. The fact that you say *sexual innuendos*, maybe. Such a preppy boy."

"What?"

Whatever he has to say is drowned out by voices and the shuffling of feet outside. Green Mask stalks in from another door to the right that I didn't notice and I stiffen.

The situation I'm in registers quickly and heat rushes to my head. I'm sitting on a random guy's lap.

Me. Brandon fucking King.

Yet I remain completely still, not wanting to draw attention to myself. I'm wearing the mask anyway. If I stay still, he won't look at me or notice me—

My jaw nearly hits the floor when none other than my baby sister rushes through the door, her cheeks red and her demeanor flustered. Glyn stares at me and I feel as if I'm being stripped naked, free falling from the sky without a safety net.

I lower my head, staring at my feet, and soon, that dark inky water swallows them whole, creeping up my calves and to my knees.

Veiny-like tendrils strap around my flesh in a vise, pulling, gripping, plunging me into the endless hole.

Down.

Down.

Down—

"She's gone," a chilling voice whispers in my ear and I jerk.

The black ink slowly dissipates and I lift my head to find that Glyn and Green Mask are disappearing out a third door to the left.

I release a puff of air, but it gets stuck in my throat when Nikolai strokes his hand on my stomach.

It's over my shirt, but it's like he's scratching at the surface of my skin, nearly peeling it off the muscles. A burn erupts at the pit of my belly and rushes to the rest of my limbs.

"Such a responsible brother. First, you came here because I made up a story about Landon, and now, you're worried about your sister. We have something in common. I like it."

My head spins, mostly due to his breath near my ear, his hand on my stomach, and his rock-hard thighs underneath mine.

Then something he said comes back to me and I narrow my eyes. "You made up a story about Lan?"

He lifts a shoulder. "How else would I have gotten you here? On my lap, I mean."

A volcano of rage splinters inside me, and I want to punch his fucking stitch mask so bad.

So, *so* bad.

But I don't, because I don't do that.

I use the energy to push against him and spring up. "Take your nonsense away from me. Far away."

That glint flashes again, but before I can find out what type of absurdity he's planning, Jeremy walks through the door Glyn and Green Mask disappeared through, holding his orange mask and a bloodied club.

He's only second to Nikolai in broadness and unpleasant facial expressions. But where the arsehole behind me is outwardly loud, violent, and generally obnoxious, Jeremy is the calmer version. The type who appears collected, but is in fact as notorious as his precious idiot friend.

He's scowling now, seeming lost in thought as he throws his club on the ground and runs his fingers through his damp hair that's stuck to his nape.

"Jer!" Nikolai jumps to my side and wraps an arm around my shoulders as if we're mates. "Meet eighty-nine. Pretty sure he's the only one who made it here and, therefore, can be a member of the Heathens."

Jeremy lifts his head and takes in the scene for the first time. He was so lost in his own head that he didn't even notice us.

He cocks his brows at Nikolai, then narrows his eyes on where he's grabbing me.

I flash the crazy bastard a death glare that he lets roll off his bloodied mask as if it was never there.

He's high. Must be.

There's no other explanation for why he'd think the twin brother of Lan, aka his worst enemy, should join his precious club's ranks. Or why he'd possibly think I would.

Now that I know Lan isn't in danger, I have no reason to tolerate his distasteful presence.

I shove his hand off my shoulder, not bothering to hide my contempt, and turn around and leave.

No, I run.

Far. Away.

THREE

Nikolai

KOLYA JR. HAS BEEN AN ADVENTUROUS WHORE SINCE HE got his first boner at the fresh age of five.

It was such a marvelous discovery when I found my then-wiener hard that I giggled with glee. Then I proceeded to run all over our house, dangling, pointing, and showing it off to anyone who crossed my path while shouting, "Look! I have a gun!"

Dad laughed his head off. Mom looked like she was going to either throw up or burst into flames.

Good times.

For me and my dad. Definitely not for my mom since she was covering my twin sisters' eyes, ushering them inside, and telling me to get my *weenie* back in my pants.

I pouted as I muttered, "But my weenie really likes the air."

Mom looked at the sky, probably to the invisible big bro up there, and when that didn't work, she directed her gaze at the actual semblance of a real God in our lives. My dad.

After he laughed his ass off—five out of five sense of humor on that man, love him—he helped me pack a pouty Kolya away, and sure as shit, my dick had every right to be offended since his first show was put to a nonconsensual halt.

Dad told me that I actually couldn't use my wiener as a gun. At least, *not yet*—see, told you that man has the best sense of humor, as expected of my dad—and stripping in front of my baby sisters is a no-no.

He also said the stupid rule where I couldn't be naked all the time. Fucking social restrictions and all that bullshit.

At any rate, that was the official birth of Kolya Jr., or Kolya for short. Kolya happens to be the Russian diminutive form of my name, but it's rarely used, and only by my very Russian grandfather, who snarls at the reality that Niko won the nickname battle a hundred to one.

And no, Grandpa doesn't know I actually call my dick Kolya or I'd need to revoke my Russian card. And that's no fun. I breathe vodka.

Anyway, ever since that boner incident, Kolya has become the sluttiest, most adventurous cock anyone would ever meet.

He's resourceful, to put it mildly, and a flat-out whore if we're being fucking blunt.

Part of his extended arsenal is being easy to satisfy. Give him a willing hole and he's weeping in joy—literally.

So imagine my goddamn bafflement when he woke up today and chose the silent treatment.

I presented an especially sexually frustrated Kolya with his favorite flavors. At the same time.

A dick and a pussy? Fucking jackpot, if you ask me.

After the initiation, I got back to the Heathens' mansion and shot three of my contacts a text to come and worship at Kolya's altar.

All three of them replied, so what the fuck? A foursome sounded like fun, so I told them to come the fuck over, and they did, stacked with weed and booze, and one was chewing on a blue pill.

Not sure you're supposed to chew on it, but I couldn't be bothered and gave him vodka to help...uh...with digestion and shit.

Don't ask me how I know those two guys and the girl. The girl is from school, probably. Again, don't ask what happens at school. I'm studying business there, but I've barely attended any classes since I've been at college. As long as I keep my GPA up, thanks to my superior genes, nobody cares. Me included.

The two guys, anyone's guess. I happen to attract a lot of attention—might have to do with Kolya's extravagant magic cross piercing that many swear made them see heaven.

Or hell. Depending on their kink.

Also, it might have to do with how unbothered I am by any request. Once, a girl was like, "Choke me, Daddy," and I nearly killed her. In my defense, she didn't specify how *hard* I should choke her, so I went with the flow—the flow being maximum violence.

Another guy sent me a text saying, "Are you looking for a doormat? Because you can step on me any day and I'd bend over and take it." So I did just that and stepped on him. *What?* He asked for it and, I kid you not, he jizzed all over my room. Then he did bend over and took it.

Fun times.

Last night, however, most definitely was *not.*

It was so far from fun, it gave me fucking whiplash.

I had three sexy-as-fuck people at my disposal and Kolya was playing hard to get like a virgin motherfucker. Which he's not.

For the first time in my nineteen years of life, I couldn't get off. Not when they offered their mouths, holes, and everything in between. In fact, I wasn't even motivated to release Kolya from his least favorite confinement—my pants.

They soon forgot about me and turned to one another while I watched, sitting on the stairs and nursing a bottle of good ole vodka. It was a threesome of epic proportions that started with making out, sucking each other off, and both guys double penetrating the girl and fucking her senseless until she nearly passed out. At some point, they pushed her aside. Viagra boy clearly couldn't get enough, so he bent the other guy over, fucked him, then nutted in his ass. Or I think he did. Because that's the point where I fell asleep.

At the bottom of the stairs.

If that doesn't tell you how desperate Kolya's state of no fun is, I don't know what would.

Not the sleeping at the bottom of the stairs part, because I swear to fuck my body can only lull itself to sleep on anything that isn't a bed. It comes with my head's fucked-up state of mind.

This is about the not-participating part. Usually, I'd be all over that shit, and, in retrospect, bringing the beautiful queer energy out of everyone. There's a reason why people say yes whenever I shoot them a text. I'm a guaranteed source of crazy *fun*.

Last night, not only did I not fuck my way through multiple holes, but I was also *bored*.

Completely and utterly *indifferent*.

Like I was earlier, when the professor was about to give me head. Hot bombshell with luscious lips and everything.

Kolya was almost hard but didn't want her lips anywhere near his goddamn annoying presence.

Fuck.

I walk through the door of the mansion after school and stop in the entrance hall, tug my T-shirt over my head, and throw it down. My necklace that Dad gifted me jostles free and I stroke the bullet that hangs from it before I let it fall to my naked chest.

There. Much better.

People should be thankful I wear pants. Fucking prude society could use a chill pill. I have a beautiful body and I would rather show it off instead of keeping it tucked away. The same applies to my monster cock. I'm usually hella proud of Kolya's size and porn star-level performance, but today is *not* it.

I narrow my eyes on the half-tent in my pants. "The fuck is wrong with you, motherfucker?"

Is it all the fucking? No. Hell no. That's what he thrives on. It's why he chose to be completely cool with any hole. Endless options and all that.

Maybe I should extend those options… But to whom? I've been literally fucking my way through any and all of the population available at my disposal.

Let's rewind.

What could've happened to trigger Kolya's silent treatment? He's been caught in this strange stage where he's about to grow a boner but never exactly gets there.

Yesterday morning, I was coming all over an ass and a pussy, or was it two asses and a pussy? Anyway, I was a bit high at the time, so who knows how many?

What I do know, however, is that Kolya was definitely pumped up for the highly awaited event—the initiation. Punching people to near death? Holding power over their insignificant existence?

Fucking ecstatic.

Kolya was most certainly feeling himself and had the night of his dickish life, especially after...

A twitch rushes to my groin and I pause.

He was feeling himself more than usual when...

A reluctant, uptight preppy boy was gliding his firm ass all over him.

"Oh no." I glare down at my pants. "Fuck no, you fucking fuck."

He twitches again as if saying, "Fuck yeah."

"The fuck are you? A masochist? He said he was *straight*. Told you to keep your *nonsense* away from him as if it were an insult."

My dick doesn't understand insults, since he has the moral compass of a used condom, and remains standing at attention like an eager kid in class.

"You need to get yourself fucking checked, dude. Preferably by an exorcist so they can get those demons out and shit."

Now that I think about it, when I was falling asleep, I wasn't seeing the hot threesome, but the up and down of a gorgeous Adam's apple as he flinched, jerked, and swallowed thickly.

Fuck me sideways.

Kolya is definitely hard and in the mood now. Maybe if I get him the same flavor as the three from last night...

He flops down so fast, I curse his goddamned maker.

It's me. I'm the maker.

"Fuck you right the fuck off, motherfucker," I mutter.

I don't fuck with straight guys.

At all.

Many of them have fragile egos and macho manly energy that pisses me off and propels me to sudden, impulsive violence. I prefer queers who are comfortable in their own sexuality, like myself, thank you very much.

The only time I hover near a heterosexual man is if he's a lost bi-curious lamb who wants to experiment. In that case, I make it my mission to take him to heaven. Like an angel did to some prophet— don't ask me what his name is; I can't even remember mine half the time.

Brandon King does *not* belong on any of my lists of interest.

He's too uptight and closed off, not to mention standoffish and arrogant. His entire existence should give me a serious case of erectile dysfunction.

Jesus fuck.

That guy could use a chill pill. Or a few. In fact, someone should shove the entire bottle down his throat and make him choke on it.

Fuck him and his *back off* and *stop touching me.*

I'm straight. Like fuck he is.

He nearly bounced on my cock *and* he sat there so prettily while I was nursing an erection of epic proportions for a whole five minutes. Not that I was counting or anything.

Or maybe I was. To prove his theory.

Straight, my ass. Or his, to be more specific—pun totally intended.

I should note that during that time, his sister walked by and he nearly lost his marbles, which is probably why he remained frozen for a long period of time, but I digress.

I'm completely uninterested in his mythical straight battle. Fuck that right the fuck off, if you ask me.

The reason I invited him to the initiation was solely to mess with his twin brother. The major asshole who leads the preppy kids in the Elites and thinks he could go head-to-head with us.

A few nights ago, Landon and I fought at one of my favorite

places on the island—the fight club. I was so pumped to pummel that English prick to the ground in front of his wannabe fans.

But then *Brandon* showed up and stood there like the prince version of his brother.

I admit that I lost concentration because he looked so fucking agitated at the prospect of Landon being beaten to death, and I also admit Kolya appreciated the view.

He's *hot*. And it's different on him than his show-off, in-your-face brother.

Brandon has a quieter presence and carries himself in a total golden-boy fashion.

Slick brown hair, groomed face, tall and slim frame, but muscled. Yup, don't let those preppy clothes fool you. Asshole has abs. All six of them. I counted them yesterday since I had nothing else to do with my hands. I would've preferred to let my hand go down a more fun path, but I doubt grouchy Brandon would've been thrilled.

Anyway…*stop sidetracking. Now, brain. I mean it.*

I almost lost that fight because Brandon got in the way. Side note, I don't usually get distracted during fights because of this lame reason, I assure you.

So, *naturally*, I had to mess with Bran the way he dared to mess with me. And it so happened that the initiation was coming up and I couldn't miss that chance.

Since he was so concerned about his idiot brother, I made up a whole drama about his participation. It was a shot in the dark. I really thought Brandon wouldn't fall for it, since he's this major snob who looks down on people like me from his high horse.

Imagine my fucking surprise when he walked right in like a lost lamb.

A *straight* lost lamb.

What I didn't expect was his subtle aggressiveness and hints of submissiveness peeking from beneath the mask of rigorous control that he wears like a second skin.

From the outside looking in, he seems too boring and snobbish and like he could use some drugs. Maybe a mixture of them would help loosen up the layer of asshole wrapped around him.

However, something changed when he was put under pressure—his body trembled and he struggled to hide behind his mask, literally and figuratively.

My dick jumps at the memory of him remaining as still as a statue on my lap. I don't think he noticed it, but he had both his palms flat on his thighs like a well-behaved prince.

But then he left before I could convince the others to add him to our club. Not that they would've agreed, and Jeremy looked fucking horrified when he found out his identity, but oh well. I just wanted to toy with him a little.

Use him against his brother if the shoe fit.

Maybe destroy his fantasies about being straight in the meantime. I've never played around with straight men, but this was too tempting to pass up.

Blood rushes to my groin and I mutter, "Fuck you, you fucking fuck. You need help."

"*You* need help, Niko." My cousin Killian brushes past me on the way inside, accompanied by his brother, Gareth, and my best friend, Jeremy.

They must've finished school and come back together, which I should've probably done as well.

But oh well, I forgot.

Jeremy stops a few inches away from me. He's an inch shorter than me and definitely the most muscled after yours truly. He's a few years older, but he's been my best friend for as long as I remember. I might have pestered him for it, though.

He pushes his dark hair away from his face and narrows his eyes. "Niko, please tell me you weren't talking to invisible people just now."

"Of course not. I was having a very frustrating conversation with my dick."

"That's even worse." Gareth shoves my shoulder and chuckles.

My older cousin, twenty-one, is the prince of our little group of mayhem. Slick blond hair, sharp jaw, green eyes like some elf, and fucking dimples. The problem with him is that he's wiser than should be allowed. It makes him a little boring, just saying.

He's worlds apart from his younger brother, Kill, who's my age—dark hair, piercing blue eyes, and possesses the personality of a serial killer. My favorite type of personality. The crazier, the better. He's a prick, but at least he's a prick who doesn't try to stop me from causing mayhem, and, under certain circumstances, he endorses and encourages it.

"Why would you even talk to your dick?" Jeremy asks, looking half curious, half petrified. Which is pretty much the standard when it comes to me.

"We're having a difference of opinion. We'll come to an agreement sooner or later."

"Or you can take care of that ED we talked about earlier. I can hook you up with one of my professors in the local hospital," Kill muses as he strolls past me and sits on the sofa, grinning like a fucker who'll have that Colgate smile smashed when I knock out his fucking teeth.

"If you wanna see my dick again, just say so." I grab my belt, ready to die on this hill.

Gareth slams his hand on mine, a terrified expression covering his features. "Don't show us your dick, Niko. Seriously, why do you feel the need to get naked whenever someone mentions your dick? We're cousins, for fuck's sake."

"Well, your brother keeps running his mouth about ED and I want to prove that I don't have it."

"We believe you," Jeremy grunts with obvious displeasure. "Keep that thing in your pants. No one in this room wants to see it."

"I don't believe you." Kill lifts a shoulder as he toys with the remote.

"Kill!" Gareth growls. "Stop encouraging his crazy or he'll be walking around naked for a couple of days."

"Good idea." I snap my fingers at him. "You're so smart, Gaz."

His face falls. "Please don't."

Killian throws his head back in laughter while Jeremy sighs for the thousandth time since he got here and then sits beside him. His state of bubbling displeasure might have to do with me, but I honest to fuck don't know what I did or am doing wrong.

"Oh, right!" I snap my fingers again and sit opposite Kill and Jer.

Gareth disappears in the background and I catch a glimpse of him going up the stairs, probably to escape my pending exhibitionism.

But that's a thought for another time.

"What now?" Kill asks with visible amusement. "You going to tell us a tale about your dick?"

"Tempting, but I'll have to take a rain check on that. I've been thinking."

"You actually do that? Maybe we should check that head of yours when you receive that treatment for the ED."

"Haha. *Hilarious*," I deadpan. "Now, shut the fuck up. I have a very important question to ask. Have you ever been attracted to a guy?"

Kill crosses his legs at the ankles. "You do know that I hook up with anyone, right? Gender doesn't matter as long as they have a hole I can use."

Right. He did go on a spree similar to mine, but that was different. I don't think he's genuinely attracted to people in any shape or form. He just loves the power.

I do, too, so fucking much that the fact that I haven't had my fill in a while—the while being thirty-six hours—is causing Kolya's friends the infamous blue balls situation.

Kill is useless. Next.

"What about you, Jer?"

"I don't find men attractive." He frowns. "What's this about?"

"Yeah, Niko. Don't tell me you're having a sexuality crisis after you've been bi for over four years?"

I ignore Kill because he's too manwhorish to offer me the angle I'm looking for and sit on the coffee table, leaning into Jeremy's space. "Why have you never been attracted to men?"

"Because I prefer women. What kind of question is that?"

My face is so close to his, anyone else would be intimidated and jerk back, but Jeremy doesn't even breathe differently or attempt to move. He's so confident in his straight sexuality that he's not fazed by my outwardly weird behavior.

"You got a boner for Jeremy?" Kill asks from the side like a witch that will be burned in hell while Satan cackles manically.

"Nope." I push back. "He's straighter than straight."

"Thanks?" Jer mutters.

"That wasn't a compliment."

He releases that defeated sigh again. "What's going on, Niko?"

"Get me someone to maim. That's what's going on." I jump up and run up the stairs three at a time, sprint down the hall, then whip the door to Gareth's room open and shove it against the wall.

He looks up from his desk, pausing on doing homework like a boring prick. Jesus. If he didn't indulge in some violence on occasion, I would've already disowned him.

No cousin of mine becomes boring and gets away with it.

"Gee, thanks for the death scare. Please don't tell me you'll start stripping…?"

I stalk toward him, eyes narrowed.

"Don't you dare, Niko, or I swear I'll tell Aunt Rai about your annoying habits—"

"Have you ever been attracted to men?"

It's subtle, and I probably wouldn't have noticed it if I'd stayed by the door, but Gareth's eyes widen a little.

He drops his pen on his notebook and exhales loudly. "What are you talking about?"

"You've always fucked women, but have you done that because you feel you have to due to peer pressure and what's defined by society as normal or because you want to?"

"What is this about?" He stands up. "What did you hear?"

"What should I have heard?"

His face falls for a fraction of a second and I step into his space. "So? What? Tell me. Tell me! What should I have heard?"

He pushes me away. "Stop doing that shit."

"Not until you answer my question."

He runs a hand over his face. "I love women. Happy?"

"What about men?"

"I...don't know. Could be." His eyes spark like a tropical forest before he clears his throat. "Why are you probing?"

"I'm testing something. When did you discover you like men?"

"I don't like men. Jesus." He jogs to the door and slams it shut, then leans against it, arms and ankles crossed "I'm not sure. I don't know. I love fucking women, but..."

"But what?" I walk up to him and then peer down at him until I can see the tiny freckles on his nose. "What changed your mind?"

"I didn't change my mind and, seriously, stop looking so intense. It's creepy."

"Blah fucking blah, just tell me what made your straight ass sway on the line. Figuratively, of course." I grin. "Or is it literally?"

"Fuck you, asshole." He closes his eyes with pure exasperation. "If you tell anyone about this, especially Kill, I'll murder you."

"I won't if you just fess up. What made you change lanes?"

"I'm not sure I did—or *would*, for that matter. It's just...one person. That's it."

One person.

One. Person.

That's it.

Fucking *interesting*.

I ruffle Gareth's hair and offer courses in butt stuff, but I'm not even done enumerating things he should know before he proceeds to throw me out and shut the door in my face.

His groans can be heard through the door as I grin and walk down the hall.

On a scale of straighter-than-straight Jer to fluid-as-lube Kill to confused-as-shit Gareth, I wonder where Brandon King falls.

Not that I'm tempted to find out.

That would be *crazy*.

Just kidding. I *am* crazy.

A week later, I'm lurking by the entrance of the Elites' mansion at five thirty in the fucking morning.

You know, where Brandon lives with his insufferable brother, Landon, and a bunch of their family/friends.

Believe me, I'd never dream of waking up this early. But I can't exactly survive on images of him trapped beneath me and wiggling his ass against my cock.

Kolya, the traitorous bitch who'd deserve castration if I wasn't a major sexual being, still twitches at those memories.

Something he wasn't interested in despite all the porn shows I presented him with, both live and recorded.

He's being a dick. Literally.

Which brings me to this amateurish stalking mission. I might have visited Bran's Instagram and seen all the stories he posts every single day at five thirty like clockwork.

Sure enough, the small gate on the side creaks open and he steps outside, stretching under the hint of sun. He's dressed in loose shorts and a fitted green T-shirt that clings to his muscles like a second skin.

Fucking *hot*.

Now, if he weren't so groomed with his shaven face, styled hair, and general sophisticated appearance, he'd be even hotter.

I love my men filthy, unkempt, and rugged around the edges.

Women are soft and pliant and should be worshipped. Men are to be used.

Who am I kidding? Both are to be used.

And he's not one of *my* men. Jesus Christ. The fuck is wrong with my thought process?

Must be the lack of sleep. *Has* to be.

Only psychos wake up this early every day for a satanic ritual.

Sure enough, he retrieves his phone from his armband—of course the prick has an *armband*. Goes so well with his pristine clean image—and snaps a picture of the sky, then his fingers tap on the screen.

I grab my phone—from my shorts pocket like a normal human being—and check the story.

It's an aesthetic picture containing part of the gate and the looming sun. *#NewDay*

That's literally the only hashtag he uses on these posts, as if he's planning to kill his audience with the repetitive caption.

Brandon tucks his phone back into the armband and touches the earbuds in his ears, elegantly, I might add, as if he's handling a million-dollar painting.

All his movements are slow, unhurried. No, not slow. Controlled. His favorite uptight behavior seems to pour from him in everything he does.

I bet he doesn't know how to have fun.

I'd feel bad for him if I weren't itching to tackle him to the ground and pummel his beautiful face a few times.

Though beautiful isn't quite the right word. He's not pretty like a girl or beautiful like a colorful flower on the side of the road. He's *handsome.*

Sharp jawline, hard eyes, straight nose, and a set of full lips that would look divine around a cock.

Kolya wholeheartedly agrees, considering the significant change in his moody state. I have to adjust my erection and shake my head.

Stop thinking about Brandon and dick. They obviously don't mesh.

In fact, the logical thing to do is turn around and leave.

But then again, I was never much of a logical person.

If I don't stay, I'll come back tomorrow. And if I leave tomorrow, I'll return the day after.

It's an itch at this point.

As Brandon starts running down the road, I release a sigh, tuck my phone back in my shorts, and follow right after.

I'm just gonna find out if he's as confused as Gareth, and if he is, I'll help offer pointers. Consider it charity work.

That's it.

That's *all.*

I catch up to him in no time, keeping a few yards between us.

His back muscles ripple beneath his shirt and his hamstrings extend and repress, causing his shorts to ride up his thighs with every step. Hypnotic.

My gaze keeps flitting to the round globes of his ass, though, all peachy and shit.

If he's straighter than straight, it's such a shame to leave that ass empty.

Brandon seems lost in whatever is playing in his ears, because he doesn't notice when I close the distance between us.

I keep running at his pace right behind him.

Now, I know I'm supposed to be on a stalkerish mission, but it's impossible to stay away from his spellbinding pull.

Fuck it.

I pluck one of his AirPods out and whisper into his ear, "Long time no see. Miss me?"

FOUR

Brandon

I'M A CREATURE OF HABIT.

Neurotically so. In every sense of the word.

Without my carefully laid-out routine, I'd crumble and crash into a million irreparable pieces.

Without my punctual set of actions, I'm *nothing*.

So every day, I wake up at five. No exception—not during holidays, not after a night of drinking or partying or doing whatever is expected from a uni student. Five. *Always*. Every *single* day.

Then I put on my clothes, do a smoothie, and go for a run at five thirty. Back at seven. Shower. Breakfast. Wallow in my studio for another hour or two. Then school. Then I go to practice with the lacrosse team. More wallowing. Talking, smiling, laughing, caring, texting, liking, being.

Existing.

Day in and day out, I have to exist. To be out there and fucking *stay* there. In the middle of people with blurry faces and names and personalities.

All day, I tell myself that I belong with them and that I'm not in fact battling with incessant nausea that saturates my lungs with every breath. That's what I do best.

Pretend. Swallow it all down. Smile.

Again and again and fucking *again* until I can crawl back to my studio, stare at my soul in the form of a blank canvas, then shower longer than necessary. I scrub myself clean, turning my skin as red as a tomato, and that's the only way I can tune out for the day.

Then I have herbal tea and go to sleep at ten thirty.

That is, if I'm not dragged to a party by my friend Remi, who likes to have fun on an everyday basis.

Sometimes, I can shoo him away and keep to my sleeping schedule, but other times, he'll be armed with our other friends and I can't say no.

Rejecting invitations constantly doesn't fit well in the pretending agenda, now, does it?

My inconsistent sleeping schedule scratches at my neurotic side like an unreachable itch, but I deal with it.

Logically.

By waking up at five the next day and resuming the cycle.

That's why I nearly lost it after that godforsaken initiation I shouldn't have set foot into.

That event was a major deviation from my usual habits, and it took me more than just waking up at five to get over it.

But I did. Eventually. Because I'm in *control*.

The whole ludicrous experience is in the past.

Or that's what I thought.

Another unexpected event just slammed into my steel wall, putting a dent in it and sweeping my perfect cycle into a ditch.

My feet come to a halt as I peer back at the waste of space of a human whom I've been trying to bleach out of my mind.

And I did.

I *succeeded*.

Until he spoke just now, that is.

My lungs heave in quick succession, chest rippling against my shirt as if hoping to escape from my own fucking skin.

Alternative rock keeps playing from my sole earbud, the loud beat pounding in my ear, but I can't hear anything over the constant static thumping in my skull.

Like whenever my carefully built life experiences a hurdle.

Nikolai isn't only a hurdle. He's a fucking wall that I can't seem to shove out of the way.

He doesn't notice the clusterfuck he's brought on with his mere presence and stands there grinning like an idiot.

Half naked.

Only a necklace with a bullet dangles on his chest.

His white shorts hang so low on his hips, one wrong move would bring them down.

A map of extravagant tattoos spread over his chest, shoulders, arms, and all eight of his abs. He's stupidly muscular in a very unnecessary way. His thick mane of hair is tied in a messy ponytail which highlights his sharp jaw, harsh features, and unhinged eyes.

I thought the bloodied mask made him seem monstrous the other time, but no, he doesn't need a crutch when he can pull off that intense and entirely unpleasant energy with his revolting face alone.

He strokes my AirPod between his fingers—*definitely disinfecting that later.* "Is it just me or are you looking at me like you *really* missed me?"

I barely manage to stop my upper lip from lifting in a snarl as I snatch my AirPod. "I don't even know who you are. Run along, boy."

There.

I threw his insult back at him. Not that I was thinking about that retort, or something similarly obnoxious, hours after the initiation.

I turn and start jogging again, hell-bent on finishing my run and going back to the schedule we all know and love. By we, I mean me and my unstable brain.

Once again, my plan plummets to the deepest pit of hell.

The damn twat catches up to me, jogging at my pace, his shoulder nearly touching mine. "It's me, Nikolai. We met the other day at the initiation… Oh, right! I was wearing the yellow-stitch mask, so you didn't see my face, but it's me! Much hotter without the mask, don't you think?"

I was intending to disinfect the AirPod before I used it again, but I don't have the luxury. I push it in my ear and blast the volume to the max and run faster, the trees lining the road blurring in my peripheral vision.

Order. Habit.

Control.

I always run the same path on the same pavement, pass by the same park, and look at the same buildings.

It's intensely infuriating when they have areas of construction on some roads, and I have to take pedestrian diversions. Right now, there aren't any.

I'm a fast runner—the fastest on the team, which is why I play midfield to perfection.

Nikolai and his ridiculous size can't keep up with me.

Now I can get back to my rhythm and forget this entire thing happened. Like I *thoroughly* forgot about the initiation—except for the fact that my baby sister was there.

I couldn't exactly text her, 'Hey, little princess, for the love of fish and chips, please tell me I was seeing things and you weren't at the Heathens' initiation,' because that would give away that I was there. Although, she did do a double-take, so she could have recognized me despite the mask.

Either way, it's absolutely *not* happening.

My love language is shielding those I love, my precious sister included, from the mess that is my existence.

So there's no way I would've voluntarily divulged I was there. I did text and meet up with her and she seemed fine. Aside from the fact that Killian Carson, another member of the Heathens, posted a picture of him kissing her—or, more accurately, eating her face.

I must admit I was alarmed and Lan lost his damn mind over it. Killian, coincidentally Nikolai's cousin, isn't the type of guy we want our sister with.

But she assured me it's okay and that she knows what she's doing.

Lan definitely didn't listen to her and made me join him when he went to threaten Killian and give him a deadline to leave our sister.

Of course, I had to apologize on his behalf when he was rude to Killian's cousin, Mia. Despite being Nikolai's sister, she's *nothing* like him.

She accepted the apology and invited me over for pancakes and gaming.

Not Lan. *Me.*

I really didn't want to go to the Heathens', but Mia insisted, and I wanted to see Killian for myself, so I went.

Fortunately, Nikolai wasn't there, but Glyn came along and I could see how she was longingly looking at Killian the whole time.

After that, I was a responsible brother and reminded her to be careful and tell me if anything happens. However, giving any sort of advice always makes me feel like a massive fraud.

So I let the whole thing go. Barely.

Reluctantly.

It's not my place anyway. It was the first time I've seen Glyn put her foot down and vehemently refuse to listen to Lan's orders—

A weight crashes against my back and I stumble as both AirPods are plucked from my ears and Nikolai stands in front of me, breathing as hard as I am.

No, he's panting, but the up and down of his chest doesn't compare to the frantic thumping of my heart against my rib cage.

"What the hell is your problem?" I snap, then bite my tongue because I don't snap.

Ever.

"I was calling your name, but you weren't listening," he supplies casually, as if he's not witnessing my temporary loss of control in epic proportions.

I shove whatever demon took over me into the darkest corner of my mind and stretch out my palm so he'll give back the AirPods.

Nikolai throws one of them in his other hand, then squeezes my palm in his, his lips curving in an unhinged grin. "Oh cool, you remember! Nice to officially meet you, Brandon. Or, hold on! I actually found you a perfect nickname. Lotus flower. You know, because you managed to bloom so beautifully while surrounded by the muddy swamp that is Landon. Isn't that so fucking poetic?"

I'm momentarily paralyzed, my neatly tucked thoughts almost topple me over into the inky-black hole headfirst.

But that doesn't happen.

Because I'm in control.

I attempt to pull my hand from his warmer one, but he squeezes, tight, as if he's attempting to crush my bones.

His grin widens, kicking the creep factor up a notch. "Do you like it? Your new name? Do you?"

"Let go," I mutter from between clenched teeth.

"But why?" He appears genuinely puzzled. "You're the one who offered to shake hands. I forgive you for pretending not to remember my unforgettable presence."

"You need to check your ego."

He looks down at himself and then smirks. "Perfectly awesome, thanks for asking."

I want to pinch the bridge of my nose, but I can't, because the bastard is holding my hand hostage, tightening his grip incrementally. The worst part is that I don't think he even notices what he's doing.

It hurts, damn it, but I'd dig myself a hole and rot in it before I'd admit that out loud.

"My hand," I say in a thoroughly unaffected tone.

He squeezes more. "What about it?"

"Let it go."

"Do I have to? It's kind of soft and nice."

He tightens his hold again, mushing the fingers together, and I have to stifle a goddamn...groan? What in the bleeding livid gates of hell?

Pain. It's only *pain*.

"I need my hand, so yes, you have to release it, Nikolai."

"Fuck. I love the way you say my name. Though everything sounds amazing in that hot accent." The gleam that I never quite managed to erase from my mind rushes back to the depths of his harsh eyes.

Turquoise blue. Brimming with sharp…curiosity? Violence? It's impossible to tell with the crazy twat.

He's intensity on steroids.

An element I have no interest in whatsoever.

"I wonder how you'd say my name in other…more *intimate* situations."

I pull my hand away so suddenly, he has no choice but to release me. "I told you to keep your gay flirtations away from me. I'm straight."

"Hmm." He tilts his head to the side, eyes watching me intently like a creep.

What does a whacko like him think about? Aside from violence, of course. The rumors about him beating people up for sport are all I heard about him prior to the initiation.

Maybe if I were more involved in the real world instead of pretending to be, I would've found out he likes men.

Though he obviously likes women as well. According to…uh, social media. I didn't search for him. He somehow landed on one of Remi's tagged pictures.

I have zero interest in where he dips his dick as long as he keeps it away from me.

"My AirPods," I demand, not making the mistake of offering my hand this time.

"You like talking in monosyllables and giving orders, don't you?"

"Give them back."

"Bossy. Told you I love it."

"Don't make me repeat myself or so help me God…"

He jumps in my space so fast, I flinch, my whole body lurching back so he doesn't touch me.

That manic look in his eyes rushes to the surface, all bright and destabilizing. Like a lethal storm.

"What? So help you God, what? What are you gonna do? Don't leave me in suspense here."

He pushes into me with every word until his naked chest heaves against mine. A dash of unknown emotions explodes and spreads through me.

It's stifling and wrong.

Like nausea 2.0. Only, much worse.

You know what? He can keep the AirPods. I'm not wearing that pair again anyway.

I step back and he steps forward, his chest still glued to mine, his heart thumping in an irregular rhythm.

Or is that mine?

Not waiting to find out, I whip around and run.

I have no idea where I'm going or if I'm keeping with my usual route as I sprint between the trees.

I run fast.

As fast as I can.

Until my muscles protest and my lungs heave.

That black ink is rushing after me in long swirls and sharp strokes. Imaginary hands grab onto my shirt and pull.

My breathing is cracked and wrong.

No.

You're in control. You're always in control, remember?

Always.

And yet I sway as those hands clutch, twist, tug, and—

A hard object crashes against my back and I'm shoved over so suddenly, I fall headfirst against the ground.

I cough and heave against the dirt, my lungs burning and my vision blurring.

Hot breaths warm my ear before the very familiarly irritating voice whispers, "Don't run away from me, lotus flower. This is the second time you've done it, the third if we count the initiation. I'm kinda hurt."

I release a puff of air, relishing the fact that I did not get caught by my twisted imagination.

But that leads me to the realization that Nikolai is on top of me.

Again.

This time, his knee is wedged on my lower back, his hand squeezing my nape as he talks in my ear.

Fucking *again.*

"Eh…?" He smiles, and I know this because his lips curve against the damn shell of my ear. "This position is a little familiar. Not that I'm complaining."

"Nikolai," I growl, my jittering nerves getting the better of me. "Get the hell off me."

"Mmm. More. Give me fucking more," he growls into my ear.

"Back off."

"That's it. Fight me. I love this energy, lotus flower."

"You won't love it when…" I trail off before I say *I bite your head off.*

Good grief. This is *not* me.

"What? I won't love it when you what?" He speaks so close, I can feel his words inside my darn ear instead of hearing them. "You need to stop cutting yourself off mid-sentence. The suspense is killing me. You're playing a bit hard to get, Prince Charming, but I'm all over that shit. Fight me. Fight me. Fucking fight me!"

I elbow him. "You're disgusting. Piss off."

Surprisingly, he releases me, choosing to let himself fall onto his arse beside me. The disappearance of his crushing weight gives me back my normal thought process. Barely.

That's when I realize I've wandered into the nearby park that I usually pass by on my runs.

Early morning light slips from between the huge centuries-old trees and hits Nikolai's face.

Something curious happens then.

Under the soft yellow light kissing his cheek and right eye, the blue lightens to a chilling turquoise, revealing tiny flecks of gray in the irises.

Blue on gray.

Fascinating.

"Whatever crawled up your ass better crawl right the fuck out," he barks, all humor gone. "Call me disgusting again and I'll pummel you against the nearest tree, then hang you by the balls so that everyone sees who's the disgusting one. Got it?"

I shake myself out of the momentary daze, realizing I actually remained lying on my stomach despite the absence of his weight.

Jumping up, I have to regulate my breathing as I glare down at him. "Don't touch me again and I won't call you that. In fact, I won't call you anything, because I'd rather not speak to you ever again."

"Why?" His grin returns as quickly as it disappeared as he stands up unhurriedly like a big cat crawling out from his cave after a nap. "Afraid I'll grow on you?"

I flash him my most fake smile. "The chances of that happening are below zero. Better luck next life, kid."

"Blah blah and fucking blah. Why wait when I have this life?" He frowns. "Also, why are you smiling like a creep?"

My smile drops and I snatch the AirPods from his grip. "Stop following me. I mean it. I have no interest in whatever you're hinting at."

He smiles wide like an unhinged maniac on drugs. Maybe he really is high. "And how do you know what I'm hinting at?"

"You haven't exactly been subtle. The answer is no."

"I can work with a no."

"You're wasting your time. I'm straight."

"That's the third time you've told me that. Someone is trying to prove a point." He slaps my shoulder. "But, hey, whatever lets you sleep at night, lotus flower."

He starts to get into my space again, his smell—bergamot and mint—filling my nostrils and clouding my senses.

Fucking *again*.

I shove him away, hard, and break into the fastest run of my running history. I eat the distance back to the mansion in no time.

Forget my routine. I need to protect something a lot more important.

My sanity.

FIVE

Nikolai

SO I'VE PICKED UP RUNNING LATELY.

By lately, I mean this is the third day. The first was when I tackled Brandon to the ground and felt the flexing of his muscles as I whispered in his ear.

Good times.

In fact, they were infinitely more than good. Fucking *hot* is the word I'm looking for.

There's something about shoving him around, messing with his golden-boy persona, but what I enjoyed the most was trapping him beneath me, having him compliant one second and fighting the next as if his life depended on it.

Kolya got his most straining hard-on in a week. The first being when Bran sat on my lap.

Once again, no amount of foreplay or greedy mouths and willing holes were cutting it for my newly picky dick. He couldn't even get it up or grow enough balls to leave my pants.

It's another story when different images play in my head, though.

I had to be a caveman and jerk off alone while picturing that blotch of red creeping up Bran's neck when I growled in his ear or the goosebumps covering his skin when I locked him in place with a hand on his nape.

He didn't fight. *Again.* He just lay there begging to be fucking used.

Though he'd tell you otherwise.

He's kind of an asshole, that guy. While I've been having a blast running with him the past couple of days, I have a feeling it's not… mutual.

I've been only greeted with the narrowing of his eyes, his death glares, and the occasional puff of air from his luscious lips.

Not to mention his monosyllabic replies and continued orders.

Back off.

Step away from me.

Do not touch me.

Remove your unpleasant presence from my vicinity.

He speaks like royalty. Not complaining, though. There's something about ruining a good boy that does shit to me.

Which is why I'm back for round three.

I wait by the Elites' mansion entrance, jogging in place and punching the air. I can't stay still.

Not when the mere thought of Bran in his shorts and fitted T-shirt sends blood rushing to my groin.

I'd like to point out that I tried to remain calm, but then again, calm and I have been at odds since I was born, and I can't possibly be expected to leave him alone. He's turning into this sweet addiction that adds meaning to my days.

Solution? Try to wear him down.

Creep beneath his skin.

Wreak havoc on his heart in the process.

He's just *so* fun to mess with. He's usually expressionless, unless he's faking this creepy smile that looks like a psycho's, so whenever I catch him off guard, he has this deer caught in the headlights expression. A flaring of nostrils here, a bobbing of his gorgeous Adam's apple there.

I'm living for that shit. *Literally.*

For two days, I've only been thinking about bugging the fuck out of him. Five thirty in the morning is my favorite time of the day until further notice.

Sooner or later, he'll fall at my feet like everyone else. Or, more accurately, to his knees.

I like to think I'm making progress in some way. Yesterday, he didn't try to run away from me, though he did attempt to use the stupid AirPods that you can bet I removed and kept hostage until the end of the run.

He did pretend I wasn't there while I asked him a shitload of questions. I can't remember many of them, but they were mostly things like, what does he do after a run? What's his favorite food? Movie? Color? Hobbies? Clothes? Hair products? Cologne?

Does he like the fight club? Violence? The crunching of people's bones?

Was that a bit pushy? Who the fuck cares, to be honest?

He wouldn't have answered anything even if they weren't pushy.

He's not exactly cooperative and lets my questions wash off him as if he never heard them until he runs back to his big castle.

But then again, I'm nothing short of persistent and fucking love a challenge.

Mom and Jeremy say I'm like a bull who doesn't stop until I get what I want, so…off I go again, I guess.

I have all the time in the world now that Kolya is going through a fucking abstinence period.

Though he doesn't seem all that uninterested when a certain brown-haired Prince Charming is in his vicinity, which boggles my mind.

Well-groomed, posh men like Bran are not my type. At all.

But something about him—

My movements abruptly stop when the gate creaks open and lotus flower steps outside dressed in black shorts and a royal-blue tee that stretches over his broad shoulders, expanded chest muscles, and lean waist.

He's not in your face, but he definitely has a superior build. He's toned in a lean way, hard and firm everywhere.

Kolya twitches in my shorts and I groan under my breath.

"Fuck, dude." I glare down at him. "Make up your mind. Are you easy or hard? Pun intended."

I get no answer. Naturally. He's literally a *dick*.

Lotus flower takes his picture of the day and posts it on Instagram. I'll peek at it later after he escapes to his prince's mansion. For now, I'd rather get my fill of him. Add new material for my daily jerk-off session and all that.

He marches with sure, slightly forced movements down the road. His gaze flits sideways, probably searching for me, but I'm well hidden behind the trees.

Can't have their cameras catching me and reporting back to the major douchebag Landon. Not that I'm opposed to pummeling that bitch to the ground and cracking his skull in two, but I'd rather not trigger any complications when I'm trying to get into his brother's pants.

Or ass.

Anyway, lotus flower keeps searching his surroundings and I remain hidden just to fuck with him.

Yesterday, I jumped to his side as soon as he rounded the corner and he was far away from the mansion's cameras. He looked at me with wide eyes and slightly parted lips, and even though that expression lasted for a fraction of a second, you can bet I added it to my mental catalog full of everything Brandon King.

Today, I'm using a different strategy. Can't let him get used to my modus operandi and quit showing me those special responses.

I want him to get as close as possible. Until I smell him. Until—

He stops a few yards away on the dirt road and I get a front-row seat of his side profile. Is he sure he's not interested? Because he dressed up so prettily for me. Though he does wear the same clothes in different colors, there's something about today's color. Blue brings out the blue in his mysterious, snobbish eyes.

Though I'd rather he go shirtless so I can get a front-row seat to his body and possibly sink my teeth into it.

Figuratively, of course.

Who the fuck am I kidding? It's definitely literally.

I'm about to close the distance between us when a convertible Audi stops right in front of him.

A blonde bombshell jumps out of the car, wearing skimpy shorts that reveal the crease of her ass and a sports bra that barely covers her big tits.

Her lips are unnatural as fuck and she's wearing more makeup than a drag queen.

She lunges at Brandon in a ferocious hug, her entire body gluing to his front. "Babe!! I'm so happy you decided to give this a go again. I promise everything will be better this time. You know how much I love you, handsome."

He pats her back, but there's no enthusiasm behind his movement. His expression doesn't change, not even a little.

Like a robot.

I got a better reaction from him by plucking out his AirPods, blondie.

Not that I care.

I *don't.*

And yet my hand twitches, demanding I throw her off the nearest, steepest cliff.

How dare she interrupt our morning ritual that's been going on for three days?

Two.

She pushes back, smiling like a model, her face soft as she coos at him and kisses the corner of his mouth. *Disgusting.*

Oh, look at that. Brandon's favorite word.

"Do we have to go on a run, though?" She pouts like a goddamn toddler. "You know I don't like that, or waking up early, actually."

A lot of *you knows* are thrown around.

Who is this chick?

I probably saw her on his IG that I spent a whole night going through, thank you very much.

Though the only occurrence I remember was two years ago when someone who looked like her, sans the bleached hair, was hanging on his arm.

The reason she caught my attention is because he never posts pictures with girls who aren't his friends.

Considering I acquainted myself with his female—and male— friends, I knew she was not on the list.

Clara.

I remember the name because I made a note to visit her IG as well, but I didn't have time since it was already five and I needed to get here.

Who the fuck are you, Clara, and what's your favorite way to die?

I'm about to step into the scene and ask her just that—or maybe just scare her away. That shit comes naturally to me.

Leaves crunch beneath my shoes and Brandon's head tilts in my direction, but he doesn't look at me.

"You don't have to run, Clara." He sinks his fingers into her hair, drags her head back, and slams his lips to hers. Her tongue peeks out and he resists for a fraction of a second, keeping his lips shut, before he opens, just the slightest bit, and she shoves it inside his mouth.

I stand still, head cocked to the side as I watch him kissing her.

Or is it the other way around?

His muscles ripple and roll, his back rigid, his biceps bulging, then his long fingers tighten in her hair.

Fighting.

That's what he's doing. He's not enjoying the act. He's *fighting.*

What are you fighting, lotus flower?

He seems to be struggling to kiss her, or maybe he's struggling to keep his libido under control.

My gaze slides down to his shorts, and no. There's no erection in sight. Kolya would've gotten that in a few seconds after a heavy make-out session.

Old Kolya, that is. The new one is clearly an idiot who will be written out of my will.

Brandon whirls her around, so I'm greeted by her back as he

deepens the kiss. I don't even look at her meaningless presence, my gaze zeroing in on his face that barely contorts.

Barely moves.

Barely feels—if at all.

He's Frenching the fuck out of the girl, but his eyes are wide open. Not once closing or getting lost in the act like she is.

His gaze flies to mine and I hold it, locking my eyes with his robotic ones as I cross my arms.

Show me what you got, straight boy.

A frown appears between his brows as if he can hear my thoughts while I remain there watching, not the show, but his face.

I relish the subtle change, how his expression morphs from control to conflicted emotions. Hate? Lust? Both fucking hot, if you ask me.

I reach down and adjust my dick, then keep my hand there and clutch it through my shorts, showing him the damning effect he has on Kolya.

He didn't even speak to me, but a mere look is enough to turn a man into the worst sinner.

Bran's eyes widen, and yeah, he's definitely not focusing on Clara one bit right now. Not even a fraction of his attention is on her.

Just to fuck with him, I roll my bottom lip beneath my teeth, then mouth, "Wanna give me a hand?"

His eyes spark a bright shade of blue as he jerks away from Clara almost violently.

"Whew, that was intense, babe," she breathes out and I'm about to bash her head in and send her over that cliff in her convertible.

He faces away from me, but not before I see the evidence in his shorts.

My, my. Is that…a fucking *erection*?

I mean, he could've gotten that because of kissing her. It couldn't have possibly been me.

He's *straight*.

Insert rolling of eyes here.

He hides away behind his flimsy walls, subtly adjusting himself before he faces Clara with the most fake-ass smile. "I just missed you."

Bullshit. I don't even think *he* believes what he's saying.

Blondie sure does since she throws herself in his arms again. "BABE! I love you so much. This time forever. I'm never leaving you again."

I have to physically force myself to turn away, because if I don't, I might go over there and punch Clara. Or accidentally kill her. And we don't want a dead bimbo on our hands.

Besides, I might have a more adequate plan for Clara.

Prince Charming better watch his fucking back.

SIX

Nikolai

S O I REALIZED THAT I NEED TO CHILL THE FUCK OUT.

Brandon who?

The guy who will take my cock between his lips and thank me for it, that's who.

No. Jesus Christ.

Chill, Kolya.

Just chill for one fucking second, dude.

Though it's impossible to convince him of that when I've been spiraling for over twenty-four hours.

Ever since I saw that atrocious scene with Clara.

While he only has that one picture of her on his IG, she definitely flaunts him all over hers.

My man x

Babe, you keep me alive x

Isn't he the most handsome man ever? x

Love you, sexy x

Blah fucking blah.

According to her posts, they've been together for about two years.

Fuck that right the fuck off.

My sister Maya, the social media detective of the family, said they're in an on-again, off-again relationship. She thought I wanted to fuck Clara, to which she scrunched her nose and told me to stay away because she was just so hung up on this Brandon guy and I could do so much better.

Couldn't care less about that. One piece of information remained in my head.

On and off for two years.

Interesting.

Anyway, I don't care, because I'm chilling. In the pool, floating face down. Living my best life.

I can fall asleep here. Sweet.

Though I'd probably die, and that's not exactly convenient.

Whatever. I'll just remain here for a bit more to relax. I sure as fuck need to stay still for a goddamn second and not entertain stupid thoughts like maybe I should go for a morning run tomorrow.

I didn't today, because if I saw pretty Clara again, I would be tempted to ruin her features. And I never, and I mean *never*, get thoughts of violence about girls in general.

Mom brought me up to respect women. Cheer them on, not bring them down.

But something about that Clara…

A commotion brings me out of my peaceful contemplations that are filled with blood. Lots of blood gushing from all her fucking holes.

I lift from the water with a gasp and check my watch. Three minutes and fifty-five seconds. Not bad.

I've been breath training for three years now and the time I spend without breathing is improving.

Aside from riding my bike with Jeremy, this happens to be the only method that helps me wind down. Probably because I'm almost dead at that time.

There's also brutalizing people, but that only pumps me up and doesn't bring me down from the blood-soaked phase.

Considering my brain's tendency to get high as a kite at

unfortunate moments, I had to find a coping mechanism to counter that *loud* phase.

I lift myself up at the edge of our indoor pool located in the underground level of the mansion. Usually, it's hard to hear anything when I'm here, but something's different now.

Is it trouble? Fuck yeah.

I walk to the bench, shaking water from my hair, then use the towel to dry the haphazard strands.

I pick up my phone and pause at the notification on the top of my screen. I open it so fast, I nearly drop the phone.

So I might have been messaging Brandon on IG. You know, because I'm a goddamn pest like that.

He didn't answer them.

For three days.

My text were along the lines of:

It's me ;)

Nikolai, in case the handle didn't give me away.

Wanna hang out? Like friends?

Ok, that was a lie. Being friends wouldn't work since you're such a delight to be around. All standoffish and grumpy and shit. The exact opposite of fun.

We could have a drink?

GIF of a bored kid tapping the table

We can do this all day, Prince Charming. Love talking to your inbox. What a fucking thrill.

Why do you always use the same hashtag? Is there a meaning behind that?

Why do you play lacrosse?

Can you send me your playlists that you listen to all the time? Not really into rock, but I love discovering new music.

Also, isn't rock too extreme for your prim-and-proper image? Not that I'm judging. I actually dig the contradiction. Kinda makes it fun to try and figure you out.

Why did you want to become an artist?

Aren't you too uptight to be into something that requires people to let go of their creativity? Or are you different when painting?

Please tell me you do that half naked. It's blasphemous to hide beautiful bodies, you know.

Want to exchange numbers? Here's mine XXXXXXXX.

Hello, lotus flower's inbox, lovely to see you again this evening.

You looked hot today.

Not that I'm hitting on you or anything since you're sooo straight.

Let's consider this my hopeless one-sided crush on a straight guy. You don't have to reciprocate.

Unless you want to *eyebrow wiggle emoji* *sunglasses emoji*

Yup. All good. My texts are still sitting prettily in here. Will check again later to make sure.

I sent that text two days ago, before I saw him with Clara.

I didn't text him after that, but now, I see the first reply from him. Earlier this evening.

Stop bugging me or I'll block you.

But he *didn't* block me. He even accepted my text that was in his requests since I follow him and he obviously doesn't follow me.

I narrow my eyes on the screen. Is there a meaning behind this?

Why would he reply days later?

Fuck this shit. Seriously. I'm losing my few remaining brain cells because of this asshole.

I put on my shorts, and yes, I was swimming naked. If any of the guys came in, well, tough shit.

When I arrive at the main hall, I'm greeted by one of my guards who my parents made follow us here. Jeremy and I use them to cause mayhem more than anything.

"Sir," he starts with a Russian accent. "I thought you might want to know that your cousin Killian was attacked. He's upstairs now."

I narrow my eyes. "Upstairs, as in alive, or upstairs, as in, in his casket?"

A crease appears on his forehead and he says slowly, almost like he's not sure, "Alive. He lost consciousness, I think."

Thank fuck.

Kill's death would probably be inconvenient. Not to mention bad. At least, for Aunt Reina, who's Mom's identical twin.

But then again, this is an opportunity for violence.

How will I punish those who hurt my cousin? Punch them to death? Waterboard them? Step on them—in a non-erotic way, of course?

Too many options.

I take the stairs two at a time and swing his door open, my head sliding in first. "Heard Kill nearly got killed. See what I did there? Also, whose head do I have to cut from their body, rip the flesh from, and hang on a stick—"

I stop mid-sentence.

Well, well, well. Guess who's here?

Killian's lying in his bed like a Sleeping Beauty, sans the beauty, and his new girlfriend, Glyn, and Gareth are by his side.

But that's not what makes me stop. It's Glyn's beautiful specimen of an older brother. Also known as the asshole Brandon.

In *my* house.

I walk inside, deliberately slowly, keeping my attention on him. For a second, his eyes widen, as if he didn't want to see me in my own fucking place.

Happy to crush your hopes, lotus flower.

He's dressed in a white button-down that's tucked into his khaki slacks. *Khaki.* Jesus. He's *so* prim and proper.

All the more reason to ruin the fuck out of that image. See what truly lurks behind his standoffish persona and control-freak façade.

I stop a small distance away. "Now, what do we fucking have here? Did a lotus get lost?"

His expression doesn't change, imitating a perfect robot, but then he lifts his hand to the back of his neck and pulls. Hard. As if he has a beef with his own hair.

That's it, lotus flower. Break for me.

This situation is amusing after the shit he pulled yesterday, so I summon my threatening tone. "Was it this one who hurt our Kill, Gaz?"

Glyn watches me with slightly trembling limbs, her eyes flying from me to her overly tense brother.

She hasn't known me for long, but even she has heard of my notorious reputation and tendencies to punch first and ask questions later. *Though I am asking first this time.*

Has her brother also heard of me? I wonder what he thinks of me, and I never wonder what other people's thoughts are.

But lotus flower is this golden boy who hides more than he shows and I'm thirsty for any crumb I can get.

Not that he makes it easy.

"No," Gareth says. "Brandon and Glyndon drove him here. They found him near their campus. For more details about the culprit, we have to wait for Killian to wake up."

"Is that so?" My attention remains on Bran, who's basically ripping his hair out at this point. "You carried the motherfucker Kill all on your own? I thought you were a dainty lotus, but maybe you're stronger than you look."

"I'm going back." His voice catches at the end as he lowers his hand and smiles at his sister in that fake-ass way. "Want to come, Glyn?"

"No, I'm staying the night," she says, her gaze falling on Killian, who's slumbering away without a worry in the world.

Thank you for your services, cousin.

If it weren't for him, Glyn's brother wouldn't be here.

Maybe Kill should get hurt more in the future, work on strengthening his immune system and shit.

Bran frowns but nods. "Call me if you need anything."

Then he turns around and chooses to brush past Gareth instead of me on his way to the door.

Someone is going to a lot of trouble to pretend I'm not here.

Wake-up call is incoming in ten fucking seconds.

I slip out behind him, not bothering to say anything to Glyn and Gareth.

Bran is already quickening his wide, controlled steps down the hall, head straight and shoulders tense. Like when he kissed *Clara.*

I catch up to him and fall in step beside him. "If you wanted to see me, you should've told me and I would've given you a tour."

"Get over yourself." He's looking ahead like a fucking robot. "I'm here for my sister and her boyfriend."

"Tomayto, tomahto. Wanna have that tour anyway?"

"No."

"How about dinner?"

"No."

"A drink?"

"No."

"Do you have another word in your monosyllabic asshole vocabulary tonight?"

"No," he says, almost on autopilot, and I jump in front of him.

He nearly walks into me and has to stop abruptly, his throat working up and down, and I can't help but stare at that gorgeous Adam's apple. I want to bite it.

Hard.

Maybe draw blood in the meantime.

The red would look fucking beautiful against his fair complexion.

He steps back faster than I can blink.

Even though he's a couple of inches shorter, he manages to look down on me with that condescension he wears like armor. "Are you allergic to shirts or something? Why are you always half naked?"

"Because I look fucking awesome and it's a pity to hide it. Also, does this mean you were checking me out?"

"Nonsense. It's impossible to miss your constant state of nudity."

"*Constant state of nudity.* Jesus. Chill, my dude. You sound like a judge in court."

"I'm not your *dude.*" He stresses the word as if it's an insult and starts to shift past me.

I get in his way again and he stops. An aura of crushing disdain radiates from him and licks my skin as he shoves a hand in his pocket and releases an exasperated sigh. "What?"

"Why did you reply to me earlier today? Did you miss my texts?"

"I was clearly telling you to stop bothering me."

"But I wasn't. I stopped after...you know, your public make-out session with *Clara*, whom you clearly asked to come to that specific place at that specific time on purpose. What were you trying to prove, lotus flower? Because the way I saw it, you got hard when you had your eyes on me. Not her."

One minute, I'm standing there, and the next, he crushes my windpipe with his arm as he shoves me against the nearest pillar.

My head hits the harsh stone and pain explodes in my skull, but I don't feel it.

I *can't*.

Not when his eyes blaze a fierce blue, savage and so out of control.

Hands down, the sexiest view I've ever seen.

"Listen to me, you thick fucker. I've been tolerating your nonsense for far too long, but enough is enough. You're not my peer, friend, or anything in between. So crawl back into your hole and stop being in my fucking space or I will crush you."

"Talk dirty to me, baby."

He growls and I shove my face in his, erasing the few inches separating us. I could easily remove his arm, but I love the pressure.

I love that he lost control enough to get physical. Up close and *personal*.

"That's what she calls you, right? *Baby*. No, it's the less glamorous version. *Babe*. Tell me the truth, did you get a boner because you were kissing her or because I got an erection for you? It's not good form to look at a guy's hard-on when you're kissing your girlfriend, don't you think?"

"Nikolai," he growls again, the sound masculine and fucking delicious. I want to reach out and suck it from between his lips and jam it down my throat.

But most of all, I love that his control is unraveling, ripping at the edges, and leaving a mess of goo in its wake.

This is the hottest I've ever seen him, and I've always found him mouthwateringly sexy.

Right now, though, I don't think I can take it slow or easy. If I'm left to my own devices, I'll fuck him all up for good. I'll throw him down and have my way with him. There won't be patience or diplomacy. There *will* be choking, grunting, fucking, fucking, and more *fucking.*

Jesus Christ. *Chill, Kolya. We can't scare him away.*

"Mmm. I love the sound of my name on your lips. Say it again, *baby.*"

"I'm going to fucking kill you." His arm presses further into my neck until it's hard to breathe, but if I have to smash my own vocal cords to egg him on, that's exactly what I'll do.

"Tell me more. I'm getting all hot and bothered with your foreplay. I love it when you curse, *baby.*"

"You fucking—" He cuts himself off, nostrils flaring and cheeks slightly flushed, but then his expression closes.

I can see him slowly pulling himself together and eclipsing behind that giant wall.

Hiding.

Retreating.

Nah, hell no. Fuck *that.*

I grab his free arm and shove him with my body mass and that's when the most beautiful thing happens.

Brandon Uptight King steps back once, twice, and lets me push him, his eyes glazed over, and a tremor rushes through his entire body and beneath my fingers.

He downright *flinches* when his back hits the opposite wall, his slightly flushed skin looking like goddamn art against the dark-red wallpaper.

His arm remains against my throat, but he lost the battle, my Prince Charming, all wound up and staring with those wide fucking eyes.

My chest presses to his and I can feel his heartbeat thundering against mine—thud, thud, and fucking *thud*—as I wrap my fingers around his throat.

He swallows, chest galloping and goosebumps erupting on the backs of his hands.

Bran would hit me if I were to say this out loud, but he's the sexiest fucking thing I've ever seen.

There's a note of innocence beneath his grouchy, standoffish edge, and I want to latch on to it, suck it dry.

Destroy him through it.

I inch my lips close to the corner of his as I whisper, "You want to know what I think, lotus flower? I think you were fighting your goddamn demons to kiss her. The deeper you went, the more forced it looked. The longer you had your mouth against hers, the more burdened you looked, so it's safe to say you weren't hard because of her."

"Shut your fucking mouth," he says and tries to push me with his other hand.

I snatch his wrist and slam it on the wall above his head.

His throat works and he shivers against me. Goddamn *shivers*.

I'm going to devour him fucking whole and leave no crumbs.

"Your bossiness turns me the fuck on, *baby*," I murmur, my lips an inch away from his jaw.

I inhale his scent deep into my greedy lungs—clover, citrus, and fucking damnation.

"Only Clara calls me that," he mutters, seeming to fight, dig, and sink his claws into that control he loves so much.

"But you didn't get hard for Clara, did you, *baby*?" I bite out, inching closer. I'm fucking intoxicated, struggling to stop myself from licking him like an ice cream cone. "I can always test it real quick."

My fingers slide from his throat to cup his jaw, my eyes zeroing in on his luscious, tempting lips.

He shudders and drops his arm from my neck to shove it against my chest.

Only, it's trembling.

Like the rest of him.

And he's *not* pushing.

His Adam's apple bobs up and down. "Don't you dare."

"Or what, *baby*?"

"Nikolai, if you don't stop, so help me God, I will…"

"What? You're leaving me in suspense again, *baby*."

He swallows again, and this time, I can't help it. I'm a fucking masochist who's hung up on this dick.

Figuratively, of course.

I dart my tongue out and lick along his jaw, all shaven and clean like the rest of him. He tastes of goddamn citrus and I want to drown in it even if it stings.

I was never good with self-preservation anyway.

He shivers again, like a leaf, his hand remaining on my pec, but now, he's digging his fingers in my skin and I'm not sure if he realizes he's doing it.

It's not enough. This is far from fucking enough.

I need more and more and *everything*.

I trail my tongue down the hollow of his throat and bite on his Adam's apple like I've fantasized. And fuck me, it tastes better than any fantasy.

He tastes like my own downfall and I'm ready to drown in it.

A groan rips from Brandon's lips and I pause, my chest expanding and my dick thickening against my shorts until I'm sure I'll burst.

More.

Give me fucking *more*.

I slide my tongue back up to his chin, his cut jawline, and stop near his lips, mine hovering, my nostrils flaring, and my breaths coming out heavy and deep.

His exhales match my own, distorted and chopped off. Unorganized and completely out of fucking control.

Just the way I want him.

I'm going to swallow those lips and feast on his tongue until he forgets all traces of *Clara*.

His eyes widen as if he can see the intention and he pushes me so hard, I stumble back.

I'm forced to release him, my body starving and needing more.

More.

More.

Fucking more.

His jaw tics and his muscles tighten. And just like that, he slips back to the uptight asshole with serious issues. "I told you not to touch me, you disgusting prick."

Aaaand he fucking ruined it.

I swing my fist back and then drive it into the side of his face. He stumbles, only held up by the wall, and I tackle him, watching in pure satisfaction as he topples to the floor, all haze leaving his face and replaced with pure confusion.

"I told you I'd beat you the fuck up if you said that again. Get the fuck out of my face, hypocrite."

Instead of waiting for him to leave, I turn around and stalk to my room.

My nerves pound, my dick hard as fuck, and my mind jittering with thoughts to go back there and pummel him.

Fuck him right the fuck off.

Straight crush is officially over.

SEVEN

Brandon

"I'M FINE, MUM. SERIOUSLY."

I pinch the bridge of my nose as I stare at the canvas filled with sharp yellow while holding the phone to my ear.

"Then let me see your face, hon," Mum says softly, almost pleadingly.

She's always pleading with me, my mum, imploring, asking, *probing*, and disturbing my routine.

I exhale a long breath.

I sound like a damn twat to the mother who only ever treated me with care, love, and understanding.

And maybe I'm on edge because I don't want her to hate me. I hate me enough for both of us.

"You know I don't like FaceTime," I grumble, then try in a more cheerful tone, "I have a school project to finish. I'll talk to you later."

"Bran." She stops, probably trying to choose her words carefully. *She never has to choose her words with the family's golden boy, Lan.* Apparently, I screw up everything, Mum's caring side included. "If you're under stress or anything, you know you can talk to me, right?

Or you can speak to your dad if you prefer. We're here for you, whatever it is. You know that, right?"

My chest expands with constricting breath and I expel it out of my lungs, but it gets stuck in my throat. Pressure builds behind my skull and I want to bang it against the nearest fucking wall.

But I don't.

Because I'm in fucking control.

Always.

"I know, Mum," I whisper back.

"Listen. I know it's too soon to talk about this, but I think Grace might be open to take you next year."

I frown. Grace, Mum's agent, is not only world-renowned but also a legend in the UK's art council and even holds the position of a Lady in the House of Lords.

Despite her reputation, she has only signed three world-famous artists, Mum being one of them.

"Why would she want to sign me?" I ask carefully.

"Because you're a marvelous talent. I'm so happy you're finally getting your chance. I know how it must've felt to see your brother get all the opportunities this whole time, but you're as talented as he is, Bran."

You have to say that because you're our mum and can't be caught showing favoritism.

"Okay," I say simply.

"I love you so, so much, Bran. My life wouldn't have been the same without you."

Her words flood my mouth with nausea, but I swallow and smile. As if she can see me. "I love you, too, Mum."

I hang up before she says anything else that will turn my stomach and send me rolling down the nearest cliff.

My hand tightens around the phone until I think it'll break into irreparable pieces. A part of me is disappointed that it doesn't and remains intact. Like my head.

My gaze slides from the phone to the canvas. I started to have a vision, made a few strokes, then had to physically force my hand down.

It was doing things my brain doesn't approve of and never will. I should be working on a landscape painting, but I couldn't bring myself to touch that.

Instead, I was thinking of eyes. I don't fucking do eyes. Eyes send my head up a fucking wall.

I stopped painting people and animals for that reason. I succeeded for years, but now, here I am again.

My thoughts were running rampant, which is why I was thankful when I got Mum's call. But then not so much when I couldn't stop myself from staring at the canvas even when I was talking to her.

Things got worse when she could tell I wasn't myself—not that I ever am—and she started probing and worrying.

I hate it when I'm a constant cause of concern for her.

It's the worst.

My gaze falls back on my phone and my heart thuds when a new text pops in. But it sinks down so hard afterward when I see Clara's name.

Fuck.

Clara: BABE! I got your gift! Love the LV bag, it's sooo pretty. I already posted it on IG and tagged you! You're so precious, handsome. Love you and miss youuu x Can I come to hang out in your room tonight? I bought the sexiest lingerie *winking emoji* *aubergine emoji* *splashes of water emoji*

My fingers are on autopilot as I type.

Me: I can't. I promised the guys I'd spend time with them. I'll make it up to you another time.

Clara: *pouting emoji* Ok. Love you, babe.

Me: *heart emoji*

My gaze remains fixated on the conversation, specifically on the last word she sent.

Babe.

I didn't care for it until someone else said it. Or a more intimate version of it.

Now, I fucking hate it.

My finger is unsteady as I exit my texts with Clara and scroll down for some time until I find the name that I hate more than *baby*.

I click on the conversation that I started two days after he called me that, touched me in ways he had absolutely no right to, then proceeded to punch my face.

> **Me:** Hey. I wanted to apologize for what I said the other time. I really meant no disrespect and I'm sorry if you got offended.

> **Me:** This is Brandon King, by the way.

He read the texts but never replied.

That was over two weeks ago.

Two weeks and I still find myself checking in case I missed a text. Like now.

What on earth is wrong with me?

I just can't seem to stop replaying what happened that night. Over and over, like a broken fucking record. Again and again, it sneaks into my head and spreads on top of other thoughts like a special torture device.

Every day, I think of why I lost control so easily. I was cursing out loud—not once or twice, but *several* times. I snapped and growled and even used violence.

But the most embarrassing moment was when he had his lips on my jaw and throat, licking and exploring. My skin caught fire and I was on the edge of something nefarious.

My heart has never beat as fast as when he bit down on my throat.

And I groaned. *Me.* Brandon fucking King *groaned* because a *guy* was biting me.

It was like existing in the skin of an entirely different person. As if I broke apart from my physical being and morphed into an alien entity.

I hate that version of myself. I fucking despise it.

But what I hate the most is what I said because I was so livid.

I've never seen Nikolai as angry as when he punched me in the face and then tackled me to the ground.

He looked down at me as if I were a pest he wished to squash beneath his shoe. The switch from flirtation, skin licking to downright violence gave me whiplash.

Then I realized maybe he thought I said he was disgusting for being gay.

I really didn't mean that.

People being straight, gay, or anything else has never mattered to me. Hell, Eli, Creigh, and Remi's granddads are the oldest gay people I know, and I've always found their bickering with Grandpa Jonathan amusing.

I have nothing against gay people. But the truth remains, I'm straight. I can only be *straight*.

The reason I said Nikolai was disgusting was because he kept touching me when I repeatedly told him not to.

It was because I felt strange, on fire, and completely out of my skin.

It was because he can effortlessly rip at my control and tear it to shreds as if it was never there in the first place.

He clearly got the hint this time, so…silver linings, I guess.

I glare at the screen, then turn it black, throw my phone in my pocket, and pick up my palette and brush, then whip a few more strokes with red. I don't even like red. I'm a fan of cool colors, blue and green.

But right now, I can't help stroking along the lines of yellow with red, giving birth to some orange. Hot, fiery.

Wild.

So fucking wild and everything I'm not.

Art has always been my damnation and salvation. I have no clue what the hell I'd be without sketching and brushing strokes on a blank canvas, but at the same time, the extent it can go to scares the shit out of me.

When I was two, I was doodling small stars anywhere I could reach. The floor, with Mum's makeup on the walls. On Landon's forehead, chest, and back while we giggled and hid away from our parents.

Then those stars morphed into sketches of our family, small dogs, and the cutest cats. Now, my artistic style has settled on landscapes. Flowers. Trees. Seas. Gardens.

Fauna.

This is far from a landscape, my brain whispers, getting freaked the fuck out, but I can't stop.

If I do, I'll have no other way to cope. I'll really have to resort to purging that ink from my veins.

Again.

Are you sure seeing the end result of this is safer than purging?

My hand suspends in midair.

The door opens and I startle, my heart lunging in my chest.

Fuck. I forgot to lock the door.

Lan strolls in, completely unruffled, comfortable in his own skin. Despite him being a bastard with not a humane bone in his body, a distant sense of comfort washes over me whenever we're in the same room.

The sad truth is that seeing Lan's face is the only way I can see *my* face looking peaceful.

We're identical twins, but Lan is a bit more muscular than me. His eyes are meaner, too, and he wears this permanent provoking smirk.

Despite having the same physical image, we're worlds apart. He's clinically diagnosed with narcissistic and antisocial personality disorder.

I'm diagnosed with being fucked up.

He's the charming twin, the one who everyone's attention flocks toward, the superstar of the King family, and the genius of contemporary art.

He's *everything* lumped into one supreme existence.

All my life, I've watched him soar and fly toward the sky while I've remained stuck underground.

I mentally shake my head. I'm *not* doing this today.

"What are you doing here?" I ask cautiously. It's not a secret that

Lan and I don't have the greatest relationship. That happens when the person I always cared about labeled me as 'Spare Parts' in his contacts. He meant it as a joke and I reciprocated it, but it cut something inside me. The illusion that we share a bond, maybe.

"I can't come to see my brother?" He slides a hand into his pocket and I take note of his black trousers that are folded at the ankles. While we both dress elegantly, we have different styles. I doubt he has any khaki trousers or polo shirts in his wardrobe.

"What do you really want, Lan?"

"You don't believe I'm here to check on you?" He grins. "I'm hurt, little bro."

"I'm not your little bro."

"I happen to be fifteen whole minutes older than you. Deal with it." He ruffles my hair as if we're back to being kids, and I knock his hand off.

I don't want to think of our once-close relationship when I destroyed it with my own hands.

Once upon a time, we slept in the same bed and he told me everything, including details I didn't care to hear.

Then everything collapsed. My mind included.

"Seriously, what are you doing here?" I ask with more exasperation than I usually show.

Might have to do with my exceptionally jittering nerves lately.

"I really just want to check on you. Mum sounded worried on the phone."

I briefly close my eyes. "I'm fine."

"Sure, Bran. If you keep telling yourself that often enough, you might eventually believe it."

"What is that supposed to mean?" I narrow my eyes, but he's not looking at me.

He physically pushes me out of the way as he stalks to my canvas.

Shit.

Fuck.

Bloody fucking hell.

Sweat trickles down my back as my brother looks at the seemingly haphazard strokes on the canvas. If it were anyone else, I wouldn't be so worried, but this is my genius twin brother we're talking about.

The top dog of REU art school and the up-and-coming sculpting talent who's won multiple awards for his devilishly detailed statues.

His head tilts to the side as he studies the canvas and I want to jump in front of him and hide it. I want to soak it in black ink. But I don't, or Lan would sense something is seriously wrong.

There are two things that scare the fuck out of me.

My image in the mirror and Landon.

"This is…fucking brilliant." He whistles.

My chest squeezes until it nearly topples me over. Lan hasn't praised anything I've done in…eight years.

His previous descriptions of my work have been scathingly critical.

Severely mediocre.

Exasperatingly tedious.

Devastatingly unoriginal.

Exceptionally mind-numbing.

Disturbingly boring.

Boring.

Boring.

Boring.

That's my twin brother, ladies and gentlemen. He pulls no punches in telling me how bad I am compared to his otherworldly talent.

It doesn't matter how much my world-renowned artist mum and the professors have liked my work. It doesn't matter how many awards I get for my technically superior nature scenes.

Lan has never liked any of them. Not even one.

"It's just a fluke," I mutter, fighting my emotions as I step to the canvas, wanting to bring it down and hide everything it represents.

For some reason, I feel completely raw and naked in front of him. Like that night he hugged me for the last time.

My brother clutches me by the shoulder and spins me around so that we're both looking at the chaos of red and yellow. The fiery explosion my fingers made in translation of the chaos brewing in my mind.

"If that's a fluke, do it all the time, Bran. Seriously, this is your best work in a *long* time." He squeezes my shoulder. "I told you everything would get better if you stopped shackling yourself."

I tense.

No. I am *still* shackling myself. I can't stop doing that.

I'm in control.

Control.

Control.

Control.

He turns me around to face him as I'm about to lose my fucking shit and spiral down that nasty road.

His eyes are narrowed. "Please tell me this isn't because you got back with Clara."

"What does she have to do with it…?" Sometimes I forget we're together. I keep making up all sorts of excuses to not meet at night—or even during the day—and send her designer bags and shoes as compensation.

"She's flaunting you all over her IG like an attention whore."

"Lan! That's so rude."

"Well, she is. A gold digger, too." He frowns. "For the life of me, I can't understand why the hell you keep going back to the bitch. She cheated on you, multiple times, and she's so toxic, it makes drugs look like unicorn rainbows."

"Very rich coming from the toxicity king."

He huffs. "Classic Bran move."

"What?"

"Always deflect, little bro. Run, hide, and change the subject whenever it hits too close to home. That's working bloody wonders for you."

I force a smile. "If you're done, kindly get out."

"Lose her, Bran. I mean it. If the bitch hurts you one more time, I'll take things into my own hands and we both know how that will end."

And then he steps out of the studio.

I continue watching the door long after he's gone.

His words sounded like he cared, or like he was doing it for me, but no. Lan has always seen me as an extension of himself, so the reason he'd take revenge against Clara isn't for me. It's for *him*, so he won't look weak.

My eyes land on the canvas and I groan. I'm so glad Lan didn't see a certain silhouette. But I do.

Clearly.

In the middle of the volcanic chaos stands a figure—tall, muscular, and furious.

My hand shakes as I run it over my face.

Fuck.

What the hell is happening to me?

And how can I stop this?

EIGHT

Brandon

A WEEK LATER, I GO OUT TO THE LOCAL PUB WITH MY friends.

Only so I don't get too stuck in my head and…do something I'll regret.

Chatter echoes around us as drinks are exchanged. We're seated at a big table in the middle, surrounded by smaller ones.

A few older locals sit at the bar, discussing their crops as they down their daily pints.

The small party is in full bloom with Remi being a clown as always. He's bouncing back and forth with a drink in hand as he verbally spars with our two childhood friends, Ava, who's about Glyn's age, and Cecily, who's a year older.

My cousin Creigh is also here, but he seems more preoccupied with his phone. Annika, the girls' new roommate and Jeremy's younger sister, tries to strike up a conversation with him, but he doesn't dignify her with a response.

He's listening, though, because he looks up whenever she stops talking.

I'm still a bit peeved about Annika recently being added to the group. She's nice, but the fact remains that she represents the Heathens, and there's often security detail outside every place we go.

I'd really prefer it if the Heathens were no longer shoved down my throat.

One small problem, though. I've sort of become close with Mia Sokolov. Or she could be just using me to get closer to Lan like all girls aside from Clara do.

I like her company and she games like a boss, so I guess we'll keep seeing each other for as long as she wants. At my place. There's no way in hell I'm stepping foot in the Heathens' mansion again.

Not after the last time I was there.

Don't think about it.

Stop thinking about it.

It's easy to focus on the people around me, but it's still a struggle to be completely present. So I throw down my third drink, mirroring Glyn, who's sitting opposite me and who's also hell-bent on drinking herself into a coma.

She just suggested playing *never have I ever* in a very slurry voice. Maybe I should call it a night and take her back to the flat she shares with the girls.

Only, I really need to drink as well. A few more and then we'll leave.

Remi holds an imaginary mic. "I'll go first."

Cecily flips her silver hair back and points an accusatory finger at him. "You always go first."

"That's right." Ava puffs out her chest. "Glyn wanted this, so let her play first."

"Play what?"

I nearly spit out my mouthful of alcohol. It's not because of Killian, my sister's boyfriend, who just said that last sentence.

Not even close.

The hairs on the back of my neck stand on end, and while I can't see the entirety of him, I can make out Nikolai's frame standing close to Killian. His hair is loose, falling thick and smooth to his shoulders. This time, he's wearing a black tee and jeans that hang low on his hips. Although it's not exactly summer, he has no jacket. Full sleeves of tattoos extend from beneath his shirt to the backs of his hands.

I can't stop looking at him.

And the more I do, the faster my throat fills with that *different* nausea. The one that's overwhelming but doesn't make me want to hit my head against the wall.

It's pushing me to nefarious ends.

Down unknown roads.

Stop looking.

Stop *looking*.

I force myself to take a sip of my drink and focus on my sister, who glances up at Killian. "What are you doing here?"

He pushes his cousin in front of him. "Nikolai was bored, so I took him out for a stroll."

"Eat shit, motherfucker. I'm not a dog. Also, he was the one who was so bored that he started vandalizing shit," Nikolai says, then speaks to Glyn, "I was dragged out against my will because he refuses to admit he misses you."

"Semantics," Killian says. "Can we join you?"

All the rowdiness from earlier comes to a halt, and I can't help hearing the doomsday sound in my brain.

Tick.

He looks murderous.

Tick.

He's not looking at me.

Tick.

He is *not* looking at me.

The upgraded nausea dies down and I'm hit with the familiar feeling of fucked-up Brandon in epic proportions.

Black ink swells beneath my feet and I feel my stomach churning.

"Yeah, sure!" Ava replies. "The more the merrier."

Killian brings a chair over and sits beside my sister, and Nikolai flops down beside him.

Across from me.

Only a table separates us, but he still hasn't looked at me since he got here. Not even once.

Killian and Glyn whisper to each other, and I know I should be looking out for my sister, but I learned that it doesn't matter what we think. She probably loves Killian.

Lan obviously doesn't agree, and it's because he kidnapped Killian and tortured him that I ended up in the Heathens' mansion.

It's all because of *him*.

Class act. Blame Lan. It's working bloody wonders like he said.

Killian finally stops trying to eye-fuck my sister and asks, "So what are we playing?"

"*Never have I ever*," I say, not recognizing my voice. "And Glyn will start."

She raises a shot. "Never have I ever done something illegal."

Nikolai shrugs and knocks down a shot. My fingers tighten around my glass. Of course he's done something illegal. His existence itself should be illegal.

He's so fucking infuriating.

Why did he have to show up in my space again?

Creighton downs a shot, seeming to have finished his obsession with his phone.

"What did you do…" Annika asks, then swallows and stares at Nikolai. "Nikolai?"

He looks at her and winks. "You know the drill."

I narrow my eyes as I stare between them. Are they a thing? Or *were* they?

Good grief. Isn't she supposed to be his best friend's sister and barely legal?

But then again, if all the posts he gets tagged in are of any indication, then he's often caught with both men and women hanging off his arm. And it's been going on for years.

Not that I went there on purpose…

My thoughts trail off when Ava takes a shot, drawing everyone's attention.

"What illegal things have you done?" Cecy asks.

"Sorry, bitches, there's no rule that says I have to explain. Should've set that beforehand."

Remi brings his shot up, then takes it in one go with an "Ahh. Drugs, those nasty little shits."

"Why aren't you drinking?" Glyn asks Killian.

"Because I'm not admitting to doing anything illegal. My father and grandfather are lawyers, thank you very much."

"That's not how it works."

"Do you have proof that I committed illegal actions?"

"Ugh, whatever."

He whispers something in her ear and she goes a bright shade of red. This is a bit uncomfortable to watch, but not as uncomfortable as the presence of the guy I'm trying to pretend isn't sitting next to Killian.

Who's still *not* looking at me.

"Your turn," she tells her boyfriend.

He pauses, but only for a beat. "Never have I ever been in love."

Ava takes a shot and I watch her with pity, my fingers trailing over my glass. My poor friend has had the worst love story to ever exist. Not that I believe in that emotion.

After all, love is just an illusion made up by empty people who crave companionship.

In reality, it doesn't exist.

My skin prickles and the feeling of being watched stabs me in the chest.

I lift my head, and for the first time in weeks, my eyes lock with the violent twat who has no business looking at me with...a challenge.

What the hell is that supposed to mean?

The way I saw it, you got hard when you had your eyes on me. Not her.

Those are the words that sent me into an epic loss of control, and for some reason, that foreign feeling is returning again.

My muscles tighten and I snatch a shot, then down it in one go and suppress a wince against the burn.

Nikolai's eyes explode in a myriad of violent intensity, and rage radiates from him in waves.

It's suddenly hard to swallow and I have to force down the need to clear my throat.

Unfamiliar anger ripples through me as he continues glaring.

What the hell did he expect?

Why the fuck is he even *expecting* anything from me?

Glyn raises a shot, but before she can drink it, Killian takes it for her and says, "You're drunk. I'll take your shots."

"I don't need you to."

"Swoon." Annika fawns over them, a stupid grin plastering all over her face.

She's seventeen and skipped a school year to attend uni this young, right? I know Nikolai is only nineteen—seriously, he's a kid—but he wouldn't have done anything with her when she was/is underage, right?

I mean, the age of consent in the UK is sixteen, but they're Americans. Isn't it eighteen over there…?

Besides, he wouldn't have done that to his best friend, right?

My throat constricts, and this time, I have to discreetly clear it against the influx of disgusting nausea.

Right?

"We need to take this game to the next level." Nikolai holds out a shot and I stare at him, my heart pounding so hard, I think I'll have a heart attack.

"Never have I ever fucked or experimented with someone of the same sex." He steals a peek at me and then drinks his shot.

My heart thunders behind my rib cage and my fingers turn clammy around my glass. Breaths whoosh out of my lungs in fractured intervals.

Fuck. Fuck. Fuck.

"Does a kiss count?" Ava asks him, and he nods. Eyes on me.

Stop looking at me.

Just *stop.*

I think I'm going to throw up in front of everyone and humiliate myself in the worst way possible.

"Well, screw it." Ava takes the shot.

Remi gasps like a drama king. "This bitch is really looking to get herself killed tonight."

Killian raises a shot and Glyn watches him with a questioning gaze.

"Don't look like you'll faint, little rabbit. Do you really believe all those kinks were done with only women? I used to experiment a lot."

As he drinks, she also picks up a shot and takes it in one go.

What...? My sister did what...?

"Don't look surprised, Killer. I used to experiment a lot, too."

I release a breath. Okay, so that was a lie to mess with Killian. She would've told me if that were the case. We're close.

I *think*.

At least, I hope we are.

"No one else?" Nikolai toys with his empty shot glass, shooting a provocative look in my direction.

I stare at Remi and Ava bickering, then at my feet, and my focus stays there. Looking at the ink swallowing my shoes.

And yet I can feel his eyes on me, intense and unapologetic.

Tick.

You're going to make a fool out of yourself.

Tick.

It's game over, Bran. Everyone will see you for the fraud you are.

A low humming sound falls from him and I can't help stealing a glimpse as he shoves a cigarette between his lips and stands. "Fucking bore. I'm out of here."

I have to tighten my grip on the glass to stop it from shaking. My gaze tracks his nonchalant movements as he stalks to the exit, lighting his cigarette and releasing a cloud of smoke in the air.

Instead of the ink retreating from around my feet, it swallows them up, then shoots up my shins and strangles my knees until that's all I can see and feel.

Black ink.

Fucking doom.

My heart simmers down almost lethargically, and I swallow another drink to numb it.

"Phew, that was intense," Annika says. "Seriously, Kill. Don't bring him next time. He's scary."

"Are you sure it's not because he could snitch to your brother?"

She laughs awkwardly. "Don't be ridiculous. I have nothing to hide from Jer."

"Uh-huh," Killian replies.

I want to ask what she has to hide. Why is she calling him scary if they were together...?

Stop it.

"So who's next?" I ask in an attempt to ignore all the chaos.

"Me!" Annika looks at Killian. "Never have I ever got my dick sucked."

"That's a low fucking blow," Remi whines, but he downs a drink. Killian and I do so as well.

"Wait a minute." Remi looks at Creigh. "Why aren't you drinking, Cray Cray? Have you missed the never have I ever for this round?" My cousin shakes his head and Remi throws his hand in the air. "Then drink—Jesus fucking Christ, spawn, please tell me you've had your dick sucked at least once?"

When Creigh doesn't reply, Remi flops on his chair with more theatrics than needed. "I think I need some medical attention. My own spawn has been missing out and I didn't know. I'm losing years of my life as we speak, I'm telling you."

"What's so special about having one's dick sucked?" Creigh asks.

"Uh, what's so special about the sun? The moon? The ecosystem? I can go on forever. Jesus, spawn, you're making me look like a bad mentor."

"You are, though." Cecily makes a face at him and they all keep talking, bickering, and laughing.

Having fun.

I zone out.

I laugh when they do, but I have no clue what's happening around me.

A fog surrounds me and seeps beneath my skin until I can't breathe.

I drink two more shots, but I'm not entirely numb.

It's not enough.

Nothing is enough.

I can't breathe.

Please *stop*.

I shake my head, trying and failing to shake away the black ink swelling inside.

When Killian decides to take Glyn home, I wait a few minutes, then make up an excuse about feeling a bit under the weather.

More like I'm crushed by my own head.

I stumble out of the pub unsteadily, my head swimming and my vision blurring. I bump into a group of people and apologize—or I think I do—as I walk in a zigzag.

The lights shimmer and turn into tiny bokeh points, moving farther and farther away.

Like my fucking sanity.

I used to pride myself on being completely in control. About everything.

Anyone.

Until this motherfucker came into my life.

And now, I'm not sure how to get that control back.

I *need* that control or everything will be over.

Every fucking thing.

I stumble into someone and step back on swaying feet. "Sorry…"

"Watch where you're going, you fucking cunt!" The guy grabs me by the collar of my shirt and shakes me a few times, and I see stars.

He sounds American. Fuck those guys. Why can't they just stay in America and leave me alone?

"You better apologize or I'll kill you," he and his twin threaten.

Oh, wait. It's triplets.

It's the alcohol, isn't it?

His friends try to disengage him from me, but he only tightens his hold until I can't breathe.

I smile sweetly like the very good person I am and then mutter, "Fuck you."

He lifts his fist and I close my eyes. Maybe I need this so I'll either pass out or finally snap the fuck out of it.

I wait for the punch, but it never comes.

The fingers disappear from around my throat and I watch in complete horror as Nikolai drives his fist into the guy's face, sending him flying.

Blood explodes all over his nose and mouth as he splutters on the ground. And then he lifts him up by his T-shirt and punches him again.

And again.

Then kicks him.

When the others try to interfere, he drives his fists in their faces in a long succession of punches.

He's in a frenzy. A craze.

He is *crazy*.

And yet as I stand here, the only feeling that goes through me is resounding relief.

He didn't leave.

He came back.

NINE

Nikolai

THIS IS DEFINITELY *NOT* WHAT IT LOOKS LIKE.
I didn't hang out around the area of the pub, chain-smoking and contemplating how to pick a fight and punch some motherfuckers.

Okay, I did.

But the next part is *definitely* not what it looks like.

I didn't beat these people up because a cunt happened to grab Brandon by his shirt or attempt to punch him.

Hurt him.

Right in front of *me*.

Yeah, so I did drive my fist in Brandon's face the last time I saw him, but only *I* get to do that.

Anyway, this bunch of assholes ended up being victims of my sour mood because they happened to be here.

Not because I followed Brandon like a creepy stalker or anything equally stupid.

Okay, maybe I did, but it was only for two blocks. Maybe three.

Fine. Five.

But none of that matters.

The fact that I get to decorate my hand with their deplorable blood does. Fucker who caught Brandon by the shirt is now spluttering blood on the ground, half conscious, while I humble his friends. One of them ran away, but oh well, I have my hands completely full with the other two. I punch and kick them, reveling in the sound of bones cracking beneath my fingers.

There's nothing I love more than having power over some cunts who happened to be in the wrong place at the very fucking wrong time.

A red haze covers my vision as I go on and on and fucking *on* until they realize I might actually kill them—great possibility—then grab each other and flee the scene.

They're limping, grunting, and cursing on their way to what can only be the hospital. Probably the police, too, but I don't give a fuck at this point.

In fact, maybe I shouldn't have let them go and introduced them to their maker instead.

Red still covers my vision as I catch a glimpse of onlookers gathered around, eyes agape, and some of them were probably filming the whole thing, considering the phones.

I flash them my signature 'back the fuck off' look and they slowly disperse, lowering their heads and continuing with their debauchery.

Now I have nothing to distract me from the actual cause of this damn ruse. I'd be lying if I said I haven't instigated violence before just because, but this time, it definitely wasn't random.

It's because of the asshole I've been tracking in my peripheral vision, even while I was having my fingers soaked with blood.

Usually, I don't see anything through the satisfying red. But this time, I was more focused on Brandon and if he'd faint or escape.

He did neither.

The whole time, he stood rooted in place, his eyes wide, pupils dilated and lips parted.

His gaze meets mine and remains there, not attempting to avoid me like he usually does.

He must be so fucking drunk, because he stares at me, mouth hanging open, without his dash of uptight disdain.

Fuck this guy, seriously.

I'm so over him and his perfectly pressed pants, tucked-in shirts, and leather shoes. I'm over the way he looks to be in control but still appears hopelessly clueless at times.

Like right now.

His flawless golden-boy image is cracked at the seams—totally because of the alcohol he kept chugging the entire time I was there—and a pink flush covers his cheeks.

A few strands have escaped his styled hair, giving him a rugged edge. Rebellious. It's safe to say he's not caught under the rigid spell of his steel-like control.

At least, temporarily.

Momentarily.

I would've been all over that shit a few weeks ago, but now, I have to remove myself from his vicinity before I finish off the night by punching him.

He got on my nerves enough by doing everything wrong earlier in the pub. From the way he pretended I was invisible, to saying he'd been in love, to denying we ever did anything.

Every. Fucking. Thing.

Now, I have to leave so I won't throttle the fuck out of him.

This is why I've stayed away. Why I've removed myself from any situation he's in or any environment where he can exist.

I see him, and I'm burning.

The harder I've tried to stay away, the wilder my obsession with him has grown.

I just can't fucking help it.

When I brush past him, I stop and swipe two fingers beneath his jaw and subtly lift up, causing his mouth to finally close. "Might want to stop staring or I'll think you have a crush on me or something equally crazy."

I expect him to push me away, but the alcohol must've numbed his brain, because he just stares. Unblinking. His Adam's apple bobs up and down with a swallow, and did his breathing pick up just now?

It takes me considerable energy to pull my fingers away, and that's when I notice I've left smudges of blood near his jaw. I have to suppress a groan at the sight, so I camouflage it with a smirk. "Oops, got blood all over your shiny image. My bad."

I don't even attempt to apologize as I wrench my eyes from him and continue on my way. I need to punch a few other things. Here's an idea, force Jeremy to give me a mission where I can torture some people and put the fear of the devil in their souls—

Something pulls on my T-shirt and I frown. If one of those sorry fucks came back for round two...

My thoughts trail off when I see two long fingers curled in the material so firmly, it stretches beneath the pressure.

I stare up at Brandon, and the way he looks at me does shit I definitely do not approve of. He's like a kicked fucking puppy, which is miles apart from his usual condescending asshole image.

"Thank you," he whispers softly, almost airily.

Fuck this asshole and that deep voice of his.

I have to get out of here.

No. Not have. It's a fucking *need* at this point or I might really do shit I'll regret.

And Jer isn't here to stop me.

"I didn't do it for you. I just wanted someone to punch and they happened to be there." I start to move again, but he tugs harder on my T-shirt.

"Now what?" I snap.

He needs to get his hand off me, because it's giving me fucked-up ideas.

And none of them are things he approves of.

Brandon swallows and my gaze goes straight to his Adam's apple. He does it again as if giving me the show I want, then clears his throat. "Did...you get the texts I sent you?"

"Yeah, so?"

"Why didn't you reply?"

"Why would I? Should I have rejoiced and thrown a party because the almighty Brandon King finally recognized my existence, decided I'm not *disgusting* anymore, and texted me? Get over your useless fucking self."

His jaw tightens and he releases me. "Don't be a dick." I apologized for what I think is a misunderstanding. I...don't believe you're disgusting because of your sexuality. I would never think that."

"Thanks for nothing." This time, I'm hell-bent on leaving. Because unlike fucker Brandon who can lie through his teeth during a useless game and keep his control in check, I have zero chill. And I need to go before I do something I'll regret come morning. I didn't even do regrets before the ill-fated meeting with this complete fucking *charmer*.

Brandon steps in front of me, or more like sways since he's as drunk as a sailor. There's only a subtle slur to his words, though, as if he can keep control despite being pumped full of liquor.

"What the fuck do you want now?" I sneer. "You're uncharacteristically clingy tonight."

"I want to ask you something."

"Why would I answer? We're not friends or anything are we, Lotus—" I cut myself off before I call him that.

Of course the bastard noticed the miscalculation despite being wasted, because his lips twitch.

Jesus fucking Christ.

I know I'm supposed to be mad—or keep up with the image, anyway—but it's impossible to hold on to the anger I've left to fester when he's smiling.

He is actually *smiling* without faking anything, his lips curving and his eyes softening. He looks happy when I could've sworn the asshole doesn't know the emotion.

It's because of the alcohol, isn't it?

Also, why the fuck does it ache behind my rib cage?

Maybe I should have myself checked, because this shit is seriously disturbing.

His smile disappears as soon as it appeared and I want to shove my hand inside his throat and drag it out. Take a picture this time and keep it forever.

"Are you going to say something or are you just going to stand there and stare at me like a creep?" I ask, using the words he's often thrown my way.

He purses his lips. *Doesn't feel so good, does it, prick?*

"Just tell me...did you have a thing with Annika?"

"What the fuck? She's like a fetus." I narrow my eyes. "Why are you asking? You better not involve her in your stupid games or I'll personally help Jeremy annihilate you."

My blood roars at the mere thought of that. I still haven't even forgotten about *Clara*, and now he wants Annika.

Nah, hell no.

Fuck that.

I'll strangle the fuck out of him.

"No, no," he says in a bit of a rush. "She's too young and I don't... I don't like anyone who's barely legal."

His eyes shine brightly and I get closer, trying to read him. "You know I'm going to be twenty soon, right?"

That smile nearly makes another breakthrough and I catch myself sucking in my breath to see it, but he suppresses it in a typical asshole move. "You're still way younger than me."

"*Way?* It's only three years."

"And a half."

"And a *half*. Jesus. We're still in the same damn generation. You need to chill for a bit, my dude."

He frowns, his lips pushing forward—fucking adorable. "I'm not your *dude*."

"Aaand the grouchy Brandon King makes a stunning comeback!" I shake my head. "You just never disappoint, do you?"

"Well, maybe you should stop giving me all these nicknames."

"Which one is your favorite?" I step closer until I can inhale the whiskey from his mouth. But alcohol isn't the only thing I smell. I'm smothered by the musk emanating from his flushed fair skin and the notes of clover and citrus in his damn hair. Fuck, his hair smells so good.

Am I sure I'm not the drunk one?

Apparently, I don't give a fuck about my resolve, because I whisper, "Do you prefer lotus flower? My dude? Oh, Prince Charming?"

"None," he says slowly, his eyes light and hooded as he stares up at me.

"Oh, right." I stand toe-to-toe with him and line my lips with the shell of his ear. "You like being called *baby*."

He trembles against me. Fucking *trembles*. Or maybe it's the alcohol and he's swaying, but I couldn't care less. I choose to believe it's because I've destabilized him.

I choose to think he's not immune to my presence and I'm getting under his skin as deep as he's penetrated mine.

He better be or I swear to fuck I'll personally amputate Kolya for the inhumane abstinence he's been forcing on me for a whole damn month.

I tighten my chest muscles for the punch or shove I know is coming and wait.

Then wait some more.

But it doesn't happen.

I step back to find Brandon pulling at the hairs at his nape. Otherwise, he's completely still. Like a robot. Eyes staring at his feet.

Not blinking.

Not moving.

Okay, I've seen my fair share of fucked up, but this vacant look in his eyes is fucking disturbing.

What the fuck did I do now...?

Bran shakes his head and backs away, rocking on his feet, and I'm not sure if it's because he's drunk on the alcohol or something else. His hand flops to his side as he swallows. "I...better go."

"Sure thing, Prince Charming. Go back to your favorite hobby of running away. If you do that fast enough, you might reach your second favorite hobby—denial—in record time."

His eyes shoot to mine. "Seriously, what the hell is your problem?"

"What's *your* problem?" I invade his space again, my chest grazing his, and we both inhale at the same time. "Why the fuck do you act as if me calling you baby is the end of the world?"

"Because you're not supposed to," he whispers, his eyes blinking slowly, but he doesn't stop running them over my face.

"You need to stop looking at me like that if you don't want me to fucking devour you."

He shakes his head once, but, surprisingly, no words come out of his antagonizing mouth.

But here's the thing.

Brandon doesn't look away and, instead, keeps staring, eyes hooded and lips slightly parted.

Fuck this asshole. He's the most infuriating man I've ever gotten to know, but he's still the only one who's started a fire at the pit of my stomach, the flames so wild, they spread to my chest and fan my dick back to life.

I'm so hard, it's fucking painful at this point, and I have to do something.

I'm back to that hopeless stage of wanting a taste.

A nip.

A lick.

Anything.

I'll take anything he allows me to have. Even if small, I'll fucking gobble it all down and store it in that nook inside me that's disturbingly filled with him.

My hand bunches in his shirt and I growl as I tug and slam him against my chest.

I can feel that loud thump of his heartbeat as his eyes widen, panic glittering in their depths like wildfire, similar to mine.

But there's something else a lot more potent.

Now that his control has wavered, I sense an avalanche of impulsiveness rushing to the surface.

And I just have to seize it. Trap it. Leave him no fucking way out.

Just once.

"D-don't," he stammers, both his hands landing on my chest as he searches our surroundings, which are full of drunk people, before he focuses on me again, his eyes a myriad of confusion. "*Please.*"

"Too late, *baby.*"

Using my hold on his shirt, I drag him into a tight alley and shove him against a grimy brick wall.

He releases the most delicious startled sound I've ever heard and I'm done for.

Finished.

Absolutely jumping off a cliff, rolling and cracking a few bones and not giving a flying fuck, because I have my prize at the bottom.

Him.

My hand slides to his throat and wraps around his chiseled jaw, my fingers digging into his smooth skin. Brandon's eyes widen to a dark, hypnotizing blue, and he rewards me with another noise, low and fucking needy.

I slam my lips to his, devouring that sound and swallowing it deep inside me.

Fuck.

Fuck *me.*

Fucking fucker of all motherfucking fucks.

He tastes like sweet surrender, all wound up and ripe for the taking.

I can't believe I didn't do this sooner. I think I've found my new favorite drug in the form of his lips. I suck the lower one into my mouth, biting down on the cushion so he feels the pain as deep as I do.

Bran shakes against me, his fingers fisting in my shirt, and I'm not sure if he's pulling me closer or pushing me away.

I don't give a fuck.

Tonight, I'm taking what I should've stolen that night I met him at the initiation.

Whether his delusional brain likes it or not.

TEN

Brandon

I'VE ALWAYS PRIDED MYSELF ON BEING IN CONTROL.
Everything has gone according to a plan, a schedule and an end goal. Spontaneity and I fell out of each other's favor years ago and I never reconciled that relationship.

And I was okay with it.

I *am* okay with it.

Losing control once threw my life in a loop of chaos and fucking destruction and I can't do chaos.

Chaos is the source of all evil.

Chaos would push me over the edge I've been walking for as long as I can remember.

And yet, right now, I can hear the cracks in my wall. While small, their deafening sound resounds in my foggy head, and I watch with complete bewilderment as the control I've nursed for years collapses all around me.

Crashing, splintering, and leaving a Nikolai-shaped hole in the outer walls of my carefully curated self-preservation.

I'm trapped, ensnared, and being held captive. I can't feel even a smidge of my autonomy or the logical thoughts that I usually wear like a badge.

There's something else I do feel, though.

Or someone.

His bruising grip on my jaw keeps me in place as he strokes my lips with his, harsh and unforgiving.

Demanding.

He bites down on my lower lip, stretching the skin until pain explodes in the nerve endings, and my heart thumps, pushing and shoving itself against my rib cage.

I must be so hammered, because when he stabs his tongue against my lips, I don't try to resist or force my mouth shut.

The scary thought is that I *want* to open.

My blood buzzes for it, my unorganized thoughts tune in for the mere possibility of it.

A feeling I've never experienced in my life.

The moment I part my lips hesitantly, Nikolai goes feral. His tongue swirls around mine, warring, plunging, and stripping me of the last smidge of control I have left.

A groan echoes in the air and I realize with depleted horror that it's mine.

His fingers dig into my jaw and he growls deep in my mouth, causing me to shudder.

He tastes of lawless violence and forbidden temptation.

He tastes like my custom-made damnation.

My fingers glide up and I swear I mean to shove him away. Put him back in his place. Shout 'How dare you touch me?'

But my hand wraps around his nape and I free fall headfirst into dangerous chaos, completely in the dark about what waits for me at the bottom.

My tongue curls around his and I fight him for control. For the sanity that he's been stripping from me one layer at a time.

His hand drops from my collar and he slides it to my side, feeling and exploring my chest and back, and I can't help the hiss that escapes when he bites down on my tongue.

It's like being kissed by a savage—a vicious barbarian whose sole purpose is to drag out the worst in me.

My eyes flutter open and that's when I realize I've had them closed since his lips claimed mine.

I blink up at him, watching his own closed eyes and feeling that pit grow at the bottom of my stomach.

Fuck.

Fuck me.

I'm not sober enough to resist, and, hell, I don't think I'm only drunk on the alcohol. My nostrils flare and I inhale sharply, filling my lungs with his mint scent. It mixes and swirls with the taste of alcohol, cigarettes, and something else that's entirely him.

Masculine and strange...

I want to think it's bad strange, but I'm far from being revolted. If anything, I've never felt trapped in a pleasure haze like I am right now.

He slides his tongue out of my mouth and bites the corner of my lip, then whispers in hot, growly words, "Who's a better kisser, baby? Clara or me?"

"Shut up..." I don't recognize how my voice comes out all choked up and hoarse.

This is so fucking *wrong*.

"I'm going to go with me." His intense eyes meet mine as he glides his tongue against my bottom lip and then nibbles down savagely. "You didn't look so hot and bothered when you were kissing her. Actually, it seemed like a fucking chore."

A guttural sound slips from me and he sucks, then bites down on my lower lip again, brutalizing the skin between his teeth before he releases it.

"You like that, baby?" He speaks so close to my mouth, he kisses me with every word.

"Don't call me that," I breathe out, shuffling and searching through the mess in my head, but for the life of me, I can't grasp at the strings of my MIA sanity.

"Don't call you what? Baby?"

"Nikolai!"

"Fuck me. I love the way you growl my name, baby."

"Don't."

"Why? Does it hit a nerve?" He rolls his hips and shoves his groin against mine, and my wide eyes meet his lust-filled ones. "Correction, it definitely hit more than one nerve, because you're fucking hard. This time, it's definitely for me."

"Stop..." The word comes out hushed, nearly inaudible, and I'm not sure if Nikolai heard it.

A small part of me is thankful he didn't, because he wedges his knees between mine and slides the length of his bulging erection against my cock.

A delicious tingle spreads up my spine and I puff out a long exhale.

"Mmm. You got so hard by just kissing." He swipes his tongue on my mouth over and over as if he's trying to erase something. "Your dick must be huge. I can feel it through your pants, all erect and begging for attention."

He rubs himself against me some more, until I feel like I'll burst, my head and body at complete odds with each other.

I tighten my hold on his nape and tug on his hair, my voice hoarse. "Don't...stop..."

"Is that don't stop or don't and stop?" He falls into a rhythm, dry humping my cock with his until my painful erection strains against my trousers.

I must release a noise, because Nikolai chuckles against my lips. "I'll take that as the former. Mmm. You feel so good, baby. So fucking perfect."

His words swim in the pleasure haze surrounding my head and stab me in the very marrow of my bones.

"Do you feel how hard I am for you?" *Kiss.* "How ravenous I turn when it comes to you?" *Kiss.* "I'll devour you fucking whole, my beautiful lotus flower." *Kiss.* "I'll make you forget about anyone who came before me, namely fucking Clara."

His hand falls from my back, slides down my abs, over my

stomach, and to the waist of my trousers. I drop my hand that was squashed between our chests and slap it on his, then frantically shake my head.

Silently.

My eyes imploring his glazed-over ones. This is the first time anyone has looked at me like this. As if they're possessed with the idea of me.

And it's fucking terrifying.

"Don't make me do this," I whisper when he doesn't make a move to remove his hand.

"Too late."

"I'm...drunk." My chest rises and falls so hard, it grazes his with every movement, every breath, and I'm intoxicated, completely out of my damn mind.

"Then blame it on me, baby." He pushes my hand away, and this time, I let it fall to my side and don't attempt to stop him again as he undoes my belt and pulls down my zipper.

My insides are cracking and smashing, and I don't recognize my lustful thoughts. I don't recognize this version of me.

Because I find myself watching his movement, anticipation coiling in me like a snake as he wraps a tattooed hand around my rock-hard cock. I don't stop him when flicks his thumb on the side. I don't stop him when he gives me a firm, delicious jerk.

I just watch.

In complete, utter fascination.

He pulls out my painfully hard cock and I hiss at the sensation of his rough hand against the sensitive skin.

"Fuck. You do have a huge dick and it's weeping for me. Mmm. Uncut. Fucking perfect." He flashes me a charming grin as he strokes me from the base to the foreskin and presses his thumb at the tip.

I think I'll make a massive joke out of myself and come right then and there, drowning in his gaze and the hair that's framing his sharp face.

Is it supposed to feel this fucking good?

"Why, hello, Straight Brandon's dick. You look pretty gay to me."

He strokes again, harsher this time, eliciting a shudder from me.

Somewhere in my mind, I know that I should stop him. I *need* to stop him.

But I don't want to.

I have no will whatsoever.

None of my bodily functions are in tune with the logical part of my brain. Not when he's jerking me off with a level of control that leaves me panting.

My ears ring and my vision blurs, but he remains in focus right in the middle, his hard strokes grounding me to the moment.

To him.

Tingles creep up my spine and all my blood rushes to where he's touching me.

"Get my cock out," he orders in a low, growly voice.

My heavy lids lift for a fraction of a second and I stare at him, dumbfounded.

What was he saying again?

"Now," he says, firmer this time, and I don't know what's come over me.

There's something about the way he orders me around that works me into an inexplicable frenzy.

I grab onto his jeans, fingers unsteady and completely awkward as I undo his button and then slide down his zipper over his enormous erection.

Every now and then, I have to stop and suppress a groan when he jerks me faster with skin-tingling control.

My hand is definitely less sure when I reach into his boxer briefs and then pause, my mind going blank.

What the hell am I supposed to do now? I don't want to make an awkward move.

"Wrap your hand around my cock and pull it out, baby." His voice is deep but authoritarian and I find myself doing just that.

It's the first time I've touched a dick other than my own, and bloody fucking hell.

The moment I bring it out, I can't resist staring at how both thick and long he is. I'm not small by any means, but Nikolai is a tad bigger and slightly curved. Four piercings protrude from the crown, shining under the dim streetlight.

"Your hands are so soft." He nibbles on my lip, my jaw, and my Adam's apple.

A groan slips out of me and he grins against it, licking the assaulted skin, then whispers, "Squeeze me, baby."

I do, carefully, not wanting to cause him pain. Though he certainly doesn't seem like he has the same concerns with my own cock since he jerks me as if he has a problem with me.

Not that I'm complaining. No one has ever touched me this roughly. This...deliciously.

"You won't hurt me, lotus flower. Do it harder." He laps his tongue at my jaw. "Mmm. Let me get the blood off you."

He bites down on the spot as if he wants to break the skin and then sucks hard until I'm lightheaded.

My skin tingles when he steps back to leave space between us.

Nikolai releases my cock, and before I can think about it, he presses his hand on mine, opens it, and rubs his cock against mine, then closes my hand on both our girths, barely. I have big hands, but it looks tiny when wrapped around our dicks.

"Let me show you how to properly jerk a man's soul out of his cock. Relax your hand."

I do, my eyes following his movements with fascination as he grips my hand and uses it to jerk both our lengths. Roughly. With a firm edge.

The visual of his inked hand on mine turns the lust into a dangerous need.

A dash of pleasure thickens my cock, but it soars into an avalanche when Nikolai thrusts his length against mine and my hand.

Our hands.

He rolls his hips and slams forward, stabbing my groin with his pierced crown. Once, twice.

On the third time, I'm thrusting as well, matching his rhythm and jerking as hard as he's directing my hand, refusing to be the recipient. Refusing to be trapped in a role that revolts me to the core.

Wetness slips beneath our fingers and I'm not sure if it's his pre-cum or mine. I obviously don't care, because I go faster, harder. Out of the control I excel at so well.

"Your hand is jerking me so good, baby." Nikolai groans, trapping the corner of his lip between his teeth and I can't help looking at his face. At the fuck-me expression. The hollowing in his cheek as he re-leases these fucked-up erotic noises that destroy something inside me.

How can a savage be so... attractive?

It's the alcohol. Please tell me this is only because I'm hammered.

"Does it feel good when I touch you?" He squeezes my hand on our lengths. "Does it feel intoxicating? Liberating?"

All I can do is stare at him. Caught in a trance. Astonished. As if my soul has left the confines of my physical body.

"You don't have to answer. Your cock is doing the job so fuck-ing well. You're leaking for me... fuck..." he breathes. "Come for me, baby. Show me how much you want me."

Oh fuck.

No, no, no.

"No... Fuck you..." I can't hold on to my lies anymore. They sound needy to my own ears.

"Correction. I'm the one fucking *you*."

My balls fill to the brim and I get no warning as my cum splutters all over Nikolai's T-shirt and even shoots up his neck and jaw.

A fever-like sensation spreads all over my body as I watch him darting his tongue out and chasing the cum on his lips and chin, lick-ing every droplet clean.

There's no other expression for what he does next. He *uses* my hand as he thrusts himself against my slowly depleting cock, faster, harder, until a shiver goes through me.

Until I forget my damn fucking name.

"Ungh... fuck... I'm coming..." His muscles tighten as he does a few more brutal thrusts, and then I feel the wetness on my groin and all over my hand.

"Mmm. Prince Charming is covered in my cum. Yum. I can get used to this view." He smears the cum on both our lengths, then reaches a hand that's glistening with evidence of our depravity and coats it all over my lips.

My head swirls and I can feel my ears heating.

No, no…

My lips part and he jams his middle and ring fingers inside, all the way to the back of my throat, forcing me to taste him.

No, it's not only him. It's *us.*

Good grief. This is so sick.

Then why aren't you fighting?

I must try to release another noise in an attempt to speak, because Nikolai shakes his head, eyes still blazed with intensity and unbound lust.

"Shut the fuck up. Don't try to ruin this with your fucking mouth. Let me keep that busy for you." He jams his fingers deeper. "Choke on my fingers instead. I want you to swallow every drop of cum down your throat."

And then he rubs his fingers on my tongue, the sloppy sound of saliva echoing in the air around us.

He keeps doing that until I start licking him.

Until I talk myself into believing this is a dream.

It was *not* a dream.

No matter how much I try to convince myself that I'm imagining things and that I couldn't possibly have done that in public—where anyone could've seen me. The truth remains that I didn't have a dream.

Not even a little. Not even close.

I pace the length of my bedroom and bathroom, nursing a pounding headache and thoughts so chaotic, they add to the migraine.

My inhales and exhales are fast, fractured, and completely repulsed by the reality I woke up to this morning.

At five a.m. Like clockwork.

Only, nothing makes sense.

I stop pacing and look at my reflection in the bathroom mirror, my hand gripping my hair tighter the longer I stare at the fucking cunt. The weak bloody wanker who couldn't stay in control, just because he had a few drinks.

Black ink covers my features, turning it faceless. What stares back at me is unrecognizable.

A monster.

My heart hammers and I storm toward the mirror, then drive my fist into it. The surface cracks but doesn't splinter, and I have to look at six distorted versions of my face.

"Fuck you," I whisper to all of them as blood drips from my knuckles, my fingers, and then splashes the white sink in red.

I want to punch the mirror again—this time, erase myself completely, but I don't, because this is also messing with my fucking control.

The ticking invades my brain until it's the only thing I can hear.

Tick.

You're useless.

Tick.

You're nothing.

Tick.

Weak.

Weak.

Weak.

I strike the side of my head with my bloodied fist until I think I'll knock myself out.

Black ink slithers from the mirror and swallows my feet, my knees, and my thighs. I grab a piece of the mirror and press on it.

Blood pours out of my fingers, and with it, the ink rushes out of my bloodstream and dissipates from around me.

I let the glass fall to the sink and exhale harshly. Streaks of red line the white porcelain and drops of blood follow in quick succession. I let my life essence pour out of me as I look at my reflection—hair glued to my temples and my eyes glassy. Dead.

It's done. I'm calm.

I'm back to being in control.

But I can't stare at myself too long. Otherwise, it'll come back.

My gaze falls on the blood that's gushing from the cuts in my fingers, soaking my palm, the back of my hand, and forming a small pool in the sink.

It's *done.*

All I have to do is pretend last night never happened.

I'm a master at pretending. Have done it my whole life and have always succeeded.

This isn't any different.

My movements are mechanical as I wash my hand, biting my lip against the pain. Dark, forbidden images invade my brain. Teeth nibbling on my swollen lip, bruising, devouring—

Stop.

My hand shakes as I hit the tap shut and bandage my cuts.

I'm about to step into the bedroom when I catch a reflection of my distorted image and I have to look away before my face becomes black again.

Wait…

Please don't tell me that's what I think it is.

I get closer, tilting my head back, and, sure enough, there's a dark-purple hickey near my jaw and another at my Adam's apple.

That fucking—

I expel a long breath and exit the bathroom, pulling on my hair and nearly toppling everything in my wake.

My movements are frantic as I put on my running shorts and T-shirt. My body is begging me to sit this one out and give myself time to recover from the hangover, but if I do that, I'll just allow myself time to think.

I *can't* think.

Not after the blood fest this morning.

I rush back into the bathroom and slap two plasters against the hickeys. If anyone asks, I'll say I cut myself while shaving.

Deny.

Forget.

Pretend.

My holy mantra will work its magic this time as well. It *always* does.

I leave my room, pushing against the headache and the fog swimming in my mind. I just need a run and everything will get back to normal.

Yet as I go down the stairs of the mansion I share with my brother, cousins, and friend Remi, I'm hit with how I felt when I took these stairs up last night.

Or early this morning.

Fuck, it's only been a couple of hours since Nikolai dropped me off near the house. On his motorbike.

I wish I didn't remember much after the colossal lack of judgment on my part, but I do. Painfully so.

He removed his shirt, which I'm sure he didn't want to be wearing in the first place, and used it to clean us up before he dragged me to where he'd parked his motorbike.

Me on a motorbike? Not in this lifetime.

But that logic apparently doesn't apply to the smashed version of me, because I totally rode on that bike and had to stop myself from holding onto his shoulders for dear life.

Nikolai was grinning like an idiot when I hopped off on unsteady feet and swayed on my way to the mansion, muttering a thanks that I'm not sure he heard.

I certainly heard his "Sweet dreams, lotus flower."

Sweet. Like fuck they were.

I rub the fine hairs on the back of my head as I exit through the gate. I didn't warm up properly, but I couldn't care less. I just need this energy gone.

Immediately.

I run down my learned path, relishing the feel of gravel crunching under my feet and the music blaring in my ears. My lungs expand with every breath, drawing in clean air.

This is my zone.

I'm fine.

Perfectly okay.

In control—

A large figure cuts in front of me and I try to stop, but it's too late and I awkwardly crash into him.

My chest takes the shock, my AirPods fall from my ears, and my senses flood with the very distinctive smell of mint, clover, and hellish damnation.

Strong arms envelop my waist, and I can feel the rumble of his chest against mine as he chuckles. "Morning to you as well, lotus flower. I didn't realize you missed me so much in such a short time."

"I...did not." I step away from him.

"Hey, you were the one who hugged me just now."

"I *fell.*"

"Tomayto, tomahto." He grins in the same way he did yesterday as he watched me tuck my tail between my legs and walk up to my place.

In a trance.

Lost.

But that's not me today.

I cross my arms and glare at him. "What are you doing here?"

"What does it look like I'm doing?" He motions at his usual half-naked state—black shorts and Nike shoes. "I'll be your running buddy."

"I don't want one."

"You might not want one, but you need one..." he trails off and snatches my bandaged hand in both of his, flipping it left and right. "What happened?"

The wounds tingle, turning hotter with every passing second he touches me, and I tug my hand with more force than needed. "None of your business."

He narrows his eyes. "Welcome back, Asshole Brandon. Can't say I missed your grouchy presence."

"Just go away." I search my surroundings for the godforsaken AirPods. "Weren't you perfectly fine with ignoring my presence for weeks?"

"That was before I made the acquaintance of your beautiful, huge dick."

I freeze and slowly direct my widened eyes in his direction. He just stands there, watching me and grinning like a damn idiot.

"Why do you look so horrified?" He steps toward me, his size metaphorically growing. "Don't tell me you forgot all about it?"

"I did. I was hammered and don't remember anything that happened."

He reaches a hand in my direction and I flinch back, putting distance between us. If he touches me again, it'll crack my newly found control.

I'm still not over the way he hugged me just now.

How can someone be so damn comfortable with touch? It's not normal.

"I see," he says without much emotion. "Is that why you covered the souvenirs I gave you last night?"

I storm forward and wrap my fingers around his neck. "What the fuck is wrong with you? Why would you leave hickeys in plain sight?"

"Next time, I'll leave them in a place that's more discreet. Mmm. Seems that, like me, you're also a fan of choking. I love it when you lose control, baby."

I release him with a shove, cursing under my breath. I lost the steel-like command of my actions and emotions.

Again.

That's not supposed to happen. Not after I released my pent-up energy in the sink this morning.

Not so soon.

Not this fast.

What the fuck am I supposed to do if even those drastic measures don't work?

How will I be able to dispel the constant sense of overwhelming nausea?

"Don't call me that," I snap, then bite my lip so hard, I'm surprised no blood gushes out.

"We talked about this." He steps into my space, blinding me with his broad, muscular build and the dark ink that ripples with each of his movements. "I pull off baby better than Clara. In fact, I think it's safe to say I do a lot of things better than her, including but not exclusive to making you come. Speaking of which, when are you going to break up with her?"

I let my lips curve into a fake smile. "Clara is my girlfriend and I have no intention of breaking up with her."

"You didn't seem to think she was your girlfriend when you had your tongue down my throat or when you came all over my cock, baby."

I want to drive my fist into his face just so he'll stop talking, but I've had enough loss of control for one day, so I breathe in and out slowly.

Just why the hell did I have to collapse around this...this...fucking *savage*?

I flash him a condescending glance. "I don't know what you're talking about."

One moment, he's standing there, and the next, his fingers sink into the sides of my throat, immobilizing me as he growls against my skin, "Don't fuck with me, Brandon. You and I both know you fell apart in my arms last night."

"Nothing happened last night," I say casually, keeping my eyes on his manic ones, and I almost believe my own words.

Almost.

"Lose the bimbo," he threatens in hot, enraged words. "Or I'll do it for you."

ELEVEN

Nikolai

S O LOTUS FLOWER DIDN'T LOSE THE BIMBO.

Sur-fucking-prise. *Not.*

It's been a week since I gave him that ultimatum, but he's not making any effort.

But then again, he's a snob who likes to be in control. Bet he takes it with his afternoon tea instead of sugar. He does that with his friends. Afternoon tea.

Christ, he's so very *British.*

My only option is to dismantle that control and shred it to pieces right in front of his mysterious eyes.

He obviously doesn't like me anyway, so what's the harm in making him hate me a bit more?

Anyway, Operation Eliminate Bimbo will soon take effect.

What I know about *Clara* is that she's an attention whore since she likes to post all her pictures with lotus flower.

A gold digger. Since she's all about the designer bags, shoes, and things he buys her.

Shit in bed—for obvious reasons.

I clearly brought him more pleasure than she ever has. He kissed me with his eyes closed.

In your fucking bimbo face.

I know because I made sure to watch him as I backed him against the wall and ate the shit out of his mouth. My Prince Charming melted, fucking *melted* even as he met me stroke for stroke.

He definitely was not fighting his goddamn demons like when he put on that show in front of me.

More importantly, he didn't seem burdened. If anything, at times, he was a bit eager...as wound up as I was.

The nonnegotiable truth is that I can give him more than Clara ever will.

Yes, he'll never admit it since he has a case of pathological denial and all that jazz, but I'm not leaving him alone until he does.

Love the way he hides and pretends he didn't moan, groan, and get hard for me. And how he likes to forget that he came all over my hand and cock.

If Brandon is not gay, I'll chuck myself down a fucking cliff.

Well, let's also include bi, because...eh... I'm not in the mood to die before I get another taste of him.

Or a few.

Several is my preferred count.

Depends on how open he is to the prospect.

I've got to say, his case of denial runs pretty deep, and I'm not sure how to get him out of his own ass—something a lot more pleasurable needs to go there.

But I digress.

Seriously, Kolya. Thinking of fucking him won't get you there faster. Let my brain solve this issue for once.

Short of getting him drunk again, I'm lost. I fucking love drunk Bran, by the way, would vote for him to be the official version in the next election.

I'm kidding. I'm never *lost*.

Sooner or later, I'll wear him down.

I always do.

No one can resist my undivided attention and constant pushing and shoving and annoying the fucking bejesus out of them.

It never happens with fuck buddies, but then again, I don't usually *chase* fuck buddies. To an extent, lotus flower is an exception in many ways.

He can surround himself with walls and I'll demolish them one at a time.

Every day, I join him for that morning run, without his approval, of course, and bite down a chunk of his steel-like control and uptight, standoffish personality.

Whenever he starts getting agitated, I get closer and call him lotus flower, Prince Charming, my dude, and his personal favorite, *baby*.

That one usually drives him crazy and forces him to lose his temper. Other times, he opts to ignore me, but I revel in the flush that creeps up his fair complexion and tints his ears.

I revel in how he steps out of the mansion, watching his surroundings with a careful expression, waiting for me to jump out from whatever nook I've chosen that day.

My all-time favorite, hands down, is when he does a quick look at me, noticing my shorts for the day, my half-naked chest, and how I choose to tie my hair.

He pretends to be angry about my constant state of half nudity, his face caught in that eternal snobbish expression, but he *notices* things. He looks at me with those needy eyes that beg me to do bad things to him.

Lotus flower is such a cock-fucking-tease, but I'll make him come around.

Even if it's the last thing I do.

Am I too obsessed? I don't think I am. This is pretty much a good amount, in my humble opinion.

Now, I've never played this type of intense push-and-pull game before, but that's what makes this a lot more thrilling.

Brandon is making himself into a war that I'll conquer and bring to his fucking knees. *Literally.*

So I don't mean to be a stalker or anything. Okay, kidding, I totally do, but I'm in REU's stadium to watch some boring sport called lacrosse.

I swear to fucking God I never paid attention to this sport until now. Seems like a failed marriage between hockey, cricket, and football, just saying. *Our* football. Not the European one.

But then again, Bran chose to play the sport, so who am I to judge?

"Why are we here, Niko?" Jeremy asks from beside me, flashing glares at the people surrounding us, who won't stop staring.

So, apparently, two big, tatted guys stand out in the midst of polka-dotted dresses, feathered hats, and tulle umbrellas. Even though I went through all the trouble to wear a damn T-shirt. The audacity of these motherfuckers.

Of course Bran would play a sport that only prim-and-proper people would attend.

My friend kicks my foot, shifting in the chair that's definitely not made for bulky guys like us.

"Shush, Jer. I'm concentrating."

"You wouldn't do that even if you were paid."

"I would, too," I say, and he raises a brow. "Fine, I wouldn't. This is different."

"How different, because I'm about to punch some Karens."

"Different enough that even *I* won't punch anyone."

"Damn. Who are you and what have you done to my friend?"

I snicker. "Just stay there as my backup."

"Backup?"

"If anyone asks, you brought me here, not the other way around. Can't look too fucking desperate."

"Who would ask? And why are you desperate?" He tilts his head to the side, studying me closely. "You're *never* desperate. You get laid more than the three of us combined."

"Used to, Jer. *Used* to. Kolya is playing the grouchy dick role to perfection. He must've caught the disease from a certain uptight presence."

He grimaces. "I still can't believe you named your dick Kolya. Seriously, Uncle Kolya is Dad's right arm. That's gross."

"Don't care. Ask him to change his name."

"Pretty sure it should be the other way around since you're younger." He shakes his head. "Are you going to tell me why we're watching fucking lacrosse? It's boring."

"I know, right? Why do you think he's doing it?"

A woman with a wrinkled upper lip glares back at us with that patronizing look Brits have when they don't want to speak their displeasure. I learned it from lotus flower since he flashes me that all the time.

"Want a picture, ma'am?" I ask and she gasps in pure horror, then turns back to her kid, who's smiling at me. I wink and he giggles.

Kids and animals like me. Adults do not. I'd rather be adored by innocent beings instead of evil snakes. I like things simple, not twisty and complicated.

And yet here you are for the most complicated man ever.

"Who's the *he* you came to watch?" Jeremy asks, but I'm tuning him out because my whole attention is stolen by the fucking bimbo who's slipping in a few rows below with two other girls.

Fucking *Clara.*

Exactly what I've been missing.

She poses for a few selfies and makes her friends take an album's worth of pictures. I force myself to ignore her—or try to—as I spot lotus flower walking with his teammates to the midfield.

Well, fuck me. I've always seen him in shorts and T-shirts, but it's different in the royal-blue lacrosse uniform, a bit tighter, maybe. Those shorts are definitely framing his ass better than the running ones.

Not that I'm staring or anything.

Okay, I totally fucking am.

His hair is styled in his signature Prince Charming look—the sides short and the longer strands on top slicked back, making his face appear sharp.

He looks serious, more so than usual, as he shoves the helmet over his head and gets to the middle with a member of the orange team. The referee throws the ball down and lotus flower fights over it with his long-netted stick.

That's some weird shit down there…

On second thought, I'm not complaining about the way he's bent over, ass on display. Maybe lacrosse isn't so bad, after all.

The crowd cheers when he gets the ball for his team. Or as much as preppy people will.

Since I used to play football, and still do at times, this is like a Mary Sue sport in comparison.

Though they do get physical. Hmm.

So he does like some roughness in his life. My cock twitches at the memory of his groans when I squeezed him with a firm grip. How he thrust against my cock at a maddening pace, trying to match my rhythm.

I have to shake those thoughts away so I don't get a hard-on and effectively get kicked out by the bunch of prudes.

My attention zeroes back on Bran, who seems to be doing well. He runs a lot from the attack to the defense, and he retrieves a lot of balls for his team. The crowd is buzzing when they score. Got to say it's not *too* bad. There's obviously adrenaline going on.

Number ten, the one and only lotus flower, gets stifling attention from the other team's defenders, who try to block him with every move. One of them pushes him and he falls as the referee announces a foul.

I jump to my feet. "Fuck that guy! Suck my dick."

"Niko!" Jeremy clutches my arm and tries to shove me down.

That's when I realize most of the people surrounding us are watching me as if I'm the personification of Lucifer himself. A lot of pearl-clutching happens, too.

I roll my eyes and sit down.

Jeremy, who doesn't give a fuck about anyone, seems like he wants to apologize to our company or something equally crazy.

Bran doesn't seem hurt. He recovers in a few seconds and resumes running all over the field.

My eyes track his every movement as I sit with my elbows on my knees and my hands forming a steeple at my chin.

He's just so elegant.

So fucking beautiful.

The definition of second-best male beauty. The first is me.

"Isn't that Landon King's twin brother?" Jeremy asks.

"Good morning, Sleeping Beauty. Might want to go back to sleep," I say, still watching Bran.

"The one you wanted to join the Heathens?"

"It was a good idea."

"More like the worst. Is there a reason why we're watching him?"

"Because he's Landon's brother. Need to keep an eye on the enemy or some shit."

"You don't look at him like he's an enemy."

I'm going to hate-fuck him so that's considered on the list.

"Shush, Jer. You're like an annoying buzzing bee that won't go away."

"Jeez, thanks."

"Anytime, we're bros."

I don't hear what Jer says, because Bran recovers the ball from the defense, runs to the attack, erasing a few players in his path, and then passes the ball to the one who scores.

"Yes! Get those fucking bitches," I cheer, laughing and ignoring the lady in front of me, who's covering her son's ears.

My smile disappears when Clara jumps and screams, "That's my man! So proud of you, babe!"

My fingers wrap around the edges of the chair so tightly, I hear a cracking sound.

He's not your man.

Definitely not your fucking *babe.*

"Niko." Jeremy places a hand on my arm. "Whatever you're currently thinking about, don't do it."

"But she'd look so pretty in a fucking casket."

"The woman just doesn't agree with your language. She doesn't deserve to die for that."

He thinks it's because of the Karen, when the fact is, I'm considering ways to add Clara's name to the MIA list.

I try to focus on the rest of the game, but it's futile. The Elites end up winning, and I don't feel that sense of triumph I experienced when Bran assisted the goal.

My mood has taken a sharp dive ever since fucking *Clara* staked a public claim on him.

Why shouldn't I kill her again?

As soon as it ends, she skips over the people toward the exit and I stand up, then follow her.

I can make out Jeremy asking me not to do 'anything stupid,' but I *live* for stupid.

Clara slips through the small crowd, pausing every now and then to take selfies. This chick needs an urgent intervention.

After a thousand pictures, she finally reaches the Elites' players' locker room and walks right in as if she owns the place.

I can't do the same since I fucking stand out and I obviously don't look the part of the British kids.

Standing by the opposite corner, I scan my surroundings, contemplating the best way to go inside. The fact that Clara is there, with him, makes my vision turn red and fills my brain with violent solutions.

Like that amazing casket idea.

Just when I'm about to walk in there and risk the commotion, she emerges, or more like she's dragged out by none other than Bran.

And he's half naked.

Fuck. Me.

I've always thought he had a firm, toned body, with all the feeling up I've practiced like a religion whenever he's within arm's reach. But I didn't think I'd be fucking foaming at the mouth just because I'm seeing him wearing only shorts.

He's lean, but well-fucking-built. A smooth plane of chest muscles and protruding abs that end in a delicious V-line that's *unfortunately* half hidden by the shorts.

Not a single blemish or tattoo in sight. He's all smooth skin and marble-like in his beauty, my lotus flower.

His fingers uncurl from around Clara's elbow when he gets her to a small corner to the side.

I tiptoe toward them in an epic show of stalkerish tendencies until I'm standing by the corner, close enough to hear and see them in full fucking HD.

"I told you not to come to the changing room, Clara. It's not a place for a woman."

She pouts like a fucking child and runs her hands, which will soon be broken, up his chest. "I was just so stoked for your win. I wanted to take a victory pic, babe."

He is not your fucking babe.

I want to drill that into her head and watch as her skull splinters to pieces.

She takes out her phone and wraps her arm around his waist, and they both fake-smile at the camera.

Once the photo is taken, his smile vanishes and he looks bored out of his fucking mind.

It's supposed to make me happy, but I can't stop glaring at her claws all over him.

"You're so handsome." She slides her fingers through his hair and gets on her tiptoes to kiss him.

Bran turns his head at the last second and her lips touch his cheek.

I can't describe the level of satisfaction that rushes through me at the sight.

He doesn't want her to kiss him.

His so-called girlfriend *can't* even kiss him.

She doesn't seem to be surprised or hurt by the rejection as she smiles and pulls back. "Will help you wind down later, okay, babe?"

He gives a noncommittal nod and she leaves hesitantly, her eyes scanning over him before she finally removes her irritating presence from the situation.

Lotus flower releases an exasperated sound and turns to go back to the locker room.

But before he takes another step, my hand shoots out and I grab him by the throat, slamming him against the wall.

He releases the most delicious startled sound, similar to the one he rewarded my ears with that night he finally lost control. I'd appreciate it more if I wasn't in the mood to punch him in his handsome face. His eyes widen and a mixture of emotions rush to his features. Confusion, anger, fear, but also lust. Fucking bright and buzzing beneath the wall of his wavering control.

Even his words are careful, unsure, and tense. "What...are you doing here?"

"Came to watch you play, but I got to watch something entirely different just now. I clearly remember that I told you to lose her, didn't I?"

He tries to push my hand away, but at this point, it'd be much easier to kill me than make me release him. I steal a look at the fingers of his left hand, and all five of them are covered in Band-Aids. He wouldn't tell me how he hurt them, no matter how many times I asked, but it's good they're healing.

"Nikolai..." His tone isn't as biting as usual. If anything, it's imploring, begging, *frightened*. "You need to go. The manager will have a meeting with us in a few and I can't..."

"You can't what? You can't have him see you being crowded into a corner by another guy? Does that scare you, almighty King?"

"Fuck you," he sneers, the words rolling off my skin like an aphrodisiac.

"You know it turns me on when you talk like that."

His eyes widen just the slightest and he pushes at my chest. This time, the roles are reversed and I'm wearing a T-shirt while he's half naked.

When I make no move to give him an inch, he releases a long, tortured exhale. "Just...go."

"Tell me why you're still with the bimbo and I might."

A frown appears between his thick brows and I can see the rage burning hot behind his usually cold eyes.

Brandon King is the epitome of a nice guy. All prim, proper, and kind. He smiles at everyone's jokes, no matter how corny they are. Checks on the people around him to make sure they're okay.

He plays lacrosse. Loves his afternoon tea. Volunteers at a fucking animal shelter on the weekends. Donates his paintings to various charities. Participates in marathons for multiple causes. Runs for women's rights. Runs for cancer. Runs for mental health awareness. Runs for abused animals. Runs for climate change.

Let's say he runs for everything. Tell him to run for a poor worm trapped underground and he'll be all over that shit.

But here's the thing that I've suspected for some time. It's an image. I'm not saying he doesn't care about all of those causes, but he's using his goody-two-shoes personality as camouflage. A crutch.

He's repressing, fighting, and struggling.

Against what? I'm not sure.

It's why I go fucking feral whenever he slips out of his self-imposed shackles and lets his true self show through.

He's still an asshole, but at least he's not putting on a fake front.

At least I get to see the real him.

Like right now.

"Why I'm still with her is none of your business. I am none of your fucking business, Nikolai. What happened that night was because I was wasted. You said I could blame you, so this is me blaming you and telling you to leave me the hell alone."

"But I don't want to."

"Are you a fucking masochist?"

"Not usually, no. In fact, some might say I'm the exact opposite, but I'm ready to wait for you to come to your senses."

"Have you heard a word I've said? I want nothing to do with you, damn it."

"Say that again and mean it." My mouth gets so close to his, I can smell the notes of musk and mint rushing from his lips in fractured breaths. "Unless...you can't?"

He glares down at me, and there's so much heat beneath that coral blue of his eyes, but he doesn't push me.

Not even once.

Bran might lash out, but my mere nearness is causing him a shortage of breath. His chest rises and falls in a quick rhythm.

This must be why he was anal about keeping some distance between us when we were running. He knew that if I got close, it would be game over for him.

So I press my chest to his. Firm muscles glue to mine and the thud of his heartbeat slams and mixes with my own.

What the fuck is this man doing to me?

Why on earth can't I keep my hands off him? Does he have witch blood? Is he made of fucking drugs?

"You're a fucking nightmare," he mutters, his throat working beneath my fingers.

"*Your* nightmare."

"I hate you."

"I don't."

"You're fucking crazy."

"About you," I whisper against his lips and claim them with a guttural moan.

He doesn't push away. He certainly does *not* turn his face or look like he's uncomfortable with the attention.

In fact, the exact opposite happens.

His lashes flutter over his cheeks as he groans, and I eat that sound the fuck up. I eat *him* the fuck up.

I swallow him whole, but most of all, I hurt him. Teeth clashing, tongues swirling, and lips chasing.

God-fucking-damn-it.

I've been fantasizing about his taste since last week. Every morning, noon, and night. Every goddamn second of every fucking day, all I wanted was to have a taste again.

But I didn't want to freak him out or send him running for the hills. I sure as hell don't give two flying fucks about that possibility right now, though.

I soak him all in, exploring, feasting, absolutely drowning in his fucking mouth.

He tastes of honey, mint, and pending fucking addiction.

I twirl my tongue against his and I'm rewarded with his hard nips.

Lotus flower kisses me as thoroughly as I kiss him, his fingers tugging on the bottom of my T-shirt to keep me glued to his naked torso.

I roll his bottom lip between my teeth and nibble on the skin until he's whimpering, shuddering, and fucking shaking against me.

Give me more.

More.

Fucking *more.*

I shove my raging erection against his shorts and sure enough, he's hard.

For me.

Again.

Hello, Satan. Is this heaven in hell? Because I could stay here forever.

"You're so fucking turned on for someone who claims he wants nothing to do with me," I speak against his red, swollen lips. "You're not drunk now, either."

"Stop touching me…" he breathes out even as his mouth seems to chase mine. "I would've gotten this way for anyone. It's called a physical reaction."

This fucking asshole. I swear he's asking to be sucker punched.

I slide my tongue down his neck and bite his Adam's apple, hard, then suck just as savagely, giving him back the hickey he hid for a whole week.

"Stop it…" He grunts, shoving his elbow against my chest.

Only, he puts no actual strength behind it.

And I'm *not* done.

I'm certainly not listening.

I trail a path of bites down to where his shoulder meets his neck, collarbone, and chest, then I scrape my teeth on his nipples.

He spits out the most erotic moan I ever heard, and I jam two of my fingers in his mouth, then spread them against his tongue.

I need him to stop fucking talking and ruining every moment with his damn mouth.

My tongue swirls around his light-brown areola, then I tug the nipple between my teeth, sucking and biting until all I hear are the muffled noises spilling from his stuffed mouth.

"You like this, don't you?" I move to the other nipple, sucking the skin around it, leaving a huge hickey before I bite down on the little bud. "You look perfect marked by me. My own piece of fucking art."

One of his hands is on my shoulder, pushing me away, but the other one is in my hair, pulling me close.

He's a fucking conundrum, my lotus flower, and I can't wait to break him into fucking pieces.

His body is flinching away from me, but his tongue swirls around my fingers, and his teeth bite down whenever I nibble on his nipple.

I'm so drunk on him and his taste. So addicted to how responsive he is.

I can't get fucking enough.

Not after one lick or two or a thousand. I want to throw him down and feast on him properly. I want to watch him shudder and whine and moan as I kiss every inch of his gorgeous skin.

I doubt he'd be thrilled with that idea, so I'll take what I can get.

My mouth leaves bites and marks all over his chest before I slide my tongue back to his jaw.

"You taste like my new favorite addiction, baby."

"Mmmff…mmm…umph…" he whines against my fingers and I remove them, then jam them in my own mouth, groaning at the taste of him.

He watches me with dark eyes, his brows dipping, his chest rising and falling in an insane rhythm.

But then he opens his damn fucking mouth. "Go away…please."

I crash my lips against his. "Shut." *Kiss.* "The." *Lick.* "Fuck." *Bite.* "Up."

He moans, the cracks in his armor growing wider and deeper, and I smash through them one by each fucking one.

I'll feast on him so thoroughly, he'll never find a way out.

I thrust my aching cock against his and whisper, "I'm so going to jerk off to thoughts of all the dirty things I want to do to you."

He shudders, and I swear I feel his cock thickening. His eyelids definitely grow heavy. He has this look of complete confusion and utter abandon. Such a fucking enigma. I want to own him.

Pull him apart.

Fucking destroy him.

I steal his lips again and we grunt at the same time as my tongue shoves its way inside, claiming his. Chaining him to me. Even temporarily.

I need more.

More.

Fucking *more*.

A commotion comes from the locker room and I hear someone ask, "Has anyone seen King?"

He goes completely still and I can feel his muscles tightening. When I wrench my lips from his bruised ones, his face is stone cold.

Panic flashes in the depths of his irises and he looks like he's on the verge of collapsing. He stares at his feet, his shoulders crowding with tension.

What the fuck…

"Hey." I tap his cheek with the back of my fingers and he blinks up at me. "What's wrong?"

"I… I…"

"Hey…breathe."

He doesn't seem to be doing that at all as he sputters and stares at me as if I'm an alien.

The commotion gets closer and he seems to be on the verge of a meltdown.

It's then I realize he's probably freaking out about the prospect of being found in this position.

I step back and he stares at me with wretched eyes that make me want to grab his hand and drag him the fuck out of here.

But that would probably make him lose it.

My eyes skim over the multiple hickeys I left on his torso and collarbone, then I lift my shirt over my head and throw it at him.

I seem to be taking off my shirt for this guy more often than not. Whenever I'm wearing one, at least.

His fingers latch onto the material and he mechanically pulls it on. It's big on him, but he looks fucking edible in it.

New kink unlocked.

"Thanks," he mutters like such a well-mannered gentleman.

He's always expressing his gratitude whenever I do the most benign gestures, like dropping him off at home, handing him his AirPods, or when I tell him to watch out for traffic.

I like to think that's his way to make up for all the shit his mouth spouts on a regular basis.

Lotus flower casts one last lingering glance at me, his expression reverting back to normal, but a smidge of hesitation lurks in his gaze.

I wait for him to say something, but he breaks eye contact and slips past me to his conversing teammates.

I stand there, my cock protesting and my muscles tensing.

This was supposed to be a little game, but I don't think I'm playing anymore.

The worst part is that I feel like I'm already losing.

TWELVE

Brandon

"I MISSED YOU SO MUCH," CLARA'S SOFT VOICE WHISPERS IN my ear as she trails kisses on my neck and jaw.

We're standing in the middle of my room as she moans softly. My hand rests around her waist just so I can force her in place when she tries to kiss my mouth.

It's illogical and makes no bloody sense, but I haven't kissed her or allowed her to kiss me since that damn night I lost all control a week ago.

And earlier today.

My eyes close in remembrance of his lips, his hard body, and the way he kissed me.

I shove all that chaos out of my mind.

It didn't happen.

It's *nothing*.

If I think that long enough, maybe this whole thing will blow over and I'll go back to my safe little bubble.

Clara doesn't mind the subtle rejection. I don't think she cares. It's why I keep her close. She's fine with the relationship staying shallow. She never probes, never asks any stupid questions. And she certainly doesn't ask what happened to my bandaged hand every day like a certain twat who refuses to give up.

Since I couldn't avoid her any longer, I invited her over to my room after dinner at a posh restaurant. Instead of eating, I spent most of the time taking her pictures and pretending I wasn't bored out of my fucking mind.

I tried dropping her off at the dorms and leaving, but she wasn't having it tonight and insisted that I *had* to see her lingerie.

I did. It's pretty, I guess. A one-piece transparent red lace thing that showcases her nipples and has an opening to her pussy. The tight, strappy material clings to her skin, complementing her curvy figure.

But I'd still rather we didn't have to do this. For me, sex has always been a constant state of mundane release. I could do without it, and I did for months, but it could have been forever, to be honest, which is why Clara went to find it elsewhere. Unlike what Lan and the others think, I don't mind. My only problem is the secrecy. I told her we could be in an open relationship, and she became mental, demanding monogamy she can't keep up with.

She can shag whoever she likes, but tonight, she's decided that's going to be me.

"You smell so good, babe."

I try to stay in the moment, I *really* do, but now that she's called me that, I can't help imagining different, crueler lips trailing kisses on my neck.

Hers are soft, his were fucking wild.

Focus.

She skips the plaster I slapped on the second hickey he gave me in the same fucking place. Like a savage. Only, now, I don't only have a mark on my Adam's apple. They're also all over my chest—dark red and purple, as if I've been bruised.

Considering what Nikolai did in that corner earlier today, I might as well be.

Clara's fingers grip my T-shirt, trying to take it off, but I pull it back down, kissing her throat and refusing to get stuck in my head again.

I breathe her flowery perfume and try not to gag. I've never liked the smell.

That's because you prefer something more masculine. The memory of bergamot and mint floods my nose and I tighten my muscles.

No.

She moans and I hate how soft it sounds. She grinds against me and I loathe how tender she feels.

Her breasts rub and slide against my chest, but all I can think about are hard muscles.

You're hard for me, not her.

The sound of his voice in my head causes a twitch in my dormant dick.

Fuck.

Fuck.

Fuck!

I pull away from Clara with a shove, my mind swimming in disturbing chaos.

She doesn't take the hint and saunters toward me again with bright eyes, her blonde hair swishing against her lower back.

I take another step back and hold up a hand. "I'm just not in the mood, Clara. I'm sorry. I think it's exhaustion from the game."

Her smile is forced at best as she reaches for my belt. "I can help you get rid of all that tension, sexy."

"No. I'm good. Thanks for offering." I grab her dress that she stripped off teasingly earlier and hand it over. "I'm sorry again."

Her shoulders hunch, but she takes the dress and starts to put it on. "We haven't shagged since we got back together, Bran. Is something wrong?"

Everything is fucking wrong.

But I don't say that and smile instead. "Just a lot to think about. I'll be fine after some time."

"Okaaay," she drawls out the word. "Love you, babe."

She waits for a beat, but when I don't say it back, she turns to leave.

"Clara."

She spins on her heel, a hopeful smile on her face. I should probably break up with her. This time for good. It's not right to lead her on when I feel absolutely nothing for her.

Ever since I was in secondary school, whenever a girl has asked me out, I've said yes, knowing they just wanted me to take them home so they could meet Lan.

I didn't mind. Because I had a girlfriend at all times, even if she was giving Lan fuck-me eyes. He never did—fuck them, I mean. But he always forwarded me screenshots of them sending him nudes and begging him to do obscene things to them.

I never responded. Just broke up with them over text and deleted whatever Lan sent me.

It didn't matter. They were all part of an image. I never stayed with one more than a couple of weeks.

I met Clara in uni, and she made it her mission to ensure we'd bump into each other by 'coincidence' in the places I frequent. I recognized her tactics from a mile away, but, again, I didn't mind. The reason I've stayed with her the longest is because, for the first time, someone came straight to me instead of Lan.

In fact, she doesn't seem to like him. Probably because he often treats her like an insignificant insect.

So I kept her. She doesn't get her nose in my business as long as I take her to high-end restaurants, buy her luxurious brands, and pose for pictures.

We broke up whenever she cheated, which happened four times that I know of, but then she said she was sorry and that she wouldn't do it again and I forgave her.

I technically cheated on her, too, so let's call it even.

Lan is wrong. She never hurt me. I'd have to have feelings to be hurt, and I don't do those.

She was just a convenience and now, she's not.

"We should take a break," I say casually.

Her face falls and she nearly drops her precious Chanel bag. "But why? I didn't do anything."

"It's not you. It's me. I cheated on you." But even as I say that, it doesn't feel right. Being with her just now felt like I was cheating on him. Not the other way around.

I need to stab a fucking shard of glass in my neck this time.

Clara's lips part and she frowns. "Wow, okay. That's shitty."

"I'm sorry." I don't mean a fucking word, but I say it anyway. Because that's what's expected. I'm nothing short of extremely considerate and spectacularly polite.

Except for when it comes to a certain wanker.

She closes the distance between us and grabs my hand in hers, nude fake nails scraping against my skin. "It's okay. We've been through this before, babe. It hurts that you went to someone else, but I can forgive you like you forgave me all those times."

I push away her hand and step back. "I don't need your forgiveness."

"Do you like her that much? I can do a threesome if that's what you want."

Desperate is exceptionally annoying.

My tone is detached as I shake my head. "We're breaking up, Clara."

"You can't do this shit to me!" She stomps her foot on the floor. "I'm not breaking up with you. This isn't how it works."

"This is exactly how it works. Please leave." I push her toward the door and open it.

She stands in the hallway and screams, "No! I refuse this."

"We're done."

She storms back inside, but she's pulled out again by a handful of her hair and tossed aside like a sack of potatoes.

My brother glares down his nose at her. "You heard him. He said you're done, so take the hint and escort your cheap presence off our property."

My oldest cousin, Eli, who followed Lan—probably after they were plotting some chaos in my brother's room—looks her up and down. "Pretty sure I've seen you before, but where?"

"I've been literally coming here for the past two years!" she screams, her high-pitched voice grating on my last nerve.

"Oh, right! You're the help!"

"I'm not!"

He looks at Lan. "She's not?"

"Of course not." My brother makes a mock gasp. "The help has more grace than this cheap rug."

"Okay, that's enough," I say, exasperated. "Just leave, Clara."

"I don't agree with the breakup. We're still together." She cowers under my brother's and cousin's menacing attention. "I'll text you later, babe."

"Don't call me that," I mutter, a migraine starting at the back of my head.

"What?" she asks, seeming lost.

"Don't call me babe. I'm not your babe," I say, clearer this time, and her eyes widen.

She starts to say something else, but Lan stands in front of me and pushes her away as if she's a prop. "Off you go. Don't show your face around my brother again or I'll cut it to pieces."

I want to reprimand him, but I'm glad his words finally propel her to move. She quickens her steps down the hall, tension rolling off her in waves.

"I'll let you know if someone else needs help!" Eli shouts after her and then asks us, "She's really not the help?"

"The degradation is unnecessary," I say with a sigh.

Eli rolls his shoulder. He's an inch taller than us and has dark hair and metal-gray eyes that excel at making people feel uncomfortable in their own skin.

Personality-wise, he's similar to my brother and they share a destructive nature, which is why they get along, although they like to pretend otherwise. They have a lot of interests in common, including a chess game at our grandfather's house that's been going on for over a decade.

But where Landon is a show-off, Eli prefers to work in the shadows.

He's still too antagonistic, though, which is why I prefer the company of his younger brother, Creigh. However, Eli has always been like a big brother to Lan and me. He made it his mission to protect us when we were growing up and he continues to do so.

Eli, Lan, and even Creigh are firm believers of the King name supremacy and consider an offense against one of its members as a declaration of war. It's not that I don't share the sentiment. More like, I never felt worthy of the superior last name.

Lan clutches my shoulder, a wicked grin painting his lips. "Congrats on kicking the bitch to the curb. For the love of Satan, don't get back together with her. She's not for you."

"And how do you know what's for me? Are you an expert?"

"Me, an expert? Nonsense. But you should at least be with someone who actually only has eyes for you."

"Aww." Eli wraps an arm around my other shoulder and squeezes me. "The help dared hurt my precious Bran? Why didn't you mention that before so I could've gouged her eyes out and fed them to the dogs?"

"Maybe that's why I didn't," I mutter. "I'm just going to sleep."

"Hell no. We need to get you drunk to celebrate." He clears his throat. "Rems!! Get the pints out!"

A few things are knocked over down the hall before a door is flung open and Remi peeks out, a Cheshire cat grin plastered on his face. "Did someone say pints?"

"Yeah, as much as you can find." Eli squeezes me. "We're giving Bran a Congrats for Dodging the Help's Bullet party."

"No clue what that is, but I'm in!" He jumps to the opposite room, wearing nothing but boxers, and kicks Creigh's door open. "Wake up, spawn! We have a partaayyy."

I'm dragged to the living room against my wishes for a celebration I want no part in. I'd rather paint for an hour or so until ten thirty.

But then again, my paintings are taking a turn I dislike and I find myself hiding the canvases as if they're a dirty little secret.

Maybe they are.

So perhaps this mindless gathering with my family members is exactly what I need.

I find solace in Creigh's silent presence, who also didn't give his approval about attending this sudden celebration.

He's around Glyn's age, but he has an old soul and he's the one I seek out whenever I need calm.

He clinks his bottle of beer against mine and lifts his chin. "Congrats on getting rid of the loose screw."

Jesus. Even he didn't like her.

I take a sip of my beer. "I didn't think you knew she existed."

"She made sure everyone knew. Not for you, cousin. You deserve someone who doesn't use you."

"Thanks, I guess."

"Even my Cray Cray thinks you dodged a bullet." Eli ruffles his brother's hair and headlocks him, at which they start to wrestle playfully.

Landon pushes them away and slides to my side, a calculative look I don't like slipping into his features. "So what prompted the breakup? Did she cheat again?"

I swallow a long mouthful of beer to avoid his inquisitive gaze. Of course Lan wouldn't let it go. He's always acting like a dog, sniffing around, and trying to locate the bone. *Bones*. Plural.

He knows I kept her around for convenience reasons, and while he didn't approve of her, he of all people is well aware of the image. The camouflage.

Now, he has no idea why I need that image, and he never will, but he couldn't have missed its existence. It's why he's never liked the way I converted to painting landscapes. He knows I'm doing it as part of that façade.

It's impossible to hide from him, no matter what I do. It's like a curse.

I let out a breath, staring at the tinted bottle. "I was bored."

"So she didn't cheat. Interesting." His intrusive eyes dig a hole in the side of my face and I pretend to be fascinated with Remi making a fool of himself.

Thankfully, Lan gets off my case with a simple "Well, I'm glad you finally got bored."

Not sure why he cares so much about my relationship with Clara, or the lack thereof, but whatever.

I knock back the rest of the bottle and then reach for a second. Maybe it's better to just get smashed tonight.

Maybe that will numb the illicit thoughts trying to tear through my brain.

Tonight, I broke up with my girlfriend of two years—though on and off—but my thoughts are infested with images of a savage ravaging me.

"Rems! Do those impressions." Eli points his beer at his cousin, snapping my attention to the present.

"Whatever do you mean, my liege?" Remi says in a dramatic medieval accent. "I shall not be accused of treason when my blood has irrigated these lands for decades."

I squirm and hide it with a sip of beer. Considering my complicated relationship with my own blood, I get a queasy feeling whenever it's mentioned. Or worse, when I see it.

"Off with his head!" Lan shouts, seeming to enjoy the theatrical play a bit too much.

"My darling." Remi reaches for Creigh and hides behind him, still speaking in the same tone. "Save me from these uncivilized barbarians."

"No one will save you from the guillotine," Eli says with an evil smirk.

"Hey, there's no guillotine in Medieval England!"

"We're in the French Revolution, *mon ami.*"

"Spawn!" Remi uses Creigh as a shield while Eli tries to bypass him. Lan laughs his head off, and I do, too.

I grew up with these guys and their antics, and I'm grateful for these mindless encounters and the cheeky banter.

They're my family, simple as that, and I'm thankful in more ways than one.

Mostly because they offered me a place where I can pretend that I belong.

Half an hour later, I need to relieve myself. I leave the rowdy living room and head to the guest toilet.

After I'm done, I wash my hands and stare at my face in the mirror for a second. The sense of nausea rolls in my stomach and I cut eye contact before I smash this mirror to pieces as well.

After I dry my hands, I lift my shirt and stare at the dark-purple hickeys near my collarbone, shoulder, chest, but mostly surrounding my nipples.

A shiver goes through me and I run my fingers over them, hissing at the shadow of pain. I honestly never thought men could have sensitive nipples or, worse, in my case, that it would turn me on when Nikolai played with them.

He didn't just leave hickeys. He brutalized my skin and created angry teeth marks on it.

Everywhere I touch, he's there. Like a constant reminder of my fucked-up mental state.

Of how far I fell and how deeply I lost control.

My teammates didn't see this because I made sure to shower after they left the changing room, pretending I had to do something first. They gave me grief about the hickey on my neck, saying that I had a wild one on my hands.

They meant Clara, of course, but she's nowhere near wild.

The one who's driving me fucking insane is none other than a man.

A rowdy, always shirtless, mountain of a man who looks at me like he wants to rip me apart.

I wonder how I look at him.

My gaze lands on my eyes in the mirror and I groan when I accidentally touch my nipple. It's still sore and aching from his attention earlier, and no matter how much I try to erase that memory, it won't go away.

I ghost my finger on the tight pebble and pinch it again, imagining it's his teeth.

My dick twitches, straining against my trousers, and I bite down on my lower lip.

I'm wasted—or getting there. This doesn't mean anything…

He looked displeased when I ran away earlier. But why? He

couldn't have possibly expected me to stay there for everyone to find us.

My phone vibrates and I freeze, then let my shirt down as I pull it out.

My heart gets stuck in the back of my throat when I see his name on my lock screen.

I should ignore it.

Nothing good comes from it when we interact.

I'm totally going to ignore it.

My thumb hesitates over the screen before I unlock it and open the text.

> **Nikolai:** Good evening, lotus flower. Thought I'd start the text like that since you love being so proper.

I resist the urge to roll my eyes and wait for the next text to come. He always has a few of them.

After the night in the alley, not only did he go back to texting me, but he also resumed testing my patience every morning on my runs.

What used to be a sacred activity is now muddied by his endless questions and constant attempts to get close to me.

I skim over his last texts, trying not feel impatient about the dots that keep appearing and disappearing.

His texts are usually long-winded, and, for some reason, he likes to tell me stories about things that happen in the Heathens' mansion as if they're any of my business.

His texts can be so sporadic. For instance, yesterday, they were along the lines of:

> **Nikolai:** Looking forward to tomorrow. Maybe this time I'll get more than five sentences from you ;)

> **Nikolai:** FYI. I'm so going to imagine your lips around my cock when I jerk off tonight.

> **Nikolai:** You're free to do the same, btw.

> **Nikolai:** Please do. I'm getting hard just thinking about it.

Nikolai: Can't help picturing you choking on my cock.

Nikolai: Fuck. Need to change the subject before I come in my pants.

Nikolai: So Jeremy woke up today and chose violence. Love that for us. Because you bet I was there with him every step of the way. Best friends and all that shit. We beat up these kids who thought they could mess with us and live to tell the story. It's the fucking audacity for me. Want me to bring you some souvenirs in the form of their broken teeth? Probably not a good idea, right? Just checking. Anyway, can't wait to see you in your tight shirt and shorts tomorrow. Running has never been so much fun.

A new text appears, and I check it with clammy fingers.

Nikolai: So I'm waiting.

Me: For what?

Nikolai: Don't fuck with me. Did you lose the bimbo yet?

Swallowing is exceptionally difficult as I recall the very obvious breakup that happened earlier tonight. But if I tell Nikolai that, it'll just go to his head, and we don't want that.

Me: Whatever I do with my love life is none of your business.

Nikolai: I'm making it mine. I told you if you don't get it done, I'll do it for you.

I stare with wide eyes as he sends me a picture of a girl sitting beside him in a pub.

Clara.

She's wearing the same dress from earlier and smiling in her drink.

Nikolai: Be at the below address in twenty minutes or I'll send you a video of her riding my cock.

My ears heat and I struggle against the wave of nausea that shoots up my throat.

I slam my hand on the sink and breathe in loud inhales and exhales, but nothing calms down my rampaging heart. A part of me knows I should either text him and tell him not to do it or ignore him altogether, but that's not what I do.

Fuck!

I storm out of the house and get into my car. I probably shouldn't be driving when I'm a little drunk, but I can't seem to give a fuck as I speed out of the property and head to the address the twat sent me.

It takes me a whole seventeen fucking minutes to arrive at an apartment complex near The King's U campus.

I punch in the code to the building that he sent me and take the lift to the penthouse. Another code. Another wasted fucking minute I don't have time for.

The lift opens in the middle of a spacious flat with a transparent ceiling that shows the partially clouded sky and some stars.

The lighting is dim and intimate, like this is a setting for a romantic night.

My anger is barely tucked beneath the surface, tearing and pulling at my precariously standing walls as I stride in the direction of what must be the bedroom.

Giggles reach me first, followed by the rumble of a very familiar voice. I stop in front of the ajar door, sucking nonexistent breaths into my burning lungs.

I should leave and put this entire thing behind me.

Forget.

Deny.

Pretend.

Be in control—

"Wow, you have such a massive cock. And, oh my God, these piercings are fantastic!"

The words purred by none other than Clara have me abandoning any form of resolve I'm grasping at. I let myself free fall, headfirst, my brain propelling past the nausea in my throat and spilling all around me.

I push the door open to be greeted by Clara kneeling between Nikolai's legs, her hands wrapped around his dick.

He sits on the bed, leaning back on his palms, and he's only in his boxer briefs that Clara pulled down to free his cock.

Now she's fisting him, watching, marveling, and admiring.

His gaze shoots to mine as soon as I stand in the doorway, his eyes darkening in an instant as his lips lift in a cruel smirk. "Call me babe, Clara."

"I can't wait for you to get this huge cock in me, babe."

The snap happens in a fraction of a second.

A red haze crawls into my vision until I can only see that fucking color.

On the way here, I thought the raging anger was because Clara was being Clara again.

I thought it was because Nikolai was touching her.

But it's not until this very moment that the depressing truth crashes into me.

I never gave two flying fucks about Clara. Zilch. Nada.

What's driving me to the edge of myself isn't her. It's her touching Nikolai.

It's not about *her*. It's about *him*.

Bloody fucking hell.

I shoulder through the door and grab her by a fistful of hair and haul her to her feet. She shrieks and stumbles, finally getting her claws off him.

"What the—" She cuts herself off when I jerk her to a standing position, eyes widening when they meet mine. "Bran…it's not what you think. I was just lonely and hurt by your rejection and…and…"

"Shut it." My voice is steady but firm, and her lips form an O.

I've never spoken to Clara in this tone. Not when she cheated. Not when everyone called her a gold-digging bitch.

All this time, I didn't hate her.

I didn't feel *anything* for her to hate her.

Now, I want to wrap my fingers around her neck and watch as the life leaves her sleazy eyes.

"Leave," I say, still speaking so calmly despite the pent-up chaos brewing inside me.

"Baby, please—"

"Nuh-uh," Nikolai cuts her off this time as he yanks her from my grip and pushes her toward the door. "He's not your fucking baby."

He's dressed now, if boxer briefs can be considered that, and I drag my gaze away from him.

If I don't, I'll be tempted to punch him, and I don't fucking do that.

Clara stares between us, brow furrowing, and I fix my eyes on her, hands jammed in my pockets, without saying a word.

"Off you go," Nikolai barks and throws the Chanel bag at her. "Don't let me see you again."

She wants to say something else, but Nikolai's glare seems to scare her to the bone, because she jogs out of the room as if she's being chased.

Soon after, I hear the ding of the lift, but her smell doesn't disappear.

Fucking flowers.

It lingers in the room and on the man behind me like a ghost.

Fuck him.

Refusing to face him, I start toward the door. "Well, good night, then."

"Fuck no." He slams the door shut with a palm on the side of my head. His chest presses to my back, jamming me against the wood as his hot breaths whisper in my ear, "You're not going anywhere, lotus flower."

THIRTEEN

Nikolai

I CAN TASTE THE FLAMES OF HESITATION AND THE WARRING conflict rolling off my lotus flower in waves, and I want to dart my tongue out and consume it.

Suck it between my lips.

Crunch it beneath my teeth.

Bran's back muscles stiffen underneath my chest like whenever he's trying to fight, escape, or reject whatever lurks in his scornful head. I've given up trying to understand how his mind works, give him space, or be logical about these emotions sweeping me away.

I *suck* at that.

My modus operandi has always been to act first and think of consequences later. There's no reason why that should change now.

Besides, he obviously wants me. I can see it in his mystic eyes that often conceal his feelings, but when the mask drops, I catch a glimpse of my reflection in that coral blue, surrounded by a halo of lust.

Sure, there's also hate and disregard as well. There's confusion and self-preservation. But who gives a fuck about those irrelevant emotions?

Certainly not me.

Tension rolls and crackles whenever we're in the same space. It doesn't matter whether it's in public or in the confinement of my bed-room. If he's here, I'm soaring and riding on the high of his presence. The beast in me wants to drag out the hidden beast in him and play. I want to shatter his control, wreak havoc on his golden-boy image, and disrupt his life.

I want to sink my teeth into his skin and feed on the lust that ra-diates from his unsaid words.

Until I drain him.

Until there's nothing left of him. Or me.

I inch even closer so that I'm covering him entirely and my rag-ing erection presses against his firm ass.

Needless to say, I've been as hard as a rock since he shoved Clara away from me. I like to think he didn't want her to touch me, not the other way around.

Because he told *her* to leave and he didn't follow.

Call me delusional, but I choose to believe the calm anger he displayed was due to being possessive of me.

He squirms, his ass brushing accidentally—or not so acciden-tally—against my cock and I groan.

God-fucking-damn-it.

Why the fuck is mere contact turning me into an animal? The thought of claiming him ticks in my brain like a bomb, drowning any trace of other thoughts. Not that I have many of those when he's around, but still.

He inches closer to the door as if he can escape me. Not possible in this lifetime and any future ones, if I have a say in it.

"Don't touch me," he orders, but his voice carries nothing of the usual haughtiness he breathes instead of air.

"But I love touching you, my Prince Charming."

"I don't give a fuck about what you love, and I'm not your Prince Charming." He swings around, the sheer mass of his body lunging forward, eyes blazing with a fire so fucking wild, I want to fan it, turn it as bright as an inferno.

He tries to push against me, but I slam my hands against the door on either side of his head, my chest shoving his. I'm so close, I can smell the alcohol on his breath and see that fire burning in his eyes.

More.

I smirk, staring down at his puffed-out lips. "Someone is mad."

"Fuck you."

"Baby, you know I love it when you talk dirty to me."

He grabs me by the throat, fingers digging ruthlessly into the sides. "You need to stay the hell away from me."

"No." I try to step closer and he tightens his grip until I can barely breathe. My lungs burn, and I can feel the veins in my neck bulging.

"I'm going to fucking kill you."

"Mmm. Love it when you get rough."

"You think I'm joking?" His short nails sink into my skin. "Touch me and I'll choke you to death."

"Tell me more. Your mouth makes me so fucking hard." I roll my hips and slam them against his groin.

And fuck.

Fuck me.

"Looks like I make you hard, too. If I reach inside your pants, will I find you leaking for me?"

"You fucking—" His face flushes a subtle shade of red and his fingers compress so hard, they shake.

He's shaking, my Prince Charming, losing his precious control one layer at a time.

And what do I do?

Trap him between my teeth and never let go. Of course.

I'm getting under his skin. The first step of being inside him.

"You can fight me, can choke the life out of me, but that won't stop you from wanting me," I strain and wrap my hand around his throat, on the hickey he's hiding as if his life depends on it. "You came here to stop me from fucking Clara. You weren't mad *for* her, you were mad *at* her. You didn't like the way she touched me and called me babe, right?"

"Shut your mouth."

"You're pissed off at me because I let her touch me?"

That beautiful rage shines bright behind his eyes, but then he says the exact opposite of what he thinks, "Why would I care what you do?"

"Always playing a role, my lotus flower. Hiding, pretending. You obviously broke up with her tonight. Why didn't you tell me that?"

"How...?"

"She told me she was going through a breakup and was looking to forget at the pub." I try to get my head closer, but he keeps me in place with his unyielding hold. "You did it for me, didn't you? You lost her because I told you to. No. You did it because you wanted to be with *me*. Because you know I'm the only one who can give you what you need."

"Stop dreaming."

"Stop fucking pretending." I remove the Band-Aid at his throat, revealing the purple hickey. "Stop hiding."

He shakes his head, but his fingers loosen around my throat. Bran isn't weak. Sure, I have more muscles, but he has strength. The reason he let me touch him the previous times isn't because he couldn't stop me. It's because he chose *not* to stop me.

Like right now.

His war for control breaks like ice beneath his feet.

I'm the lake waiting to swallow him fucking whole.

My fingers spread on his sharp jaw, my lips an inch from his, breathing notes of alcohol and mint off his fractured exhales.

"Don't you dare..." he whispers and it's shaky, breathless.

The asshole clearly wants me, he's *burning* for it. His body language gives him away. Eyes darkening, nostrils flaring, and fingers holding my neck so lovingly—though he'd argue otherwise—and his huge dick is performing a standing ovation for me.

But he's still fighting tooth and nail, still refusing to admit the inevitable.

"Want to blame me again?" I murmur against his skin.

A puff of air leaves his mouth and he nods once.

"Then blame me all you want, baby."

I slam my lips to his, taking what's mine.

Because he is fucking *mine*.

It doesn't matter that he doesn't know it yet and would probably deny it till kingdom come. It doesn't matter that he's a fucking asshole.

He's my asshole. Literally.

Bran opens with a groan, his hot, wet tongue clashing against mine as he moans. He moans like the most erotic fucking thing I've ever devoured.

He's so pliant and passionate when my mouth speaks to his, so fucking wanton and responsive. His hips roll and he brushes his cock against mine as I kiss the living daylights out of him.

I nibble on his bottom lip the way he loves, then plunge my tongue back inside, seeking his greedy one, stroking, rubbing, and twirling.

His jaw flexes with every kiss, every nip, and every savage sound I release down his throat.

I love how his hand glides from my neck to my hair, fisting to keep me in place so he can shove his tongue against mine, searing me to him in ways so foreign and addicting.

More.

I need more.

I jam my knee between his and wrap a leg around his thigh as I grind my cock against his rock-hard one.

The new position gives me better access, more friction, and he groans down my throat as he clenches his fingers in my hair, letting me know how much he likes that.

His cock thickens against mine as I stroke him up and down, rubbing, fondling us until tingles erupt in my spine.

I growl when he picks up on my pace and meets me stroke for stroke. He grunts, pants, and tugs at my hair. It's the most beautiful pain I've ever felt.

How the fuck is he able to drive me crazy by just kissing?

My hands slide down his chest and he groans when I brush his nipple that protrudes from beneath the shirt, so I twist it. He bites on my tongue.

Fucking savage.

I hiss with a grin.

I love it when his beast collides with mine in a fucked-up symphony of violence.

So I slide my hands beneath his shirt, over the smooth planes of muscles, and it's his turn to hiss when I pinch his nipples. The longer I torture, the more his dick thickens, and the faster he dry humps me, making me drip in my boxer briefs.

I'd love nothing more than to indulge in nipple play and drive him fucking insane, but there's another part of him I'd rather play with.

Twisting one nipple, I let my other hand travel down and I unbutton his pants. He releases a small gasp when I unzip his fly over his bulge.

This Prince Charming is fucking packing.

I shove my hand inside his briefs and fist his cock at the base with a firm hand, then squeeze.

"Umph...fuck..." he breathes against my mouth, his eyes dazed, eyebrows drawn together, and face dripping with pure fucking desire.

No one should look this edible.

"You like it when I touch you roughly, baby? Do you feel how you thicken in my hand?" I pull him out and stroke him firmly from the base to the tip, teasing the foreskin with my thumb.

"Shut your mouth." He does it for me, his lips devouring mine, and he kisses me with unbound lust, his hips jerking as he fucks my fist. "Fuck you..." He bites the corner of my lip and stretches the skin. "Fuck you...Nikolai... Why the fuck did you come into my life... Fuck..."

"I'm in your life because you're fucking up mine, baby." I lower myself to my knees in front of him.

His eyes widen as he stares down at me, his hand still lost in my hair. He removed the band at some point and is fisting it into a ponytail.

"What are you—" His words end with a groan when I slide his huge cock into my mouth, relaxing my jaw and steering him as far back as possible.

God-fucking-damn-it. He tastes so good.

"Ffuuck..." He releases a long curse, throwing his head too far back, it bangs against the door. His eyes shutter closed and he wraps his free hand around my nape, fingers digging into my skin.

"Mmm," I mumble around his cock, rubbing it against the back of my throat, then sliding it all the way out to swirl his foreskin. I push it back to fuck the tip with my tongue and lap against the opening. Precum explodes in my mouth and I drink it greedily, which makes him leak some more.

"Mffuckk...fuckkk..." he breathes out, his hips jerking in an irregular rhythm.

"Look at me," I order.

Bran's eyes flutter open the slightest bit, but he looks down at me, one hand brutalizing my hair, but the other strokes my nape. He's a fucking riddle of opposites, my Prince Charming.

Hot and cold.

A storm in the summer.

A fucking beast in the form of a gentleman.

"That's it, baby. Eyes on me as I choke on your cock."

He grunts, the sound deep and masculine, and makes my own dick stand at painful attention.

My gaze locks on his as I slurp on his cock, licking, and making sloppy noises as I swallow him alive.

Then I pull his length inside until I gag on it. His lips part, breathing shallow and loud as he thrusts, demanding more of the friction.

Of me.

Keeping a hand at the base of his cock, I cup his balls, teasing at first, then I squeeze until he jerks, pounding harder into my mouth.

I can't stop looking at his lust-filled face, at the way he watches me with both hate and wonder.

Lust and confusion.

That's it, lotus flower, give me your emotions. Feed me your cracked control.

"Oh fuck... Oh fuck..." he repeats as a mantra, his thrusts turning crazed, and I let him take his pleasure, squeezing his balls and slurping on his length.

He uses his fist in my hair to shove me harder against him so he can fuck my mouth.

I reach beneath his shirt, spreading my palm on his hard abs, and latch onto his nipple, pulling and squeezing.

He hisses and groans. "I... I'm...coming, Niko...fuck... I'm coming..."

His thrusts turn animalistic as he drives into my mouth with urgency. I scrape my blunt nails against his nipple and squeeze my throat around his tip.

That sends him over the edge.

Bran releases a long grunt that reverberates over my skin as his cum explodes on my tongue and down my throat. The salty taste of him lingers in my mouth and forms a mess on my lips.

I continue sucking him and swallowing every drop, even as his dick depletes and he thrusts his hips a few more times, riding his orgasm.

After a while, he blinks twice, eyes wide open as he reluctantly removes his hands. "I...fuck. I'm sorry I made a mess."

Such a gentleman, my Prince Charming. Only he would apologize for that hot-as-fuck show.

I release his cock with a pop and can't resist teasing the hidden opening with my tongue before I stand up and grab his jaw. "I'm not sorry. I will definitely make a mess out of you as well."

My lips press against his and he doesn't hesitate. Not even for a fraction of a second as he lets me kiss him. He doesn't hesitate as he strokes my tongue with his, tasting himself off my mouth.

His arms wrap around my back, a palm riding up to my head as he strokes my hair, slowly, sensually, as if he's making up for how he pulled at it just moments ago.

Bran doesn't look like it, but he's a passionate kisser. He goes deep and furious. Sometimes deep and slow, like now, nibbling and stroking, touching and exploring, as if he wants to take his time getting to know every nook of my body and mouth.

When I pull away, he releases a protesting sound that I'm not sure he's even aware of.

I suppress a smile as I grab him by the hand and drag him toward the bed. "Your turn to choke on my cock, baby."

FOURTEEN

Brandon

A FOG OF PLEASURE SWIRLS AROUND MY HEAD, HUNGRY AND dangerous, as yellow spots line my vision.

Nikolai slides his boxer briefs down and kicks them away until he's only wearing his bullet necklace.

I try to look away, but I realize with daunting clarity that it's virtually impossible to ignore the man in front of me.

During the past week, I had to stop myself from studying his extravagant tattoos, because that would mean I was staring.

And I couldn't possibly be caught doing that.

Right now, however, I don't seem to care. Could be because I just let him give me the best blowjob of my life.

And I don't even *like* blowjobs.

I could deny it all I want, but the truth is, Nikolai Sokolov is… good-looking.

Sorry. Fucking hot is the expression I'm searching for.

He's all muscles, proportionally placed over his tall frame and broad build. His tattoos are a mixture of artistic bleeding roses, skulls, and intricate designs. My favorite is the tattoo of a serpent wrapped around a skull that covers his shoulder and bicep.

My gaze flits to the sophisticated infinity tattoo that twirls down his hip and over the side of his thigh. That's also a favorite.

I attempt to get my fill of the rest of his tattoos, but it's impossible when his cock stands fully erect, nearly touching his abs.

I've often seen my teammates naked, but I've never felt this on edge around them. Or anyone, really.

Then again, Nikolai is nowhere near average. His whole presence is effortlessly intimidating, but I'm far from being intimidated.

It's much, much worse.

I'm burning to touch those muscles.

My nostrils flare at the thought of leaving my smell on him. Not anyone else's.

Mine.

He's naked, but I'm the one who's being stripped by his intense gaze that he slides over my open trousers and my soft dick that's twitching beneath his attention.

He darts his tongue out and swipes it across his bottom lip, and my gaze flashes there, and once again, I'm hit by the reminder of my cock in his mouth.

I can't help replaying the image of the way he touched me, but more the way he looked at me. The way he topped from the bottom and handled me roughly but also sensually.

That was definitely the strongest release I've ever had. Only rivaled by that time in the alley.

Sex is supposed to be meaningless, mild at best and torturous at worst. But with Nikolai, it's hands down the most intense, mind-numbing experience. With Nikolai, my releases breach the physical and extend to an unknown, frightening universe.

And I'm hit by the survival instinct to run away.

To open the door and sprint into the night, then do what I excel at.

Pretend. Avoid. Deny.

However, my feet remain rooted in place as I stare back into his eyes. But because I'm so far out of control, my attention falls to his bruised lips and mine tremble in remembrance of the way he kissed me.

And the way *I* kissed him.

The way *I* devoured him as if I were attempting to fuse my soul with his or something similarly ridiculous.

"I know I'm hot, but you have to stop watching from afar and get your sexy ass over here, baby." He sits on the edge of the bed and grins in that slightly evil way. "Strip for me. Let me see you."

My fingers wrap around the edge of my T-shirt's collar of their own accord and I pull it over my head, then toss it on a chair. My shoes and trousers follow before I push the briefs all the way down.

I have a nice body as a result of all the running and working out, but I don't go out of my way to showcase it. Definitely not to the extent of exhibitionism that Lan loves so much.

In fact, I prefer being clothed at all times. But right now, I feel a sense of triumph when Nikolai studies every inch of my skin, his greedy eyes taking me in from head to toe as if he hasn't seen a naked man before.

"You're so fucking beautiful." He marvels and opens a hand in my direction.

I walk toward him, but I don't take it. That just feels weird. This entire thing does. From the moment I realized I was possessive of him, not Clara, all the way to when I came down his throat.

And yet, for some reason, I don't want to put an end to it.

Not now.

I'll keep this up for a while longer.

He said I can blame it on him afterward. So it's not on me.

This is a dream and I'll enjoy it until I'm forced awake.

I cross my arms. "I'm not a girl. Don't call me beautiful."

"Men can be beautiful. I am, for one." He winks and grabs my wrist, forcing me to uncross my arms.

"Your arrogance knows no bounds."

"You love my arrogance."

"Keep dreaming."

"You love the way I look at you," he continues, biting the corner of his lip as he slides his hungry gaze over me. "You love how I touch you." He flicks a finger over my nipple, drawing a shudder from me. "You definitely love playing hard to get."

I swat his hand away. "Nikolai!"

"Call me Niko like you did earlier."

"I did no such thing."

"You totally did while you shot your cum down my throat. You said *Niko* in this sexy, needy voice."

"No idea what you're talking about."

He narrows his eyes, but before I can burst into flames, he tugs on my wrist. "Come on. I need your lips around my cock."

I steal a quick glance at his dick that's so hard, purple veins bulge on the sides, and a transparent liquid shines at the tip.

"What…" I clear my throat. "What should I do?"

"What I did to you."

"I will *not* get on my knees."

"I went on my knees for you just fine."

My hand rubs the back of my head and I release a sigh. "I don't know how to do this, okay? I've never…"

"Sucked off another guy?"

I nod slowly. The thought of making a fool out of myself gives me worse nausea than the fact that I actually want to do this.

A part of me is buzzing with the possibility of giving him pleasure as intense as he gave me.

Nikolai's eyes darken, the blue appearing unhinged, possessive, even, as he wrenches me forward and I fall on top of him, my chest pressing to his.

His heartbeat thunders against mine, and I hiss when my cock brushes against his thigh.

Good grief. I just came, so why the hell am I getting hard again? I never get hard after a release. *Never.*

His coarse fingers stroke my jaw, and I'm in awe at how a shiver goes through me at that. Or maybe it's because of the hooded look in his gaze.

"Just do what you think you'd like when getting a blowjob."

That's the fucking problem. I don't like those.

Well, until now.

"If at a loss, mimic what I did." He winks. "Now, kneel on me."

Before I can ask what he means, Nikolai lies on his back and directs me so that I'm turned around and on all fours on top of him. His hard cock is within reach and mine is near his face.

I have never been in such an exposed position before. Have never been comfortable with sixty-nine and, therefore, haven't done it. I've always liked to be in control of every sexual act, even if I was bored out of my mind during it.

Now, however, I don't feel uncomfortable. It's more…apprehension mixed with a surge of a foreign thrill.

Before I can think about what it means, Nikolai thrusts his hips up.

"Wrap your lips around my cock, baby."

His orders send me into a weird frenzy and I fist his dick at the base and stroke it a few times like he did to me. I can't resist teasing the crown and one of the piercings to test if it feels sensitive.

A drop of precum coats my thumb and I'm rewarded with Nikolai's grunt. So I do it a few more times while I jerk him until his hips lift off the bed and his delicious noises of pleasure fill my ears.

I register and pay attention to every sudden hitch in his breathing, every movement of his hips, and even the goosebumps that erupt on his thighs.

That way, I know what he likes and keep doing it rougher.

"You're killing me." His lustful voice rushes through me like an aphrodisiac.

I smile, loving the idea of killing him.

The thought of a notoriously frightening man like him being so into me is a strange turn-on.

After a few more tugs, I guide him into my mouth and groan around him. I don't mean to, but I can't help it when his skin explodes on my taste buds.

Maybe it's because I've wanted to do this for longer than I would like to admit. Maybe it's because he does taste, and mostly *feels*, bloody fantastic in my mouth.

"That's it, baby. Get my cock sloppy and wet," he rumbles from beneath me, his fingers sliding up and down my balls, teasing, squeezing. "Loosen your jaw. Let me fuck that throat."

A shiver goes through me and I do as he says, turning into a wanton entity I can't recognize while I lick the sides of his dick. Precum drips on my tongue and I swallow, squeezing the pierced crown at the back of my throat and keeping it there.

Nikolai grunts, jerks, and thrusts. "Your mouth feels so fucking good. Jesus Christ. Look at you, baby. You don't even have a gag reflex."

His hips lift and I can tell he's holding back, trying not to hurt me or something. So I go harder, jerking his cock at the base and testing what he just said. I bob my head up and down, taking as much of him as I can to the back of my throat with every slurp.

"Mmm. Fuck. Your mouth is made for sucking my cock. You're doing so well."

I growl around his skin and he thickens even more against the vibration. For some reason, the praise sends me into a frenzy. He's breaking me, crushing my very foundation to fucking pieces, and I'm overwhelmingly addicted.

Undeniably fucking screwed.

I suck his cock like it's a sport, going deeper and harder, then relax my jaw and let him use my tongue for friction. It's sloppy in the beginning; my saliva runs down his length and onto his balls, but then I mix it with his precum on purpose as I lick and tease his piercings so enthusiastically, it's as if I was born to suck cock.

Not just any cock. *His* cock.

I drown in the lustful moans spilling from him. My balls tighten and my dick thickens as his growls rumble through me, turning me into a fucking animal.

The opening of a drawer breaches my ears, but I don't pay attention as I get the hang of what I'm doing. I twist the base of his shaft, pull it out of my mouth, then swirl my tongue on the crown, teeth tugging on a piercing.

"Mmmfuck, baby…fuck…" He releases a thick, lustful sound and feeds me more of his precum.

I can feel him getting close, his dick growing huge in my hands, and even though my jaw aches, I take him in again.

There's no ending this until he shatters as hard as he broke me earlier. I'll give him pleasure as intense as he gave me—

A cold, slippery finger trails a path on my balls and then my arse cheek is pulled to the side and that finger circles my rim.

I buck, the movement taking me so completely by surprise, I don't know what to do. My head is swimming in so much overpowering lust from sucking his cock that I didn't even realize what he was doing.

Nikolai rolls his hips and thrusts all the way to the back of my throat. Pressure forms at my back hole as he traces the rim some more, then slides his finger in.

"Shhh. You're doing so good, baby. Your ass is taking my finger so well." He drives his cock in my mouth as he penetrates me from behind.

The intrusion makes me close my eyes, my knees shaking, and a part of me demands I fight.

Somehow.

Anyhow.

I need to—

He drives his finger in slowly, breaching me so wholly, I can't think straight.

"Mmmf… Ffuck…" I mumble around his cock, saliva and precum dripping on his balls.

Another lubed finger joins the first and the fullness clouds my head. All I can do is remain still, mouth open, arse in the air as he thrusts in me.

The pain slowly disappears, replaced by an acute sense of… pleasure?

Oh fuck.

"That's it, baby." He thrusts his cock in and out of my mouth, hitting the back of my throat with the piercings. "Fuck your ass on my fingers."

I realize with utter shock that I'm rocking back and forth, lips parted so he can fuck me with his cock and I'm helping him drive in and out of my arse.

Fucking fuck.

He's dragging out a foreign version of me, clawing and tearing at every safety measure I had in place.

He gets close and I'm giving up control.

He touches me and I'm stumbling, rolling, falling, falling, falling…

Nikolai's fingers scrape something inside me and I nearly lose balance.

"There it is." The lust in his voice undoes me, shoving me to the edge. "Fuck… I'm gonna come…"

He pegs his fingers against that secret part once.

Twice…

On the third time, heat engulfs me and any sounds I want to make are drowned by the cum that explodes all over my mouth, lips, and face.

But that's not the part that makes me want to scream. It's my own dick shooting cum on Nikolai's chest, face, and hands.

It goes on and on, spraying everywhere and decorating the sheets.

Please don't tell me I just came without any stimulation to my cock.

I jerk away from Nikolai and he slips his fingers from my arse. My hole clenches around them as if wanting to keep them there. What the—

"Mmm." Nikolai traces his other hand over the cum on his chest, smearing it on the tattoos before he drags his fingers to his mouth. "You definitely made a mess this time. Hot as fuck."

I try to escape, but I end up tripping on his limbs and I fall beside him on the bed.

Nikolai doesn't seem to sense my feelings of trepidation, because he rolls, flips around, and hovers on top of me. His majestic body, while huge, doesn't feel threatening. The tip of the necklace skims over my throat like a caress. His loose hair frames his face and I have to stop myself from touching it.

"You're going to kiss me, aren't you?" I ask, my defenses depleted.

He grins, eyes shining with mischief. "You know I will."

"What if I ask you not to?"

"We both know your mouth is a fucking liar unless I'm devouring it." He darts out his tongue and licks his cum off my jaw and lips, then thrusts it into my parted mouth, feeding me his cum, making me taste him again and swallow every last drop.

Whenever he kisses me, I feel like I'm losing a piece of myself that I'll never recuperate. And yet I can't help sinking my fingers into his hair, moaning in his mouth, gliding my tongue against his, sucking, biting, and forgetting.

For one moment, I forget and let myself get lost in the dream.

He pulls his mouth from mine and I have to physically stop myself from chasing his tongue and hooking it against mine.

Nikolai gives my bottom lip one last tug before he releases it and pushes off me, his finger teasing my nipple on his way up. "I'll be right back, baby. Don't move."

My head turns to the side, watching his inked back muscles flexing, his hair messed up from how much I pulled and fisted the inky strands.

Somewhere in the center of my chest aches.

Why the fuck is he so beautiful and why am I...this attracted to him?

Wasn't I supposed to be broken?

I stare at the white platform ceiling for a few seconds, but then as the pleasure haze disappears, I blink away my confusion and sober up.

My legs barely carry me as I stand up and snatch my clothes, then put them on awkwardly as I jog to the lift.

I pause inside, my forefinger hovering over the yellow ground-floor button, and then I do what I've done my entire life.

Run away. Deny. Pretend.

Nausea rushes up my throat when I push the button.

As the door closes, my fingers find the hairs at the back of my head and I pull, but no amount of pain drowns out the sense of loss crawling up my limbs.

I couldn't sleep last night.

For the first time in eight fucking years, I didn't get a wink of sleep. Not one.

I tossed and turned, took three cold showers, drank more herbal tea than in Victorian England, and went to my studio, but nothing helped to put me down.

I even jammed my Swiss Army knife in my arm, but the sharp point only caused a small cut and the blood that dripped out didn't manage to chase away the ink that swallowed me up to my waist, murdering any form of pleasure I'd experienced the previous night.

What makes you think you can enjoy anything when you're fucking defective?

Despite those thoughts and the black face in the mirror. Despite the blood that rushed out of me and the strokes of red on my canvas, I can't help the jolt of hope or the simmering expectation that envelops me as I step out of the mansion and snap my usual picture.

I wasn't going to bother with the AirPods since Nikolai always removes them, sometimes not so nicely, but if I don't wear them, then he'll think it's because of him.

Isn't that the case?

I ignore the voice in my head as I put the music on pause, my heart beating faster the farther I get from the mansion.

This is the first time I've been excited about something and desired it with every fiber of my being. So much so that it's starting to freak me out.

The first time I've considered taking the pain as long as I get the pleasure first.

At least, for a while.

My feet come to a halt when a large figure cuts in front of me and I remain still as he plucks both AirPods from my ears.

Nikolai is shirtless, which isn't anything new. What is new, however, is the savage look in his eyes. His tone comes out sarcastic, though. "A very good day to you, lotus flower. Do you have anything to tell me?"

I swallow the dread that gathers in my throat as I speak in my calm voice. "No. Why should I?"

He takes a step forward and I take one back. If I don't let him get close, everything will be fine.

Things only get worse after he touches me.

Nikolai stops and fingers his necklace, tugging on the bullet until I'm sure he'll break the thing. "I clearly told you not to move last night, so why did you run away and ignore my texts?"

He texted? I've had my phone on *Do Not Disturb* since I got back to the house and only took it out to snap the picture just now. But before I can offer up the flimsy excuse, Nikolai runs his fingers through his loose hair.

"Your push-and-pull game was adorable the first few times, but you need to cut it out. Don't make me do it for you. We both know my methods don't agree with your proper manners."

I suck in a deep breath. "Get out of my life, Nikolai."

"The answer is no."

"I want you gone."

"It's still no."

"Do you have no pride?"

"What the fuck is that? Is it edible?"

I release an exasperated sound. "I don't know why the hell you're obsessed with me, but I'm telling you that it's impossible. I'm not gay."

He bursts out laughing, the sound scraping at the edges of my sanity, and I want to reach out to stop it, but I can't move.

Shut up.

Shut the fuck up—

"Not gay?" he sneers at me. "Baby, you came three times on my hand, mouth, and fucking fingers. You choked on my cock and came because of a mere prostate fucking. If that isn't gay, I don't know what is."

"Stop talking," I grit out, trying to fight the pounding in my head. I need to leave before he sees me for the ugly monster I actually am.

"What the—" He snatches my hand, and for a fraction of a second, I feel like the world is tilting back on its axis.

I inhale his mint scent and spit out disgusting nausea until my stomach settles back down.

Nikolai inspects the plaster on my forearm. "What happened to your arm?"

"It's just a scratch." I try to retrieve it, but he tightens his grip on my wrist. Over the watch I never remove.

He narrows his eyes. "Why do you seem to get hurt a lot? The other day, it was your hand, and this time, your arm. You don't strike me as clumsy."

I watch his hair flying in the wind and I hate that the only urge I have is to touch it, run my fingers through it.

But I can't.

Wanting him is a painful struggle. Wanting him is ripping a hole in the very marrow of my existence and making me question everything.

I can't afford to question *everything*.

I need my system and routines, and he simply does not belong there.

He's an error in the matrix.

A plot hole in a story.

"Why do you want me, Nikolai?" I ask instead of answering his question. "We're nothing alike—I'm too proper for your liking. You're too violent for my preferences. So why are you this obsessed with me?"

"Do I need a reason?"

"Of course you do."

"That's where you're wrong. I don't need a reason to want you, lotus flower. I just do. And if you put a pause on the useless thoughts cramming that head of yours, you'll also admit that you just want me, too. Simple. Normal."

"You don't even *know* me."

"I know you're such a gentleman and you love running at the same time every day. I also know you're different from your psycho twin brother and have a good relationship with everyone. Except for Clara, because she's finally out of the fucking picture, but here's the most important part." He smirks. "I also know you love kissing me."

"I do not."

"Wanna prove it?"

"Don't..." I slam a hand to his mouth and he kisses my palm, then licks my fingers, thrusting his tongue between them.

I jerk my arm away. "Why the hell would you lick me? Are you a dog?"

"Woof." He grins and I can't even muster the emotions to be mad at him.

Bloody wanker is mental.

"Is there a way I can get rid of you?" I ask, my shoulders hunching.

"If I die, maybe. Scratch that, I'll haunt the fuck out of you until you join me, my Prince Charming. Then we can have a fuck fest in ghost land."

"You need help."

"Then help me, baby."

I release a groan of frustration, but I can hear my walls cracking and a door opens despite my attempts to slam it shut.

All this time, I've refused the very notion that I'm attracted to him. But last night proved me terribly wrong.

I could blame the alcohol or him, but that only worked the first time. *Barely.*

Pushing him away is futile since he's a fucking elastic band that keeps snapping back twice as hard.

If I want to remain in control, I need to absorb him into my system. Take things into my own hands. Get bored. Toss him aside.

The end.

A grunt leaves me and he watches me closely as if he's attempting to read my mind.

I can't believe I'm doing this.

"If this happens, and it's only an *if*." I meet his gaze. "No one knows."

"Not even Jeremy?"

"No."

"Not even your sister? She's all cozy with Kill and we get along."

"No one."

His lips push in a pout. "Okay."

"We'll only meet in a place no one else knows about."

"My penthouse. I bought it recently and still haven't told anyone else about it."

"Except for Clara."

"You still jealous about that?"

"I'm *not* jealous."

"Whatever floats your boat, my lotus flower."

"Nikolai."

"Yes, baby?"

"Don't call me any of those nicknames in front of anyone else. Don't act like you know me in public."

"But why? I want to hang out with you."

"I don't. We're not friends and this is only physical."

"We'll see about that."

"What?"

"What?" he repeats, pretending to be oblivious. "I want to see you all day."

"Don't you have school?"

"Not important."

"Your silly club shenanigans?"

"Not a priority."

"Have you forgotten that my brother's club is at odds with yours?"

"What do you have to do with your asshole brother?"

"He's my twin."

"Still can't see why you have to be lumped with him."

I stare at him for a beat. Nikolai doesn't hide his disregard for Lan, but he's also not subtle about his obsession with me. Does he not see that we're *identical* twins?

"We're strangers in public, Nikolai. I mean it."

"Fiiiine. Any other dictatorial conditions?"

"That's it for now. I'll let you know if I come up with anything else."

"Since we're done with that stupidity. It's time for my condition." He wraps his fingers around my neck. "Don't run away from me again. If you do, I'll flip the world upside down to find you. You're mine now, baby."

FIFTEEN

Nikolai

TODAY IS THE PERFECT RECIPE FOR VIOLENCE.

It started with Jer and me riding our bikes into the wind and beating up a few Serpents, doing some old-fashioned house cleaning on the island and teaching them a few valuable lessons. Naturally, that included drawing blood and breaking bones.

While I felt a rush at the time, and Jeremy had to stop me from beating a fuckwit to death, the intoxication disappeared as soon as we got back to the mansion.

I slept in the pool—sorry, I mean *meditated*—but that didn't stop me from spiraling down that chaos-driven hole.

There are these times when I'm in the mood to destroy everything—myself included. A high without the drugs. Insanity without the straight jacket.

And it is some form of a mental illness—at least, according to the hotshot psychiatrists my parents took me to the first time I beat a kid to near death for calling Mia a mute. At the age of ten.

Apparently, it's normal to feel offended on my sister's behalf and want to rip the other kid a new one. Everyone feels anger. It's okay, it's *normal*.

What's abnormal, however, is me insisting that the kid should die, have his tongue cut out and shoved down his throat.

Yeah, that one didn't go over well with any of the people dressed in white in that spotless room. Even my mom, who's a goddamn leader in the Russian mafia, was concerned about my violent tendencies that manifested early.

More concerned than the time I used my wiener as a gun.

I seem to do that a lot to my dear mama. I worry her to no end and probably keep her up at night thinking about my shenanigans. She's supportive, though, and often softens her voice when she tells me to be careful when I'm in this mood.

The destructive mood. The red haze mood.

The mood in which the world is full of featureless people with black plastic bags strapped around their heads, waiting to be punched to death.

A mood where everyone and everything grates on my last fucking nerve and I'm better off staying away from the people I love, namely my sisters, my cousins, and Jeremy.

But Kill insisted on fighting me tonight. He's the only one without enough brain cells to avoid me when I'm like this, but then again, he always says I'm much more fun when I'm exhaling chaotic violence into the world.

It's the only time he can relate since he's a bit of a psycho himself.

Now, don't get me wrong. I love this mode, especially this morning when Jeremy gave me the chance to embark on that thrill of hunting down slimy cunts and teaching them a lesson. Jeremy knows what I need, which is why he's like the best bro ever.

The only friend who can tolerate my crazy and gives me methods to counter the way my chaotic brain presses on my sanity.

I'm not a docile kitten outside this state of hyper mania—I'll always want to beat up things for sport. However, at least then I can tell my thoughts apart. I can see the world in colors other than red.

I can see people's features.

Having had manic episodes since puberty, I'm used to it. I'm so used to it that I have it completely under control.

Today is different.

Today, I jumped off a tree, rolled down a cliff, and fell from my bike. I swam until I nearly had a heart attack.

But that's the problem. My heart rate hasn't gone down. Not once. Not when I tried to inhale and exhale slowly. Not when I forced myself to remain still for...five minutes.

I haven't been able to fucking breathe properly, and whenever I do, my lungs fill with the same fucking red mist that's blinding my eyes.

Every second of every minute, I'm itching and burning to erase it. And for years, the only way I've been able to do that is to beat people the fuck up.

There are also pills, but fuck those right the fuck off. They kill my mind, take away my inhibitions, and nearly drowned me in the pool the last time I took them.

I know how to keep myself in check without their unwanted help. They're not helping anyway. They just turn me into a fucking zombie, and no one likes that fucked-up guy.

I pace the length of the locker room back and forth, back and forth like a caged gladiator in Roman times.

The crowd's cheers reach me from outside, buzzing on my skin as if I'm being stung by a thousand bees.

People love the adrenaline of seeing violence. They love the crunching of bones and the spilling of blood. There's something intoxicating about watching two people shred each other a new one.

And I get off on the screams. The chants. The enchanted look in their eyes. It's why I usually take a few of them home for a fuck fest that always takes place afterward.

Sex and violence go hand in hand with me. A high. A release. A perfect synergy of fucked-up energy.

Tonight, however, I have absolutely no intention of continuing this tradition. I haven't for several weeks.

Fucking Kolya and his stupid imaginary chastity belt.

Though he's not chaste—it's blasphemy to call him that. He's just become selective and is only into a certain reluctant asshole.

At the mere thought of my lotus flower, my cock twitches to life, tenting against my shorts.

See. He's still a dick, just not for everyone.

Pacing the length of the dimly lit locker room, I stare at my phone that's been gripped in my hand for the past…fuck knows how long.

I should be out there, beating Kill to a pulp and getting beaten in return, but I can't stop looking at my conversation with Bran.

It's been four days since the day he finally agreed to stop running from us—well, he didn't say that exactly, but he laid out all those fucking conditions, so he can bet his ass that I took that as an agreement to my sole condition.

I went running with him the past three days, and he was still stalling, being the epitome of an asshole and refusing to come to the penthouse.

Every day, he came with a different excuse. Practice. Meeting with friends. Art project.

He finds those so easily, the lies slipping out of his beautiful mouth without a second thought.

Fucking liar.

He's just trying to avoid the inevitable, which I told him in not-so-subtle words over texts yesterday.

> **Me:** You know you're stalling, right?

> **Me:** You can hide for as long as you wish, but I'll eventually drag you out, baby.

> **Me:** So I've been thinking. I don't do that a lot, but it's become a habit lately. You know, since you love all that smart shit.

> **Me:** Wanna know what I've been thinking about?

> **Bran:** Don't care.

Me: Glad you asked. I've been kind of replaying the image of your ass swallowing my fingers as you came all over my stomach. So fucking hot. I came to that image in fucking waves, picturing your erotic face.

Bran: Why on earth do you have to speak that way?

Me: Does that mean you were thinking about it, too? I knew I liked you. Serious question. Wanna do it again? This time, maybe replace my fingers with my cock? I'll make you feel good when I fuck you, baby, I promise.

Bran: You're not going to fuck me, Nikolai.

Me: Eh, what do you mean I won't fuck you? Isn't that the whole point behind your exasperating conditions?

Bran: Why do you have to be the one who fucks me? Maybe I should be the one who fucks you.

Me: Baby, you've never fucked a guy before and I only top. Besides, you obviously enjoy receiving, judging by the way you came apart on my fingers.

Bran: Doesn't mean I'll let you fuck me.

Me: Are you still weirded out about being touched by a guy? You clearly loved it, no?

Bran: Love is a strong word. I just...didn't mind it.

Me: *eye roll emoji* Then you won't MIND the fucking either. I'll prime you really well and try not to make it hurt. Though you do enjoy a bit of pain, since your cum flooded my mouth when I handled you roughly.

Bran: Stop talking.

Me: Penthouse tonight?

> **Me:** Tomorrow?

> **Me:** Tomorrow. It's a date.

He left me on fucking Read.

That was yesterday. I didn't go on the run today because of all the demons perching on my shoulders and whispering nasty things in my ear.

It's the first time I haven't pounced on the chance to see his face, annoy the fuck out of him, and crawl deeper beneath his skin.

I don't want him to see me this way. I also can't trust myself not to fuck him the fuck up the moment he's in front of me.

My finger is stiff as I exit the text exchange and call the only person I'm comfortable speaking to when I'm in this situation.

The only person who told me, "Fuck the pills. If they erase your fire, don't take them."

He picks up after a few rings and speaks in a British accent. "Talk to me, son."

I pace faster, my feet slapping against the tiles. "It's coming back, Dad. It's fucking me up in the head and I want it gone."

"You're okay. Breathe." His voice is calm and firm, but I can sense his affection beneath the control.

My father is a high-ranking member of the New York Bratva, the best hitman anyone has had the misfortune to know, and the number one man in my paternal grandfather's family.

But most importantly, he's my number one supporter. I love my mom, but she's a fan of science, of doctors in white coats who love to slap people with labels. She's also an advocate of the fucking pills. Not my dad. He, like me, believes that I can control it. And I did.

For fucking years.

Doesn't feel like I'm in control now, though. Fucking far from it.

I'm teetering on the edge of destruction. It pulses beneath my skin and roars in my veins.

"I'm going to snap, Dad. I can feel the pressure gathering and intensifying behind my eyes. Someone will touch or look at me the wrong way and I'll fucking explode. How do I stop it?"

"Maybe you shouldn't, Niko. Just fall into it, absorb the shock, and release some steam. You know how to do that the best, no?"

"It's not fucking working." I slam my fist against the locker and the sound bangs in the eerie silence like a bomb. "Jeremy gave me the setting I needed this morning and it still didn't fucking work."

"What...changed?"

My movements come to a halt as I trace the necklace my dad gave me when I started to need a crutch. Something to touch when I feel my mind spinning, screaming, and turning against me.

"What do you mean?" I ask in a quiet voice.

"Did something happen recently that triggered this? Perhaps a stressful situation? An outcome you don't approve of, maybe?"

Fuck.

I stroke my fingers over the bullet on my necklace, fast, uncoordinated.

"What is that something, son?" Dad asks cautiously.

"Someone. Maybe."

"Who is it?"

"Not important," I lie through my teeth, my movements turning jerkier and more out of control.

"In that case, get rid of them."

The very foundation of my fucking sanity, or whatever remains of it, revolts against that idea.

"Nikolai. You need to promise me that you'll get rid of whoever drove you to this state," Dad says more firmly. "The key to keeping you in control is *not* to provoke you. If this person is doing that, they need to be gone."

"Yeah, I know."

"You'll do it?"

"Yeah."

"Promise?"

"Yeah, Dad. I promise."

"Good." He releases a breath. "I love you, son, and I'm glad you could confide in me."

"Love you, too, Dad." I hang up with a scowl.

He's right. I should get rid of the provocation. Technically, Bran means nothing. So what if I want to fuck him? I wanted to fuck a lot of people before him and I'm sure I'll go back to my old ways soon if I give myself time.

The only difference is that I've never wanted to make someone mine as much as I want to chain him the fuck up to me.

But I can remove him from my life.

I *have* to remove him, because Dad is right. He's provoking me. I was supposed to get under his skin, but he's the one spreading beneath mine like poison. It won't be long before he reaches my heart and slams it to a halt.

His constant rejection and running away is messing with my head in ways I don't approve of.

I've always kept things physical, but that's far from being the case with Bran. I'm spending more time with him than I have with anyone, and I actually like it.

No. I *love* it.

I can't imagine my days without seeing his face first thing in the morning and that little smile he hides so soon after spotting me.

He rejects me, and I keep going back for more like a junkie who needs a hit of the drug that's sucking my life dry.

But this can't go on anymore.

Throwing my phone on the bench, I storm out of the locker room and jog to the ring, where Kill is waiting.

The crowd roars to life as I jump in from between the ropes, wearing nothing but my black shorts, my necklace, and a few bandages.

"Welcome, princess." Kill flashes me a vicious grin, running a bandaged hand over his naked chest and the band of his red shorts.

"You might want to fuck off, Kill," I say over the pressure gathering in my head. "I could actually hurt you."

"Show me what you got, Niko."

I crack my neck, thankful for having a crazy motherfucker for a cousin. Like Jeremy, he knows how much I need this and will fight me whenever I'm in this fucked-up state of mind.

The referee announces the start of the match. My cousin circles me, but I don't have time for that shit.

Hurt.

Maim.

Kill.

I pounce and punch him in the face so hard, he reels a few steps back. A collective gasp echoes from the crowd as blood drips on the mat. My cousin wipes the side of his cut mouth, a bloodied grin slipping through. "That's it, Niko. Unleash the fucking crazy."

I pummel him, all thoughts disappearing from my head and replaced by pure, bloody violence.

Kill tries to defend himself and actually lands a few blows, but it's of no use. I feel no pain in this mode. No fucking remorse or reprieve or the need to press down on the fucking brakes.

The only thing that saves him from me is the referee forcing us back to our corners. And even after that, Jeremy and Gareth jump into the ring and shove me away from him.

Gareth wipes the blood off his brother's face, but Kill keeps grinning as if I'm not on the verge of murdering him.

Jeremy is also cleaning some of the blood that I didn't know I had on me, but he has to stay in the ring because I'm not fucking sitting down or staying still.

I can't.

My feet are moving of their own accord, my mind is racing, and my blood is pumping.

Let me back in there.

Let me back.

Fucking back!

"Niko!" Jeremy shakes my shoulders and I finally look at him through my hazy vision. "Maybe you should leave."

"Fuck no."

"You don't look good, man." He pauses, the silence punctured by all the fangirls—and fanboys—calling my name. "I don't know how to describe it, but this is different from your other times. Maybe you should take the pills."

"Fuck. No."

"Fuck this, Nikolai." Jeremy clutches me by the nape, nearly shoving my forehead against his. "I don't care about the lowlifes you beat up this morning. Fuck those people. Fuck them, okay? But Kill is your cousin. He agreed to this because he saw you were struggling, but you're beating him to a pulp."

"He's fucking enjoying it…"

I trail off when I feel an intense gaze at the back of my head. For a moment, I think Kill is letting his psycho demons loose so they can try to intimidate mine—and fail miserably—but no.

It's coming from the crowd.

My gaze flits through the undefinable faces, not lingering on any so that I don't see them as people with bags strapped around their heads.

In a few seconds, my eyes find those intense blue ones.

I'm dreaming.

Fuck.

I'm too far gone to imagine Bran actually coming to the fight club when his brother isn't involved. Pretty sure he's allergic to violence, blood, and craziness. Which is why I stayed away today despite how every cell in my body protested at the prospect.

I blink once, but he's still there, standing out like a sore thumb in his polo shirt, pressed pants, and slicked-back hair.

A dash of dark blue fixates on me and I completely forget that I have to lose him like Dad said.

I have to *remove* him from my life.

How the fuck will I be able to do that when he looks at me like that? I'm getting fucking hard the more he watches me with undivided attention, his gaze sliding from Jeremy to me.

A leggy blonde taps his shoulder and he cuts eye contact and forces a smile, then she throws herself in his arms. He hugs her back.

My eyes narrow on his hand on her.

Is that the next Clara? She doesn't look like a Clara type. More sophisticated, happier, and definitely not cheap.

Pretty sure I've seen her before, but where…?

Who gives a fuck? He's using someone else for his stupid public image. God forbid the fucking asshole actually accepts he's gay or bi or what-the-fuck-ever and gets over his fucking self.

"Nikolai!" Jeremy brings my attention back to him and slaps my cheek with the back of his hand. "Where the fuck did you go, man?"

Somewhere not nice.

"Hey, Jer?"

"Yeah?"

"Will you stop me if I have this crazy idea about killing innocent girls?"

His lips part. Jeremy is this big mafia prince who doesn't hesitate before inflicting pain, but he's looking at me as if I'm the Mad Hatter.

"What girls are you thinking about killing, Niko?"

"Anyone who gets in the fucking way of what I want." My gaze flies back to the crowd, but he's not there.

The spot beside the blonde is now empty as she drinks from a can of beer and joins the excessive cheers.

Where the fucking fuck did that asshole go now?

You know what? It's fine.

It's better I don't see him when I'm this way.

I'm fucking *fine.*

Maybe if I rip a page from Bran's denial book and tell myself a lie for long enough, I'll be able to believe it.

Once the fight resumes, I'm back at Kill's throat. I beat him the fuck up and he takes it with taunting smirks and provoking words as if he wants to drain my energy—and get himself killed.

By the time the fight finishes with the absolute destruction of my cousin, the crowd is going wild. My name echoes and reverberates, but the thrill doesn't touch my skin.

Nothing fucking does.

I storm to the locker room, my shoulders tense and my throat dry. Every swallow feels as if I'm slowly cutting at my insides, curling and twisting them into a huge pool of fucked-up red.

Whenever my mind goes into overdrive, violence is usually enough to root me back in place. Not this time.

This time, I want out of my fucking head.

My fist slams into the locker, leaving a huge dent in the metal, and I breathe harshly, my exhales rebounding around me like animalistic growls.

A light catches my attention in the corner and I pick up my phone to find a string of texts from none other than my lotus flower. My heart beats faster, harder, tugging at the strings that are keeping it in place.

The first text arrived soon after I left the locker room for the match.

Bran: I heard you're going to fight tonight. Can you not?

Bran: Okay, listen. I didn't mean to ignore you. It's just that I didn't know what to say. It's weird to ask a guy to fuck me.

Bran: I don't mean you're weird. Really, I don't. Though you are. But that's not the point. What I'm trying to say is that you're not weird for your sexuality. I apologize if it came out that way. I just meant that it feels weird to me. I'm not used to this.

Bran: I'll come to your place tonight. If you want. Just don't fight, please.

He stopped texting after that and probably got his ass here.

His next texts appeared just now.

Bran: So you did fight and you looked like you were enjoying yourself. Should I take that as a no?

Bran: You know what? I'm going to your place. You're the one who said this was a date.

Ah, fuck.

Fuck it.

Fuck. Me.

I know I should be pushing him away. I really, *really* should. But he's so fucking irresistible.

Looks like my lotus flower will meet the crazy Nikolai.

God save his soul.

Or, more accurately, his body.

SIXTEEN

Brandon

MAYBE I SHOULD LEAVE.

That's the dozenth time I've had that thought since I invited myself to Nikolai's penthouse.

After I left my Tesla in the car park, I contemplated not actually invading his place. That's just rude.

But the other option was to wait in the reception area, where anyone could walk in and see me.

Not happening.

Getting myself in was safer. If he's mad about that, then, well, maybe he should've changed the code.

Or not asked me to come here ten times a day like a mantra.

Still, I'm uncomfortable as I sit on the sofa, my uneasy breaths only interrupted by the creaks of the leather beneath me.

His place is proper huge compared to the rest of the flats on the island and would definitely be considered a penthouse anywhere in London.

The decor is modern, slick, and polished. Everything is in perfect shape and the decorations seem untouched, probably because it's a new building. I don't think he lives here most of the time, though, considering the lack of life anywhere in this place.

Feeling a bit stuffy, I shrug off my jacket and place it neatly on the chair's armrest. I'd rather hang it instead, but I don't want it to feel like I'm taking liberties in his space.

I removed my shoes at the entrance as well so as not to track in any dirt.

The other day, I was a bit too preoccupied to remember my manners. Not that I'm in a better state of mind today, but he's not here so…

I run a hand over my face and stare up at the cloudy sky through the transparent ceiling. What am I doing, seriously?

This will inevitably lead to a disaster that will undoubtedly push me to purge the pain.

This will hurt. Again.

This will make the black ink submerge me and shove me to the darkest corners of my soul.

And yet I can't move.

I don't want to.

I lift my phone and stare at the texts I sent Nikolai. My chest constricts when I see that he read them, but he didn't reply.

What does that mean?

He never ignores my texts, aside from when he ghosted me. This morning was the first time he didn't glue himself to my side despite my grumbles and attempts to push him away. In fact, he didn't show up at all.

Maybe he's done chasing me. He definitely didn't seem that interested in me when Jeremy was all over him between rounds of the fight.

Bloody hell.

I cover my eyes with my arm. What the fuck is wrong with me? Why can't I remove the image of Jeremy touching him so intimately from my head?

In fact, that was part of the reason why I left the fight club. The first part was being unable to watch him being punched by Killian. Even if he punched back twice as hard.

The ticking sound goes into overdrive in my head, driving me up the wall.

Tick.

He's not coming.

Tick.

Why would he? No one really wants you.

Tick.

You look pathetic. Just leave already.

A migraine starts to form at the back of my skull as the demons run rampant, spouting their hatred and telling me what they think of me without mincing their words.

I know I should leave. I do. But for some reason, I'm rooted in place.

The reality of the situation bursts through me without warning. *I don't want to leave.*

The lift dings and a rush of adrenaline spreads through my chest. *Simmer down. Desperate much?*

Not sure the reprimand works, because when I stand, my feet barely keep me upright. My skin prickles when I feel his overwhelming presence, but then I see him, and my lips part.

Splashes of blood cover some of the tattoos on his chest and decorate his handsome features. His hair is tied in a messy bun, strands escaping and framing his face with a sheen of savagery.

I haven't seen him this unhinged since the initiation. But even back then, he was more pushy and playful than...desolate.

His eyes are uncharacteristically empty, a blue so dark, I can't see the Nikolai I've come to know over the past couple of weeks in them.

"Hey, sorry I let myself in—" The words are barely out when he smashes his body against mine.

The breath is knocked out of my lungs as we both go crashing down on the sofa. I lift my hand to try and get some balance, but he grabs my wrists and slams them above my head and shoves his knee between my legs, forcing them apart.

"Nikolai, what are you—"

"Shut. Your. Mouth." He bites my lower lip with every word, eliciting a shudder from me.

My head spins and a shiver spreads across my skin and ends in my dick.

Am I supposed to feel this turned on by a kiss? It's not even a *full* kiss.

Fuck.

I exist in his vicinity, then I'm on edge.

He touches me and I catch fire.

This is why I did everything in my power to put some distance between us. Get back control over my shameless reaction to him.

Nikolai doesn't understand the concept of distance, though.

His teeth pull rougher than usual and tingles explode on the skin trapped between them.

But I like this type of pain. This pain isn't mental or emotional. This pain means I'm right here, not swallowed up by black ink or pulled under by disgusting nausea.

"Who the fuck is she?" he growls against my mouth, his coarse words vibrating on my skin.

I try to clear my head, which is impossible under the circumstances. "Who's who?"

"The girl who was throwing herself in your arms at *my* fucking fight."

"A-Ava?"

"Ava. Her name would look fucking pretty on a gravestone."

"What the…" I sober up a little and try to release myself from his grip. His fingers dig into my skin, prohibiting me from moving.

Christ. I've always loved how big he is, but it's a nuisance when I try to get him off me.

"Didn't take you long to find a replacement for *Clara*." He snarls her name as if it's a curse word and bites my jaw, my throat, and my Adam's apple. "But I'm going to make them all disappear. Mark my fucking words."

I groan at every nip, my cock thickening until it's straining painfully against my trousers. Why do I love it so much when he's rough?

"A-Ava…is my childhood friend. You…met her during that game at the pub."

He lifts his head abruptly, eyes flicking and brow furrowing. I still don't like the look on his face, but it eases a bit, harsh but recognizable. "So that's where I've seen her. She's not Clara's replacement?"

"What? Of course not. My cousin would kill me."

"I will fucking kill *him* or anyone who dares to touch what's fucking mine."

I gulp past the lump in my throat as I search his wild features, and my lips part when I realize he means every word.

It should repulse me, send me running again, but my cock has turned as hard as stone and I'm delirious.

My lungs fill with his scent—mint, blood, and all male. It coils and rattles inside me with overwhelming strength.

No one has ever said that to me. No one has ever been so obsessed with me that they act like they'd move heaven and earth to protect me.

I shouldn't even want protection or this toxic connection.

But the reality I've been trying to ignore crashes into me.

I want him.

I fucking *crave* him. So much it hurts.

So I lift my head and capture his lips in a punishing kiss. I thrust my tongue inside his mouth and taste the metallic blood. I taste the desperation. The aching lust.

I fuck his mouth as hard as he fucked me over.

The constant fear of falling apart vanishes when he gives back as ferociously as he takes, robbing my breath.

The constant pain that I breathe day in and day out crumbles and caves like it does every time Nikolai touches me. My insides don't feel as hollow or as desolate, and I can breathe air that's not soaked in black ink or filthy nausea.

It scared the shit out of me the first time and every time after, but now, I couldn't care less about the aftermath of the pleasure.

If fear and pain are the price I must pay for another taste of him, then so be it. I wrench a hand out of his grip and sink it into his hair, tearing the elastic band away and letting the strands fly free.

He's right. I fucking love kissing him.

But most of all, I love how he kisses me. It's hard and dominating but also overwhelmingly passionate.

His tongue slurps on mine and his fingers dig into my jaw so that he can feed me his.

I'm intoxicated.

Enamored.

Absolutely fucking *unhinged*.

How can a simple kiss feel so good…?

He wrenches his lips from mine with a growl and I release a protesting sound. "I'm going to fucking ruin you as badly as you've ruined me, my lotus flower. I'll get so far beneath your skin, you'll never fucking get rid of me."

For some reason, that makes me smile.

I've always lived on the right side of things. Perfect scores. Perfect manners. Perfect image. I never toyed with danger. Never wanted to live outside of my little bubble. Never crossed a line.

But then this man bulldozed through my walls, and now, I'm breaking apart piece by piece.

My fingers tighten in his hair. "Shut up and fuck me."

A spark rushes to his previously dead eyes and he growls, "Bedroom. *Now*."

He drags me by his grip on my hand, but the moment I stand up, his mouth is claiming mine again and we stumble over the table, only breaking the kiss to tear each other's clothes off on our way to the bedroom.

Or more like *my* clothes. I'm way too overdressed, damn it.

By the time we reach his room, we're finally naked. I want to study his glorious muscles and tattoos, but he presses his chest to mine and thrusts his hip forward, rubbing his hard, thickening cock on mine

I groan in his mouth.

The sound shatters when he pushes me onto the bed and lands on top of me. He kisses his way down my throat, my collarbone, and my chest.

"Fuuck…" I breathe out when he bites a nipple, teeth nibbling on the tip. Precum slides down my length and drips on my abs.

"Mine. Every inch of you is fucking *mine*." He grunts against my skin, making my cock harder, my muscles tighter, and my head lighter.

He moves his attention to the other nipple, sucking and biting and probably leaving all sorts of marks, but I can't seem to focus on that.

Later. I'll think later.

Now, I want to *feel*.

His dick slides up and down my length. Our precum trickles over the skin and he uses it as lube. The maddening friction heightens until I'm releasing unintelligible noises, groaning and moaning. My hips jerk, instinctively rubbing my cock against his. Drops of our precum coat our abs as we hump and rub and growl in unison.

"Niko…" I rasp, writhing against the pillow as I pull his head down with a handful of his hair. "Just…fuck me."

I'm reduced to begging for it, but I'm too far gone to care about it at this point.

My heart nearly spills from its confinement when he flashes me his sexy grin. "You called me Niko. Fuck, baby. I'm really going to fucking devour you."

The friction of our cocks grows in intensity. More rubbing, grinding, and humping, until I think we'll come in an absolute mess. But then he reaches beneath the pillow and pulls out a bottle of lube, then sits on his haunches between my legs.

"Bend your knees," he orders, and when I do it, he squirts lube in his palm, then circles my rim with a slippery finger. "Mmm, your hole is getting nice and wet for me, baby. So fucking beautiful."

My breath hitches and my cock gets even harder the more he circles my hole. He thrusts a finger inside me and a shameless moan spills out of me. His intense eyes remain on mine as he adds the second.

It's that look that drives me insane. I see my reflection in those dark blues, and for the first time, I don't hate what I see.

Not when he looks at me like he can't get enough. Like I'm the center of his universe. Even temporarily.

He works me open with firm pumps of his fingers. I jerk my hips, dick bobbing on my abs.

"That's it. You're taking my fingers so well."

My exhales puff out in a long, fractured breath and I wiggle my arse against him, matching his in-and-out.

"I need your hands." Nikolai throws the lube within reach. "Make my cock all slippery so I can fuck you, baby."

It's a miracle I don't come then and there. I take obscene pride in how steady my hand is as I fill it with lube, lean over, and slide my palm on Nikolai's length.

When I reach the tip, I stop and—like a junkie who can't help it—I take the crown in my mouth and tug on a piercing with my teeth.

His growls of pleasure are music to my ears. "Mmfuck...baby...I'm going to come if you keep doing that."

I release his crown with a pop and continue lubing him up from base to tip.

"I love the way you fucking touch me, but I also love—" He scissors his fingers inside me and thrusts a third finger. "How you swallow me in your ass."

My hand pauses on his cock and I throw my head back with a moan. "Ah...fuck... It's so full...Niko, fuck..."

"Stay with me, baby. If you can barely take my fingers, how will you fit my cock in this tight ass?"

I squeeze his cock, jerking him faster, and wiggle on his fingers. "Put your cock inside me. I want you in me."

"I love your fucking filthy mouth." He slams his lips to mine and kisses me hard and fast as he pulls out his fingers.

My back hits the bed, but he doesn't break the connection. I don't let him.

He covers my hand with his and makes me guide his cock to my hole as his tongue batters mine, his teeth sinking, nibbling, claiming.

The piercings tease my opening before he thrusts the first inch in.

"Ummph..." I mumble against his lips, and the idiot takes it as a sign to tear our mouths apart.

"Relax for me, baby." His eyes are clearer now, more in tune with the Nikolai I know as he kisses my jaw, my nose, and my lids.

What is he doing?

Fuck...

I tug on his hair. "Stop kissing me everywhere like I'm a girl, Nikolai."

He merely chuckles and bites down on my lower lip. "I don't kiss girls everywhere—or boys, for that matter. But I will kiss you wherever I fucking please, lotus flower. Get used to it."

Then he sucks on my lip and kisses, then bites his way down my throat as he thrusts his hip forward, feeding me a few more inches.

My arse clenches around him and I wince at the burning intrusion. Despite the lube, he's fucking huge and I can feel the piercings scraping at my insides. Though it's not a bad sensation, just new.

Maybe even a little...thrilling.

Okay, a *lot*.

"Mmm...you're so tight, baby. The way your ass milks my cock is majestic. I don't think I can hold on anymore."

"Go all the way."

"Baby... It's your first time."

"I said. Go all in. Don't treat me like I'm weak."

"I know I promised not to hurt you, but you're making it fucking impossible."

He drives his hips forward, burying himself inside me, and I jerk, shuddering in his embrace.

"Fuck, baby, fuck. Are you in pain?"

I hide my head in his neck, studying the contours of the snake on his shoulder, and wiggle against him, then bite the lobe of his ear. "More. Give me fucking more."

"Oh, baby. You're well and truly fucked," he whispers back as he wrenches my mouth into his and thrusts into me, slow and long. The burning sensation disappears and tingles of pleasure spread down my spine.

As if feeling that I'm well adjusted, Nikolai slowly ups his rhythm until my dick leaks precum all over our abs.

He fucks me hard, not taking it easy or slow, and I meet him stroke for stroke, jerking my hips and fucking his mouth with my tongue. Alien noises leave my lips whenever I feel the scrape of his piercings inside me.

Little by little, his mouth, hand, and cock undo me, leaving me desolate and desperate for anything he has to dish out.

"Christ. Mmm. Your ass was made to swallow my cock."

"S-shut your mouth." I chase his lips, but he pulls away only for a second before he tugs my lip between his teeth, then reaches between us and slides his fingers over my nipple.

I shudder and writhe, sinking my teeth in his tongue when he slows down.

"What are you doing—"

My words die out when his crown bumps into that pleasurable place in my arse.

All the blood rushes to my dick, and my spine stiffens. Lust and need soar high until I think I'll never come down.

"Niko…fuck…fuuuck…"

He squeezes my dick and whispers, "Come for me, baby. Show me who you belong to."

I don't think I could control it even if I wanted to. My cock thickens and hot cum sprays on my abs, and I thrust my hips through it, forcing my eyes open to look at him.

"Come in me, Niko."

"Holyfuckingshit," he groans in one breath as his thrusts turn dangerously animalistic, going rougher and faster until I almost can't keep up.

He shudders on top of me and calls me baby and beautiful and all these other nicknames he loves giving me as he comes inside me.

Despite my own hazy head, I can't look away from his face as he empties his load. He's just so fucking hot.

My hand runs up the ink on his hard abs, fingers wrapping around his nape as I shove him down and claim his lips again.

I can't get enough of kissing him.

Devouring him. Inhaling him into my fucking lungs.

He pounds into me with shallow thrusts until his cock is depleted, then he pulls out. I groan as cum leaks out from me.

Is it supposed to feel *this* good?

My hand slides from his throat to his hair, tugging and pulling. It must hurt, but Nikolai doesn't complain as he kisses me harder, his chest glued to mine. Both of us are a mess of sweat and the cum on our abs.

We keep kissing until I can no longer feel my lips. Until the cold air forms goosebumps on my damp skin.

Reluctantly, I let him go and pull away. Nikolai gives me space and I sit up, wincing, before I scoot to the edge of the bed and stand with a bit of difficulty.

Cum drips down my thighs and I have to bite my lip to stop myself from moaning.

An inked hand wraps around my wrist and a large chest presses against my back, his half-erect cock nudging on my sore arse. I ignore the shiver that spreads through me as I glance at him. Nikolai leans his chin on my shoulder, head cocked to the side, watching me with that slight manic expression from earlier. Though it seems a bit subdued now.

"Where do you think you're going?"

"Uh…shower." Why do I sound so hoarse?

His lips curve in a slightly evil grin. "Can I join?"

"No." I pause when his smile disappears, then sigh. "I'm sorry. I'm not comfortable with that."

"I'll wait until you're comfortable, then." His grin returns and I want to kiss it, but I don't, because that's just fucking desperate. "Thanks, baby."

"For what?"

"For bringing me back."

"Bringing you back from where?"

"Somewhere unpleasant." He smacks my arse. "Go get that sexy body all soaped up and try not to think of me."

"Nikolai!" I swat his hand away, resisting the tingles that rush through me as I escape to the en suite bathroom and hop into the shower.

It's a bit weird to get the cum off me, but I manage to do it, hissing when I touch my rim and literally fuck myself to wash away the evidence of the best sex I've ever had.

I have to stop before I start moaning and Nikolai decides he's not going to wait outside, after all.

Is that what I want him to do?

He told me not to think of him, but here I am completely taken by the bastard. I blame his vicious determination. In hindsight, I had no chance against him.

Some might say what happened just now was only a matter of time.

A smile pulls my lips as I step out on the foot towel, careful not to drip on the floor.

I catch my reflection in the mirror and my smile instantly drops.

What gives you the right to be happy after everything you've done?

I try to swallow, but the lump gets stuck and I feel my airways closing.

Fuck.

Fuck.

I cut off eye contact, mindlessly pulling a towel from the rack and quickly drying myself, then wrapping another towel around my waist.

My vision is blurry, but I can't get out of there fast enough.

Run away, Bran. Just run the fuck away—

My movements and thoughts come to a sudden halt when I find a massive man sitting on the floor right by the bathroom door, still naked, and...is he...

I lean over and tentatively stroke his hair away from his face. No doubt about it. He's actually *asleep*.

I can't resist the chuckle that leaves my lips.

Why am I not surprised he'd fall asleep anywhere and in any position?

Though...does this mean he was waiting for me?

Get over yourself.

I reluctantly release his gorgeous hair and head to the bed so I can get him a blanket, but that's when I notice he didn't change the sheets and pinch the bridge of my nose.

This man-child, I swear.

I locate the clean sheets in the cupboard and meticulously change them. I manage to support his stupidly muscled body against my shoulder, then drop him on the bed.

Through it all, he doesn't even groan. Deep sleeper, it is.

He sprawls his legs all over the super king-sized bed and uses his hand as a pillow. His hair spreads out on the sheet like silk, and I can't help ghosting my hand over it before I pull the blanket over him.

I pause when I see my dried cum on his stomach. I should probably clean that…

No. I like the sign of ownership.

After I cover him, I shove the old sheets into the washing machine and then hit the cold cycle.

Once that's done, I hunt for my clothes and put them on. For some reason, I find my feet leading me back to the bedroom like a magnet. I stand at the entrance, staring at Nikolai.

A part of me wants to stay, maybe not in the same bed since that's…strange, I suppose. But just around.

That contemplation shatters when the image from earlier comes back like a curse and I physically force myself to walk to the lift.

This small moment of pleasure is all the reprieve my demons can offer.

I can't let him see me like this.

And he won't.

Because I'm fucking *fine*.

SEVENTEEN

Nikolai

I KNEW SOMETHING WAS FUCKING WRONG WHEN I WOKE UP IN bed.

Me? In a fucking *bed*?

Hello, Satan. This is Kolya reporting live from somewhere in hell and telling you to kindly fuck off. We're not ready to go yet.

I blink a few times and the room, that's definitely not some edgy hellhole, comes into view.

The penthouse…?

I sit up with a sudden jerk, all sleep disappearing from my eyes.

Nah, fuck no. I was clearly sitting outside the bathroom waiting for Bran to finish his shower and then…what? I don't remember going to bed.

I *wouldn't* go to bed or cover myself, not even if I were drunk. That's just blasphemy.

My face breaks into a grin. Does this mean Bran carried me to the bed? I inspect the clean sheets that I certainly didn't change and yup, definitely him. He's organized to the point of being a bit neurotic. Or a lot, depending on your definition of the word.

Now, I want to kick myself in the ass for not feeling him carry me, wrap his arms around me, and cover me. Fuck. I'm getting hard at the thought.

My Prince Charming is actually stronger than he looks. Even Jeremy and my cousins don't carry or move me when I fall asleep in unusual places or situations.

The images of him touching and placing me up here are muddied by the other lingering thought. I stand up and don't bother putting any clothes on as I stride to the living room. "Lotus flower?"

I know he's not there before I search. There's no trace of his clothes, his presence, or anything remotely similar. If it weren't for the itch he left beneath my skin last night, I wouldn't think he'd been here. He even washed the sheets that carried his scent, as if he wanted to erase what happened from memory.

Not fucking possible.

Last night was the best sex of my life, and it's not about the sex per se, though that was fucking hot. It's about him.

The way he cried out my name and held on to me and kissed me. The way he let me in. Even *demanded* it.

Why the fuck did I think he'd choose to stay this time?

He doesn't. It's not what he does.

It's not what I usually want, either. I don't like sharing space with my fuck buddies outside of sex. They're welcome to stay the night in the Heathens' mansion, but only if they're not in my immediate vicinity.

So why the fuck do I feel any other way about Bran?

Maybe it's the fact that you call him that and a few other nicknames, not to mention the fact that you got this fucking place just so he'd feel safe away from everyone else?

Yeah, so I did that. He's always paranoid about people and their meaningless fucking opinions, so I thought he'd feel more comfortable in a place that's only for us. I mean, for him to meet me here.

There is no *us*.

Apparently, he didn't feel safe enough to stay.

I stroke my necklace and catch a glimpse of the clock. Ten a.m.

Motherfucker.

I missed the morning run for the second morning in a row.

It's true that I haven't been sleeping much the past couple of nights, but I shouldn't have overslept and missed the highlight of my day.

My movements are lethargic as I search for my phone. I scan the texts at the top, but ignore them when I don't find his name.

Then I open IG and find his usual story at five thirty sharp. *Jesus Christ.* The man is a fucking running machine.

The first story ends and the second shows a canvas with a few haphazard red lines. Not sure what those mean, but red is good. Right? Well, it's good to me because it represents blood and violence. Not sure golden-boy Bran feels the same.

I pull out the text exchange I have with him and type, *Why the fuck did you run away again?*

But then delete it.

That sounded desperate and clingy even to my own ears. Fuck me. *Chill, Kolya, dude. You're giving the Sokolov name a bad rep.*

Though that's fucking impossible now that I've claimed Bran. It was supposed to be just a fuck. I've always fucked. Fucking ended at the moment of release.

Not with *him.*

Last night, I came here with the sole intention of fucking him all up, taking what I wanted, then discarding him like he usually does me.

I intended to fuck him and then make him disappear from my life like Dad told me to.

But that was before he kissed me and asked me to fuck him.

That was before he looked at me with those soft eyes.

He pulled my anger apart with every touch, every kiss, and every groan and grunt. I couldn't hold on to that rage when he put his hands on me.

The battered cells in my hyper brain didn't mellow out, but his presence provided them with tunnel vision. A target for my monstrous energy.

Others fuel that energy.

My lotus flower tamed it.

I feel more like myself than I did during the past twenty-four hours.

So instead of blaming him for leaving again, I send a different text.

> **Me:** So... I have a question. Did you feel me up when you carried me to bed?

He reads it immediately and I think he'll ignore it, if not permanently then at least for a few minutes. If push and pull were a game, my lotus flower would be the undefeated champion.

So imagine my fucking surprise when he replies immediately.

Bran: I did no such thing.

Jesus. He's fucking adorable. An asshole but adorable all the same. I can imagine him turning all serious when he typed that.

> **Me:** Love it when you talk posh to me, baby. Another question, did you miss me this morning?

Bran: Why would I? You didn't come yesterday, either.

> **Me:** Aw, you're counting? I didn't think you were this hurt by my absence.

Bran: Get over yourself. In fact, I'm happy to finally get my space back.

> **Me:** *sulking GIF*

Bran: What are you? A five-year-old?

> **Me:** Would you prefer it if I never came along on the runs?

Bran: Do what you want. It's not like anything I do or say will make you change your actions.

> **Me:** You're right, it won't. You're too standoffish anyway, so I wouldn't trust you with my decisions.

Bran: Because they're sooo bright?

> **Me:** They can be.

> **Me:** Hey! Was that sarcasm?

> **Me:** Anyway, you didn't answer my question. Should I come to the morning run tomorrow or stop altogether?

Bran: Why are you asking me about what you should do?

> **Me:** Answer me. Do you want me there? Yes or no.

Bran: Yes.

My lips pull in what must look like the most stupid grin ever. I knew my efforts would come to fruition. Now, I need to work harder to make myself indispensable in his life. My mind might have quieted down today, but that dark thought about never giving him a way out stays the same.

> **Me:** Just so you know, I would've come even if you said no. Bwahaha.

Bran: I'm going to block you.

> **Me:** You know you can't stay away from me, baby.

This time, he definitely leaves me on Read. So I send another one.

> **Me:** Going to shower now, though I'd hate to get your cum off me. Mmm. Might rub one out while thinking of your ass swallowing my cock.

Bran: Stop talking, Nikolai.

> **Me:** Why? Getting hot and bothered?

Bran: I'm in class.

> **Me:** And yet you're texting me? Oh, wow. You must really miss me.

Bran: Dream on.

Me: I prefer reality. You know, like when you begged me to fuck you.

Bran: I didn't BEG you. Jesus.

Me: We must remember it differently *eggplant emoji* *peach emoji* *water splash emoji*

Bran: Just go away.

Me: Fuck. I'd pay to see your face right now. Real talk. You okay?

Bran: Why wouldn't I be?

Me: It was your first time being fucked and you didn't let me take care of you afterward, so I'm a bit concerned.

Bran: I'm fine. I can look after myself.

Bran: Do you do that a lot?

Me: Do what?

Bran: Take care of your fuck buddies.

It hits me then. I don't. Not necessarily, I mean. Most of them are experienced and I don't like the hassle of baby bisexuals unless they've prepped themselves beforehand.

Me: Not really. You're special. And so is your big dick and sexy ass. You really okay? I know I'm huge.

Bran: Arrogant much?

Me: You know I am. And you didn't answer my question. Are you really okay? Tell me the truth.

Bran: A little sore, but I'm fine.

> **Me:** Pictures or it didn't happen.

Bran: Nikolai, no.

> **Me:** Baby, please? I need a glimpse of you.
> Even if it's just your face.

Bran: Did you miss the part where I'm in class?

> **Me:** Fine. I'll do it for you.

I wrap my fingers around my thickening length and take a few selfies, then send them over.

Bran: Nikolai! Why the hell are you sending me dick pics when I told you I'm surrounded by people?

> **Me:** To keep you company. You better think about my cock, because I can't stop thinking about yours. I need to fuck you again, baby. I'm getting hard thinking about pounding your ass.

Bran: I'm muting you.

I smile, imagining his flustered expression, then decide I've tortured myself enough for a while and stop texting. It wasn't a lie. I'm really hard now.

Bran: By the way, I noticed you had no food in your place, so I ordered you some Italian pastries for breakfast.

I grin.

He *loves* me. I just know he does.

Okay, he doesn't, but he cares, and that's a good start.

Turns out, everyone was worried about the way I disappeared last night.

I kid you not, Jeremy put out feelers with the police and shit because he took what I said about killing innocent girls seriously.

He can be dramatic.

Okay, so maybe when I was in that mood, I could've accidentally hurt someone if Bran did actually use them as a crutch.

Don't blame me. It's not my fault I only think in black and white.

Kill and Gareth were checking all the places I would usually go to—clubs, another fighting ring. The Serpents. No shit—they actually knocked on the Serpents' door and were like, "Hi, I know we hate each other, but have you seen this massive idiot motherfucker who's covered in tattoos?"

I didn't make that up. Gaz relayed it back word for word.

My sisters were going crazy, calling me all night. Maya left a dozen VMs, screaming and then begging and crying.

Jesus Christ.

"Where were you really?" she asks as we sit in her favorite coffee shop downtown.

"Spill, Niko," her twin, Mia, signs with more attitude than need be.

"Yeah, spill, cousin. What made you disappear all night long?" Killian, who's sporting a black eye, asks, lounging back in his chair.

"Busy," I say while sipping some disgustingly not-sweet-enough coffee, then add one more sugar cube. Make that three.

Maya gasps in outrage and flips her long hair over her bare shoulder while Mia stares at me with a concerned frown.

My sisters couldn't be more different. Where Maya is a self-proclaimed diva with expensive taste and a thirst for attention, Mia is a little daredevil who couldn't care less about people's opinions and doesn't shy away from flipping her favorite middle finger.

Even now as they sit on either side of me, they look nothing alike despite being identical twins. Maya wears a strapless top, a tight skirt, and high-heel stilettos. Mia is in a goth Barbie black dress, complete with lace and shit, a choker around her neck, blue ribbons in her hair, and gigantic chainy boots covering her feet.

Sometimes I forget they're actually identical, because they have vastly different personalities. Guess that's also the reason why I can't fucking stand Landon but would fuck his brother to eternity all day, every day.

My dick twitches to life and I curse internally.

Seriously, Kolya. The fuck? My baby sisters are here. Behave yourself, dude.

"What made you too busy to reply to our texts?" Maya asks. "I had a mini breakdown."

Judging by her begging for me to come back through sniffs and tears, I'd say it was a *major* breakdown, but I don't tell her that.

I sip my now sickeningly sweet coffee and contemplate an answer that's not "I was busy having the best fuck of my life."

Not only is that insensitive when they really had a scare, but also, there's that annoying tidbit where Bran said no one could know.

Still, I don't have to identify him…

No. Nope.

It's better I reveal nothing since I'm shit with secrets. If I reveal something, I'll end up blurting out everything and that could seriously end things between us before they even start.

"I went somewhere to cool down," I say and it's not a lie. Although cooling down wasn't the first item on my list.

"Sure thing, Niko. Kick my face in, then go cool down as if nothing happened."

"Hey, you wanted that fight. Don't go blaming me, Satan's heir."

"I told you not to hurt my face, you little fuck."

"Yeah, Niko." Maya grins mischievously. "That's the only thing his girlfriend likes."

He grins back. "At least she likes something. You, however, seem to be out of luck with the person *you* like."

I narrow my eyes. "Who do you like, Maya?"

"No one," she says, her voice a bit high-pitched. "You know how Kill likes to talk shit."

He searches his surroundings. "*Moi?*"

Mia inches to my side, ignoring their bickering, and watches me closely as she signs, "Are you really okay?"

I ruffle her hair. "Never been better, baby sis."

Her expression eases and she hugs me. I know not to take her affection for granted. I'm close to both my sisters—Maya because I let her practice her makeup skills on me when we were growing up. But Mia...Mia is special. We both deal with our demons in our own ways and know we'll slaughter each other's enemies if given the chance.

She's badass like that, my sister.

"Incoming boy toy," Killian says with apparent disdain.

For a second, I'm confused as to why Bran would be here and why Kill knows about him. Only to remember my lotus flower isn't a boy toy and there's no way in hell my cousin figured out things.

Sure enough, Maya is pulled away from my side and a slender, pretty guy sits on my lap, batting his lashes. "Missed you, Daddy."

"Eww. You're so cringe," Kill says.

"Can't believe I'm agreeing with Kill, but you so are." Maya jams her finger in her mouth and makes a vomiting sound.

Simon holds out a palm without looking at them. "Talk to the hand, bitches."

"Get off. And don't call my sister a bitch or I'll choke the fuck out of you."

"Love it when you choke me, Daddy."

Jesus. I'm getting flashbacks. Do I sound this desperate when I talk to Bran?

"You're, like, a year younger than him," Maya says. "In what world is he your daddy?"

"Daddy is a state of mind, ignorant."

"Simon, stand up before I knock you off," I say.

"But I missed you. You haven't been replying to my texts. I'm so lonely without you." He leans in to whisper in my ear, "I can't wait to have your monster cock rail me all the way to heaven, Daddy."

I swear this used to do something for me.

Now, he's just annoying and clingy.

You're annoying and clingy, too, in someone else's eyes.

I start to push him away but pause when I sense eyes digging holes into my skull.

Who has the audacity to glare at me—

I lift my head and my gaze clashes with none other than Bran's.

He stands at the cashier with his cousin Creighton and friend Remington. The latter is talking animatedly. Creighton doesn't seem to be listening, but Bran...

Bran's entire attention is on me.

Fuck me.

He's watching me, openly, his body turned in my direction as he narrows his eyes on me. And for a second, I think he'll come over here and remove Simon or something.

I think he'll stake a public claim on me.

Instead, his walls build around him one by one. That stupid fucking fake smile curves his lips as he turns to his friends, grabs his drink, and walks out of the coffee shop as if nothing happened.

As if he didn't even see me.

That fucking—

Rage swirls inside me and I knock Simon over, needing to peel his fingers from my clothes before he finally lets go.

I'm thankful to Maya and Mia, who stop him from following me, because I can't be responsible for his safety if he gets in the middle of the hurricane coiling inside me.

By the time I get outside, there's no trace of Bran.

Motherfucking fucker.

I pull out my phone to send him a text and then stop. What the fuck will I say? Offer excuses?

Why the fuck would I when he obviously doesn't give a fuck?

Jesus fucking Christ.

I feel myself spiraling down that black hole.

Fuck this.

I need to find Jeremy and go on a goddamn hunt. Either that or I will actually hunt my Prince Not-Fucking-Charming down.

And I'm not *that* desperate.

EIGHTEEN

Nikolai

AT THE END OF THE DAY, I'M SPENT.

Violence might be frowned upon by a bunch of ethical elites, but it's actually the only method that manages to calm me down.

But that's not exactly the case right now.

I should've stayed at the mansion and bugged Jeremy for another mission, to give myself something to do, but I found myself driving my Harley to the penthouse.

The moment I step out of the elevator, I sense something different.

No—I smell it or, more accurately, *him*. Clover, citrus, and a fucking conundrum.

Sure enough, Bran is sitting on the sofa, legs wide apart, elbows on his knees, and his fingers forming a steeple at his chin.

God-fucking-damn-it. He's hot.

I can barely stop myself from reaching over and messing up his perfectly styled hair and put-together dark-blue polo shirt and khaki pants.

Mr. GQ reporting for fucking duty.

Upon seeing me, however, he doesn't seem to be here for round two. His expression is calm and composed, but I can sense the waves of a malicious storm whirling beneath.

Still, I take an immense amount of pride in the fact that he let himself in for the second night in a row.

"I got you something." He reaches into his pants and throws something at my chest.

I catch it and then frown. "A pack of condoms?"

"Figured you'd need it so you don't give people STIs."

"What…?"

He stands up with the same infuriating calm. "Good night, then."

"Wait—"

The moment I touch his wrist, he whirls around fast and slams me against the wall with an elbow on my throat.

"Don't fucking touch me," he grits out, his lips so close to mine, he almost kisses me with every word.

I suppress a groan at how fucking sexy he looks when he's enraged. I take a shit ton of pride in the fact that I'm the only one who sees this side of him—rugged at the edges and different from the golden-boy image he wears in public.

He's perfect to the outside world but himself with me.

So what do I do? What I do best, of course.

Provoke him more.

"Are you mad about something, my lotus flower? Maybe a certain scene you saw earlier today?"

"Who the fuck do you think you are that I would notice you?"

"Oh, but you did." My fingers dig into his nape. "It's why you're losing your precious control right now. Tell me, Bran, are you jealous?"

"Jealous? Over you? Not in this lifetime."

"In that case, should I call Simon to join us? That's his name, by the way, Simon. He's gay and *loves* threesomes. Or maybe you can sit down and watch as I rail him."

He lifts his fist and punches me in the face. Oh fuck. He's really losing it, my Prince Charming.

More.

Give me more.

I grin up at him. "I take that as a no?"

"I'm going to fucking kill you."

"Promises, promises."

"Nikolai!"

"Yes, baby?"

"Don't baby me. In fact, we're done." He releases me with a shove. "Go to your Simon."

"No, fuck no." I clutch him by the wrist, then shove the condoms back in his hand. "I'm clean, asshole. I wouldn't have done that to you or anyone. In fact, I only fuck with condoms. Last night was the only exception."

He faces me, his eyes dark and shining with rage. "Was Simon also an exception?"

"No. Besides, I haven't been with anyone since the initiation."

"No one?"

I shake my head. "What about you? Should we get you tested, considering the *Clara* situation?"

"I'm tested and clean. I haven't had sex for...six months."

Fuck me.

Holy fucking hell.

I knew he only got back with her just to mess with me. I knew he didn't want her. I *knew* it.

My grin is wide as I stroke his nape. "Did I mention that you're so adorable when you're jealous?"

"Shut your fucking mouth, Nikolai."

"As you wish, baby." I press my lips to his, teasing at first, and then bite down and breach his mouth with a growl.

He puffs out a shuddering breath and I swallow it deep in my throat. *Christ.* It doesn't matter how many times I kiss him. It always feels like it's the first time.

His taste explodes in my mouth and I inhale him deep in my fucking lungs and keep him there.

He tastes of tea, citrus, and lust as fucked up as mine.

I push him toward the bedroom and we stumble inside, his fingers tugging on my hair, removing the band so he can mess it all up. I enjoy every spark of pain, every push and fucking pull.

He can shove me away all he wants, but I'll trap him again.

Own him again.

Once we're inside, I make quick work of removing his T-shirt and run my gaze over his smooth muscles that are only tainted by my marks. "You're so hot, baby. I want to lick you up."

He tugs my hoodie off, his fingers touching my chest, exploring my muscles. "I fucking hate you."

"Mmm. Talk dirty to me." I nibble on his bottom lip and drag his zipper down over his hard cock agonizingly slowly.

I torture him, reveling in every shudder and tormented sound that slips out of him.

Bran squeezes my dick through my pants, then loosens his fingers, slides his hand in, and fists my length, stroking me with a tight grip.

"Fuck, baby. Your hand feels so good."

He leans over and whispers in my ear, "Better than Simon?"

"Better than anyone." I fight the grin that's rushing to the surface as I kiss his throat and suck on his Adam's apple. He hisses between his teeth and cocks his head to the side to give me better access.

I continue my way down, kissing, nibbling, and biting on his collarbone and nipples until he's shaking, but he keeps stroking me with a firm grip.

Still feasting on one nipple, I pull out his cock, teasing the fore-skin with my thumb until I find the opening, then push it against my crown and guide him to thrust me against his cock.

"Umph… Fuck," he breathes out, his lips parted as my piercings dig into the pretty hole, and I fuck his cock with mine.

"That feel good, baby?"

He nods, but I don't think he's conscious of what he's doing as he falls in rhythm with me. His lips find mine and he kisses me loudly. The wet, sucking sounds match the in-and-out of our precum mixing as we leak all over each other.

How can the asshole be so pliant when his body talks to mine?

He acts as if I'm invisible outside, but when I'm touching him, kissing him, he's all mine.

Mine for the taking.

Mine for the owning.

Fucking *mine*.

"I have to get inside you, baby." I pull away and drag him toward the bed.

Bran doesn't protest as I push him to a kneeling position in front of the bed, his chest on the mattress and his muscled ass in the air.

"Mmm. Stay like that." I slap his ass cheek and I don't miss the way he bites his lip as he follows my movement.

After I grab the lube from the drawer, I slip behind him and squirt it between his ass cheeks. My fingers circle his rim, then slide inside at the musical sound of his groan. My Prince Charming loves having his ass filled, whether by my fingers or my cock. I can feel his hole swallowing my three fingers, clenching and pulling and tempting my fucked up side.

But I take my time priming him for me. I slowly fuck him with my fingers, my cock sliding up and down the crack of his ass as I pepper kisses on his nape, his spine, and his ass cheeks, kissing and nibbling and leaving so many of my marks, he'll never be able to remove them.

Not now. Not ever.

Mine. He's fucking mine. And everyone who sees these marks will know he's taken.

Owned.

Fucking *claimed*.

"Niko…"

Jesus fucking Christ. I have to pause and shake my head or I'll come all over his ass like a fucking pubescent kid.

I'm fucking doomed.

He moans my name and I'm going feral.

"Yes, baby?"

"Do it, please."

"Do what?"

"Put your cock inside me."

"Mmm. Fuck." I wrench out my fingers and pull his ass cheeks apart. "Say it again."

"Just fuck me already, you fucking bastard."

"You drive me fucking crazy, baby." I nudge my crown inside and he jerks, his ass wiggling against my cock, trying to swallow me fucking whole.

"Your greedy ass is made for me." I thrust all the way in, eliciting a growl from him. "Only me."

"Umm... Fuck... Fuck..."

"Look at me, baby."

Bran twists his head to the side, his hooded eyes meeting mine as I grab his hips and drive forward with shallow thrusts.

"That's it. Feel me fucking you."

He moans, the sound so fucking erotic, I'm surprised I last. Bran might be quiet, but he's fucking loud in bed. He releases these blabbering noises that I can't understand most of the time, but that means I'm fucking him good. I'm fucking him rough, like he wants.

And I go feral for it.

There's something about owning a standoffish, uptight asshole like Bran. It's thrilling but also *rewarding*. The fact that I'm the only one who can see him fall apart on my cock is better than any drug.

"Harder," he mutters, his hips jerking as he rubs his cock against the bed.

"What was that?"

"Fuck me harder. Don't take it easy on me."

"Baby. If you keep talking like that, I'll break your ass."

"Promises, promises."

I burst out laughing and he smiles, but it morphs into a grunt when I pull out until only my crown is inside and then drive all the way in. The headboard bangs against the wall from the force of it.

"Ummf... I'm...fuck..."

"You like that?"

He loses the battle and buries his head in the sheets, nodding and releasing muffled noises.

Keeping one hand on his hip, I reach over and pull him back by a fistful of his hair. "Eyes on me when I fuck you. You wanted hard, right?"

He nods, his face turning red, lips parted.

"Kiss me, baby."

He tugs on my lower lip with his teeth and plunges his tongue into my mouth as I drive into him with the intensity of a madman. The sound of his ass slapping against my groin fills the air and obliterates my sanity.

I fuck him hard, I fuck him deep, until he's blathering in my mouth, releasing noises and words I don't think he even knows the meaning of.

I love the way he completely lets go when my lips meet his. I love the way his muscles grip me like a vise, milking and swallowing me whole.

"Y-your piercings..." he grunts, voice hoarse against my mouth as he reaches for his dick and strokes himself savagely.

"What about them, baby?"

"They feel so fucking good... Fuck...you feel so fucking good, Niko."

I'm done for.

A goner.

Absolutely decimated.

My hips jerk and I drive into him faster, harder, rougher. The way he likes it. "Come with me, baby."

He groans, releasing a long moan as he works himself faster, matching my crazy rhythm.

"I'm... I'm... F-fuuuck..." His words end in a growl as his skin flushes and his lips part, his cum spraying all over the bed.

I devour his noises with my lips and he shudders, but he keeps rolling his hips and slapping his ass against my groin as I empty inside him with a groan.

"Fucking fuck...baby," I breathe out as I bite his lower lip and he bites back with the same animalistic energy. His beast matches mine as he kisses me with a similar fever, still moving against me and milking me from my orgasm.

We keep kissing for some time until I realize the uncomfortable position he's trapped in. He doesn't complain about that, but he does protest when I wrench my lips from his and pull out of his ass.

His hole clenches around me and I moan at the feel of him. Jesus Christ. I can survive on fucking him alone.

My gaze follows the cum that spills out of him, trickling down his thighs and smearing his balls and spent cock.

I kneel behind him, pull his ass cheeks apart, and feast on the cum, licking and fucking it back inside him.

"Niko…what are you… Oh fuck… Jesus…f-fuuuck."

He wiggles, but I slam a hand on his lower back to keep him in place. "Stay still, baby. We can't waste any cum."

I rumble against his rim and he shudders as I lick every drop clean.

By the time I'm done, his voice has turned hoarse and his cock is getting thicker by the second.

He's sluggish as he turns on his back, his skin flushed red. A sheen of sweat covers him, and his face is caught in a pleased daze. I lick my lips and his gaze falls to them. I can't help staring at his swollen mouth.

"You'll kiss me?" he asks cautiously, hopefully, even.

"I'll always kiss you, baby." I fall on top of him, my lips crushing to his, my chest pressing on his muscles, and our limbs entangling.

Bran slurps on my tongue, drinking me, tasting me as he tosses my hair and messes it the fuck up.

The kiss is sloppy at best, but it's fucking erotic. I've never kissed anyone after sex, but it's vital with Bran.

I have to kiss him to feel him. To get beneath his skin and dismantle him.

Kissing had no meaning before this motherfucker. Now, it's the damn center of my existence.

"Want us to be exclusive?" I ask against his mouth.

The lust slowly withers from his face, replaced by whatever demons that force him into autocratic control.

I curse myself for ruining the moment.

He blinks a few times and pushes me away. "You're crushing me."

I scoot to the side, falling back on the bed and propping myself up on my elbow. "You weren't complaining about me crushing you when you had your tongue hooked on mine."

"Jesus…" He stands up and I follow so that I'm in front of him. "What do you say?"

"About what?" He faces away, seeming distracted as he studies his surroundings, looking anywhere but at me.

"You fucking heard me, Bran. Want us to be exclusive?"

"Why would I? I don't want a relationship with you."

Motherfucker. I can't believe I was fucking this guy a few seconds ago. Now, I want to drive my fist in his goddamn face.

"So I can go fuck Simon and the dozens of others waiting in my contact list?"

This time, he whirls around and faces me, that menacing danger dancing in his coral-blue eyes.

Yes, baby. Feed me your fire.

"Fuck another person and we're over, Nikolai."

"That's the definition of exclusive. Would it kill you to admit you want that?"

"Fine, whatever."

He starts to head to the bathroom, but I clutch his wrist.

"Now what?" he asks, watching me slowly.

"Why are you so adamant about hiding your sexuality? Being bi or gay isn't a taboo, you know. This isn't the sixties."

"None of your business."

"You're such a dick. I'm just asking."

"Well, don't. I told you this is just physical, so stay in your lane. My problem with my sexuality is my own. If you can't accept that, I can go somewhere else."

"Like fuck you will." I grab him by the throat and relish the pop of his pulse beneath my fingers. "My cock is the only cock you'll sit on, got it, baby?"

"You need to stop talking to me in that language."

"But you enjoyed this language a few minutes ago."

"I give up." He releases a sigh. "Let me go so I can shower."

"Can I join?"

"No."

"Are you going to run away again?"

"I'm not running away. I'm leaving."

I let him go with an exasperated breath and I expect him to fuck off to the bathroom, but he faces me.

"Don't do this, Nikolai. I'll see you in the morning?"

I release an affirmative noise and he smiles, but it's tight, like my fucking insides.

He opens his mouth to say something else, but he shakes his head and slips into the bathroom, closing the door behind him with a fucking lock.

Locking me out.

Figuratively.

Literally.

NINETEEN

Brandon

A BIT LONGER THAN TWO WEEKS PASS IN THE MOST BEMUSING blur.

What started like a temporary loss of control has categorically turned into the most tragic addiction.

Every night, I say I won't go to the penthouse and I manage to hold out for a few days—nightmare-riddled, completely sleepless, and absolutely torturous days.

I bury myself in the studio, in practice, in being outside of my skin. Day in and day out, I manage to lie to myself for a few hours, only to relapse to daunting bad habits again.

The blood and the penthouse. Both are dangerous addictions of different proportions.

Both are pulling me apart and leaving me completely desolate and unable to look at the distorted face in the mirror anymore.

Only one addiction can actually lead to my decimation. One addiction forces me to forget everything else whenever he's in my vicinity. Whenever he touches me, kisses me, fucks me. I pretend my outer skin doesn't exist.

I'm not Brandon King. I'm not the broken entity who sees black ink instead of his reflection in the mirror. Not the weak man who's more often than not swallowed by disgusting nausea and the terrifying notion of nothingness.

I'm just *me*.

His lotus flower. His Prince Charming. His *baby*.

But that vacuum of emotions only lasts for the duration of the mindless release and the unbound lust. It lasts until I lose his touch and I'm forced back into my own skin.

I do the forcing—every time. I just rip off the plaster and walk away, but it's getting harder to willingly lose his lips, his touch. I'm almost scared of that moment when I have to lock myself in the bathroom and battle my demons. They're rather vicious lately.

The more I enjoy myself, the more painful the aftermath.

But it's not as painful as forcing myself away from that damn penthouse. It's not as painful as waking up every day and having this queasy feeling in my stomach because I know he's waiting outside the mansion's gate. Grinning.

Nikolai isn't really a cheerful man. I've seen him outside, multiple times, even though I like to pretend I don't. And yes, he's loud, but not in Remi's carefree, funny way. He's notoriously violent and curses a lot.

Killian often kicks him so he'll shut up, or Jeremy will whisper or speak to him calmly so he'll stop drawing attention or rein in his infamous bursts of violence.

He doesn't show them the version he shows me. Always smiling, grinning, and being an infuriating ray of sunshine, as if my mere presence makes him happy.

That part boggles my mind. Why would he be happy with me when I can't stand myself most of the time?

No matter how often I ask that question, I can't quite find an answer.

Still, I enjoy whatever I get, even if it hurts.

Even if every day, I want to watch the blood endlessly flow out of my wrist.

Today is one of those days. I didn't go to Nikolai's penthouse yesterday and I feel like I'm sucking breaths through a straw.

I stare at my painting and feel the urge to topple it over and light it on fire. The perfect silhouette of a mountain and a lake that I've been working on for weeks feels fake, completely at odds with what my fingers actually want to create. I've made more paintings that I don't want to admit exist, but this perfectly manicured scenery has been a fucking struggle to work on.

Mum said maybe it's because I'm not focused, but what she doesn't know is that I couldn't have been any more focused. It's just that this thing feels wrong.

Painting landscapes has been my crutch for years. My way to avoid creating anything with eyes. But it's not working anymore.

If anything, I'm starting to see them in the same light Lan does. Pathetic. Mediocre. Unoriginal. Boring.

Boring.

Fucking *boring*.

I pull out my phone and stare at the text I sent Nikolai earlier today because he didn't join me on my run this morning.

The first time he didn't—the day of that fight—I felt a hollowness so deep, I didn't know how to explain it. That hole got bigger the following day and I ignored it.

Today, however, I had trouble breathing. The twat has left his mark in every corner of our running path with his endless questions and shameless flirting so that I can't go there without feeling his shadow.

Why did he make it a habit if he wasn't going to keep it up?

So I sent him a text.

> **Me:** Slept in?

> **Nikolai:** Nope.

> **Me:** Then why didn't you come over?

> **Nikolai:** Missed me?

> **Me:** You wish.

He left me on Read. The audacity of the bastard.

Me: Are you ignoring me?

Nikolai: Doesn't feel so good when the roles are switched, huh? And to answer your question, I borrowed a page from the Brandon Asshole Dictionary and decided not to show up for the fuck of it. Just like you ghosted me last night.

Me: We never agreed that I'll be there every night.

Nikolai: Then be here every night. Just like I go to see you every day.

Me: I can't. You know that.

Nikolai: I know nothing.

Me: You're being ridiculous.

Nikolai: Me? Ridiculous? Jesus fucking Christ. Have you seen your hypocritical face in the mirror lately?

I do. Every day. I have to force myself away from him to see that fucking black hole in solitude. And his pointing it out doesn't make me feel any better about this damn situation.

Breathe.

Fucking *breathe.*

Me: This is going nowhere. Let's stop talking.

Nikolai: Aaaand you're back to your favorite hobby. Run away, baby. You're a champion of that bullshit.

Nikolai: You know what? Fuck that. If you don't feel the need to come over every night, I also don't need to see you every morning. In fact, don't show me your fucking face today.

Me: As if I want to see your fucking face.

Nikolai: Fucking great.

Me: Wonderful.

Nikolai: Awesome.

Me: Fantastic.

He left me on Read. *Again.* Nikolai never leaves me on Read.

I keep checking the exchange every half an hour like a junkie, but there's nothing from him.

No stupid, entertaining story of the day. No memes. No dick pics that he loves to send at the most random times.

It's late evening, around the hour when I'd usually sneak out of the house and go to him like a druggy in need of a hit, but I doubt he's there today.

Besides, he doesn't want to see my *fucking face* anyway.

Good grief.

My hand finds the back of my neck and I tug on the fine hairs until pain explodes all over my skin.

But it's not enough.

It doesn't hurt enough or provide enough relief. I'm neurotic, my brain ticking and my skin prickling at the lack of him.

I really went ahead and made myself addicted, didn't I?

The impulse to destroy the painting in front of me tingles under my skin and I'm about to give in when my phone buzzes in my hand.

My heart lurches and I'm taken aback by the force of my reaction.

Right. He can't stay away. After all, he's the one who's obsessed with me.

I'll forgive him for acting like a thick cow...

My heart falls when I find out it's a text from Annika. But it's for a different reason than disappointment.

Anni: Hey, don't be alarmed, okay? But there was a fire in the Heathens' mansion and Creigh came to save me, but he got himself in trouble with the others. He's okay, just unconscious. Can you and Remi come to pick him up?

The Heathens' mansion is in full chaos—half of it is burned and almost unrecognizable. A madness of students, firefighters, and medics crowd the circular driveway, but Remi and I manage to carry an unconscious Creigh out and to the car.

Anni is with us every step of the way. Her face is covered in snot and smoke, and she's wearing Creigh's hoodie.

She seems distraught, her usual cheerful expression muted, and her eyes don't leave Creigh, even after he's in the back seat.

I lean against my car and pretend to watch the firefighters, the Heathens' guards, and any individual who comes into my vicinity.

However, no matter how much I search, I can't find a trace of Nikolai. The lump that I haven't quite been able to swallow remains unmoving at the back of my throat, obstructing my breathing.

Maybe he's not here. Maybe he's in the penthouse.

But even I know that's wishful thinking.

Pretending to be nonchalant, I face Anni. "Is everyone else okay?" That sounded innocent enough.

"Jer got hurt." She sniffles, tears gathering in her eyes.

"I'm sure he'll be fine, Anni." Remi rubs her shoulder.

I can't even bring myself to comfort her as the doomsday feeling spreads in my brain like wildfire. He's always with Jeremy, so what if…what if…

"If it weren't for Nikolai and Creigh, I don't know what would've happened to him," Annika says with a sniffle.

"Nikolai helped?" I take an obscene amount of pride in how collected I sound.

"Yeah, he barged in with these smoke masks and stuff like a bull." She smiles, but it soon drops. "I don't like that he beat up Creigh, though."

I release a breath. If he has the energy to hit someone, that means he's fine. My gaze flits to Creigh, who's probably unconscious because of that fucker.

Jesus.

After we say our goodbyes, I'm about to get in the car, when I feel the hairs on the back of my neck stand on end.

I don't know why I do it, but I look up at the balcony where I first saw the Heathens and Nikolai on that initiation night. It feels like forever ago.

One thing hasn't changed, though. He's still far away. It doesn't matter how many times I touch him, how many times I kiss him. At the end of the day, we go back to our respective worlds.

And who made it that way, genius?

Nikolai's hair is loose, haphazard strands framing his face and flying in the wind. Smudges of black cover his cheeks, his nose, and his naked chest.

He's crossing his arms and watching me with narrowed eyes. I run my gaze over him and he seems okay.

Probably.

Nikolai slams both hands on the railing, fingers tightening around the metal, and leans forward as if he wants a better look at me. Even from this distance, I can almost feel his muscles tightening.

"Bran?"

I startle and turn my attention to Remi, who's frowning.

"What are you looking at?"

Shit.

Fuck.

Was I too obvious?

"Nothing," I say in my eternally calm tone. "Let's get Creigh home."

I'm thankful that Remi follows without a word. When I steal another look at Nikolai, his expression is murderous as he slips back inside.

Remi talks all the way home about how inhumane the Heathens are for hurting his 'spawn' and I'm thankful that he fills the silence. But nothing could dull the tension in my shoulders.

We manage to carry Creighton to his room and he soon wakes up and tells us he's okay. Remi refuses to leave, but once I make sure my cousin is fine, I slip back to my room and pace the length of it as I fetch my phone.

> **Me:** Are you okay?

Nikolai: You ask as if you care.

Me: Don't be like this. I'm asking if you're okay. Can you just answer the question?

Nikolai: You could've asked in person, but that would kill you, right?

I close my eyes and pull at the hairs at the back of my neck.

Nikolai: If I say I'm not okay, will you come to the penthouse?

Me: If you want me to, yeah.

Nikolai: Then I'm not okay.

Me: On my way.

Nikolai: I'll be there in an hour or so. I have some shit to do here first.

Me: Should you be doing anything if you're not okay?

Nikolai: Love it when you worry about me, baby. See you.

I want to tell him I'm not worried, but even I don't want to send that lie.

The drive to the penthouse is only fifteen minutes. I wait on the sofa as usual and turn on the telly, then settle on one of the late-night reruns of Agatha Christie's adaptations.

Unable to stay still, I stand up to fetch a bottle of beer from the fridge. He started stocking it up and ordering groceries that he knows nothing about. I told him to stop after the first time and began to buy my own groceries. I usually make him something before I leave. Breakfast or dinner, depending on how late it is.

I guess a part of me is trying to make up for how I leave every night when he doesn't seem like he wants me to.

He doesn't say that out loud, but I can feel the crushing disappointment in his voice whenever he asks, "You leaving?"

Every night. Every time. As if he expects the answer to change.

And every night, it gets harder to say "Yeah" or "You know I am."
So I just nod now. And even that is excruciatingly difficult.

Watching the murder mystery that I've learned by heart at this
point, I give up on the beer and prepare a quiche in case he's hungry.

I've always loved cooking and used to do it with Dad all the time.
Mum isn't much of a cook and neither are Glyn and Lan.

Dad and I bonded over cooking. He often told me it's an art and
he only learned it to ensure his place in Mum's heart.

*"She'll eat other people's food and be like, nah. No one can cook like
my Levi. Watch and learn, son. The best way to chain someone to you for
life is to own their stomach."*

I smile to myself as I methodically mix the ingredients and do
everything just right. I guess part of the reason why I love cooking
is because it suits my meticulous personality. And it's one of the few
things I do better than Lan.

After I put the quiche in the oven, I set a timer and clean the
kitchen. Nikolai always insists that he has someone who comes over
for cleaning, but I just can't stay in a place that's not spotless.

He calls me a clean freak, but he doesn't seem to mind. If anything, he'll usually be sitting on the sofa and watching me with a stupid grin.

Other times, he tries to help, and that turns into a disaster. He's
just too chaotic. Whenever I tell him to do something, he takes a short-
cut. He's the type who mixes white and colored clothes and then says,
"Well, they're all clothes. Who cares?"

He drinks milk from the bottle and eats tuna from the can. Like
a savage. Good grief. I get twitchy eyes just thinking about it.

But I guess he does mean well. He asked what my shampoo and
body wash are and then bought them for me, although, really, I love
his body wash. It makes me smell like him.

But then again, that's not ideal when I'm trying to keep this whole
thing a secret.

He also got my hair products and loves watching me get into my
'Prince Charming' look, as he calls it.

And he even taught me how to perform an enema. So…eh, that's a thing for gay sex apparently.

The first time he did it for me, and that was…*interesting*.

He teased me the whole time while I was face down on the bed, arse in the air, and I might have come.

I later found out there's actually another position, and when I confronted him about that, he wasn't apologetic in the least and said, "But I like that one better."

Twat.

By the time I finish cleaning, the oven dings and I turn it off, then sit down in front of the telly, watching the happenings of "The Murder of Roger Ackroyd."

I must fall asleep, because when I open my eyes, my head is lying on a muscled thigh and long fingers are stroking my hair.

My heart thumps loud in my chest as I look up at Nikolai's masculine face, his eyes focused on the telly. I can hear the actors speaking, but I can't make out a word. I just know it's still the same murder mystery, which means I haven't been out for long.

A part of me is fighting to get up. I hate it when he treats me so delicately like I'm some girl. It's enough that he fucks me. I'm still not fully comfortable with the fact that I like being fucked by a man. It makes me feel less manly, less…normal.

But at least I can tune those thoughts out during sex. I can give in to his dominance and relinquish control for a while.

It's different when he kisses my nose and eyelids and strokes my hair. It's different when he lays me on his thigh, like now, with one hand resting on the middle of my chest and the other lost in my hair. There's no sex involved and I don't like how horrifyingly comfortable it feels.

Still, I don't attempt to move.

I clear my throat. "When did you get here?"

He smiles even before his eyes meet mine. "About twenty minutes ago. Your snoring reached me from the elevator."

"I don't snore."

"Christ. You should see your offended face."

"Well, I don't."

"If you say so." His fingers continue the same soothing rhythm in my hair, lulling me back toward sleep.

"Are you okay?"

He slides his other hand from my chest to wrap it around my neck. "I am now."

"You lied about being hurt?" I ask with a ball lodged in my throat.

"I never said I was. I just mentioned that I was not okay."

"You clearly are."

"No, I'm not. I'm lonely without you, baby."

I suppress a smile. "I thought you said you didn't want to see, and I quote, 'my fucking face.'"

"I lied. I always want to see your face."

"I lied, too," I whisper, then clear my throat. "Can you tell me why you beat up Creigh?"

"We thought he was sent by your fucking brother to burn down the mansion."

"Creigh wouldn't do that."

"But Landon would?"

"Not personally, no. He likes to delegate his dirty work to others."

"Not to Creighton?"

"I don't think so?"

"You're not even sure."

"Not about that, but what I am sure about is that Creigh would not start a fire that would harm Annika. He cares about her. And I really hate it when you hurt my family members."

"Hmm. I won't hurt Creighton again if he doesn't get in the way. Jeremy is injured and I wasn't thinking straight."

There it is again. That bond with Jeremy that makes me feel strangely hollow.

"You care about him that much?"

"Fuck yeah. He's my best bro." He smiles with nostalgia. "If it weren't for him, I would've gotten myself killed a long time ago. He gets me, you know?"

I don't, but I need to change the subject because this is starting to feel uncomfortable. "What happened tonight?"

"A small disturbance from the Serpents. Nothing to worry about."

"They burned down your place. How is that nothing to worry about?"

"We'll get back at them and pummel them to the ground."

"Do you have to?"

"Of course. How else will they learn not to mess with us?"

"I'm sure there's another way…"

"There's no other way in the mafia. It's either kill or be killed. Those little fuckers will one day lead the Bratva branches in Chicago and Boston, so they're challenging us to gain ground. If we back down, we'll look weak."

Sometimes, I forget that he's a mafia prince. One day, he'll inherit his parents' legacy and live a life that's completely soaked in blood.

"Do you enjoy it?" I ask. "The violence and paybacks I mean."

"Fuck yeah." His eyes shine until it's almost blinding. "I feel most like myself when I'm teaching some assholes a lesson or two."

"Right."

"Don't worry, lotus flower, I won't be violent with you. Except sexually, of course, since you love it."

"Shut up."

He chuckles and jerks his head in the telly's direction. "So what are we watching? Seems dumb."

"Agatha Christie is *not* dumb."

"Who's that? An ancient actress?"

"Nikolai, please tell me you know who Agatha Christie is."

"Your godmother?"

"Crikey. Seriously? She's a famous novelist."

"Did she write any of the Marvel movies?"

"No."

"DC?"

"Of course not."

"Tarantino, then?"

"No."

"Never heard of her."

"You're seriously an anomaly."

"Maybe you are. This shit seems boring. Why are they talking all the time? Where's the action? The cars flying and people jumping in the air?"

"It's a murder mystery. They talk to give clues about the murderer."

"Neat. I'll use this to lull myself to sleep."

I hit his chest even as I suppress a smile. "Let me guess. You like action films?"

"Hell yeah."

"But they're mindless."

"The more mindless, the better. I'm a simple man. I see good violence, I rate it five out of five."

"You need help."

He licks his lips, eyes twinkling. "Then help me, baby."

A fire erupts at the base of my stomach and spreads all over my body. I stare at his moist mouth and gulp. "You're going to kiss me, aren't you?"

"I'm starving for your lips."

He dips his head and steals my lips and I just give in. It's impossible to fight the pull he has on me, and at this moment, I don't want to.

We kiss for what seems like hours, tongues stroking and teeth nipping. Only, this time, it's not urgent or leading up to sex.

Once we break apart, we don't go to the bedroom. We don't tear each other's clothes off.

We just stay in that position, with my head on his lap as we watch Agatha Christie.

And it feels peaceful.

Right.

At least, until my demons demand that I leave.

For now, I just soak in his presence and do what I excel at.

Pretend that everything is okay.

TWENTY

Nikolai

"**L**ET'S START A FUCKING WAR!"

That's what I shouted this morning, to which everyone rolled their eyes as if I was being unreasonable, when the fact is, we should've started this war two weeks ago, after those fucker Serpents thought it was a good idea to attack our home.

But I'm cool. I can roll with it.

Lie, fucking liar.

Except for a little arson and chucking one of their cars down a cliff, I didn't get much action. *Fine.* So Jer did give me a few targets to eliminate and I go to the fight club like my life depends on it.

But none of that is enough for the war machine brewing inside me.

It might also have to do with other particular circumstances that I can't seem to fucking understand anymore.

Instead of giving us what we all need—the war—Jer told me to calm down, and Kill said it would be better if he takes me on a walk, to which I replied that I'm not his fucking dog.

Still, we walk down the island's cobbled streets, throughout the old town, attracting more attention than necessary. Or more like, I do, even though I put a shirt on, for fuck's sake.

"You need to stop glaring at anyone who looks at you," Kill says with his usual calm, looking every bit the dignified gentleman that he most definitely is not.

"Maybe they need to stop looking at me." I snarl at a lady who keeps walking and glancing behind her.

She runs inside one of the stores as if her ass is on fire.

"Jeez, Niko. Way to scare the locals."

"This is dumb. Let's go to the fight club, where I can beat you the fuck up."

"Pass. I'm meeting my Glyn and I can't suffer from a black eye."

I stare at him with mock disbelief. "Are you telling me your girl is more important than me? Your cousin with whom you grew up?"

"Why is that a question? Of course she is."

"Kill, you motherfucking—"

"Oh, please. Quit the dramatics. You already have someone who's more important than us."

I pause and narrow my eyes. "What the fuck are you talking about?"

"Your failed attempts at sneaking around at night and at the crack of dawn. Care to share where you go?"

"Fuck off."

"Oh? Didn't know you had the ability to be secretive, dear cousin. My, my. I'm officially intrigued."

"Un-intrigue yourself."

"That's not a word. Hmm. It can't be your fuck buddies since you didn't shy away from flaunting them in our faces and disturbing us with your excessive porn shows and extravagant orgies. The fact that they disappeared altogether and you told the guards to kick out your toys whenever they come to the mansion means one thing."

"Which is?"

"You really do have that ED."

"Don't make me flash you in public, because I'll totally fucking do it."

"There are a bunch of prudes here, Niko. You'll end up in jail."

"Don't fucking care."

"If it's not ED, the only other option is...you went exclusive."

Fucking Killian and his psycho mind should be banned from existing around me. I'm struggling as it is and barely stopping myself from shouting that "I'm off to fuck my lotus flower" every night and "I'm gonna give my lotus flower a good morning kiss" every day.

It should be blasphemous that I'm expected to keep any sort of secret. I'm a muscles guy who prefers speaking with his fists. Everything else needs to fuck right the fuck off.

I don't like complicated. I don't *do* complicated.

Anyone who entrusts me with their secrets is a fool. Bran is a fucking fool. But he believes in my discretion, so I can't just advertise the whole unorthodox relationship.

Though he'd lose his marbles if I were to call it a relationship.

It's a situationship.

A deal at best and a whoring contract at worse.

Sometimes, it feels like a relationship. Especially after the fire. He's started coming to the penthouse more often than not, and the times he can't, he sends me texts like:

My cousin and brothers are dragging me to this party. If I leave, it'll be suspicious. I'm sorry. Will I see you tomorrow morning?

The girls invited me to their flat and I can't make up an excuse this time. Glyn is asking if I'm okay because she's growing worried, and I don't want to put that burden on her. I'm really sorry. Can I still see you in the morning?

So yeah, the first time he didn't come to the penthouse, I ghosted him the next morning as well, but I couldn't keep doing that when he was apologizing and basically begging me to meet him for our runs.

He's so fucking adorable. Though I wouldn't tell him that out loud or it'd freak him out. He gets antsy whenever I treat him gently outside of sex.

It's like he's scared of the prospect of us growing closer or something. And yet he's the one who does my grocery shopping and cooks for me.

I don't remember what all the fancy dishes are called, and I'm pretty sure I don't eat them the right way, considering the way he shakes his head in disapproval, but they taste awesome. Which is the whole point behind food, if you ask me.

He's the one who stays a bit longer every night, as if he's finding it harder to leave. He comes up with excuses about cleaning up and cooking or finishing the late-night murder mystery, but I know it's because he loves me and wants to be with me more.

Okay, he doesn't exactly *love* me. But I'm totally growing on him.

I catch him smiling at my antics, and he does that more now. Smiling, I mean.

He also tolerates my flirting more and replies to my texts in a timely manner. I think he even likes filthy texts now. He's become a fan of the dick pics as well, though he often tells me to stop sending them.

Sometimes, I find him looking at me with this cryptic expression when I'm watching his boring movies.

Other times, however, he looks at me as if I'm an alien, which is usually my cue that he'll leave. Other times, he locks himself in the bathroom for more than half an hour and comes out distraught, his real expression hidden behind the disturbing control that he wields so well.

It doesn't help that whenever I ask him if everything is okay, he lies through his teeth with that fake smile and says the word that I hate the most now. *Fine.*

He's anything but *fine*, but I don't know how to get him to talk. That is, if I'm supposed to do that when we're not in a relationship.

Bran is a vault. No matter how much I bang on the surface, it never cracks. He always, without a doubt, slips behind the steel walls and closes himself off.

A tap on my shoulder brings me back to the present and I find my cousin staring at me. "Are you thinking about them? A man? A woman? Both?"

"Fuck off, Kill."

"Honestly, I can't imagine you in a relationship."

"Why the fuck not?" I snap.

He pauses, raising an eyebrow. "You're too volatile. Besides, you

said you don't want a partner. Ever. Since you're a free soul and refuse to be tied down."

Right. I did say that.

Fuck. I completely forgot that I actually used to think that way
not too long ago. What is it about Bran that makes me want to fucking tie him to me?

It's the conquest, right?

Just because I have his body, I don't have his soul, and I'm on the
edge because I want his everything.

Once he hands that over, I'll discard him.

Right?

"So?" Kill shoves my shoulder with his. "Who changed your precious set of anti-monogamy rules? You can tell me. Must be killing
you to keep it all to yourself."

"You really want to know?"

He nods.

I beckon him with one finger. "Come here. It's a secret."

He inches close and I smack him on the nape. "Mind your fucking business and stop being nosy."

My cousin massages the assaulted spot. "You'll regret that."

"Take it as payback for all the times you throw shit at me." I break
out in evil laughter and continue strolling down the street.

Kill grabs me by the arm and pushes me in the opposite direction. "Let's grab a coffee first."

"And croissants." I stroke my stomach. "You think they have
macarons?"

"Don't think so." He watches me. "Since when do you like
macarons?"

"I always have."

"No, you haven't. Your sweet tooth usually ends at donuts."

I hum but say nothing. I might have started indulging in them
since Bran bought some once. I finished the whole box in one night
and had a mini sugar coma.

He's started hiding them from me since then and only leaves two
pieces out like a stingy asshole.

"Kill!"

My grouchy cousin's face breaks into a rare genuine smile at the sound of his girlfriend's voice.

She's waving us over to her table with... My, my.

My lips curl into an automatic grin when my eyes meet those stunning blues. For a fraction of a second, he looks like a deer caught in the headlights, his fingers loosening from around his cup.

It's a bit similar to his expression last night when I pressed him against the wall as soon as he was out of the elevator and fucked him there until he couldn't stand up straight.

Chill, Kolya. Jesus, man. We're in public.

Does he understand that logic? No, because he's twitching against my pants in pure dick fashion.

I know Bran is allergic to being labeled beautiful, but he so is. He's also so elegant and well-groomed. The collar of his shirt is perfectly folded, his cuffs are symmetrically rolled, and every strand of his hair falls into the right place.

He's always dressed in refined fashion and he carries himself with silent charisma. He might bottom and enjoy it, but he's the control freak outside the bedroom. Hot-headed, too, to the point of madness. Bet no one looks at his fancy manners and can guess he loves it rough.

While Glyn and Killian are busy sucking each other's faces off, I slide a chair over and sit beside him. I purposefully sit with my thighs so wide apart; my jeans touch his pants.

He continues watching me as if I'm a world wonder, his lips slightly parted.

The need to devour those lips beats inside me like an urge, but I force it down and whisper, "You're drooling. Am I that hot?"

He swallows and quickly diverts his gaze, choosing to focus on the absurd PDA across from us.

Typical Bran. To be honest, I don't know why I keep hoping he'll one day come out in epic fashion and kiss me in front of the world like he loves to do in private.

That's just impossible.

I suspect he'd rather keep this going for years instead of finally being honest with himself. Not that I care. Once I graduate, I'll be back to my life in New York and he'll return to being the prim-and-proper London boy.

"What a coincidence," Glyn says after she finally breaks apart from Kill.

He taps her nose. "You really think it's a coincidence? Looks like I have a lot more to teach you, baby."

Kill. You evil genius.

So he knew she was in this coffee shop with Bran all along, which is why he insisted we grab coffee here.

It's nice to know I have a successful stalker cousin. Some might say it runs in the family since I'm pretty sure I caught Gareth stalking a Mercedes the other day and he used one of the bodyguards' cars for the mission.

What's not nice, however, is the fact that he also uses *baby.* Couldn't pick another nickname?

I steal a glance at Bran, and he's busy staring at his coffee as if searching for an answer to the fucking universe. Black, no sugar like his soul.

He's interlinking his fingers, letting them rest on his lap and I rest my hand on my thigh, close to his, and inch closer, getting high on the warmth emanating off him.

Fuck me. He's intoxicating.

I simply can't exist in his vicinity and stop myself from touching him.

It's torture.

"How are you, Niko?" Glyn asks me with an easy grin.

Sometimes, it's hard to think of her as Bran's sister. Though they do look like siblings, she's more carefree than he'll ever be. She acts spontaneously while he counts his every step. Every word. Every action. Like a psycho.

Except when my body talks to his, of course. That's when I get the uncut version of my lotus flower.

"Nikolai," Killian says. "His name is Nikolai."

"But I love Niko," I say with a smile.

To give Bran credit, he pretends that I didn't say a word as he sips from his coffee. However, I can see his hand twitching on his thigh.

"Right?" Glyn says. "It's much easier to call him Niko instead of Nikolai. Don't be jealous, Kill."

"Yeah, don't be jealous, cousin. Glyn and I are friends, right?"

"Uh-huh." She grins and I wink at her.

I swear I catch Bran glaring at me from my peripheral vision, but when I look at him, he's busy watching his coffee.

"Watch it, Niko," Kill threatens in mock calm. "You're digging your own grave."

"Let me search for the fucks I have to give." I pretend to check my pockets and then produce two middle fingers. "Oh, here you go."

Glyn bursts out laughing, Killian is nowhere near amused, and Bran is still lost in his phone.

Christ. His mental door-slam game is strong.

"So what were you doing here before we interrupted you?" I ask Glyn.

"Nothing much. Bran and I love to catch up."

"You must be close," I say and feel Bran stiffen beside me.

"We are," she says with glee. "We're a team against Lan."

"We're not against Lan." He speaks for the first time, voice calm and clear like an unmovable mountain. "He's our brother."

"Yeah, well, he doesn't act like one."

"This is not the time or place for this discussion," he says point-blank, and although he sounds composed, there's a firm edge beneath it.

Hearing him speak in that tone is how I figured out his kind image is just that—an image. He's actually a bit controlling. Okay, a *lot*. Neurotically so.

He acts like he's okay with everything, but deep down, he tries to manipulate the situation so it works the exact way he wants it to. He's picky, standoffish, and meticulous. Difficult and grumpy, too. The quiet ones are the fucking scariest.

"Whatever." Glyn pouts. "You always try to give excuses for him anyway."

"He's my twin brother."

"Yeah, okay." She rolls her eyes and slurps aggressively from her cup as Kill strokes her shoulder.

I see an opportunity and I sure as fuck take it. Since the lovebirds are busy, I plant my hand on Bran's and he goes still, his hand slightly trembling beneath mine.

He's so fucking warm that I can't help threading my fingers through his, digging the pads in his thigh.

Bran goes still, and here's the thing; he doesn't try to push me away. So I go further, stroking his skin with my thumb, trying and failing not to get turned on by a mere stolen touch in public.

I really love how his hand is big but still slightly smaller than mine. It's perfect size. *He* is perfect in every physical aspect. Anyone who says otherwise is clearly a blind fucking idiot.

Glyn looks up and Bran subtly pulls his hand free and shoves mine away then grabs his phone, building that wall around himself.

Not so fast.

I pull out my phone and text him.

> **Me:** You're not paying me any attention, baby. I'm jealous of Kill and Glyn.

He reads it immediately and I can see him glaring at his phone as if it's my face.

> **Bran:** Go away.

> **Me:** Aww, but I don't want to.

> **Bran:** Don't be a baby, Nikolai.

> **Me:** I thought you were the baby, baby.

He covers his mouth with a palm, but it's too late, I can see him smiling. It takes everything in me not to lean over and feast on that smile and pull on his lip with my teeth just the way he loves it.

> **Me:** You smell so good, I want to lick you up.

> **Bran:** Nikolai!

> **Me:** You look so hot, I want to eat you up. I can't wait to fuck you until you're a blithering mess, baby.

Bran: Shut up.

> **Me:** Love how you're prim and proper in public but turn into a filthy-mouthed sex god in private. How you're all quiet now, but you become loud when your ass swallows my cock. Mmm. Getting hard thinking about your face when you choke on my cock.

Bran: STOP.

> **Me:** Oh, one last thing. I forgot to do this earlier today.

I send him a dick pic I took this morning.

Bran squirms in his seat and immediately exits the chat. I suppress a smile as I keep staring at my screen.

"Is it Simon?"

Kill's words pause my attempts to send another dick pic just to mess with my Bran.

I slide my gaze from my phone to my cousin, frowning. "Simon?"

"Is he the one you're exclusive with?" Kill asks.

Bran pauses with his cup of coffee near his lips before he slowly sets it down.

"You're in an exclusive relationship?" Glyn asks with apparent glee.

"He is and wouldn't tell me who with." Kill pauses. "I'm going through your toys, and Simon is the only one clingy enough to want that."

"Who's Simon?" Glyn asks.

I steal a look at Bran and his lips are set in a line. He knows *exactly* who Simon is, even though it's been several weeks. After all, he agreed to be exclusive because of his jealousy.

"He's the one who walks and talks like a diva and calls Nikolai Daddy," Killian answers her.

"Oh, Simon." Glyn smiles. "He asked me to call him Sim."

"More like a simp." Kill twists his lips. "He's so cringe. Please tell me he's not the one you're with."

"Maybe he is," I say as I hit Send on the second nude.

This time, it's a full-body mirror selfie where I'm fisting my cock and biting my lower lip.

Then just to fuck with him, I type:

> **Me:** Thinking of your ass makes me drip, baby.

Bran stands up all of a sudden, hand clenched around his phone, but he sounds composed when he says, "I'm going to pop into the toilet."

I suppress a smile as I watch the dots appear and disappear.

"Stop smiling like a creep," Kill says. "It's disgusting."

"Don't be jealous of my sexy smile, Satan's heir." I slide my phone into my pocket. "I need something sweet. Be right back."

I head to the cashier, pretending to be checking out their sweets. No Italian pistachio croissant, no baklava, and no macarons. Not interested.

After I catch a glimpse of Kill and Glyn eating each other's faces, I slip to the restroom. I find Bran standing in front of a sink, his face twisted and his fingers holding his phone in a death grip.

I slip behind him and whisper in his ear, "Careful, if you glare at it hard enough, it might break."

He flinches and whirls around so fast, he nearly falls. I wrap an arm around his waist. "Easy, baby."

His wild eyes search our surroundings with tendrils of panic. "What are you doing, Nikolai?"

"I figured you could use a hand." I glide my palm to his erection and fist it through his pants. "Mmm. Did you get hard looking at my nudes, baby?"

"Nikolai…" He struggles for control, his voice hoarse. "This is a public place… Stop…"

"But the possibility of getting caught is making your cock thicker."

I lean over and slide my tongue over the shell of his ear. "Or is that because of me?"

"You need to get over yourself…" His words end with a moan when I bite the lobe of his ear, then his jaw, and his bottom lip.

"You were saying?"

"Cut it out…"

"What was that?" I stroke his erection, making it as hard as stone. "Your cock is so fucking hard for me."

"F-fuuck…bloody hell."

"Mmm. Love it when you curse, baby."

"Nikolai—"

Whatever he has to say is cut off when the sound of footsteps comes from outside.

Bran freezes, the lust replaced by a sense of panic so steep, it baffles me. Even his erection starts to deflate.

Why the fuck does he act as if it's the end of the world if someone catches him kissing me?

I grab his wrist and drag him to the last stall, then shove him inside, slam the door shut, and back him up against the wall.

A few male voices reach us from outside, discussing the Premier League and whatnot.

"Leave," Bran whispers.

"Shut your fucking mouth."

"Niko—" I crash my lips to his and he groans into my mouth, the sound small but enough to make me hot and bothered.

The kiss is hard and fast, meant to make him stop talking. I don't want to hear his grating words right now.

"I'm going to need you to be real quiet for me, baby." I unzip his pants and pull out his hard cock. "Seems you really get off on this, don't you?"

"Nikolai, don't…please…" He shakes his head frantically, but I jerk him from the base to the tip, relishing how he turns rock-fucking-hard.

And just because I can't help it, I push on the foreskin and tease the hole.

"Mmm. You're dripping for me. How cute."

"Fuck you…"

"Love it when you talk dirty." I lower myself to my knees with a bit of struggle. We're big guys, especially me, and this place is small.

Once I'm in an okay position, I slide him into my mouth.

Bran growls and I press a hand to his lips.

"Shh," I whisper around his dick. "I love it when you're loud, but this isn't the place for those sexy growls. Be quiet for me as I choke on your cock, baby."

He throws his head against the wall, eyes rolling as I take him to the back of my throat, then out again and in again. I tease the tip, thrusting my tongue against it a few times.

"Mmmfff…" He curses against my palm as he buries his hands in my hair, shoving me against his groin.

I suck him in a frenzy, wanting to get him off. I choke on his cock and squeeze his balls until he's writhing against the wall and his pre-cum spills on my tongue.

God-fucking-damn-it.

He's a sight to behold when chasing his pleasure. Flushed skin, hooded eyes, and demanding fingers.

He has an obsession with my hair, and just like every time, he yanks away the tie to sink his fingers against my skull, fisting my hair, then stroking it, then fisting it again.

I can feel his muscles tightening as he thrusts in my throat faster. His teeth sink into my fingers as his cum explodes in my mouth and down my throat.

He comes for a long time and I keep sucking him dry until I swallow every last drop.

He sags against the wall, fingers clenching in my hair. Once I'm done, I pull him out and lick my lips as he watches me with feral eyes.

"Stop looking at me like that or I'll fuck you, baby."

As I stand up, I remove my hand from his mouth, now sporting a red half-moon over the tattoos from his teeth.

"What the hell do you think—"

My lips seal to his. "Unless it's a thank-you, I don't want to hear it."

He watches me for a beat. "Can you stop kissing me randomly?" I lick his lower lip. "Nope."

He tucks himself in, fighting against the redness creeping up his skin.

Once he's back within his boring element, he glares at me. "What's with Killian finding out about you being in an exclusive relationship?"

"He just loves playing detective." I lick his throat. "Don't worry, he doesn't know it's you."

Bran's hands land on my chest and he tries to push me away, but he tilts his head to the side, giving me access to that pounding pulse point. "Why does he think it's Simon?"

"You heard him. Simon is the one who makes more sense."

"Why? Because he calls you *Daddy*?"

I chuckle against his neck, trying to be quiet even though there are no voices outside. "Jealous, baby?"

He fists my hair and tugs me back. "Don't mess with me, Nikolai."

"Don't mess with *me*." I wrap my fingers around his throat and squeeze. "You have no right to act butthurt when you're the one against a public relationship. If you don't like people thinking I'm with Simon, boo-fucking-hoo. It's your fault."

A smudge of pain passes through his eyes and I want to kick myself in the ass when he releases my hair.

"Baby..."

"No, you're right. I'm the one who wanted it this way and I need to deal with the consequences."

"But why does it have to be like this? We can—"

"No!" he cuts me off so harshly, I actually step back.

"You didn't even hear what I have to say."

"The answer is no, Nikolai," he says with a note of panic, and I want to reach inside him and drag out whatever demon is making him feel this way, then beat it to death.

What the fuck happened to him? Why does he go into this mode sometimes, as if he's being chased by a monster?

"Just drop it, okay?" He's breathing harshly. "Go back first."

"Hey...what's wrong?"

"Nothing. I'm fine."

"You look anything but fine."

"Why is that any of your business?" he snaps. "Why do you have to care? Just leave me alone."

"You know, you're pushing me too far and I might let you fucking drop, Brandon."

His lips part and I think he'll at least apologize like he usually does, but he whispers, "Please go."

"Fuck you," I mutter, then whip the door open and leave.

My movements are forceful as I wash my hands and stride back to the coffee shop. I pause by the table when I notice the atmosphere is not as sickeningly sweet as when I left.

The reason is that Bran's clone is in my chair.

I place a hand in my pocket and stand beside him. "You're in my spot."

Landon's head whips in my direction, sporting his slimy smirk. Although he shares Bran's physical traits, Landon is buffer and much more loathsome. If it weren't for the identical features, no one would think they're siblings. Where Bran is calm and a fucking asshole behind closed doors, Landon is an asshole openly. Antagonistic and completely unhinged.

I still haven't forgiven him for kidnapping Kill, even if my cousin let it go to keep his relationship with Glyn intact.

"Don't see your name on it, big man," he says with that same smirk, and the only reason I don't punch him in the face is because it's a mirror of Bran's.

Can't stand the fucking guy.

"Lan?" Bran shows up, looking not one bit flustered. As if he didn't get on my last fucking nerve a minute ago.

He carefully slides into his seat, keeping his attention on his pretentious brother. "What are you doing here?"

"I heard you and Glyn were catching up, so I wanted to join. I didn't think there would be unwanted company, though."

"Watch your mouth," Kill grits and Glyn presses on his hand as if stopping him from punching her brother, who definitely deserves to be sent to the moon with a hole in his goddamn face.

"Bran, little bro." Landon wraps an arm around his shoulders. "Why were you sitting beside Nikolai? Stupidity can be contagious, you know."

This fucking—

Before I can kick him, Bran pushes him away. "That's rude. Apologize, Lan."

"Me? Apologizing?" He bursts out laughing. "Good one, Bran. You're effortlessly funny."

"I apologize on my brother's behalf," he says, barely looking at me.

Christ. This fucking asshole, I swear. I glare at him and he ducks his head, cutting off eye contact like the coward he is.

"What's going on here?" Lan snaps his fingers in front of my face. "Hey, you. Eyes off my brother before I fucking blind you."

"Lan!" Glyn chastises.

Bran lifts his head and the fear I see in his gaze makes me sick to my stomach.

He's so terrified about the notion that anyone could find out about us that he looks like he's on the verge of throwing up.

"I'm out of here," I announce and leave without a look behind.

Fuck the lot of them. Starting with Brandon fucking King.

I walk back to the mansion and then take my Harley on a ride along the seashore. But neither the air nor the vibrations of the bike lighten my mood.

After half an hour, I park by the beach and pull out my phone.

I find a text from the bane of my fucking existence.

Bran: Thank you and I'm sorry.

Motherfucker.

Me: What for?

Bran: I'm sorry for how I spoke. Thank you for leaving and not clashing with Lan.

Bran: Listen, I think he's suspicious about something.

Me: So?

Bran: It's best I keep my distance from the penthouse for now.

Me: Typical Brandon. Running away at the first sign of danger seems to be your modus operandi.

Bran: You don't know Lan. He's like a dog. If he comes sniffing around, he'll find out everything.

Me: And that's such a fucking tragedy?

Bran: Nikolai, please. Don't do this.

Me: You know what? I am doing this. I don't have time for spineless, indecisive assholes. I'm neither your plaything nor your booty call.

Bran: What does that mean?

Me: Go find yourself another toy. We're done.

Me: Oh, wait. We were never anything in the first place. Delete my number.

TWENTY-ONE

Brandon

I'VE NEVER BEEN ADDICTED TO ANYTHING, SO I DIDN'T REALIZE how notoriously painful it is to go through withdrawal.

It's been two weeks since Nikolai told me we were done—in a text—and I'm still not over the bursts of loneliness.

Two weeks and it's getting worse, not better.

It's not your common withdrawal, after all. Or maybe I'm just a newbie at this entire thing and don't have the foggiest clue about how to handle these types of situations.

Sometimes, the pain and nausea get too much and I'm smothered by the black ink and have to purge it out.

Somehow.

Anyhow.

I've seen my blood more often than not in the past two weeks. The other day, I let it flow and flow until I lost consciousness in the bathroom. A part of me wished I'd never wake up.

A part of me prayed for it as I lay on the bathroom floor, my eyes blurred with moisture and my heart too tired to keep pumping life into my useless body.

My brain checked out and my thoughts came to terms with how utterly fucking tired I am.

Of myself.

Of everything.

I still am.

My brush ghosts over the canvas, adding strokes of warm colors, intertwining and mixing them until they match my hollow insides.

Art is the only thing that keeps me grounded. I don't even go to practice anymore after I purposefully sprained my ankle.

I'm withdrawing from social circles with all sorts of excuses. Studies. Work. Pending deadlines.

I just don't have the energy to deal with anyone or anything at the moment. But more alone time only pushes me toward bad habits.

Cutting and blood and fucking self-loathing.

I'm spiraling and I can't stop it.

I'm falling and can't hit the bottom.

My hand trembles and the plaster that I covered with my thick watch burns. The injury tingles and my blood pumps into the barely healing cut.

The doomsday feeling racks my brain and saliva floods the inside of my mouth.

Tick.

You're so fucking weak.

Tick.

A disgrace.

Tick.

Fucking useless.

The brush falls from between my shaky fingers and hits the floor, leaving an orange stroke on the plastic.

I open the drawer to my right and grab my Swiss Army knife almost on autopilot. If I just open it one more time, no one will know.

If I just purge the black ink surrounding me, I won't feel trapped in my own skin and it'll be over.

Except that I repeated those same words the last five fucking times I did this. Five times in the span of two weeks. Five.

Bloody hell. I'm losing control.

And yet my fingers wrap around the handle and I remove my watch and then place it on the table. I peel off the plaster and stare at the dark-red skin. The last time I did this, the cut was so deep, I lost a lot of blood. I thought it'd never heal and I'd need stitches.

The skin mended itself back together again, fruitlessly hoping for closure, for healing, like a fucking masochist.

The first time I cut myself was by accident when I was shaving at seventeen. I watched the tiny droplet of blood rolling down my jaw and neck and felt an immense sense of relief.

It was the first time I looked at myself for a solid minute without feeling the need to smash the mirror.

So I became a bit careless with my shaving and cut myself here and there just to see more of my blood. The harder the blood flowed, the more the black ink receded.

But I didn't do it often. I was extremely careful not to make my parents suspicious. So when Dad joked that maybe he should teach me how to shave again, I stopped doing those small nicks on my face and neck.

I started shaving down there and cutting between my thighs where no one could see. I would sit in the bathtub and watch the blood trickling out of me, close my eyes and suck in clean air.

After I started uni, I began cutting my wrist, but only in the exact same spot, drawing over the three lines that could be hidden by a watch.

But I didn't let myself do that often, either. No more than once a month, maybe. When the nausea constricted my throat and I couldn't breathe without gagging on the black ink.

When it hurts to the point I can't exist within my own fucking skin.

The frequency hiked up in the past couple of weeks to the point that I can't control it anymore.

When I was with Nikolai, I didn't do it, because he was awfully perceptive. He could sense something was wrong with my hand and arm and kept asking about it for weeks. I kid you not, he would be like, "By the way, how did you hurt your hand? It looks serious."

Considering all the sex, I didn't dare cut my thighs, and the weird part is that I wasn't really overwhelmed by the urge to see my blood. It was manageable, until it wasn't.

Until now, where I'm fantasizing about cutting my fucking wrist off.

"Hon…please. I'm so worried about you. Please talk to me. Tell me something. Anything."

Mum's words from earlier rush into the fog and I release a shaky exhale. I told her I loved her and then hung up, because I couldn't deal with the pain in her voice.

Dad called me and I didn't pick up, because hearing the concern in his voice would undo me. It scares me that I'm the disappointment who's nothing like him in any shape or form. He might have been strict with Lan, but, really, that's because he reminds him of his younger self.

I'm the fucking anomaly who only ever caused my parents' concern. A fucking hurricane of disappointment and failed potential.

A vibration pulls me out of the trance and I blink twice, then reach for the phone with my injured hand, slightly trembling, my heart lodged in my throat.

Over the past couple of weeks, my coping method to get over the never-ending withdrawal was texting myself as if I were texting Nikolai.

I have enough pride to not contact him after he dumped me, but it didn't hurt to send those texts to myself. Pretending it was him. At least, that way, I got to express what I felt in words.

Daft words like:

Why did you come into my life if you were going to leave?

Why did you make me addicted to you if you didn't plan to stay?

If I say I'm sorry will you come back?

You were never a booty call. I don't even do those. And I'm the fucking toy, not you.

I don't even like running anymore. You ruined it like everything else. Fucking bastard. Fuck you.

I'm messed up, Nikolai. Extremely so. You should be glad to have dodged a bullet.

I hate myself. Why don't you hate me, too?

Oh, right. You do now. Finally. Congrats on the wake-up call. Better late than never.

Are you back with Simon and your other friends with benefits? Did you find a replacement already?

That last thought often crams me down the black hole of my mind and I can't shake it off, no matter how much I try to.

I've seen Nikolai in the fight club a couple of times, mainly because I can't handle *not* looking at him anymore, but I always leave before he takes notice of me.

Just like I wrote those texts to myself instead of him.

But here's the thing.

Last night, I got hammered with Remi, and when I came back to my room, I was on edge. So I went through Nikolai's chaotic Instagram, which he fills with the most random nonsense.

It's a habit I indulge in lately and it helps to quiet down the demons. At least, for a while.

Around ten thirty, which is when I usually go to the penthouse, he posted a picture of the telly on a scene from the nightly murder mysteries. The hashtags were *#Watching #Alone*

My heart revived from the ashes at that moment, but only for a fraction of a second before I saw all the comments from men and women thirsting over him and offering to accompany him. Including fucking Simon.

You can watch me, Daddy ;)

So remember the part where I was drunk? I wasn't thinking straight, so I kind of texted him.

Me: Do you miss me?

I kept pacing my room back and forth, waiting for his reply. My mind, heart, and fucking body were a mess of epic proportions. I wanted to drive to the penthouse and see him.

I wanted to throw away whoever he'd invited to our space.

But I would've definitely gotten into an accident if I'd driven in that state, and while I couldn't give two flying fucks about my life, I wouldn't endanger other people's lives.

He replied after a whole two minutes, even though he read it immediately.

Nikolai: Who's this?

My heart plummeted and I stopped in the middle of my room, staring at the text as if it were a knife that had plunged itself into my chest and protruded through my back.

Maybe I read the post wrong. He's already moved on and I'm the one stuck in this fucking prison of my own making.

Me: Wrong number. Sorry.

I was about to throw down my phone and indulge in my self-destructive hobby, but it vibrated in my hand.

He was calling me.

I swear I never felt so shaken up as when I swiped up and placed the phone to my ear.

"Why the fuck—" He inhaled sharply and I felt the vibration of his voice in my ear.

Then I stopped breathing altogether as if that would make me hear him better.

"It's obviously not the wrong fucking number. What the fuck do you want from me, Brandon?" His tone warred with calm, but I could hear the agitation beneath it.

I smiled and closed my eyes briefly in relief as I listened to his breaths and soaked in his voice. He didn't forget me or delete my number.

"You never call me by my full name," I whispered. "I don't like it when you do."

"I don't give a fuck what you like. I don't give a fuck about you or how you're doing. I told you we're fucking done, so stay the fuck away from me."

"But I don't want to," I threw his words back at him, too drunk to care about how desperate I sounded.

"What the fuck did you just say?"

"I don't want to. You obviously don't want to, either, or you wouldn't be talking to me. You're that obsessed with me, huh?"

"I'm so over your bullshit."

"Liar. You can't stay away from me, Niko." I used another one of his sentences. "You know you want me. No matter what I do, you come crawling back to me."

He hung up then, and I cursed myself for the overconfident tone I used when, really, I just wanted to hear his voice, even angry and wrong. Even if he was calling me by my full name, it was still his voice that I'd spent way too long without.

Then I went to bed, imagining his strong arms encircling me and his chest beneath my head.

For some reason, I thought he'd text me today and had my hopes up when I felt the vibration just now, but it's not his name that's on the screen.

> **Dad:** Call me as soon as possible, Bran. No matter how hard it is, I want you to remember that you have a family who loves you and would stand behind you no matter what. You're not alone, son. Okay?

Pressure builds behind my eyes and I let the Swiss Army knife fall to the table, then rub the heels of my palms against my eyes.

I don't think he knows how much I needed to hear that. Or maybe he does. Dad has always been really good at reading the atmosphere and providing me with the right support at the right time.

> **Me:** What's normal, Dad? And please don't call. I don't want to talk on the phone.

> **Dad:** Normal is whatever you decide it is.

> **Me:** What if my notion of normal is drastically different from everyone else's? I don't like being different. I hate it. I can't cope with it.

Dad: Bran, listen. Society's perception of normal is a learned concept. It's an opinion that was passed down through generations until it eventually became a tradition. It's rooted in people's minds because it's been taught for a long time, but fundamentally, it's just an opinion. It means nothing just because people conform to it. You being different is fucking fantastic, son. You've risen above their sheep mentality and you can choose to be proud of your difference instead of hating it. It might take time to shake off society's perceptions, but that's okay. I'm here. Your mum is here. Your whole family is here to help you. All you have to do is say the words.

Me: I don't want to be different, Dad. I want to be like Lan. Why can't I just be like him?

Dad: Lan is different, too, Bran. He's so different, it drives me insane. He's so different, he wears it like a badge of honor. You know this. He's literally been diagnosed with narcissistic and antisocial personality disorder.

Me: Yeah, but he seems normal.

Dad: Because he fakes it.

I fake it, too, but I don't tell him that.

Me: Thanks, Dad. I'll talk to you later.

Dad: Come over when you can. I have a lot of new recipes to teach you.

I send him a few heart emojis and then hide the knife, add a new plaster, and put on my watch.

On my way out of the studio, I congratulate myself for stepping back from the edge. Though it was all Dad's work, really.

But for how long can I keep up this façade before it explodes in my face…?

Loud voices reach me as soon as I'm close to the living room. Lan—of course, he's ninety-nine percent the reason behind all trouble—Eli, and surprisingly, Creigh, who barely speaks.

He's shouting now.

"What's with all the commotion—what the…" I trail off when I see Creigh beating Lan to a pulp against the sofa.

I storm toward them, but Eli grabs me by the nape and pulls me back. "This isn't your place."

"What the actual hell? Lan's bleeding."

"Aw. You worried about me? I should've asked Creigh to beat me up earlier." My brother can barely speak, teeth bloodied, but he drops a hand on his chest. "So touched, I could cry."

I wiggle against Eli's hand, but my cousin keeps me in a death grip while Creigh continues punching my brother.

"Stop them!" I bark at Eli. "Why are you letting this happen?"

"Your brother needs to be put in his fucking place."

"He's going to kill him!"

"Small price to pay for all the fuckery he does."

My heart lunges harder the more Creigh beats Lan. The sound of his punches echoes in the air like a haunting symphony of violence. The fact that I can't help fills my throat with nausea.

Through it all, Lan steals peeks at me and even winks. Fucking twat.

Lan and I are different and I've always suffered from an inferiority complex when it comes to him. Where he's the god, I'm the unknown peasant.

Where he excels at everything and makes a show of it, I excel at everything silently.

One would think his actions would make me hate him, but I don't. Seeing him hurt is no different than me being punched in the gut.

I'm thrown back to the first and only time Lan ever begged as he held me close while I cried in his chest.

"Please, Bran, please! Tell me what's fucking wrong."

Though that happened during the darkest time in my life, his words and his hug are my favorite memories.

That was almost eight years ago, and no matter how we change, whenever I look at Lan, I see his face from when we were fifteen as he kept me together.

So I always want to keep him together as well, even if he puts himself in the worst fucking situations.

I have no doubt that he wronged Creigh in some way. He wouldn't hit Lan for no reason.

Is this because of that fire at the Heathens'?

I'm about to hit Eli and go to Lan's aid when Remi walks in, stops at the entrance, and stares at the scene while blinking several times. "Not sure what type of freak show—or kink, not shaming—you King men are into, but I have a serious question. Am I too drunk or is there actually a guy tied up in our basement?"

I go still in Eli's hold, that doomsday feeling trickling back to my mind. "A guy is tied up in our basement?"

"Sure as fuck, and if I'm not too drunk, then I'm pretty sure it's Nikolai Sokolov."

My lips part.

My heart falls.

What the fuck—

"That's the surprise I kept for you, Cray Cray." Landon grins like evil incarnate. "He's your path to vengeance. Told you I had everything figured out."

I came up with a plan to save Nikolai.

I don't give two flying fucks about Creighton's need for vengeance against Jeremy. Which is the reason behind this whole thing, as Eli explained.

Lan used Creigh in one of his games and concealed information about his past.

A past that Jeremy's family has to do with.

To make up for his shenanigans, Lan concocted a plan to lure Jeremy into our house. And what's better than using his best friend as bait?

Apparently, Lan managed to drug Nikolai, which is how he could transport him and lock him up in the basement.

I know I said I don't hate Lan, but I'd really love to punch him in the face for all the rubbish he keeps pulling.

The thought of Nikolai drugged and tied up for my family's entertainment sobered me up immediately.

I spent the whole night and half a day trying to think of how to get him out of here unscathed.

The problem is, Lan and Eli have strictly forbidden me from getting close to the basement since, well, they know I won't stand by.

I asked Remi for help and he categorically refused to get involved in whatever this is.

"Mate, Lan is your brother, so he won't hurt you no matter what you do. I, on the other hand, could be skinned alive. And that psycho Eli is also in on this. Hell no, I'm just going to lock myself in my room and watch porn. Thank you very much."

So I went on my own to the electricity generator room, studied the blueprint, and managed to cut the power in the basement, where they're keeping Nikolai.

That way, the cameras won't work.

Then I stole the key from Lan while he was taking a shower, fetched a knife and a flashlight from the kitchen, and snuck to the basement.

Once I arrive in front of the door, I search my surroundings before I unlock it and slip inside.

My heart beats so loud in my chest, I barely manage to keep my hand steady as I'm overwhelmed by his scent, his presence, just him.

I've always frozen up when I'm in a state of shock, and that happened more often than not when I was with Nikolai.

His massive unconscious body lolls on a chair in the empty room.

Thick ropes swirl around his chest and dig into his inky arms, binding him to the chair, and his head is slumped forward, his hair camouflaging his face. It's longer now, wavier.

My fingers twitch, wanting—no, *needing*—to touch it again, feel it, see if it'll still bring me peace like it used to.

I can't stop it. Even if I know I shouldn't do it. Even if I'm sure this is just a recipe for disaster.

My hand moves of its own accord as I sink my unsteady fingers in his hair and glide it back.

The moment I see his face again this close, I want to throw away my pride, fall between his knees, and beg him to take me back.

I want to kiss his lips and feast on his tongue.

Two weeks without him has been a fucking eternity. I didn't care before him, but after him, it's torture to go day in and day out without his touch.

Survive without his presence, his flirtatious nature, and his clingy texts.

Without his grins and his daft jokes.

Without...*him*.

I stroke my fingers in his hair and contemplate kissing him. Just once.

No one will know—

He releases a groan, the sound vibrating and striking me in the chest. I let him go and pull at the hair on the back of my neck to keep my hand busy and stop me from touching his cheek, or, worse, actually kissing him.

Nikolai opens his unfocused eyes, pupils dilated, probably because of the drug Lan gave him.

My heart thunders so hard behind my chest, I'm surprised he doesn't hear it.

"Lotus flower...? What are you doing here?"

My hand stops its incessant pulling and I swear I've never felt so relieved as when he called me that instead of my real name. But then again, his speech is slurred, so maybe he's still drugged and doesn't know what he's talking about.

I let my hand fall from my nape and fetch my knife, then start cutting the rope, trying to remain composed, to not actually stroke every slope of his muscles as I speak in my signature detached tone. "You're the one who came into my house. You just couldn't stay away?"

I feel the rumble of Nikolai's chest against my hands and make out his grin from the corner of my eye as he drops his voice. "How else would I see you so adorably worried about me?"

"I am not worried about you, and don't fucking call me adorable again."

"Wow. The posh boy can curse."

"Shut it or I'll leave you to my brother's and cousins' nonexistent mercy."

"If I'd known I'd see this side of you, I would've gotten myself kidnapped long ago."

I stare at him, my chest aching and my heart begging for something. Anything. "Are you insane?"

Nikolai rolls a shoulder. "Probably."

I puff out a long sigh. "I'll release you and leave the back door open, and you'll have to find your own way out."

"No."

The new voice makes me freeze and I start panicking. How long has he been there?

I straighten and slowly turn around. "Creigh."

Shit.

This whole thing is happening because of his revenge. I need to get Nikolai out of here. Now.

I have a terrible feeling about this.

Still turned sideways, I cut on Nikolai's ropes, trying to keep my movements as minimal as possible.

Creigh, however, notices and barks, "Step back."

"This isn't right and you know it—"

"Step the fuck back, Bran. I won't repeat myself another time."

I do, letting my hand with the knife fall to my side as I face my cousin.

"Get out," he orders.

This isn't like him. He's blinded by revenge and isn't even seeing me. I'm the only person he actually seeks for company, because we're both comfortable with silence and don't feel the need to fill it.

He's easygoing and prefers sleep over anything else, but he also fights and takes after the King genes more than I do.

This is the first time I've seen Creigh so unhinged and out of control. I'm worried Nikolai will be caught up in the madness he's planning with Eli and Lan.

And that sparks a loathsome feeling inside me.

Fear.

The need to protect him beats under my skin like an urge.

"Listen..." I take a step toward Creigh. "I know you feel the need for revenge, but this whole thing is wrong."

"No one asked for your opinion. Stay out of this."

"I won't allow you to throw your life away for parents you've never known and a past you're better off without, Creighton." I speak in a firm tone. "I'm letting Nikolai go and then we'll talk about this. *Rationally.*"

I turn toward Nikolai and I feel like I'm melting when I find him looking at me with those hooded eyes.

I'm sorry, I say with mine. *For everything.*

I grab the ropes, but a blow lands at the back of my head, and the world is pulled from beneath my feet.

The last thing I see is Nikolai's wide eyes as I fall on top of him. But I manage to slip the knife between his thighs so he can save himself.

Or at least, I think I do.

My last thought is just how much I've missed his smell. Maybe losing consciousness isn't so bad after all if I get to hug him.

TWENTY-TWO

Nikolai

THE SITUATION TURNED INTO A SHITSHOW.

Two people left that basement in a fucking ambulance that day.

One of them was me due to that motherfucker Creighton. But hey, karma is a little bitch who works very fast, because he also got what was coming to him.

I might have made my fate worse since I pushed my throat against his blade. No regrets, though. I refused the very notion of being used against Jeremy. That's just not going to happen under my fucking watch.

Anyway, that was over a week ago.

I'm fine now, didn't need many stitches, and in a few weeks, I can wear the new scar as a badge of honor. Yes, bitch.

My sisters and Jeremy don't agree about how I view the whole incident, but who gives a fuck. I'm alive.

I'm fine.

Or I was. Until I found out a tragic fact that I'd been blind to see this whole time.

My baby sister Mia is apparently friends with Bran.

Friends.

Why the fuck would he be friends with my sister? Unless he has an ulterior motive and is using her for another diabolical plan by his fucking brother or his whole fucked-up family.

He didn't even visit me in the hospital.

Not that I'm butthurt about that or thinking about it on a daily basis or anything equally crazy.

We're *done.*

Yeah, right. You haven't moved on a fucking inch.

I could swear I heard his voice when I was sleeping and even saw him sitting in the chair beside my hospital bed and felt him stroking my hair. But then again, I've often been delusional when it comes to him.

Sometimes, I pictured him walking out from the penthouse elevator.

Other times, I imagined he came up to kiss me in public.

The few times I fell into a deep sleep, I dreamed of his heartfelt smiles, erotic noises, and his head on my thigh.

He invaded my every waking and sleeping moment.

The harder I pushed my mind to forget him, the more persistently he haunted me. Oftentimes, I found myself in the penthouse just to be able to smell him or see his shadow in the kitchen fixing God knows what.

But I was *fine.* Fucking *perfect.* Except for bugging Jer to give me problems to solve and being at the fight club on a daily basis, everything else was *awesome.*

I don't deal with complications, so removing the major complication from my life was the most logical decision I'd ever made. I was proud of myself for making that choice. For extracting the tumor that was growing inside me. I no longer had to deal with his grouchy presence, his push-and-pull games, and his stupid mixed signals.

There was just his pesky fucking ghost that followed me everywhere and wouldn't leave me alone, but I was *handling* it.

I was fucking *okay.*

Until he sent me that goddamn text.

Just like that, the thin layer of ice I'd surrounded myself with melted away.

The asshole was right. I *can't* stay away from him.

I can force myself away, I can try to be the very thing I'm not—logical—but then I'll stalk him on social media and sometimes in real life.

From the shadows, like a motherfucking creep.

Now is one of those times.

I lean against my Harley, arms crossed and helmet on. I'm even wearing a leather jacket to be anonymous.

My gaze is on an NGO's building. This is his favorite charity—the one that organizes marathons and performs volunteer work around the island.

Naturally, Bran is one of their top volunteers since he has that kink for running.

What I love about this building is that the windows are large and I can see what's going on inside, even if I'm across the street pretending to be having coffee. I haven't touched the cup since I bought it, considering the helmet and all.

My eyes track Bran's movements as he carries some chairs to the other side of a giant hall and smiles at something his colleague, a rosy-cheeked curvy brunette, says.

It's his golden-boy smile, not exactly fake, but it's not genuine, either. He's mostly polite as he listens to her blabbering on and on like a fucking chatterbox.

He better stop smiling at her or she'll do a fast climb to the top of my shit list.

Would she stop fucking talking already?

I need to chill for one second, because we're not even together anymore.

Not that we were before.

He says something to his male colleague, and I also think about ways to make him die in his sleep, but the guy is not the problem. He mostly seems to engage in the conversation politely like most British people do.

The brunette, however, keeps following Bran from one end of the room to the other, buzzing around him like an annoying fucking bee.

She's obviously flirting—her eyes are droopy and she keeps twirling her hair and giggling like a fucking schoolgirl. Bran's body language never changes, though. He's smiling, yes, but he's in complete control of the situation.

I know exactly what he looks like when he's interested, and the girl isn't getting anything. Not a flaring of his nostrils, a bobbing of his Adam's apple, or even continuous eye contact.

Either he's too oblivious to her attempts at catching his attention or he doesn't care.

Now, it'd be interesting if it was the second option—

She places her hand on his arm and I narrow my eyes. If she doesn't remove it, that hand will be broken into fucking pieces.

We need to rectify this situation.

I pull out my phone and stare at the text he sent me after the last time I saw him in the Elites' mansion basement.

> **Bran:** I'm sorry I couldn't get you out before everything that happened. I'm also really sorry about what my family did. I wish I could've stopped it.

> **Bran:** Are you okay?

> **Bran:** I know you don't want to talk to me, but can you please tell me if you're doing okay?

> **Bran:** ?

I ignored him.

If he really wanted to check on me, he should've gotten his ass to the hospital.

Not that I'm salty about that or anything.

Now, I type.

> **Me:** What the fuck is up with your 'friendship' with Mia?

He's still exchanging pleasantries with the girl as he takes out his phone from his pocket. His smile disappears upon looking at the screen and I take pride in how he looks a bit distraught at receiving a text from me.

There are more emotions in his face now than in the past hour. And yes, I've been here for that long.

Call it an unhealthy fucking obsession.

He distances himself from the girl—*in your face*—and leans against a table, ankles crossed, as he continues staring at the screen. He does that for a full fucking minute. I know, because I'm looking at the time.

Finally, my phone lights up.

Bran: We're just friends. We love gaming.

Dry as the fucking desert.

Bran remains in the same position, watching his phone. From the outside looking in, he seems composed and unaffected, but the fact that he's waiting is a sign of his messed-up equilibrium.

Me: You want me to believe that?

Bran: Why wouldn't you?

Me: The fact that you suspiciously became friends with MY sister? How do I know you won't use her to get revenge against me or as your fucked-up version of camouflage like you did with Clara?

He glares at his phone and I can see the fire spreading from his eyes in waves.

Bran: I won't do that. Mia is really just a friend. Besides, why would I want revenge against you? We're already over, aren't we?

As I read his text, I watch him pulling at the hairs on his nape, his face tight, his shoulders hunched.

And the scene does something to me.

I know I'm falling back into the same pattern that I left—or pretended to. I'm letting him have his way because I can't fucking stay away from him.

Because ever since I sent him that text, I've been thinking about him more than if I were meeting him every day.

Because I haven't been able to fucking breathe since he disappeared, and now, I watch dumb Agatha Christie episodes because they remind me of him trying to explain the bland characters.

> **Me:** Do you want it to be over?

He stares at the phone, lips parting, and the incessant pulling at his hair comes to an abrupt halt.

> **Bran:** What is that supposed to mean? You're the one who told me we're done.

> **Me:** But you never told me what you want.

> **Bran:** Don't fuck with me, Nikolai.

> **Me:** You're the one who fucked with me first. You texted me and were talking big on the phone and even came to save me. Maybe you're the one who can't stay away from me.

> **Bran:** You're right. I can't. I tried and it's not working.

My jaw hits the floor as I read and reread his text to make sure this isn't another one of my delusional episodes.

Fuck. I can't believe he admitted that out loud.

Through text. But it still counts.

> **Me:** Does that mean you're miserable?

> **Bran:** Are you enjoying this?

> **Me:** Maybe. Gotta up my asshole game so I can match your energy.

> **Bran:** Rub it in, would you?

> **Me:** Oh, I will. You can count on it.

Bran: Are you okay? Glyn said you were, but I want to hear it from you.

Me: Meet me in the penthouse and I'll tell you.

Bran: When?

Me: Now.

I expect him to send me an excuse so we can meet later after he's done playing the golden boy and being with his friends. But then my phone lights up.

Bran: I'll be there in twenty.

Me: Come out now.

Bran: ?

Me: Look across the street.

His head whips up and then he looks at me with that adorable stupefied expression. I wave at him and he searches his surroundings before he texts me.

Bran: What are you doing here?

Me: Come out. I have a helmet and I'm fully dressed. No one will know it's me.

Bran: Go first. I'll follow in my car.

Me: You have two minutes to come outside or I'll go in there and it won't be pretty since I might actually break that girl's hand for touching you.

Bran: Don't. I'll be right out.

He mumbles something to an older lady in the back, and a few moments later, he storms out of the building. I expected him to be panicking about the possibility of being seen in public with me, but he seems more angry than panicked.

Interesting.

My gaze continues tracking his movements as he strides toward me, and fuck.

I missed seeing him up close in his elegant shirts and pants, looking so hot and fit. Though a part of me wishes he was a bit disheveled like I've been this entire time.

But then again, Bran has always been the personification of perfection. He handles himself with rigorous discipline and neurotic control. It's who he is. That's why he can be falling apart and look like he's detached.

I always thought it was a defense mechanism he'd developed, but against what, I don't know. Since he's a closed-off asshole and all that.

As soon as he stops in front of me, he watches me for a beat, even though he can't see anything.

After I throw away the untouched cup of coffee, I pass him the spare helmet and he shoves it on so that only his eyes are visible. They're intense and fucking angry, but I sense something different there. Lust as ferocious as mine. Longing that almost matches my own.

Almost.

"What on earth are you doing here? Are you a stalker?" he snaps.

"Maybe."

"You could've told me to come over."

"And you would've?"

"I am now, aren't I?" He releases a long sigh. "Let's just go."

"Hop on."

I throw my leg over the seat and rev the engine as Bran climbs on behind me and grabs the back of the seat for balance. Like he did the first time he was on my bike, which was coincidentally the first and only time anyone has ever been on my Harley.

No matter how many times others expressed their desire to ride it—and then me—I didn't like the idea of anyone else but me touching this baby.

For some reason, I don't mind when it's Bran. In fact, I wanted to get him in this position again after that first night he gave in.

The night after which I messed with his control in an irrevocable fashion. In return, he completely fucked me up.

I rev the engine again. "You can grab onto my shoulders. I don't bite."

"Sure about that?" he asks with a note of sarcasm.

"Okay. I don't bite when I'm riding."

I expect him to refuse since he's allergic to any public touching, but he must be comfortable with how the helmets disguise us, because his hands curl around the tops of my shoulders.

It's not on purpose, but my lips pull into a smile behind my helmet. Fuck. It's been so long since he had his hands on me, and even though annoying clothes separate us, I soak in the feel of his hands and his warmth radiating down my back.

He shifts behind me and I suck in a sharp inhale, breathing in his citrus and clover scent.

Fuck me.

The smell goes straight into my brain as if I sniffed a line of cocaine.

I slide down the road before I haul him over and do something that will definitely send him running.

It's windy and I don't reduce my speed. Gravity forces Bran to be glued to me, his chest pressed to my back, his fingers digging into my shoulders, and his thighs rubbing against mine.

Note to self: I should take him on more rides.

Though that depends on what he says tonight, because I won't let him have his way anymore.

It's time we do it *my* way.

I take a longer route to the penthouse, relishing the feel of his body pressed up against me. And just to fuck with him, I speed up.

His fingers grip my shoulders tighter.

"It's easier if you wrap your hands around my waist," I shout over the wind.

"No way in hell."

"No one will know it's us. Chill, my dude."

"I'm not your dude! And I'm not wrapping my arms around your waist like some girl."

"No girl has wrapped her arms around my waist while I'm riding. Simon might have, though," I taunt.

His blunt nails dig into my shoulders and I can feel them through the jacket. He's definitely not doing this to hold on to me.

"One more reason not to do it." He sounds strained, battling against the anger rolling off him in waves.

Did I mention that I love pushing his buttons?

"What if I tell you no one but you has been on my bike?"

"You just said Simon wrapped his arms around you."

"I was messing with you."

"Fuck you."

I hit the brakes for a bit and he slams further into my back. This time, he wraps his arms around my waist, fingers interlacing at my abs.

I could get used to this.

Just when I'm considering delaying the trip home, the floodgates open and rain pours down, and we're drenched in seconds.

"Fucking UK weather, am I right?" I shout.

I can feel the rumble of his chest against my back, but he speaks evenly. "It is what it is."

"Take it or leave it, huh?" I ask, and I'm not sure if it's about the weather anymore.

"I guess," he says quietly.

I get us to the building and park my bike in the underground parking lot, then hop off and remove my helmet.

Thankfully, I didn't get my hair wet. The rest of me is another story, though.

My movements come to a halt when I'm slammed by the most erotic view.

Bran's white T-shirt has turned transparent, sticking to his muscles and flashing his nipples in a striptease show. My dick twitches and I have to look up so I don't get an unwanted and entirely embarrassing erection.

I'm trying to prove a point, damn it.

Be cold.

Stay cool.

Don't fucking give in.

"This is a bit inconvenient," Bran mutters as he tries to unhook the strap at his chin.

I push his hand away and do it for him, then remove the helmet.

"I could've done it myself," he grumbles

"Or you could say thank you."

"Thanks."

Fuck me.

I'm not used to this docile part of him. Yes, he's polite and shit, but he's being extra careful today.

Almost as if he's walking on eggshells.

He glances at me and his eyes widen as they focus on my neck, probably on the Band-Aid there.

My gaze follows his hand as he reaches toward it, but then he fists it and jams it in his pocket. "Is that really okay?"

"Don't pretend that you care."

A frown appears between his brows. "Why wouldn't I?"

"Why would you?"

"Think what you will of me, but I don't like seeing you hurt."

"If that were true, you would've visited me at the hospital."

"I did—" He cuts himself off and looks away. "Doesn't matter."

"It does matter. Look at me."

He slowly does, and an uncharacteristic sheen of pain covers his face.

"You visited? How come I never saw you?"

"You were sleeping." He rubs the back of his head. "I managed to sneak past Jeremy and Gareth when they were speaking to the doctor. But I had to leave soon after since Lan came looking for me and was about to start more drama."

So he *was* there.

I wasn't imagining him sitting beside me and stroking my hair.

Is that tidbit supposed to make me feel this fucking giddy?

Cold. You have to be cold or this won't work.

I head to the elevator, not waiting to see if he follows. He does, trudging behind me. The trip is spent in suffocating silence aside from the sound of water dripping from our clothes onto the floor.

Or my struggle to stop myself from ogling his transparent shirt.

A part of me wants to corner him and feast on his lips, take my fill for the weeks he's been out of my life.

That's a lie.

Since I first saw him, he's never been out of my life. Not really.

I have to hold myself back and not touch him, not fall first this time, because if I do, I'll just slip back into the pattern I ended things for.

This time, it'll be different.

The elevator dings and I stroll inside the penthouse. Behind me, I can sense Bran watching the space as if relearning it or searching for something he left.

I go into the bedroom and come back with towels and a change of clothes.

He nods and clears his throat as if chasing away something stuck there. "Thanks."

I say nothing as I walk back into the bedroom, strip down, dry myself, and then put on shorts.

Forget about the shirt. I don't like them and I won't pretend to now.

When I return to the living room, I find Bran has also changed into the gray shorts and white T-shirt I gave him. They're loose and unflattering, but he'd look annoyingly hot in a potato sack.

Also, I really, *really* love seeing him in my clothes. I have to look away because I'm starting to get hard at the view.

He's putting his things in the washing machine and calls out, "Nikolai, bring your wet clothes when you're finished."

Even though I'm already here, I go back and get everything I left on the bathroom floor.

There's no other way to describe the look he gives me other than snobbish disregard.

"You couldn't put them in something? They're dripping all over the place."

"Okay, Mom," I mock.

He yanks the clothes from my hands with an exasperated sigh

and puts them in with his—except the white shirt that he has on the rack near the balcony door. No whites with colors is apparently a rule when doing laundry.

He reaches into the cabinet above him and brings out the detergent, softener, and some other thing that's apparently good for the skin. Once he's done with that useless routine, he sets the washing machine program.

Then he walks to the kitchen, puts the kettle on—that he bought, because I couldn't care less for tea—and retrieves some herbal tea infusions that have remained untouched since he stopped coming here.

I can't help standing there and watching him move around the area as if he never left. His movements are easier now, and he no longer looks like he's walking on thin ice around me.

"You don't have milk?" he asks, head shoved in the fridge.

"No, Grandma," I mock again.

He glares at me. "Why are you like this?"

"Like what?"

"Completely unorganized. You're no different than a savage."

I throw my weight on the sofa and splay my arm on the back. "More like you're neurotically organized."

"I just like things in order."

"Isn't that a thing called OCD?"

"No, it's not. Don't throw those terms around if you don't understand them."

"Yes, sir."

He grabs the kettle and gives me the side-eye. "Are you done being sarcastic?"

"Are you done nitpicking?"

He shakes his head with clear displeasure.

Usually, I'd grin and even get in his space, but I'm trying to be cold, so I just watch him.

I missed having him here, even if he's always being an asshole about everything. It was like a fucking prison without him.

Right now, it feels as if he never left.

He pours the hot water in a transparent pot over the herbs, then he puts it on a tray with two cups and brings it over.

Bran sits across from me with the tray on the coffee table between us. The sound of the thunderstorm and pouring rain is the only noise for a while.

"What's the stupid herbal tea name this time?"

"Lemon and ginger," he says and then looks at his watch to measure the time.

If it were the past, I would've filled the silence and pounced on any opportunity to talk to him, be near him. I would've been right beside him by now, either coaxing his head on my thigh or using his as a pillow.

Right now, however, I force myself to remain both still and silent, my fingers digging into the back of the sofa to stop them from doing something stupid and ruining my plan.

Bran stares at his watch for what seems like forever before he finally looks up and releases a long sigh. "Why did you bring me here?"

"To hear your answer to my question earlier. Do you want us to be over?"

His Adam's apple bobs up and down as he swallows. Lightning strikes, casting a harsh glow on his handsome face as thunder rumbles in the distance. The silence stretches for a few heavy seconds before he bows his head and shakes it once.

I have to suppress a smile because, fuck me, he's so damn hot.

Can I just fuck him?

No, Kolya. Control your fucking libido for once and stay on standby.

"Use your words. And look at me."

He slowly lifts his head, his eyes plunging into mine. Rain beating down on the roof lingers for a few agonizing beats before he speaks in a strained voice. "Do I have to say it?"

"Uh-huh."

"I don't want to end it." His voice is so low, I can barely hear him. "Happy now?"

"No."

"What... Why?"

"I won't go back to the way things were."

His lips part and he pulls on his stupid hair as his voice comes out strained, choked, even. "Then why did you ask? Why did you bring me here? Is this…a game?"

"Maybe."

"If you think you can play me—"

"Why the fuck can't I? Didn't you play me enough?"

"I…did not."

"We have different opinions about that." I lean closer in my seat. "Here's how it will go, Brandon. I don't give a fuck if you come out or not. That's your decision. But you will *not* leave after every time either."

"But everyone at home—"

"I'm not hearing it. If you want me, this is how you'll get me."

"And if I can't?"

"The door is right there. Don't let it hit you on the way out."

The veins in his neck nearly pop and he grabs his hair tighter, pulling, tugging. I can see the war in his eyes and I don't like it. I don't like that he's hurting himself, and part of me wants to stop it.

But I don't. Because Bran is the type who needs to be pushed off his high fucking horse.

He's teetering on the edge, I can feel it and taste his conflict in the air.

One more shove.

I take out my phone. "What's it going to be, posh boy? Let me know if you're leaving so I can call someone else."

His eyes flash in terrifying rage and he drops his hand as his muscles tighten. No more conflict or anxiety rolls off him in waves. The only thing that remains is the coiling anger that hardens his eyes.

"So that's your goal? Getting rid of me to return to your fuck buddies?"

"Why would you care?"

He jumps up, rounds the table, and climbs on top of me. He fists my hair, his knees pressing on either side of me. His body hovers over mine, vibrating with tension even as his voice comes out steady, threatening. "Have you touched someone else, Nikolai? Hmm?"

I stare up at him, clenching and unclenching my hand on the sofa to keep from grabbing his hip or his back. Anywhere I can touch him. God, I fucking missed the heat rolling off him and the feel of his skin on mine.

Just one more push. A tiny one.

"Why are you asking? Jealous?"

"Don't fuck with me. I didn't even agree to the damn breakup, so technically, we were never done. So tell me, Nikolai. Who did you fuck? Simon? Someone else? Couldn't keep it in your pants, right? You're pathetic."

"If I'm pathetic, then what are you? Delusional?"

"If you don't tell me, I'm walking out right now. Who was it? Who took my fucking place?"

"No one."

His eyes widen and his grip loosens around my hair, even as he keeps me in place. "Really?"

"Really."

"No one came here?"

"No."

"Why?"

Because this is our place and no one else is allowed in it.

But instead of saying that, I lift a shoulder. "What about you? Did you fuck anyone else? I'm going to need names and addresses."

"You're mental." He smiles a little before he shakes his head. "There was no one. I don't even like sex."

"You obviously do."

"Only with you," he whispers, his fingers stroking my pulse point beside the bandage.

Only with you.

Pride swells inside me and I want to probe about that, but that's not for now, so I ask the most important question. "Does that mean you'll stay?"

His answer comes in the most beautiful form.

My lotus flower sighs with resignation as he crashes his lips to mine.

TWENTY-THREE

Brandon

I HAVE SURVIVED WEEKS BARELY ABLE TO BREATHE, SO THE RUSH of life that ripples through me feels foreign.

Intoxicating.

Addicting.

I'm trapped again, completely helpless in the arms of the man who flipped my world upside down and refuses to leave.

The man because of whom I've barely slept since last week, sick with a level of concern I've never felt. Not even for myself.

I plunge my tongue against his and kiss him deeper, my fingers tugging and pulling on his hair until he groans in my mouth.

Until I'm drunk on his taste, his smell, and his warmth. On his breath and the feel of his flexing muscles beneath mine.

But most importantly, on the pulse that beats in his throat.

He's alive.

He's here.

His hands land on my hips, tugging me against him as he kisses me with the same ferocity, digging himself into that nook in my chest even *I* have no access to.

But I don't care.

As long as I can feel his heartbeat thundering against my chest, as long as I can hear his growls of pleasure, as long as I can smell his intoxicating scent, I can flounder in self-hatred afterward.

I can take on those vicious voices.

I can pretend I'm not an entity of emptiness with no sense of identity whatsoever.

I can take *anything* as long as I have him.

Because Nikolai is the only one who kisses the pain out of me, even if temporarily.

I trace my lips over his jaw, his high cheekbone, and then down his neck, careful not to touch the plaster covering the injury.

The vibration of his groan sends a shudder through me that ends in my hardening cock.

"I'm sorry," I whisper, kissing around the plaster over and over. "So sorry."

And it's not only because I couldn't save him in time.

I'm sorry about being a coward who can't kiss him in public but hungers for him in private.

I'm sorry that I retreated after he ended things when I should've fought for him.

But most of all, I'm sorry that he even wants me.

I need him in ways words can't express, and he's the only person I can do this with, but he can have anyone he wants, considering he's infinitely secure in his sexuality.

I'm not secure in my body, my sexuality, or my own fucking head.

But he touches me as if he's blind to all those flaws.

He touches me as if I'm normal, and I need that. I fucking *crave* it.

"It's not your fault." He speaks in that low, growly voice as he reaches a hand beneath my shirt and digs his fingers into my sides. "Stop apologizing for shit you didn't do."

Instead of replying, I kiss my way down his inky chest, over his necklace, and nibble on his nipple. I'm rewarded with the rumbling of his voice and the clenching of his muscles.

"You like that?" I ask as I pinch his other nipple.

"Mmm. I like your tongue anywhere."

I smile against his nipple, tugging on it before I continue down, peppering kisses all over the different shapes and forms of his tattoos. He's criminally attractive and he knows it so well, which is why he often parades around half naked.

The thought of others enjoying his beauty turns me murderous.

But he's had no one since me.

That thought makes me hum with pleasure against his abs. No one can touch him but me.

His noises of desire are mine.

His body is mine.

He's all *mine.*

I tug on the drawstring of his shorts with my teeth and look up at him.

My breath catches when I find his eyes darkening with unhinged lust as he watches me.

"Fucking beautiful."

My heart thumps louder. I've missed those words and that look. I've fucking missed being looked at as if he really thinks I'm beautiful.

I never even considered that I could be beautiful until him.

Maintaining eye contact, I undo the drawstring and pull his shorts down.

And fuck.

He's gone commando. Of course he has. This is Nikolai and he's deeply allergic to clothes.

I drop to my knees between his legs and fist his hard cock, jerking him up and down in a slow rhythm.

"Mmm." The noise he releases makes me fucking ravenous and my dick thickens against my shorts. "You're on your knees."

"For you."

"For *me.* I like the sound of that." His fingers thread in my hair. "Choke on my cock. Make it sloppy and wet so I can fuck you."

"Call me baby." I flick my tongue over his crown, teasing the piercing and licking the precum.

"Missed your nickname?"

I squeeze until he groans, but I'm not sure whether it's in pleasure or pain. With Nikolai, it could easily be both.

"Do it." I speak around his crown, sucking it inside and then nibbling on the piercings with my teeth.

"Stop fucking around and put my cock in your mouth, baby."

A shudder spreads through me and I take as much as possible of his length, all the way to the back of my throat, and swallow around his pierced crown.

Nikolai curses in long, unintelligible strings of words and I squeeze his balls.

"Ummm," I moan when he thickens against my tongue.

"Jesus fuck, baby. Your mouth feels so fucking good…"

I lick him faster, armed with the knowledge I've gathered during all this time. Nikolai loves to be sucked, but there's something else he goes feral for.

I pull his cock out, tugging on a piercing with my teeth before I release him with a pop.

My eyes meet his hooded ones. "Hey, Niko?"

"Mmm? Why did you stop?"

"I want you to fuck my throat."

His eyes widen the slightest bit before they flood with twisted desire and something else I can't put my finger on.

"Fucking fuck." He fists the top of my hair and tugs my head back. I follow, lips open and my fingers still squeezing his balls. "You're the hottest fucking thing I've ever seen."

Bloody hell.

He *means* it.

Why…?

Before I can think, he thrusts all the way to the back of my throat. I widen and loosen my jaw so he can go as far as possible. I'm extremely proud that I don't have a gag reflex.

I want to bring him pleasure as intense as he gives me.

"Holyfuckinghell. You're taking my cock so well. Mmm, I fucking love how you swallow around my crown…" His hips jerk back and forth against the sofa as he fucks my throat.

He takes and takes and gives me the most beautiful view in return. His face.

I love that I'm the reason he looks elated, *high*, even, as if he, like me, is addicted to the mad friction that happens whenever we touch.

"Open wider, baby. That's it... Jesus fuck...I love how you choke on my cock. Mmm... Did you miss this?"

I nod, but I'm not sure if it's visible with the harsh grip he has on my hair.

"Good. Because I missed your beautiful little face when it's stuffed with my cock."

My own cock leaks in my shorts at his dirty mouth.

His rhythm turns wild, his piercing bumping at the back of my throat with every thrust. Pressure forms behind my eyes, but I don't give a fuck. I take whatever he has to lash out at me. I need it.

I need *him*.

Precum and saliva gather in my mouth and I swallow the way he likes it, causing the muscles of my throat to constrict around his crown. His growl is music to my fucking ears, so I do it again and he tightens his grip on my hair, messing it up as much as he's screwing my entire life over.

"You need to stop that or I'll come down your throat."

I squeeze his balls, encouraging him, trying to push him over the edge. I'm so close myself. When he comes, I'll just need to stroke myself a few times and I'll join him.

All of a sudden, Nikolai drags his cock out of my mouth and I'm forced to release him.

My lungs burn from the sudden rush of air and I pant as I swallow thickly. "Why...don't stop..."

"I love your mouth, but I need to come in your ass, baby." He jerks up, kicks away his shorts so that he's standing in front of me in his full, beautiful glory.

Ah, fuck.

I didn't realize how much I missed his shameless nudity until now. I've become so accustomed to the view and the feel of his marble-like, extensively tattooed body that everything felt colorless after him.

Using his grip on my hair, he tugs me up and pulls on the corner of my T-shirt. "I love how you look in my clothes, but this needs to go."

He helps me remove the shirt and I fumble with my shorts until they're pooling at my ankles and then I kick them off.

Yes. I'm commando as well.

I won't make it a habit, but I like the savage look in his eyes as they take in the entirety of me.

"Hot motherfucker." Nikolai leans over and bites on my Adam's apple, making me gasp. "I missed your voice and even your annoying fucking nagging."

My fingers find their way to his hair and I press him to my chest. I can't have him close enough. Touch him deep enough. Soak in him long enough.

"Arms around my neck," he orders.

When I do that, still stroking his hair, he slaps his palms on my arse cheeks and presses his cock to mine. I bury my face in his hair, inhaling his smell as I groan and hump against him. Sparks of pleasure pool in my groin. With every slide of flesh against flesh, our precum trickles over our cocks and we rub a few more times.

Nikolai pushes me up. "Hop on. Wrap your legs around my waist."

"I'm not light…"

"Do it. Now."

Grabbing onto his neck, I maneuver myself and Nikolai helps me up and I cross my legs at his back, heels digging in his arse.

I thought it'd feel awkward, but surprisingly, I hold on to the balance, and Nikolai doesn't seem to mind that I'm wrapped all around him in a koala embrace.

In retrospect, I might be enjoying this a bit too much since my hard cock that's trapped between us pulses and drips all over my abs.

He kneads my arse and nibbles on my jaw as he walks to the bedroom. "That's it. Good boy."

"I'm not a boy. I'm *older* than you."

"Age is a number, and you're definitely my good boy, baby."

He tilts forward and we drop into a mess of limbs on the bed.

His chest collides with mine, but I don't mind. He could crush me and I wouldn't complain.

It's okay.

If it's him, it's okay.

That thought fills me with a different type of dread.

Does this mean I *trust* him? The mafia prince who winds down by punching people?

My thoughts scatter when he reaches beneath the pillow and produces a bottle of lube.

"Do you always have that on the ready?" I ask and hum a grunt when his piercing scrapes my cock.

"Yup. I never know when you're going to grace me with your presence."

He pushes back so he's kneeling between my parted legs, and I mourn the loss of his body against mine, but then I'm distracted when he squirts the lube straight on his cock.

I lean on my elbows, watching him as he rubs himself up and down in violent strokes that leave my mouth agape.

"Aw, you drooling baby?"

"Shut up…"

"You love my cock that much, hmm?"

"Stop talking, Nikolai."

"Mmm. Love it when you get all bossy and wound up." He swirls his slick, shiny fingers against his crown and I want to push them away and take over the task.

"Here." He throws me the bottle of lube. "Make your hole dripping wet so I can fuck you, baby."

"Jesus," I breathe out as I struggle to open the thing.

He really knows how to undo a man with his words and damn fucking presence.

I squirt the cold gel on my palm and open my legs farther, then lift my arse before I press it against my rim.

A gasp falls out of me when I find Nikolai watching me with depraved intensity and flaring nostrils, his strokes slowing down.

"Fuck yourself for me. Let me see your fingers plunging in and out of your hole."

A rush of lust overwhelms me and I bite my lower lip as I breach myself with a finger. My muscles tighten around it and I groan.

"Did you touch yourself back there while we were apart, baby?"

I nod, focusing on his tattooed hand that squeezes his length. My cock leaks all over my stomach at the view.

"Mmm, naughty. Did you imagine it was my fingers driving into you?"

I shake my head and add another finger, fucking myself in the same rhythm he touches himself and trying not to get too excited, because I want to come while he fucks me.

"Then what did you imagine?"

"I imagined...ummfuck... I imagined you were fucking me with your cock."

"Fuck, baby. I need inside you. Now."

I remove my fingers and trace them on his chest. "Stop talking and fuck me."

"Mmm. Talk dirty to me."

"I need your cock inside me."

"More."

"I want you to pound me until I'm screaming."

"Fucking more."

"Fuck me until you fill me with your cum."

"Oh fuck. Where did you learn to talk like that?"

"From you."

His face erupts in a gorgeous grin as he lifts my legs and throws them over his broad shoulders. Our eyes collide as he drives into me. Agonizingly slow. So slow that sweat beads on Nikolai's forehead and sticks his hair to his temples. His brows furrow as he obviously restrains himself to not thrust all the way in.

A shiver goes through me and it feels like forever before he's fully sheathed inside me.

It's been a long time since Nikolai last fucked me, and I almost forgot just how huge he is. It often burns when he first buries himself in me, but he always, without exception, gives me time to adjust.

We're both panting, our chests slick with sweat as we bask in the moment, our ragged breathing echoing in the air.

The only other sound is the rain beating down on the ceiling.

A droplet of sweat rolls down his brow and falls on the corner of my mouth. I dart out my tongue and lick it then bite my lip. Nikolai's eyes rage a dark blue as he expels a large breath.

"Fuck. I missed your ass. I love how it swallows me whole. Mmm. Can you feel how you're welcoming me home?"

"Ummfuck..."

"You're my favorite fuck hole, baby."

"S-shut your mouth, Nikolai."

"Make me."

I grab a handful of his hair and tug him down, smashing his lips with mine.

It's a mess of tongues, teeth, and lips as he drives into me. Slow and shallow at first, but the longer I kiss him, the faster he finds his rhythm and pounds me like a madman.

The back and forth of his abs creates friction on my rock-hard dick, milking it until precum splutters all over us.

Through it all, he doesn't stop kissing me, doesn't stop binding me to him one thrust at a time.

My body is a mess of overstimulation, but it's my battered heart and nonexistent soul that are fucked over.

I dig my fingers in his back, feeling my balls fill up and my cock ready to burst.

Nikolai pulls away from my lips and reaches between us, then squeezes my cock, his thumb pressing savagely on the tip.

"Don't come until I tell you to."

"Fuck... No..." I tug on his hair, wiggling my arse to chase the pleasure. "I'm going to come..."

"Not yet." His thumb blocks my opening as he goes harder, his piercing brushing against my sensitive spot with every thrust.

I thrash on the mattress, mumbled voices slipping from my throat as the pleasure builds to an exasperating high.

"Niko…please…please…fuck…"

I want to come. I want to come. I want to come.

The thoughts repeat in my head like a chant. My vision becomes blurry and I let out what sounds like a pathetic whimper.

"Let me come…please…please…" I'm begging at this point, my whole body tightening, my abs contracting, and my balls aching.

"Say you missed me."

"W-what?"

"During the time we were apart, tell me you fucking missed me. Even if it's a lie, say it."

"I did…I missed you… I missed you so fucking much." I feel a rush of air whooshing out of me with the words.

I don't think I've ever said anything that I felt to my core like those words.

Because yes, I missed him. I missed him to the point of insanity. I missed him until I couldn't breathe.

And the only reason I can suck air into my starved lungs is because he's touching me again.

"Come for me, baby." He releases my tip and squeezes my balls.

"Ummfuck…Niko…fuck…I'm coming for you…" My cock jerks and my cum splatters all over my abs, his hand, and the sheets. Everywhere.

"Love it when you make a mess." He thrusts faster, his muscles tightening and a vein popping in his neck. "I love it when you come."

"Umm…" I'm still groaning, riding my orgasm as my cock slowly withers to half erect.

"Wanna know what you look like when you come?" He speaks against my lips, his breath stroking my skin and his intense eyes swallowing me in their depths. "You look like fucking mine."

My cock twitches, trying to force its way back to life as he bites my lower lip and fills my arse with his cum.

He comes hard and he keeps coming, until I milk him of every last drop.

Our slick chests press together and I glide my fingers into his half-damp hair, bringing him closer and wrapping my legs around his waist. Then I do what we both love.

I kiss him deep and hard, trying to brand myself under his skin so he'll never leave me again.

Nikolai pulls out of me and I can feel cum dripping onto the mattress. But before I can fall into that sensation, he wrenches his lips from mine and flips me onto my stomach.

I glance behind me and my lips fall open at the decadent desire shining through his eyes.

Blood rushes to my groin and my cock stands at full attention.

"Get on your hands and knees, baby. I'm going to fuck you again. This time, like an animal."

TWENTY-FOUR

Brandon

AFTER A LONG BATTLE WITH THE IMAGE IN THE MIRROR, I manage to cut eye contact and drag myself out of the bathroom.

The more intense the pleasure, the more crippling the pain.

The longer I forget, the more cruelly my head torments me.

But I'm done with my daily dose of self-loathing now. I'm fine.

Probably.

Hopefully.

I step into the bedroom with a towel wrapped around my middle and another one drying my hair.

My feet come to a halt when I don't find Nikolai waiting. Usually, he'd be doing push-ups, punching the air, or pacing like a caged lion.

Though he did say he'd take a shower in the second bathroom down the hall. Maybe he also takes long showers.

I put on a pair of his shorts and a gray T-shirt, then pause when his cologne fills my nostrils. My fingers bunch the cloth and I lift it to my nose to drag in a long inhale.

For some reason, his rich, masculine scent has a calming effect on me.

He has a calming effect on me.

I linger in the bedroom and stare at the bed. Earlier, I made him help me change the sheets as he grumbled about my OCD, but now, I can't help thinking about the fact that I'm staying the night.

What do people do in these situations? I've never stayed the night with anyone before. It's just not me.

I loathe the idea of being too close, of letting myself too loose.

But I guess I'll have to cope for Nikolai.

I'm terrified that once he cracks me open, he'll find me revolting. He'll see me as I see myself in the mirror—as a black hole of nothingness.

I want to run and hide, but that means losing him.

So I stay.

It's the least I can do.

Better pray he doesn't finally see you for the basket case you truly are.

I try to ignore that voice as I walk out of the bedroom. Should I go check on him in the shower?

Honestly, I wouldn't be surprised if he's punching the air as if it's his demons. I just want to make sure he's okay, considering he falls asleep in weird positions.

My steps are silent as I walk down the hall and knock on the bathroom door. "Nikolai?"

No answer.

I knock again. "Is everything okay?"

Nothing.

My breaths are choppy as I grab the doorknob. "I'm coming in."

My heart nearly hits the floor when I find the water flowing out of the Jacuzzi bathtub and Nikolai submerged.

No, no, no…

A ringing floods my ears as I run toward him, drop to my knees, and thrust my hands into the water to grab his shoulders.

I should've checked on him earlier. If anything happens to him, I'll never forgive myself—

His eyes pop open and he grins, then speaks in the water, bubbles erupting everywhere before he lifts his head.

I fall to my arse, air leaving me in long doses. Jesus Christ. Why does it feel like I just died and was resurrected?

"Lotus flower? What are you doing here? Oh! Wanna join me?"

"Why the fuck—" I cut myself off and speak in a calmer tone. "Why were you underwater?"

"Meditating."

"Meditating?"

"Yeah." He grins. "I can hold my breath for over four minutes."

"Let me get this straight. You meditate by holding your breath underwater?"

"Yup. Want me to teach you?"

"You're seriously fucking mental."

"Is that a good thing?" He shakes his head, sending water flying everywhere.

"No, it's not. And *stop* that. Are you a dog?"

"Woof." He grabs my cheeks with wet fingers. "Let me lick your face."

"Hard pass." I push him away and stand up, shoving my hand behind my back to hide how much I'm shaking. "Don't do that again. It's dangerous. You could fall asleep and drown."

"I love it when you're worried about me, baby."

"Just come out." I head to the door and throw a glance behind me. "And you better clean up this mess."

"Okay, Mom!" he shouts behind me.

I head back to the bedroom and change into a dry T-shirt and shorts.

Wearing his clothes feels is like I'm wrapped up in the cocoon of his arms. It's weirdly intimate.

A good weird, though.

Sitting on the edge of the bed, I check on my cousin Creighton. Uncle Aiden took him back to London after he nearly managed to get himself killed. And while I hate that he dragged Nikolai down with him and he's the main reason why Nikolai even slit his throat, Creigh got the short end of the stick. We really thought he wouldn't make it.

Although he's alive, he's been in a foul mood, and I worry about him.

He does reply to me, though it's monosyllabic. It's enough for now.

I text Remi, then tell him and Lan that I'm staying the night at the school's art studio to finish a project.

They reply right away.

> **Remi:** Mate, I'm telling you this with the sincerest love, but the only time you should spend the night somewhere is if you're shagging. Don't be a nerd.

If only he knew the truth.

> **Lan:** What project?

Of course he'd be suspicious. It wouldn't be Lan otherwise. But for some reason, I like that he checks on me all the time. Even if he's doing it out of a sense of narcissism. Being his identical twin means I can't reflect badly on his pristine image.

> **Me:** One of those you call boring. Sorry I'm not up to your level.

> **Lan:** Little bro, I'm telling you for the millionth time that you are up to my level if you quit restraining yourself. You used to make masterpieces without a single thought, but now that you're THINKING instead of CREATING, it's a fucking chore to see your work. But then again, no one listens to Lan, even though he's always right.

The door bangs against the wall and I lift my head to see Nikolai walking in, entirely naked while drying his hair with a towel.

I place my phone on the side table and release an exasperated sigh. "You couldn't put clothes on?"

"Clothes are overrated. People should thank me for wearing them in public." He tilts his head to the side. "Besides, we've already seen each other naked, so maybe you're the one who should strip."

"No, thanks."

He lifts a shoulder. "Worth a try."

I reach into the wardrobe's drawer and toss him a pair of boxer briefs. "At least put those on."

"Fine." He throws the towel on the bed and mutters, "Prude."

"I heard that and, seriously, hang up your towels, Nikolai."

He rolls his eyes as he slides the boxer briefs up his muscular thighs and snaps the elastic band with a playful tug.

I drape the towel on a clothes hanger. "Can I ask you something?"

"Why do you need to request permission to ask me something?"

"It's the polite thing to do."

"Don't do that with me. I don't ask permission when I bombard you with questions."

"You don't say."

"Hey! Was that sarcasm? The infamous passive-aggressiveness?"

"I don't know what you're talking about."

He chuckles, the sound smooth and so joyful, I can't help the smile that twitches my lips.

"Ask away, baby."

"Why do you sleep in weird places?"

"I don't like beds." He sits on it. "It's not that I don't *want* to sleep in one, I just can't."

"Is it because of something that happened?"

"Hmm." He shakes his head, sending droplets of water everywhere.

"Nikolai!"

"What?"

"Dry your hair."

"Why? It'll dry on its own."

I pinch the bridge of my nose and point at the stool in front of the vanity. "Sit down."

He jumps up and plops down on the seat and grins at me through the mirror as I turn on the hairdryer on the lowest setting, medium heat, and start drying his hair.

"So?" I ask, not meeting his gaze. "You were going to tell me if sleeping in strange positions has to do with a certain incident."

"Oh! Sorry, I got distracted by how fucking hot you look with your hair messy."

"Nikolai, focus."

He releases a sigh. "I started sleeping this way in my teens. It was around the time my episodes began."

My fingers pause in his hair. "What type of episodes?"

"High energy. Racing thoughts. Uncontainable need for more, more, and fucking more. I had it that day when I fought Kill and beat him to a pulp while you were flirting with Eva."

"Her name is Ava and I was *not* flirting with her." My mind goes back to that time, to when his eyes were red and he looked to be on edge. So I was right to think something was wrong. His gaze was empty and for a moment, I thought he didn't see me.

"She was hugging you."

"We're childhood friends."

"Still don't like it." He pouts like a fucking child and I have to stop myself from smiling at how adorable he looks. Jesus. He's this big tattooed guy who's larger than life and part of the mafia, but he still acts this way.

Around me.

Only me.

I glide my fingers through his hair, lingering in every spot a bit too long. "Back to the subject at hand, do those episodes happen often?"

"Not really. I have them under control."

"You didn't look that much in control that day."

"That was because you were being an asshole."

"Me? What do I have to do with it?"

He strokes his necklace. "Nothing."

I want to probe some more, but he meets my gaze in the mirror. "Oh, right. I wanted to ask you something as well."

"Hmm?"

"Why do you not like sex?"

My fingers freeze in his hair and I swallow as I meet his gaze. "What do you mean?"

"You said you don't even like sex, but you do with me. Why didn't you before?"

"Not all of us enjoy the activity."

"Why not? Is it because you only did it with girls?"

God. I can't believe he's the first person I'm telling this. But he's been so open with me, the least I can do is share something in return. I don't like the rejected look in his eyes whenever I refuse to answer his questions.

"It's not that. I never looked at a person, of any gender, and felt attracted to them or wanted to have sex with them. I never got hard by external stimuli unless I forced myself into the mood. The concept of being aroused due to seeing erotic images or watching people fucking is foreign to me. I never touched myself unless I needed to get myself hard for sex. Never liked porn or understood other men's need to shag all the time. If it were up to me, I'd happily go celibate for years."

I stop before I say 'Or I would've in the past.' I clearly missed his touch while we weren't together.

The thought of being without it again triggers a queasy feeling at the base of my stomach.

"Baby, I don't want to put a label on you since you hate that shit—I do, too, by the way—but that's a bit ace. Uh, I mean asexual, if you've heard of that term."

"I figured I am. Or I *was*. I don't even know what I am anymore."

"But…you did have sex."

"Because it was expected, not because I wanted to. My releases were always a physical reaction that never affected me mentally. I just never enjoyed the act. It was more of a chore, really… Why are you smiling like a fool?"

"I just can't help but feel proud that I made you enjoy the glorious act of fucking."

"Shut up." I turn off the hairdryer.

"You just needed a good fucking by yours truly."

"Nikolai!"

He stands up and wraps his arms around my waist, then glides his fingers beneath the shirt to stroke my skin.

I can't believe I'm thinking this, but I missed his clinginess.

"Bet if I kissed you a little bit, you'll get in the mood right away. Want to test it?"

"No."

"Baby, please?" He speaks against my lips and presses his chest to mine.

I breathe heavily even as I plant both hands on his chest. "We already went three rounds."

"I can do ten. I can't get enough of you. How about this? Let's bet how many times I can make you come."

"Don't."

"Your body and mouth sing a very different tune. Your push-and-pull game is spot on." He darts out his tongue and licks my bottom lip and it trembles beneath his touch. "Did you play it with others before me?"

"No..." I'm surprised my voice comes out steady.

"Because you didn't want them, but you want me?"

"Shut up."

"Since when did you start to want me?" he whispers against my ear. "Was it when I pinned you down in the forest? Or was it after you sat on my lap?"

"You wish."

"Mmm." He bites on the shell of my ear and I let out a groan. "I love that I'm the only one who sees you like this, all hot and bothered and fucking mine."

I sink my fingers in his silky strands and tug his head back so that I'm looking down on him. "You're mine, not the other way around."

"It's not a competition. I can be yours while you're mine." He grins. "Love these sudden bursts of possessiveness, baby. You better not have had them with others."

"Hypocritical much? You literally shag everyone."

"Not everyone... Well, I'm open, I guess, but that was in the past. I'm no longer a manwhore, I swear on Kolya's honor."

I fist his hair tighter. "Who the hell is Kolya?"

"Hi, lotus flower." He rubs his erection against mine. "My name is Kolya and I'm obsessed with your huge cock and beautiful ass."

I burst out laughing. I can't help it. "You named your dick?"

"Everyone does."

"No, they don't."

"Yes, they do."

"If you say so. Why Kolya?"

"That's the Russian diminutive form of my name. No one but my grandpa and my dad's side of the family uses it, though."

"And how long has *Kolya* been active?"

"Since I was five?"

"Please don't tell me you had sex at five."

"No. I had my first gorgeous boner then. Didn't go well with my mom and everyone in the house when I ran around naked showing it to everyone and pretending it was a gun."

I chuckle. "Why can I imagine that?"

"You also think it was hilarious, right? I was seriously proud. Only Dad backed up my shenanigans."

"He seems cool."

"Coolest dad ever. Before I hit puberty, he sat me down and said, 'You're about to go on that adventure you've waited for since you were five. Now is the time you can actually use your dick as a gun. Do your thing, son. Just use protection and don't make me a grandpa.'"

"How…did he take your sexuality? If you came out to them." I pause. "If you don't mind me asking?"

"I don't mind any of your questions, baby. Seriously, stop being annoyingly British. To answer you, I didn't have to come out. Mom and Dad walked in on me fucking a guy and kissing a girl at fifteen. They were shocked, but not in a judgmental way. Mom already felt I liked guys since I'd wink at them like I did girls. She just wasn't sure. Dad…well, he was like, 'Of course you would like the variety. It wouldn't be you otherwise.' Then he hugged me and whispered, 'You better use protection and not make me a grandfather when I'm this young, motherfucker. I mean it.' He's effortlessly hilarious, my dad. Oh, he's also British."

"Really?"

"Well, he has a complicated family history and he definitely has Russian blood, but he was raised in the UK and speaks in your accent."

"What's his name?"

"Kyle Hunter."

"Hmm. I think I might've heard of him in Grandpa's circle. Wait. Your last name is Sokolov, not Hunter."

"It's after Mom. Since Dad had a few last names and Mom's last name belongs to Russian Bratva royalty, they decided to give it to their children. Nikolai Sokolov is actually my late great-grandfather's name. I'm his gorgeous incarnation."

I smile and shake my head. "I'm glad your family is acceptant despite, well, being in the mafia."

"Mom and Dad are. My aunt and uncle—Kill and Gareth's parents—too. Everyone else…meh, they're still backward. I wouldn't take a guy to meet my grandpa or uncles, for instance. That'd just turn ugly and no one needs that."

"Does that mean you took a guy to meet your parents?"

"Does it count when they walk in on me? Because that was the only meetings that happened."

"Jesus. You have more sex than Zeus."

"Who's that? A porn star?"

"Please tell me you're kidding."

He squints. "Pretty sure I've heard about him before. Is he an actor?"

"He's a Greek god."

"And he was a porn star?"

"No. He just…let's say he shagged a lot. Like you."

"Don't be jealous, baby."

"I am not."

"Well, I am."

"Of who?"

"Fucking Clara and everyone who saw you naked."

"You need help." I suppress a smile. "You're the one who's had more sex than me."

"Yeah, but I've never had a relationship and I don't feel fucking murderous about them like I do with you."

My lips part and I clear my throat. "My relationships were a façade. I never...cared about them."

"And you care about me?"

"Shut up." I wiggle free of his hold. "I'm going to sleep."

"Wait for me!"

A huge body slams into mine, crashing me into the bed. I groan as I try to push him off me, but it's impossible.

Partly because I don't want his weight gone.

Nikolai lays his head on my chest, wraps his arm around my middle, and throws his leg over mine.

"You're not going anywhere anymore." He kisses my Adam's apple. "Night, baby."

A lump constricts my breathing and I can't swallow past it as I stare sideways to find his face buried in my neck, his hair falling on the pillow.

His breathing soon evens out and I smile to myself.

Didn't he say he doesn't sleep in a bed?

I stroke his arm and kiss the top of his head. "Night, Niko."

When I wake up, I realize two things.

One, somewhere in the middle of the night, our positions changed, and right now, my head is on Nikolai's chest as he hugs me to him, his tattooed arm thrown over my middle—beneath my shirt— and his leg is between mine.

Two, if the clock on the nightstand that shows seven a.m. is correct, then I fucked up.

For the first time in eight years, I didn't wake up at five. I don't even do alarm clocks anymore. I am the clock. I always wake up at five. I always run at five thirty.

Not today.

I shattered my holy routine, and now, all the chaos will come rushing in.

What the fuck have I done?

Panic sobers me up in an instant and all the sleep haze disappears.

I start to get up, but Nikolai shoves me back down in his embrace.

His fingers spread on my back and he strokes the skin as he murmurs in a husky tone, "Ten more minutes."

My exhales are fractured and choppy, and I'm forced to breathe in his body wash. I'm surrounded by his all-encompassing warmth, and it calms me down, for a very strange reason.

I shift and tilt my head to stare up at his face.

"Don't go," he lets out in a sleepy rumble.

And my heart swells so much, I'm surprised it doesn't burst.

How can I go when he's asking like that?

I caress his sharp jaw, swiping my thumb on his lower lip, and Nikolai releases a blissful moan that tucks its way between my bones.

His eyes slowly open, and I swear I can hear the shatter somewhere inside me when he grins. "Morning, baby."

Shit.

"Morning," I whisper, not trusting my voice or myself at this moment.

I try to get up and he tugs me down again. "Let's cuddle some more."

"You like cuddling?"

"With you, I do."

"Is that supposed to make me feel special?"

"You know you are. You don't need me to stroke your ego more."

I smile. "Come on. I'll make us breakfast."

"Ten minutes."

"I already missed my morning run. I don't want to miss class."

"It's okay to miss a run. It's not the end of the world."

It is to me.

"I like my life in order."

"Too bad I'm in it."

"Does that mean you admit you're chaotic?"

"Never denied it. I love corrupting you."

"More like I'm leading you to the right path."

He bursts out laughing, the sound husky and rich. "Good fucking luck trying."

"I'm nothing if not up for a little challenge."

"You mean *huge.*"

It's my turn to chuckle and he pulls me closer against him, pressing my chest to his, tightening his hand on my back as if he's scared I'll disappear or something.

"Nikolai. You need to let me go."

"Five minutes."

"Fine." I trace my fingers over his tattoos and stop when I reach a blank spot near his left pectoral muscle. "Is there a reason why you left this place empty?"

"Oh, that. It's on my heart so I want to wait until I can think of something extra special."

"Does that mean you plan to be covered in ink?"

"Fuck yeah. I have a lot of space on my back and thighs. Maybe you can sketch me something."

"You'd want that?"

"Why not? You're an artist, right?"

"I do landscapes."

"I'm sure you can think of something as unique as me."

"Your arrogance is astounding."

"Don't act like you don't love it." He strokes the back of my neck. "Have you ever thought about getting a tattoo?"

"No. I don't like them on me. I prefer to leave my skin unblemished."

"You're so prim and proper."

"Not all of us can wear tattoos. They look good on you, though."

"Did you just admit to liking my tattoos?"

"I didn't say I *like* them."

"Fuck me. You *do*. You're blushing, baby."

"You're dreaming." I push away, and this time, I manage to disentangle myself. "I'm going to make breakfast."

"Aw, don't be shy. Come here." He opens both arms, grinning like an idiot as I stride to the bathroom.

I manage to wash my face and brush my teeth without looking in the mirror, but I have to escape Nikolai again when he tries to grope me on my way out.

He's seriously impossible.

Since there are virtually no groceries, I manage to make scrambled eggs and I stumble upon a half-eaten box of macarons and put the rest on a plate. He only knows how to buy pastries like a sweet-toothed monster.

I'm pouring water in the kettle for morning tea when a heavy arm wraps around my middle, a large chest presses to my back. Nikolai drops a kiss to my throat over a hickey he left last night before he rests his chin on my shoulder. "Can't we go back to bed?"

"Stop being a baby and let me go. I can't do anything when you're all over me."

"That's the point."

I lift the plate of confection and he grins, instantly releasing me to grab it.

"Macarons!"

He's so easy to read, it's heartwarming. Nikolai might be notoriously violent and a crass heathen, but he's actually a staggeringly simple man, and I love that about him. I'm complicated enough for the both of us.

Pushing up against the counter beside me, he crunches two macarons in one go. He's only in boxer briefs, his large muscles on full display and his hair falling in smooth waves to his shoulders. Honestly, I'm not complaining. It's always a feast to look at him this way and know he's all mine. This monster of a man belongs to me.

"Lotus flower?"

"Hmm?" I click the kettle and retrieve two tea bags.

Nikolai never liked tea before, but when I offer him a cup, he drinks without moaning about it. I'm converting him slowly but surely.

"I'm going to ask you a serious question."

"What?"

"You said you were in love once. Who were you in love with?"

"Huh?" I stare at him as if he's grown two heads.

"That day during that never have I ever game. You took the shot when Kill said 'never have I ever been in love.' Who stole your heart? I want to know."

Fuck.

He looks so serious and wounded, I want to kiss him.

So I do. My lips seal to his and I swipe the crumbs of the disgustingly sweet macarons from his lips. "I lied. I was never in love."

His smile is blinding and he licks his lips as if chasing away mine, then he frowns. "Why did you lie?"

"You were looking at me weird."

"How weird?"

"Like you wanted to devour me on the spot."

"I always wanted to devour you, baby."

"Oh, *really*? I must've missed that."

"Christ. Was that sarcasm again?"

I grab the kettle and pour water into two mugs. "Make yourself useful and help me set up the table."

"Give me another kiss first."

I fist his hair and shove him toward me, then claim his mouth in a slow, sensual kiss, twisting his tongue and tasting the sweetness.

Kissing him outside of sex is different. *New.* It makes my chest hurt and my brain fog up, but I was always a sucker for pain.

When I release him, he groans. "Mmm. From now on, I'm going to need you to kiss me good morning this way."

I release him with a push. "Go."

"Okay, going, going." He smacks my arse on his way to the opposite counter.

"Nikolai!"

He just grins and rummages through almost all the cupboards until he finally finds two damn knives and forks.

I end up doing most of the work because the way he messes everything up drives me bonkers.

Once we sit down, I sip my English Breakfast tea and go through an e-newspaper on my phone while Nikolai devours the macarons like a monster.

"Who are you texting?" he asks after he swallows.

"Not texting. Reading the news."

"Why?"

"Because I like to stay informed about what's happening in the world."

"But what's the point?"

"Seriously? You don't care?"

"Would it change something if I did?"

"Doing something is better than doing nothing."

"Is that why you participate in all that volunteer work?"

"Yeah. I was born into a life of privilege and I try to help those who weren't as lucky."

"Hmm. What about lacrosse? Why do you play it?"

I put my phone down and take a sip of my tea. "I'm good at it."

"And that's enough reason to play it?"

"I suppose."

"I used to play football in high school, but I didn't only do it because I was good at it. I loved the adrenaline."

"American football, I presume."

"The only football."

"The *only* football is the one kicked by an actual foot and is the most popular sport in the world."

He shrugs. "You mean *soccer*?"

"Don't call it that in my presence. Disgusting."

He chuckles, the sound echoing around us with rare ease, and I can't resist smiling.

I woke up this morning thinking my life would be flipped upside down because I missed the most important part of my routine, but it's not as apocalyptic as I thought it'd be.

If anything, I like the easy conversation we have.

"Seriously, though. Do you really like lacrosse?" he insists.

"I wouldn't play it if I didn't."

Though the actual reason is that it's the only sport Lan didn't play. We used to play polo together when we were growing up, but I distanced myself from that and him as soon as I hit puberty.

I needed to play something he had no interest in. Football, cricket, and my beloved polo were out. Rugby is too physical for my taste. So that left me with lacrosse.

But I don't say that out loud. I can't have Nikolai sensing my inferiority complex and thinking I'm less perfect.

He's watching me with those intense eyes and I don't like it. I need to change the subject so the focus is on him.

"Hey, Nikolai."

"Yeah?"

"If you could be anywhere in the world, where would you go?"

"Inside you, baby."

I nearly choke on my tea. "I'm serious."

"I'm also serious. I take Kolya's demands to heart, thank you very much."

Lifting the cup to my mouth, I pause before I take a sip. "You said you always top. Did you ever consider bottoming?"

"Why?" He raises a brow. "You want to fuck me?"

I can feel the heat rising to my cheeks and I gulp the tea trapped in my mouth. "That's not what I meant. I was just asking."

"I don't like it, but I'd let you if you wanted to try it out."

"But you just said you don't like it."

"I'd rather let you fuck me than you running off to experiment with someone else."

My lips part. Wow. He'd really go that far for me?

I don't think about it as I stand up, close the distance between us, and stop between his parted thighs. My fingers sneak beneath his jaw and I look down at his beautiful eyes. "I don't want to fuck you. But thank you for offering. Really."

His hands land on my hips. "Tell me if you feel like it. Don't suppress it just because you know I'm not a fan."

"You don't have to worry about that. I really prefer being fucked by you. I like the feeling of…uh, letting go and losing control."

"You sure?"

"Positive."

He tugs me forward and I release a startled noise when I land on his lap. My hands grab his shoulders for balance. "What are you doing?"

"I lied. I don't only want a morning kiss." His lips ghost over mine. "I need a morning fuck as well."

This man will fucking destroy me.

I just hope I don't destroy him in the process.

TWENTY-FIVE

Nikolai

NOT TO BE A STALKER, BUT I KIND OF ENDED UP AT THE grocery store Bran frequents.

What? It's his fault that I miss him as soon as we're apart.

It's the afternoon and guess what? He's coming over to the penthouse this early. It's been about a week since he agreed to stay overnight, and I've been the happiest fucking man alive.

Not that I'm still thinking about that night and morning or anything.

Anyway, the reason I'm outside this local organic grocery store is because of a conversation I had with him about half an hour ago. When I was in class.

> **Bran:** What are you in the mood for tonight?

> **Me:** What kind of question is that? I'm always in the mood to do dirty things to you, baby.

> **Bran:** I meant food. FOOD.

> **Me:** You mean aside from your cum?

> **Bran:** Jesus. Yeah, aside from that.

> **Me:** I'm happy with anything you cook.

Bran: You sure? If you fancy something to eat, tell me. I'll go grocery shopping in a bit.

> **Me:** Nah. I love anything you cook. Do what you want. Also, you're getting groceries right now? It's the afternoon.

Bran: I finished classes early, so I'm heading to the penthouse.

> **Me:** Hell yeah. I'm on my way.

Bran: Don't you have uni?

> **Me:** Not important.

Bran: Don't skip classes, Nikolai. I'll see you later.

So yeah, I totally skipped classes. I actually left that class while reading his last text and rode my bike all the way here. I left it at a local parking lot and followed him around on foot.

He can't possibly expect me to stay away when he's going to the penthouse this early. It's true that I last saw him this morning, but I've been going through withdrawals.

My mood is dangerously dependent on him and that's not even funny anymore, but I'm done trying to figure it out.

I'm just obsessed with this man and everything about him. Some would argue it's something a lot more dire than obsession.

He consumes me, but he also grounds me. I've never felt as mentally strong as when I'm with him. Even the most mundane things we do together—having meals, watching movies, listening to him read the boring morning newspapers—bring a huge smile to my face.

Brandon King is ravaging me alive, and I can't wait until I'm fully inside him.

In the meantime, I'm content with indulging in my stalkerish tendencies. I wait by the corner of the grocery store. I'd love to go inside, but it's one of those small shops where I'd totally stand out, and while I don't mind, he would.

My lotus flower fits right in with the locals. I catch a glimpse of him putting a few tomatoes in his basket while smiling at something the shop owner says. Now, she's an older woman, but not *that* old. Maybe in her thirties, and I don't like the whole interaction.

Lady better stop giving him heart eyes if she's in the mood to live another day.

I'm about to creep up into her field of vision and scare the bejesus out of her when I catch a peculiar view from off to the side.

Since Bran turned me into a professional stalker, I always pick the best spots to watch him up close and personal, and for that reason, these locations are…rather obscure. I often run into all sorts of bizarre views, including couples, druggies, and homeless people.

This one, however, is different.

Usually, the couples who lurk in corners are doing some heavy petting, if not actual sex. The current scene is nowhere near that image.

A larger guy shoves another one against the wall with a tight grip on his T-shirt's collar, and I hear, "Shut the fuck up."

Any other time, I'd ignore this and change my position to continue stalking my Bran.

Something stops me, though.

The guy who's been shoved against the wall is familiar. Wait… is that…?

"Gaz?" I ask, walking toward them.

Sure enough, my cousin looks up, his fist clenched in the other man's shirt. An older man—at least early to mid-thirties—who's dressed in a white button-up shirt, black slacks, and leather shoes. His dark hair is slicked back and his expression is solemn.

He looks at me with complete disregard, as if I just intruded on his fun.

I flex my fist and make sure he sees it. This fucker will be buried six feet under before he attempts to harm my cousin. "What's your name, motherfucker, and what's your favorite way to die?"

"Niko, it's not…" Gareth trails off on a wince when the asshole tightens his grip on his shirt.

"Step the fuck away from him." I stride toward them. "*Now*."

"Who the fuck are you?" the man asks, his accent distinctively American, his expression entirely murderous.

I'm going to break his face for daring to touch my family.

"My cousin, Nikolai." Gareth shoves him away. "Please leave, sir."

"Sir?" I echo. "Why the fuck are you calling him sir?"

"He's my professor. Kayden Lockwood." Gareth stands beside me, his expression closed off as he stares at the man.

He narrows his eyes on me before he looks my cousin up and down. "We are not done, Carson. I expect you in my office tomorrow morning."

As he walks away, a wave of tension rolls off Gareth before he puffs out a long exhale.

I stand in front of him. "Why the fuck would your professor corner you in an alley?"

He glances up, his green eyes large and his blond hair sticking to his temples with sweat. "We…had a slight disagreement."

"And he couldn't solve it in the classroom like all other professors?"

"I…uh, I pulled something outside of law school and he was pissed."

"That still doesn't give him the right to attack you. Want me, Jer, and Kill to add him to the MIA list?"

"No, no. That's not necessary. I can take care of this situation."

"Didn't look like you were doing a very good job at it. Kill and I will maim the fucker."

"Niko, no." He grabs my arm. "Don't…tell Kill. Don't tell *anyone* about what you just saw."

"Why not…? Fuck me." I pause. "Is this that man you told me about that time? The only one you're attracted to?"

Gareth's lips part. "N-no."

"You just stuttered. You never stutter."

"Just forget it. Since when are you this perceptive?"

"Since now. It's him, isn't it?"

"No," he says with more force than needed.

"In that case, I guess I can discuss this further with Kill and Jer and see if it's true or false."

"Nikolai!"

"Or you can just tell me."

"Fine! It's him." He looks more relieved than burdened as he puffs out the words. I relate to him in more ways than one.

I know what it's like to be in a secret relationship where no one is allowed to know. It's suffocating sometimes, but it's worth it.

And from the look in Gareth's eyes, I think he feels the same as I do. It's not ideal, but like me, he wouldn't have it any other way.

"A much older professor, huh?" I grin. "You're much more adventurous than I thought, cousin. I'm actually impressed."

"It's nothing serious, so don't tell anyone."

"You sure about that?"

"Yeah."

I grab him by the shoulder. "Want me to continue my lesson about butt stuff?"

"No, thanks." He pushes me away. "I'm…going for a walk."

He storms away before I can question him some more. I consider following him, but immediately shut down that idea when I see Bran walking out of the store carrying a few bags.

Forget about Gareth. He can survive. I, on the other hand, need to recharge by strangling my lotus flower.

I stay a safe distance behind him as he walks by the small stores in the town center. He's dressed in dark pants and a light-green shirt, and his eyes are covered with elegant sunglasses. I can't wait to unwrap him later.

He stops by a pastry shop and I grin when he buys a box of macarons.

Bran then proceeds to walk in the direction of the penthouse. Despite having a car, he doesn't usually drive it and prefers to use his legs whenever possible. It's about a half hour walk from town, but I'm not complaining. I love watching him from afar and seeing how he stops and plays with dogs or checks in on the elderly people he does volunteer work for.

He's such a golden boy. At least, on the outside. I'm actually proud that I'm the only one who knows how much of a control freak he is.

Instead of going down the main street, Bran takes a secondary route and I follow, frowning. Does he have someone to visit around here?

He stops near an alley and turns around so suddenly, I don't have time to hide.

Bran removes his sunglasses and hangs them on the opening of his shirt. He gives me a once-over, his gaze lingering on where my biceps meet my T-shirt, and I can't help flexing them. I really, *really* love it when he checks me out.

That way, I can take some comfort in knowing he wants me. Not to the point of my utter obsession with him, but I do often catch him looking at me lately.

The other day, he was tidying up the bathroom while I was soaking in the Jacuzzi, but then I caught him ogling me as his shorts tented. He didn't agree to join me in the bathtub, so what did I do? The most logical thing, of course. I bent him over the counter and fucked him as he brought the house down with his moans and groans.

He's so loud, I love it.

I love that he lets go when around me.

Now, he releases a long breath. "You need to quit the habit of stalking me."

"I thought I was being subtle."

"Subtle? I could sense your eyes digging a hole in the back of my head."

"More accurately, your ass, baby."

"You're not even going to offer an excuse?"

I shrug. "Do I need to? I'm a simple man. I missed you, so I came to see you."

"We were together this morning."

"I need a dose of you at all times."

A pink hue covers his cheeks and he clears his throat. "Don't you have school?"

"As I said, not important. You can't expect me to picture you walking around the house while I'm not there." I grab the heaviest-looking bags. "I'll carry these. Go first."

"We can walk together. This area is usually deserted this time of day."

"Really?" I grin, gluing myself to his side.

"You don't have to if you don't want to—"

"Of course I want to."

He steps away, keeping a short distance between us, but I don't focus on that and choose to watch his small smile and the way his face radiates under the rare sun. His eyes shine a bright-blue color and some of his hair looks lighter.

Christ.

How can a man be so fucking beautiful? The urge to kidnap him and keep him all to myself beats like a need beneath my skin. I've given up thinking this is only a phase that will go away or that there will be a day when I'll see Bran and not have this queasy feeling in my chest.

I'm so screwed.

Bran clears his throat. "Stop looking at me like that."

"Like what?"

"That. Whatever *that* is."

"Don't think I can, baby. I have no self-control when it comes to you."

He swallows and I can't help watching the up and down of his Adam's apple. Fuck. I flex my hand around the bag to stop myself from hauling him over and kissing the fuck out of his full lips.

"Does that mean you have self-control when it comes to everything else?" he asks, and his slightly husky voice does nothing to disperse Kolya's attempt to rise to life.

"Yeah."

"So all the rumors about your penchant for violence are incorrect?"

"They are correct. I love beating things and people up, but I have enough agency to stop. Can't do that with you. It's impossible."

"Hmm. So I'm more important than violence?"

"Fuck yeah."

He smiles a little. "Good."

"You like torturing me?"

"It's only fair."

"What is that supposed to mean?"

"Nothing."

We spend the rest of the way in comfortable silence, and I find myself reveling in every moment I spend in public with him. I never liked silence, and wasn't really given the choice considering how loud my brain is. Even with Bran, I often filled up any silence with gibberish. Admittedly, I talk too much. He doesn't.

My Bran is one of those people who don't talk unless he has something meaningful to say and I grew accustomed to his brand of comforting silence. It's not tension-filled or brimming with unsaid words. It's peaceful, relaxing, and fulfilling in its own right.

It's his way of soaking up the moment, as he told me once, and I'm strangely picking up the habit.

I'd love to thread my fingers through his, but that's not an option right now. One day, I'll be able to hold his hand on the street.

One day.

When we're inside the penthouse, I hurry to put the bags on the kitchen table so I can devour him. If I just drop them at the entrance, he'll start nagging.

The sound of something hitting the floor reaches me first, then a strong grip lands on my bicep.

I whirl around, but I don't have time to focus when Bran fists a hand in my hair and captures my lips in a violent kiss. His tongue invades my mouth and he feasts on me. I'm stunned for a second, but then I wrap my arms around his back and claim what's fucking mine.

My hand falls to his ass and I nudge him up. He doesn't complain as he hops on and wraps his legs around my waist.

God-fucking-damn-it. I love it when he lets me carry him. I've been doing it religiously since I first did it last week.

Bran kisses me for what seems like hours, his fingers stroking my hair, his breaths and his entire fucking being fusing with mine.

He pulls away and smiles against my mouth, then wipes something at the corner of my lips.

"Fuck, baby." I pant. "What was that for?"

"I've wanted to do that since I saw you." He strokes my cheek.

"Let me down. I'll wash up and prepare dinner."

"No way in fuck am I letting you go after that. Buckle up, baby. Kolya would like to say hi."

I walk him to the bedroom as his laugh echoes in the air.

One day, and I mean very, *very* soon, Bran won't be content with only kissing me behind closed doors.

He'll be proud about being with me just like I'm over the moon about being with him.

What the...?

I pause when I feel a weight on my shoulder and comforting warmth snuggled up to my side.

The last thing I remember is sitting on the floor with my back against the wall while waiting for Bran. He said he was running late because he was meeting up with his brother and sister, and you can bet that I grumbled and threw a fit about having to share him with anyone. So what if they're his siblings?

It's getting tragic at this point.

It's been a week since the day he kissed me senseless after I stalked him then fucked him like a madman before allowing him to do anything. Good times.

Since then, I've been shamelessly insatiable for any glimpse of him. I need to see him every night, but even that isn't enough, so I follow him around whenever I get the chance. But I have to keep a distance—not too difficult considering I've become a seasoned stalker at this point.

Anyway, I haven't seen him at all today because of stupid tests that I couldn't skip and was fucking desperate for ten p.m. to come since that's when he usually shows up. However, my hopes got crushed when I received the text about his plans. I must've fallen asleep on the floor because right now, I'm on my back on the wood and Bran's head rests on my shoulder, his body pressed up to my side.

And the best part? His hand covers mine over my chest.

He's in a light-blue shirt and black pants, which means he didn't change into pajamas. I check my watch and it's two in the morning.

Fuck me.

I can't believe I slept for so long and missed the chance to see my Bran.

I demand a redo, now and fucking thank you.

A frown appears between his brows and I smooth it with my index finger. His eyes pop open and I have to swallow something stuck in my throat, because fuck. How can a man look hotter with each passing day? This isn't good for my uncontainable obsession.

"Did I wake you up?" I ask.

"It wasn't a good sleep anyway," he grumbles in that husky voice that goes straight to my dick and somewhere in my chest.

"Uh, baby? Why are you sleeping on the floor?"

"You were sprawled all over the ground when I came in and I wanted to experience it like you do, see if it's as comfortable as you make it look. The answer is a definite no." He sits up and kneads his shoulders and neck. "Don't do this again, Nikolai. It's not good for you in the long run."

"I can only sleep in a bed when you're there." I sit behind him, extending my legs on either side of him, and massage his shoulders. "Be here and I won't have to sleep on the floor."

"Deal." He leans into my touch and releases a soft sigh. I'm ravenous for the way he lets me touch him outside of sex now. I know he wasn't comfortable about the prospect in the beginning, but he now does it so naturally that I have to stop myself from devouring him whole and leaving no crumbs.

How the hell is he able to get me worked up with a few sounds?

How did he mold the almighty Nikolai Sokolov into this strange entity that can only survive in his presence? I don't even remember myself before him anymore. I certainly refuse the very notion of being separated from him.

"How was your night out?" I ask to put an end to this queasy feeling.

"One can't complain."

"So you enjoyed your time while I was being miserable."

"You're so dramatic. Besides, I thought you'd be busy with your shenanigans in the fight club."

"I didn't go. I wanted to see you."

"Is that so?" he says in a slightly mocking tone.

"What is that supposed to mean?"

"I don't know." He turns sideways so he's facing me and raises a brow. "Have you done something I don't approve of today?"

"Me? You're the one who ghosted me."

"Earlier today, did you or did you not take a picture with some leggy brunette?"

"No. Why would I do that?"

He reaches into his pocket, pulls out his phone, and opens my IG in the tagged posts section and shows me the picture in question. A girl—that I honest to fuck don't remember her name—is glued to my side, pushing her tits up against my arm. The captions is, *Miss you, my hunk.*

"Care to explain yourself?" Bran asks in an eerily calm tone. I've noticed that he becomes scarily collected when he's mad.

"Uh, baby. That picture is months old, probably from before I met you. Not my fault she decided to post it today."

"One of your fuck buddies?"

"*Ex*-fuck buddy. I barely remember her face. She's from school, I think."

"And yet, she has the liberty to call you her *hunk*?"

I grin. "Jealous, baby?"

He doesn't smile back as he fists my hair in a painful grip. "You belong to me, Nikolai. I do *not* share, are we clear?"

"Fuck. I love it when you get all possessive."

"That's not an answer. I don't want to see you with girls or guys hanging onto your arm or sitting on your lap. I don't want anyone to touch you, period."

"Only if you don't let anyone touch you."

"I won't."

"Are you going to delete that one picture with *Clara* on you IG?"

"You went that far back?"

"So what if I did? I'm going to need you to erase her existence from your life."

"I've already deleted that post a long time ago."

"In that case…" Grinning, I take out my phone, go to the post, and type a comment.

Nah, not your hunk. Delete this.

A smug smile curves Bran's lips when he sees it and he nods with approval before he turns away and I resume massaging his shoulders. Fuck me. I love the feel of his relaxing muscles beneath my fingers and the content noises he releases.

"By the way, I googled the meaning of Brandon, and it literally means prince or king. Don't I get brownie points for calling you Prince Charming?"

"More like stalkerish tendencies points. Who googles the meaning of other people's names?"

"I do because it's you. I'm curious about everything that concerns you."

He leans his head on my shoulder, and my movements come to a halt when his eyes meet mine and he flashes me a little smile. That feeling lurking in my stomach lurches up and I feel trapped, completely and utterly taken by him and his rare smiles.

Jesus fucking Christ. What's happening to me?

"Aren't you curious about me?" My voice comes low, a bit vulnerable, and I don't even do that. Why is it that Bran looks at me and I feel this sense…of doubt? Not in me, but in his feelings for me.

I can sense myself falling deeper and harder, but he's still a blank board most of the time, and that does shit to me.

"I am," he says softly.

"Are you going to google the meaning of my name?"

"No need. It's the Slavic version of Nicholas who was the Greek god of victory."

"I didn't know that."

"Seriously?"

"Yeah, I just know it's a badass Russian name and means victory or something like that."

"Do you speak Russian?"

"Sure as fuck. My grandad made sure my sisters and I do or else he wouldn't have given us our Russian card."

"I never heard you speak it."

"I do sometimes with Jeremy and especially the guards since most of them are Russian-born."

"Tell me something in Russian."

I cup his chin and stare deep into those eyes that have become my undoing as I say the words Grandpa said Russians take seriously and literally. *"Ya nee ma goo bees tee byah zhit."*

"What does that mean?"

"You're so cute," I lie through my teeth.

He frowns. "Don't call me that."

I wrap my arm around his waist, trapping him in my grip. "Tell me something you noticed about me no one else knows."

"What type of request is that?"

"Just do it."

He lifts a hand and traces a line from my forehead over my nose. "Not sure if no one else knows this, but you have a perfectly symmetrical face. Most people have an eye or ear that's slightly bigger that the other. They have a good side because it's proportionally better than the opposite one, but you look perfect from any side, because everything is well-balanced. Even your upper and lower lip are the same size. Actually, your entire body is perfectly symmetrical."

He strokes his fingers over my lips and they willingly part. God damn. He says a few words that imply he's been watching me and I feel like I'm being torn apart. "You're an artist's dream muse."

"Then make me yours."

He laughs. "Maybe you already are."

"Fuck yeah. That's a good thing, right?"

"Maybe." He continues stroking my face. "Your turn."

"My turn to what?"

"Tell me something you noticed about me no one else knows."

"Hmm. You have eleven moles on your body."

"Okay..."

"I'm not done. You have two hundred seventeen lashes on your right eye and two hundred twelve lashes on your left one."

His lips part. "You...counted them?"

"Almost every night since you stayed over. That's last night's count. Might change today. You tend to lose some on your left eye."

"But why would you count my lashes?"

"I love them. They're dark and long and so fucking pretty when you're sleeping. Besides, no one but me can count them, so that's a huge bonus."

He chuckles softly, the sound echoing around us like a lullaby. "You're so weird."

"I've always been."

"That you have."

"The only difference is that you're not running away anymore."

"No, I'm not." He leans completely against my chest and closes his eyes. "Give me five and then I'm taking you to bed. From now on, you're not allowed to sleep on the floor anymore."

I have no words to say, so I lower my head and capture his lips in a slow kiss. That queasy feeling only gets more intense the longer my mouth ravages his. My insides melt when he meets me stroke for stroke, grunt for grunt.

If I wasn't sure before, I am now.

I'm completely and irrevocably in trouble because of Brandon King.

TWENTY-SIX

Nikolai

THREE WEEKS PASS BY IN BLISS.

And by bliss, I mean the most erotic, beautiful fuck fest. Just kidding. I love the fucking, I really, *really* do. Ask Kolya and he'll be giving a standing ovation.

But Bran and I have always had the fucking at the center of what we are. It's why he even gave in to me in the first place.

Give yourself a pat on the crown for being a motherfucking elite seducer, Kolya.

However, that's not the only strong element in our relationship anymore. Something changed after the first time he stayed over. Although I was the one who put forth that condition, I think he felt a sense of relief that I was forcing him to stop running.

I could be imagining it or deep into my delusions, but he really has this peaceful expression when I fall asleep strangling him or when he wakes up stroking my jaw.

Oh, I actually sleep on a *bed* now. Shocker, I know. It's like the eighth world wonder and one of those mysterious breaks in history. I'm sure my previous useless therapists would have a field day with the causes.

I'm a simple man. I smell Bran and feel his hard muscles molded to mine, and I'm a goner. It's blasphemy to expect me to sleep separate from him when he's lying there like a beautiful prince.

He might attempt to push me away or pretend that I'm annoying and crushing him, but here's the thing. Whenever I pull away from him in my sleep, I wake up to find his head on my chest and his arm wrapped around my middle. Or he'll press his chest to my back, throw his arm on my waist, and bury his face in my hair.

He's so fucking cute, I always want to swallow him whole, and I do, *often.*

I usually wake him up with my lips around his cock or my cock nudging inside him. He picked up on it and started trying to wake up before me just so he can suck me off first thing in the morning.

It's not a competition I'm complaining about. In fact, I love how he gets that smug look on his face while giving me the sloppiest of sloppy blowjobs.

Over the past few weeks, Bran has become a bit more comfortable touching me and I don't always have to initiate sex anymore.

If he's in the mood, he definitely makes it known either by attacking me as soon as I walk inside the apartment or with his constant texts that mimic my clingy nature.

He can also be surprisingly possessive—though not as unhinged as I am since I literally threaten to break the arm of anyone who touches him. The other day, I ran into Simon at one of the coffee shops and he started being touchy as usual before I pushed him away.

Turns out, Bran saw it and sent me this gem of a text.

You better remember who the fuck you belong to, Nikolai.

Did I print that text and frame it? Possibly.

I fucking love that he's been more forward lately. Not to the point of talking to me in public—God forbid anyone knows about us. But he's getting there.

I don't mind. *Much.* I love that I'm his secret. I love that he's aloof and in complete control when in public, but he falls apart on my tongue, fingers, and cock in private.

I love that he steals glances at me when everyone is looking, then whispers how much he needs me to fuck the daylights out of him when it's only the two of us.

He's mine and that's all that matters.

I'm the only one who knows he's a noisy motherfucker during sex, and that's all I care about. Still, I make sure to decorate his skin with hickeys so others know he's owned. I take my time turning them deep purple until he's whining and add new ones every night. The earful he gives me afterward is worth it.

There'll be a day when he'll come out. I know it. I *feel* it in his eyes when we're in public. I see it in his body language when he angles himself in my direction as if he wants to walk to me, hug me, and kiss me. He stops himself every time, but that's looking more painful for him lately.

He'll break one day and I'll be there to pick him up with open arms and an open mouth.

I'm wearing him down and he's totally falling for me.

Okay, I'm being delusional again. While he doesn't actually *love* me, he cares.

Sometimes more than necessary.

So here's the thing, Bran despises the fights and makes that known every time as he patches me up and puts ointment on the bruises.

He also hates how chaotically beautiful I am—though he probably wouldn't call it that. He can't stop nagging about all the shit I leave lying around or the dishes in the bathroom—what? I had a snack while soaking in the Jacuzzi—or whenever I shake my wet head. I only do that so he'll dry it for me. Some would argue I also fight so he'll be so adorably worried about me.

Most importantly, he replies to my ridiculous texts that go the line of:

> **Me:** Did you know there are like so MANY Greek Gods?

> **Bran:** Is that so?

> **Me:** Yeah. How am I supposed to keep up? Why are there so many?

Bran: How dare they?

Me: Right? Speak some sense into them, especially that dick Zeus. He needs to stop having so many children and raping women left and right. Father of gods, my ass.

Bran: I'll have a very stern conversation with him.

Me: Do you really think of me as him? I'm wounded.

Bran: My sincerest apologies. It was bad form to even make that comparison.

Me: You're going to have to repeat that apology with your lips wrapped around Kolya. You know, since he's sulking and shit.

Bran: You could've said you wanted me to suck your cock instead of starting a whole drama.

Me: No, no, it's not about that. Kolya is REALLY hurt.

Bran: I'll make it up to you.

Me: Now?

Bran: I seriously can't with you.

Me: Is that a yes?

Bran: See you in an hour.

I jump down through the ropes after I've pummeled someone to near death, ignoring all the screams and the roaring crowd as I drink from a bottle of water Jeremy passes me.

"You okay?" he asks.

I pour water on my head and shake it, then smile—imagining Bran pinching the bridge of his nose and saying, "I seriously can't with you."

"Niko?" Jeremy watches me closely. "Don't tell me you're thinking about another fight?"

"Nope. One is enough." I shove the bottle against his chest. "Laters, Jer."

"Wait." He falls in step beside me as we walk down the tunnel and throws an arm over my shoulder. "What's up with you lately? You barely come back to the mansion and you're acting suspicious."

"Busy, busy."

"With what? Or more accurately, with whom?"

I pause, coming to a stop in front of the locker room, then face Jer. Hmm. He's my best friend, and usually, I'd tell him all about the fuck fests and the weird adventures. Even though he couldn't care less for the details, he listens without judging. Except for telling me that I'm crazy sometimes, which is true.

The point is, I'm starting to feel a little bit restless about this secret. I love having Bran all to myself, but I don't like that *no one* knows. Sometimes, Kill looks at me weird as if he figured everything out, but he always has that psycho look and I definitely don't trust him not to broadcast everything to the world if I tell him anything.

If there's anyone I can trust with my secrets, it's Jeremy. I was fourteen when I realized I really loved both dick and pussy. That young, yup. Jeremy is straighter than straight—no doubt about that—and he's five years older, but I always bugged him. Everywhere he went, I was there, annoying the fuck out of him with my antics until he liked me. It's my modus operandi, deal with it.

Anyway, he's the first one I told that I thought I liked both girls and guys and he wasn't surprised. Let's just say he and Dad understood Kolya before I came to terms with his moody-prick era.

Jer kept it a secret for like a year, until my parents found out and I held a coming-out orgy party. Jeremy definitely left that one as early as he possibly could. Kill stayed.

So, the thing is, he's like Secret Keeping 101.

I stroke my necklace and narrow my eyes on him. "How do you know it's *someone* who's keeping me busy?"

"The smiling at your phone like an idiot more often than not. Also…" He taps his nape. "You usually have a hickey here. You can't see it, but whenever you pull your hair up, it's visible."

I touch the back of my neck. That sly fucking bastard. He's been leaving hickeys all this time? And here I thought he just loved kissing me there.

"Jer."

"What?"

"I can't take this, he's so fucking adorable."

"For leaving a hickey?"

"For staking a claim and being sneaky about it *while* complaining that I leave too many."

"Okay," he says slowly. "It's a guy?"

Ah, fuck. I didn't plan to disclose the gender, but hey, as long as he doesn't know the name, all is good. No one would suspect it's Bran. He's such an uptight dickhead and anyone with two brain cells would think I'm nowhere near his type.

I nod with a grin. "The most beautiful guy ever."

"You like him?"

"Sure as fuck."

"How much do you like him?"

"Enough to be exclusive."

"Wow. A first."

"I know, right? I'm all for monogamy now."

"And you still haven't introduced him to me?" He raises an eyebrow. "And here I thought I was your bro."

"Well...thing is. He's still all chained in the closet and shit, so that's a no for now."

"I won't tell. I didn't when you wanted to keep your sexuality a secret."

"This is different."

I was never *ashamed* of my sexuality. I just wanted to make sure it wasn't an experimentation phase before telling my family. Bran seems to struggle with how much he loves sucking dick and being fucked in the ass. Like he really, *really* gets all panicky whenever we're close in public or when I go to watch his games and try to see him after. So I stopped that altogether so as not to stress him out.

I'm not sure why he's so scared about admitting it out loud.

I wonder if it has to do with his long showers and the damn locked bathroom door.

Sometimes, I catch him looking at his feet, completely zoned out until it turns a bit freaky. Other times, he'll have these random nicks of the razor against his neck and even his thighs and balls. He shaves down there—*of course*. He's so groomed and loves being spotless. He also started shaving my face for me because, apparently, I don't do it well enough. It feels so fucking hot whenever he sits on the counter and traps me between his muscular thighs to shave my face.

He's never cut me, not once, but he seems clumsy with himself.

I bought him a new electric shaver that doesn't cause cuts, but he says he prefers the razor.

It's starting to give me the creeps for real whenever he has those, as small as they are.

Jeremy watches me for a beat, arms crossed and brow furrowed. "You're okay with that?"

"With what?"

"Being in the closet with him. You already came out, so you're under no obligation to be shoved in the dark with him."

"He'll come out one day."

"And you're happy to wait? As long as it takes?"

"If it's him, yeah. I guess."

"Okay." He clutches my shoulders. "I just want you to know that you deserve to be loved in the light, Niko. Just like everyone else."

"Pfft. He doesn't *love* me."

"I don't like this guy." Jeremy narrows his eyes. "You're being exclusive for the first time in your life and keeping it a secret for his sake and he doesn't love you? What is he? An idiot?"

"Hey, don't call him that."

"You're defending him? Wow. Where's my brutish friend Niko and what have you done to him?"

"I'm a changed man, Jer." I grin. "Gotta go. Don't tell anyone."

"Do you have to go? I thought we were discussing how to bring Landon down after everything he's done."

I wince. So I might have been the one who delayed the Heathens' plans to take vengeance against Landon King. I have to do it, and I will, because he's a motherfucker, but I can't help thinking about Bran's reaction.

All this time, I'd hoped they were enemies, and while they don't hang out much, they text each other all the fucking time.

Or more like Landon checks on Bran in a neurotic fashion, and my lotus flower gets this little smile on his lips whenever he reads his asshole brother's texts.

He said they're different but they're twins and that's a bond for life.

I suppose he wouldn't appreciate me punching his brother into an early grave, even if he deserves it.

"Just plan it out and let me know," I tell Jer. "I have more important shit to do."

"Baby, I'm home!"

Did that sound so domesticated?

Well, I do think of the penthouse as home now, which is weird. Bran also texted 'I'll see you at home' earlier today, so at least I'm not the only one thinking it.

I remove my T-shirt and toss it on the floor, then, thinking about the asshole's nagging, I pick it up and dunk it on the chair. Not ideal, but it's a compromise.

My brow furrows when I don't find him in the kitchen busy being a Mary Sue. He's so anal about the meals he makes. Bran is the type of cook who'll go out at ungodly hours just to have his perfect ingredients.

He's an excellent cook. I just wish he'd cut himself some slack.

And not only about cooking, but also lacrosse, his gazillion charitable activities, and painting. He's meticulous about everything, and he's so ridiculously hard on himself, it's starting to raise red flags. No one should be that perfect and think they're not. Literally no one.

Sometimes, I doubt that he even likes his body, because he's so quick about putting on clothes the moment we're not fucking. It's as if he doesn't like looking at those gorgeous, perfectly toned muscles. It's impossible to see him half naked. The guys at the Heathens' often parade half naked after showers or around the pool. Bran isn't a fan of swimming, probably because he has to dress down for it.

I wish he'd talk to me more. While we often have conversations during breakfast or dinner, there's a pattern I've noticed.

Whenever I ask something about him, he subtly turns the conversation so it's about me instead.

He loves asking me questions about my parents, my siblings, my life in NYC, and even my role in the Heathens. Whenever I talk, he always listens with keen interest.

However, when I try to get to know him, he's like a blank slate. He prefers talking about his friends and asshole brother instead of himself.

Which is annoying, to say the least.

It's strange that he's not in the kitchen. Is he not here yet?

I narrow my eyes. He said he was playing stupid video games with Mia earlier, so he better not have lost track of time.

And no, I'm not jealous of my baby sister.

Much.

I head to the guest room down the hall that he turned into a mini art studio. He said that since he's spending more time here than at the Elites' mansion, he can at least be productive and work on his art.

And seriously, that's one of the best decisions he's ever made. I love sneakily watching him being all concentrated as he does these bold strokes of color. I don't understand them, but they look pretty and, most importantly, he looks hot as fuck when he's in the zone.

He has this picturesque mountain painting that he's been working on, but he doesn't look pleased in the least when he does.

I open the door, ready to jump him from behind and attack his ticklish sides until he bursts out laughing. The sound is so rare that I can't resist any chance to make it happen.

Usually, he laughs or smiles effortlessly whenever I'm telling him about my past adventures in school or with Mom and Dad, so I need to narrate more of those tonight. I even called Mom to ask about any shenanigans I might not remember...

My hand falls from the knob when I find him standing in the center of the room, in front of a canvas full of chaotic black strokes. His palette is on the floor, smudged in black as if he poured it out to murder all the other colors.

Splashes of black stain his feet and his khaki pants and even his usually spotless white shirt.

This isn't like him. Bran is so organized and despises the idea of chaos. So to see him standing in the middle of it is not normal.

I slowly approach him and catch a glimpse of him staring at the canvas with a blank face. His hand pulls at the back of his hair so harshly, his nape is red, and his knuckles are white.

"Lotus flower?" I call, but he doesn't make any sign of acknowledging my existence.

So I move in front of him, blocking his view of the canvas.

He looks straight through me as if his body is here, but his soul is floating somewhere else. I reach for his hand and pause when I feel how stiff he is, as if he's hardening his body against a threat.

What the fuck is messing with you, Bran?

I have to apply pressure to peel his fingers from his hair one by one. My chest squeezes when I see brown strands in his hand.

"Brandon?"

I circle his nape, stroking the spot he abused. "Baby, look at me."

My lips brush against his and they twitch. When I pull back, I find him watching me with bemused, lost eyes.

"Nikolai? When did you get here?"

"Just now," I lie, my fingers still caressing his nape. "You okay?"

"I'm fine."

"You don't look fine. Your skin is pale and you're standing in the middle of a mess."

He looks at his surroundings as if he's seeing it all for the first time.

Little by little, light blooms back behind his irises and he winces. "Bloody hell. Sorry."

"Stop fucking apologizing." I breathe harshly, watching him closely, trying to find a trace of the zombie version from a moment ago.

"Sorry...uh, I mean sorry. Jesus..." he trails off. "You should go. I'll clean up."

He starts to move, casting his gaze anywhere but at me.

My hold tightens on his nape and I clutch his jaw with my free hand so he'll look at me. "What happened?"

An unnatural shine covers his eyes and it's so similar to when he becomes panicked after I touch him in a semi-public space. "It was... an accident."

"It doesn't look like an accident."

"I just dropped it. It's nothing."

He pulls away from me and grabs the palette then carefully places it on a few tissues on his sketching table.

For a few seconds, he remains there, hand gripping the edge of the table and his back crowding with tension as if he's fighting his demons and shoving them back to where no one can see them.

When he turns around, he seems more like himself, and this time, he looks at me, like *really* looks at me, and instantly, his lips purse with disapproval. "Were you fighting again?"

I make an affirmative sound, not bothering to use my state as an excuse for him to touch me.

There's something wrong with him, and the more he hides it, the clearer I see it. But if I ask him about it outright, he'll just deflect and retreat behind his high walls. Or worse, he'll revert back to his old habits and run away.

But I can't take this anymore. I can't watch him break in silence and do nothing.

Bran glides wet wipes over his hands, cleaning away the black paint, then walks to me, clutches me by the jaw, and rotates my head from left to right. "You seriously need to stop fighting. One day, you'll really get hurt. You're not immortal."

He presses his finger against a bruise on my jaw and I wince.

"Does it hurt?" he asks with a note of concern that he obviously doesn't have for himself.

"If I say yes, will you kiss it better?"

"I give up." He releases me with a sigh. "I'll go get the first aid kit."

"I'll do it myself. I need a bath anyway." I walk to the entrance and glance back.

Bran watches me with a wretched expression, his body is angled my way like every time we're in public, and then he opens his mouth, but just like all those times, he closes it again.

"You have something to tell me, baby?"

I expect something. Anything, but he shakes his head. "I will… clean up and fix dinner."

I say nothing as I storm out and into the bathroom. I should be used to his methods at this point, but I don't like it.

The whole fucking thing is making my skin crawl.

I sit in the Jacuzzi for what seems like forever, but it must be like half an hour. The bubbles echo around me, but there's nothing relaxing about them, so I turn them off to think in silence.

My mind fills with thoughts about the reason behind Bran's state from earlier, but no matter how much I think about it, I come up empty.

With a sigh, I lean back and grab my phone from the side of the tub and check my texts, mostly from the group chat with the guys.

Killian: Where are you, Niko?

Jeremy: He's busy. Let him be.

Gareth: Niko busy? And you're not there to keep him in check?

Jeremy: Let's say he doesn't need my services with his recent endeavors.

Killian: It's the ED situation, isn't it?

Gareth: Kill, the fuck? He'll just flood the group chat with dick pics.

Me: Kolya says hi, motherfuckers.

I send one just to fuck with them.

The door opens and I look up to find Bran standing in the entrance. He's changed into flannel pajama pants and a white T-shirt, looking like a Christmas present.

"I...wanted to make sure you weren't meditating in the water."

"I'm not." I close my eyes and lean my head against the cushion.

No idea why, but I'm mad. It's not the first time he's hid himself from me, but I've never seen him in that state, either.

The fact that he refuses to let me in even though I'm a damn open book is messing with my fucking head.

I really, *really* hate fucking complicated.

Movement echoes around me and I remain still, vehement about trying to ignore him for once.

The splashing of water forces me to open my eyes just in time to see Bran climbing into the bath, entirely naked.

"What are you doing?"

"You always ask me to join you. Is it different this time?" he asks even as he sits down and stretches his legs out on either side of me.

"Do what you want." I try to sound unaffected, which is hard when he looks so stunningly beautiful.

At this point, it's safe to say I've learned every ridge of his muscles and where his moles are—upper left shoulder, above his right hip, behind his right knee, on his left knee, and just beneath his jaw.

Not that I'm obsessive or anything.

He nudges my thigh with his foot. "Are you mad at me or something?"

"What gave you that idea?"

"You're not jumping my bones, for one." He smiles, but it's forced. "Are you losing interest?"

"Are you?"

"No."

"Hmm."

He's silent for a second. "What's this about? Is it because I told you to stop fighting?"

"I won't do that."

"I can tell."

"As soon as your cousin Creighton comes back to school, I'll bloody his face, not because of what happened to me, but because he dared to punch you that day. I'll also fight your precious psycho brother and beat him to a fucking pulp, so you better mentally prepare yourself."

He gulps, his throat bobbing up and down. "Don't do that… please."

"What are you willing to do to stop me?"

"What do you want?"

"Tell me what happened when I got here, and don't say it was an accident or it was nothing, because I don't buy that bullshit."

His face pales and he goes still, his chest rising and falling in a fast rhythm before he breathes slower. "It's…really nothing."

"We're done here. Get the fuck out and leave me alone."

Bran's lips part as he blinks at me. So, no, I've never really spoken to him in that tone. I always clown around when he's his grumpy, uptight self, but I'm just sick of this.

I can't help thinking about what Jeremy said, and it's messing with my head.

"Nikolai…" Water splashes as he scoots over so that he's kneeling between my legs and then wraps his arms around my neck.

I meet his wide blue eyes, and for the first time, I don't soften at the mere view of his face or the heat radiating from his body.

For the first time, I don't melt into a puddle just because he's saying my name or touching me.

"Get out."

He shakes his head and tightens his grip. "I'm sorry."

"Why the fuck do you keep apologizing as a knee-jerk reaction? It's fucking pathetic."

He flinches and drops his arms to either side of him. "I'll…just leave."

"Go right ahead. Run away like you do best."

"What the hell do you expect from me? I try to make it up to you and you lash out. I've done nothing to be spoken to in that tone."

"Nothing? You're literally hiding me away like I'm your dirty fucking secret. Like you're ashamed of being with me in front of your precious friends and family, and on top of that, you're concealing yourself from me. You call that fucking *nothing*?"

"You said you were okay with it."

"Maybe I'm not anymore."

His lips tremble. "Are you…leaving me again?"

"You'd love that, wouldn't you?"

"I wouldn't! I wouldn't love it!" His voice rises and his hand shakes as he looks at me with eyes so fucking sad, it pulls on the heart I'm supposed to be hardening. "Don't leave me."

"Then give me something. Anything. I won't be kept outside your walls. That's not how this fucking works."

"Why would you want to learn about me?" He pulls on his hair, fingers tugging until his face is all red. "Just *why*?"

I get on my knees and shove his hand away. "Stop hurting yourself or I swear to fuck—"

My words are cut off when I catch a glimpse of a Band-Aid beneath his thick watch that he always has on—even when he sleeps. He said it was a gift from his Mom and holds sentimental value and I figured he's a momma's boy who loves having a memory of her at all times.

Right now, however, I realize how naive I've been.

I clutch his wrist and his eyes grow in size as I start to remove it. Bran goes ballistic and tries to wrench his wrist free. He even punches me in the chest and tries to kick me.

But he doesn't have a chance. He might be an athlete, but I'm much bigger than him.

I shove him against the side of the tub, my knees on either side of his thighs, caging him in place as I snatch his wrist.

"Don't, Nikolai. Don't!" He speaks in a tone I've never heard before, all broken and full of panic before he whispers, "Please, I beg you, don't see that part of me…"

I keep my eyes on his lost ones as I tug the watch free, sending it flying across the floor.

Sure enough, there's a Band-Aid around his wrist.

"Please," he begs again, his hand in mine trembling, curling, flexing, twisting away. "Please…"

I rip it off in one go and all air whooshes out of my fucking lungs. The skin is red over a cut that slashes through the line in his wrist. A few other older cuts line his skin, horizontal to the first, methodically put so they're never wide enough to exceed the strap of his precious watch.

His hand goes limp in my grip and I stare at his face. Only, he's looking down at the water, his head bowed, his shoulders defeated.

Jesus fucking Christ.

All my anger disappears. On its behalf, a loathsome feeling rips through me like wildfire.

Fucking fear.

Those nicks of the razor were not a coincidence. They were a sign.

"What's the meaning of this?" I ask in a voice I don't recognize. "Fucking look at me, Brandon!"

He slowly raises his head, his lips trembling.

"You cut yourself?" My words are low, but they're so loud in the silence. "Why?"

"Because I'm fucked up." His voice sounds like death's lullaby, anguished and shattered. "Because I look at myself in the mirror and get the urge to shatter it to pieces. Because I've been haunted by the bitter taste of nausea and self-loathing for so long, I don't know how to live without them. I was doing fine, pretending and putting on a façade, so why the fuck did you ruin that? Why did you come into my life and destroy every wall I built and ruin every lie I told myself? Why do you touch me like I'm beautiful? Why don't you hate me when I can't stand my-fucking-self?"

"I can't hate you, baby. It's impossible." I lift his wrist up and brush my lips at the edge of the cut.

A whimper falls from his mouth and he throws himself at me. I stagger but he keeps me in place by wrapping his arms around me.

His fingers dig into my skin and it hurts as he squeezes me against him. His trembling body fuses to mine and he breathes harshly into my neck.

"Baby? You okay?"

"Please…" His voice is muffled. "Please let me hold you like this. It doesn't hurt when you touch me."

I grab onto him, pressing him further into me, harder, closer, until I'm not sure where I end and he begins.

Seems that Bran runs way deeper than I thought, but as he hangs on to me as if I'm his only anchor, I know that I'll never let him go.

Not even if I burn with him.

For him.

In him.

I'd willingly catch fire if he so much as asked me to.

TWENTY-SEVEN

Brandon

"IT DOESN'T EVEN MAKE SENSE."

I nod along, although I have no clue what Cecily and Glyn are talking about. I agreed to meet them for afternoon tea out of habit and I regretted the decision almost immediately.

My head is a fucking mess and I'm barely functioning. I can't muster the energy to put on a façade, let alone fake my smiles properly.

"Don't you think so, Bran?"

I lift my head from my cup of tea and stare at Cecy. "Hmm?"

"About the fact that Ava is up to no good. She's making a lot more trouble lately and keeps going to all these fights."

"You know how she is," I say, tracing the rim of my cup. "Just give her space and she'll come around."

Besides, judging by what I witnessed the other day when she 'pretended' to come see me, I'm exceptionally aware of what's going on between her and my unruly eldest cousin. In fact, at this point, everyone but her knows what's up. Her inability to submit to reality or at least acknowledge it is possibly why she's been spiraling out of control. I tried advising her, but she's too hotheaded to listen and prefers indulging in Lan's plots of mayhem that target Eli.

My brother's aim is entirely to egg Eli on and have fun, but she's digging her own grave. Whether intentionally or unintentionally, I have no clue.

"I'm worried, though," Cecily says with a frown.

"Me, too." Glyn stuffs her face with a macaron and my chest twists into a knot.

I can't help recalling the sweet-toothed monster who's always stealing from any box of pastries I bring.

He hasn't touched any lately, though.

My heart aches and I clear my throat, but it does nothing to alleviate the lump stuck in there.

It's been a week since the day I had a breakdown and nearly splintered to pieces. But I didn't, because Nikolai held me through it.

And he did it for a long time.

Until my knees went numb and I became lethargic. Until the cut stopped burning and itching and driving me fucking mental.

Then he made me lean on him and carried me out of the tub because I couldn't stand upright. I was a pathetic mess, a shadow of a person, and the very fucking thing I was terrified he'd see.

I expected disgust or, worse, pity, but I couldn't see any on his face.

He looked extremely focused as he dried me off, helped me put on some clothes, then let me sleep while strangling him.

The thought that he'd leave triggered a panic so deep, I was hyperventilating. I think I hurt him by how hard I clung to him, but he didn't seem to mind. If anything, he held me tighter and kissed my eyelids, my nose, my cheek, the top of my head—anywhere he could reach.

That's when I finally fell asleep.

He left me alone the day after, although I could tell he had a lot of questions.

But then I found out the reason he didn't get in touch was because he was fighting my brother the following night.

I asked him not to. I *begged* him, even, but he went along with it anyway.

There's something Nikolai doesn't know that I've been keeping a secret—aside from my fucked-up state of mind. His sister Mia is in some sort of relationship with my brother.

When I found out about that, I tried to warn her away, but she was as hard-headed as her brother and wouldn't listen. Lan is also acting uncharacteristically possessive of her, which he's never done with his previous conquests.

So I hid that from Nikolai because I could tell he holds a massive grudge against Lan—rightfully so.

But even without that information, he still went on with the fight.

I had to stand there and watch Nikolai and Lan go at each other's throats and nearly beat each other to death.

To say I was livid after that would be an understatement. Not only because Nikolai still went on with the fight despite me begging him not to, but also because of Lan.

He suspects something and he was positively murderous after the fight. He wouldn't stop asking, "Why the fuck was Nikolai looking at you like that?"

While he didn't specify what the 'that' was, I could see the accusatory look in his eyes and hear it in his tone.

Telling him anything is just a disaster waiting to happen, so I deflected, and it's working for now.

That night, I naturally couldn't go to the penthouse, because Lan was watching me like a fucking hawk. I was sure if I'd left, he would've followed me. No doubt about that.

So I texted Nikolai.

> **Me:** Why on earth did you fight Landon? Now, he won't stop pestering me and asking about why you kept looking at me.

> **Nikolai:** And it'd be the end of the world to tell him the truth?

> **Me:** If I do, he'll kill you.

Nikolai: Not if I kill him first.

Me: He's my twin brother, Nikolai. You can't just talk about killing him and expect me to be okay with it.

Nikolai: But it's okay if he attempts to kill me?

Me: No, of course not. I'd much rather you stay away from each other.

Nikolai: Is that your way of saying you'll never tell him about us?

Me: That's just a recipe for disaster. He's not exactly your biggest fan.

Nikolai: The feeling is mutual. I hate the motherfucker.

Me: Can't you just ignore him? I'm sure he'll ignore you, too.

Until the whole thing with Mia hopefully blows over.

Nikolai: Let me ask you. Do you ever plan on telling him about us?

Me: I don't think that's a good idea right now.

Nikolai: How long do I have to wait? A month? A year? A decade? How long should I prepare to shove myself back into the closet with you?

Me: I'm sorry.

Nikolai: Fuck you and your fucking brother.

That was the last text he sent me. Six days ago.

Six whole days.

I've waited for him in the penthouse, but he never shows up.

I've texted him a few times, but he's never replied.

Every night, I hope he'll come home. Every night, I sit on the sofa across from the lift until I fall asleep. Sometimes, I spend all-nighters obsessing and having to physically stop myself from bleeding my fucking wrist dry.

The fact that he ghosted me after I opened up to him, even partially, has been messing with my head in ways I don't like to admit. Nikolai has always communicated with me. This is the first time he's not being an open book and it's fucking me up.

It's not like I can go to his campus or house. Though Mia invited me to her birthday party tonight, so this is my only chance to see him.

"Bran!" Glyn waves in my face and I blink. "Where did you go?"

"Nowhere. I'm just a bit exhausted."

"I get it." She sighs. "Lan's been shadowing you lately, hasn't he?"

"Yeah."

"That must be so annoying. What's his plan now?"

"I don't know." Though I do know, but it doesn't matter now that Nikolai isn't in the picture anymore.

What if he really is done with me this time? What if he finally gave up after seeing that ugly side of me?

The thought sends a rush of nausea to my throat and I feel like I'll throw up.

"Poor Bran is just existing, but psychos won't leave him alone." Cecily pats my hand, bringing me back from the edge.

"Psychos?" I frown. "Do you mean Eli? He doesn't really bother me. He's actually pretty content when he's around me."

"Not Eli. Nikolai."

My heart thuds against my rib cage and I have to remind myself to breathe.

Jesus. How desperate could I be to get so flustered at the mere mention of his name?

"Nikolai?" I ask with the same nonchalance that I fake so well.

"Yeah, he was asking me about you the other day when Jeremy took me to the Heathens' mansion. He calls you lotus flower." Cecily winces. "It gave me the creeps to see him that interested in you."

"Right!" Glyn snaps her fingers. "Whenever I go to visit Kill, Nikolai asks about my brothers and I thought it was because of how much he hates Lan's guts, but he seems more interested in any tidbits about Bran. Did he always love art? When did he make his first painting? What does he like to do in his free time? What's his favorite color? Movie? Parent? Jeez. It feels like a police interrogation."

"What makes it creepy is how intense and insistent he gets. Jeremy said that's how he is and if I don't feel comfortable, I shouldn't answer him, but still. Why do you think he does that?"

"If I didn't know better, I would think he's crushing on you, Bran." Glyn giggles and bumps my shoulder with hers.

My body stiffens and I reach a hand to my nape, pulling at my hair until pain explodes not only in my scalp, but also deep in my soul.

"Bran?" Cecily watches me carefully. "Are you okay?"

"Not really," I murmur, battling against being suffocated under the weight of my own admission.

I am not okay.

Have I ever been okay? I don't remember the last time I was okay. No. I do. It was when Nikolai hugged me to sleep. I was okay that night.

Fuck it. I'm falling apart anyway. Might as well do it spectacularly. I let my hand fall to my side and face my sister. "You're right. He's crushing on me. Or he was."

Her eyes double in size. "How do you know? Did he tell you?"

"You could say that. Actually, I've been with him for a while now."

I regret my decision to just let it all out when Cecily spills her tea and Glyn looks at me as if I'm an alien.

And these two are supposed to be the least drama-free and understanding people in the group.

Bloody hell.

I tighten my grip on the teacup. "Are you going to say something or just continue to stare? Not that it's uncomfortable or anything remotely similar."

"Sorry..." Cecily dabs at the spots of tea on the table with a napkin. "I'm just making sure I heard you correctly. Did you just say you've *been* with Nikolai for a while? Like the way you were with Clara?"

"Don't compare him to Clara. I couldn't care less about her." *I'm losing myself because of him.*

"Oh my God," Glyn breathes out and cups her mouth, but that does nothing to hide her smile. "That day in the coffee shop when Kill said Nikolai is exclusive with someone, could that, by any chance, be you?"

"Yeah."

"Are you, like, coming out to us, right now? What am I supposed to do? Can I hug you?"

"I'd rather not," I say, feeling a bit lighter that she's smiling. That's good, right?

Cecily takes my hand in hers. "I'm so happy for you, Bran. I feel like a proud mama seeing you find someone you like."

"Yes! I hated that bitch Clara," Glyn agrees. "She was such an opportunist. You know, I didn't want to tell you this, but that night we had a party in the Elites' mansion, I saw her trying to kiss Lan and she was rubbing herself all over him. He threw her out and asked me not to tell you since it would just hurt your feelings. I despise her so much, I can't even begin to express it."

Lan never mentioned that. But then again, he never tells me anything.

And what do you tell him? You locked him out a long time ago.

"You..." I watch them closely. "Don't think it's weird that I like a guy after only dating girls all this time?"

"What does gender have to do with it?" Cecily strokes my hand. "I'm just happy you're happy."

"Me, too." Glyn interlinks her arm with mine and leans her head on my shoulder. "Whoever you like doesn't change who you are. You'll always be the coolest older brother ever."

"Best friend in the land of the living." Cecily scoots her chair over and grabs my other arm.

"Thanks." My voice catches and I clear my throat. "I'm lucky to have you both."

Cecily smiles up at me. "So, how long have you been with Nikolai?"

"Yes!" Glyn rests her chin on my shoulder. "We need deets."

"A couple of months."

"Wow. You guys really kept it under wraps." Cecily shakes her head. "I didn't suspect anything."

"*I* kept it under wraps. *I* am the one who didn't want to say the words aloud."

It's not really about coming out. It's about everything else I have to admit when I come out.

The reason why I didn't want to believe how so *not* normal I am.

"You needed time. It makes sense," Glyn says. "You were always with girls, so I never really suspected you were bi."

"I don't think I'm bi. I'm just gay." The words flow from my mouth easier than I thought. "Asexual, too. Or I was. I think the right term is demisexual. I can only feel sexual desire toward someone I like."

"I kind of suspected the ace part." Cecily smiles. "You were never attracted to anyone, no matter how hot they were. You looked at animals with more affection than you looked at your girlfriends."

"Animals aren't gold diggers." Glyn punches the air. "I want to beat those bitches for using you."

They didn't use me. I used them. But that's not a conversation I'm willing to have.

"I can't wait to see Mum's and Dad's reactions when they find out." Glyn grins and then pauses. "That is, if you want to tell them?"

"I will."

"They're going to flip their shit."

"In a good or a bad way?"

"Bran, you could literally be an alien and they'll love you. You're their favorite."

"No, I'm not."

"You totally are. Mum worships you, and Dad loves you so much, he's always like, Bran did this and Bran did that." She pauses. "Not sure he'll like Nikolai, though. He's a massive menace."

I wince. "It doesn't help that he's Kill's cousin."

"Kill can be civilized. Nikolai is...well, *not?*"

"Why Nikolai?" Cecily asks. "No matter how much I think about it, you guys are worlds apart in character. Where he's chaotic, you're organized to a fault. He's unhinged, you're methodical. You're, like, opposites."

"Maybe that's why it worked. Besides, he didn't really leave me much of a choice. He invaded my life and wasn't budging no matter how much I pushed him away...well, that is, until now."

"What's wrong?" Glyn pulls away, frowning. "Please tell me it's not because of Lan."

"They fought the other night, right?" Cecily winces. "Jeremy said Nikolai hasn't been himself this past week."

"It's not Lan, it's me. He didn't like the fact that I was hesitant."

"But this whole thing is new for you, Bran. It's okay to take your time." Glyn rubs my shoulder.

"Not if it means I could lose him. I think I hurt him whenever I do that, because he believes I'm ashamed of him."

"Oh."

"I'm not," I blurt out quickly. "I just... I can't help thinking about all the other factors, namely Lan."

"Ugh. Seriously, you need to get over your fixation on Lan's re- action to everything you do. I love you, Bran, I *really* do, but you give him so much leeway for all the shit he does." Glyn sighs. "He doesn't even care."

She's wrong. Or maybe I'm also holding on to another myth that was never true.

But seriously, what does it mean if I'm more worried about Lan's reaction than my damn parents'?

Not that I'm not concerned about Mum and Dad—I get a queasy feeling just thinking about that conversation, but Lan...

I can feel my stomach dipping when I imagine the haughty, dis- appointed expression he often gives my art.

He's always been perfect, and his disapproval gives me fucking nightmares.

"I mean, not to be the devil's advocate." Cecily grimaces. "But nothing good will happen if Lan knows about Nikolai. That'll be like when he learned about Killian and Glyn all over again."

"That's what I said." I rub my face. "Nikolai doesn't seem to agree. I really don't want them to fight again."

"You're right…" Glyn's shoulders droop. "It won't be pretty."

"You bitches!" A loud voice comes through and we all groan as Remi slides to our table, dragging Ava behind him. "I can't believe you're having afternoon tea without my lordship. If I hadn't seen Glyn's story, I would've been none the wiser. And then I find this one lurking in the house like a thief. You bitches will be the death of me, seriously."

"I'm not a thief, I was just looking for Bran." Ava kisses my cheek. "Hi, Bran."

"Hey."

Ava sits beside Cecily and hugs her. "Missed you, bestie."

Cecily rubs her arm. "Everything okay?"

"Yeah." She smooches her cheek.

Remi pulls up a chair and invades the space between me and Cecily, and they fight about who gets to sit beside me.

Since I'm the most levelheaded of the group, they always want to be with me. I often get texts like, *It's boring without you, Bran.*

Even though I'm not a clown like Remi or hyper like Ava, I have a special place in the group.

Why did I ever feel like I'd be judged by my closest friends? My intimate circle of support?

No, it's not them I was scared of. It's *me.* It's always my-fucking-self. I'm my own worst enemy.

"So what were you talking about before my lordship's spectacular arrival?" Remi steals Glyn's macarons and Cecily's tea.

"Nothing." Cecily winks at me.

I shake my head at her and take a deep breath. "Remi, Ava. I want to tell you something."

Though I'm joined by Cecily and Glyn, my movements are stiff at best as we walk into the Heathens' mansion.

My sister and my friend have been here countless times, considering their boyfriends, but that's not the case for me.

I remain in my element as we push past the partygoers. The Heathens went all out with this birthday party. Countless lights cover the ceiling, casting violet and blue lights on the people jumping to the trendy music.

Alcohol is thrown around everywhere and I would really like to be wasted for this, but that's just cowardly, so I stop myself from snatching a drink.

I catch a glimpse of Maya, who's wearing a glamorous white dress, dancing with a group of people in bizarre outfits. But I don't see Mia.

A few weeks ago, Mia introduced me to Maya, and she's nice, but I prefer Mia's company. We're both introverts and get along without talking much.

Glyn leads us to the second floor and we continue pushing our way through.

My chest aches when I catch a glimpse of Mia dressed in the black version of Maya's dress and dancing between Killian and Nikolai. Though they seem to be kicking and punching each other.

I really don't like it when Killian hits him. I know it's their dynamic and they've been like that their entire lives, but he needs to stop putting his fucking hands on him or I'll break them.

Good grief.

Where did that violent thought come from?

"Hey you." Jeremy slides to our side, smoothly, if I might add, and kisses Cecily a bit longer than I'm comfortable with watching.

"Hi," she breathes as he wraps an arm around the small of her back.

My gaze strays back to Nikolai of its own accord. He looks so damn well-built in a black T-shirt and jeans. A few rebellious strands escape his ponytail and fall on his forehead. His muscles ripple with every move and the intertwined tattoos running down his biceps and arms instantly distinguish him from the crowd.

I've always found him beautiful. No, not only beautiful. He's categorically *hot*. It just took me some time to realize that I was becoming hopelessly attracted to everything about him. The fact that I haven't been able to touch him for days on end is messing with my head.

My gaze studies him closer, taking in his sharp jawline, full lips, and—

I frown when I get a clear look at his face. His eyes are dark, almost bottomless, his mouth is set in a line, and he seems…off.

Like that time during the fight.

He must be having one of his episodes. Though I'm not sure what type of episode it is, he mentioned they come and go. I haven't seen him in this state since that night of the fight. Only, now, he seems more closed off.

And I want to…what?

What the fuck do you think you can do when you're broken yourself?

Killian notices us, or more like spots Glyn and stops dancing. Mia and Nikolai do, too. My friend smiles at me. Nikolai scowls.

My nape burns and my skin starts to feel black, inky, and foreign.

It's been a week since I last saw him, and while I didn't expect a welcoming ceremony, I also didn't think he'd look this displeased.

Glyn hugs Mia and hands her a bag. "It's small gifts from the three of us. Happy Birthday."

"Thank you. You didn't have to," she signs, then grins at me and types on her phone before she shows me. "I didn't think you'd come."

"You personally invited me. I wouldn't miss it." I smile, fighting the need to ogle her brother.

"What the fuck are you doing here?" Nikolai shoves Mia behind him and gets in my face, his voice harsh, face closed off. If it weren't for his familiar smell, though now mixed with cigarettes and alcohol, I'd think I was looking at a stranger.

Is this how he felt every time I pretended not to see him in public? Because it's no different than having a fucking knife lodged between my ribs.

"Another elaborate plan from your brother? What is it this time? Arson? Assault? Murder, maybe?" The coldness behind his words leaves me speechless.

Nikolai never speaks to me in that tone. He never *snaps* at me.

And the fact that he's done it twice now makes the grim possibility of losing him a terrifying reality.

But you know what? Fuck him.

Why the hell is he angry when he ghosted me for a whole week?

"Bran is my friend. I invited him to my birthday," his sister signs, her movements smooth and determined.

"It's okay, Mia," I tell her and keep glaring at him. "I couldn't care less about your brother's opinion of me, but it's probably better that I leave."

She shakes her head frantically.

"Mia is right," Jeremy says somewhere behind me. "You're our guest."

Killian clutches Nikolai's shoulder. "If you can accept Glyn and Cecily, you'll have to accept Bran, too. He has nothing to do with Lan, despite the creepy physical resemblance."

"He's right." Glyn looks at me with an encouraging smile. "Bran is completely different from Lan. I promise."

Jesus. She sounds like she's selling me for some position.

Nikolai's eyes never leave my face, and I can't help staring back. While I don't really like the anger, I like that he can't look away from me.

It's the least he can do after disappearing on me as if I'm nothing.

Mia jumps in front of him and signs, "Please don't ruin my birthday."

Nikolai flashes me one last glare before he releases a throaty sound and snatches his pack of cigarettes from the table.

My frown deepens. Things aren't good if he's smoking. He told me he's a mood smoker and only resorts to them when the chaos in his head is too massive to contain.

I really need to get him alone, talk to him, and make sure everything is okay.

Just when I'm thinking about the best way to do that, the last person I need waltzes right in the middle of the scene like he owns the place.

Lan scans his surroundings and then flashes us a diabolical smirk. "What's with the tense atmosphere? I thought this was a birthday. Also, did someone mention the word 'ruin'?"

TWENTY-EIGHT

Nikolai

FOR THE FIRST TIME IN FUCKING EVER, I DON'T HAVE MYSELF under control.

And that's saying something since everyone always thinks I have a loose screw and can't be labeled sane by any stretch of the imagination.

It's different this time.

I knew it was *disastrously* different when I didn't want to talk to my dad. If I did, even he would be insisting on the pills.

A part of *me* is insisting on the fucking pills.

I hate the fact that I'm even thinking about that possibility. But there's no other way to kill this state of chaos. I haven't been sleeping, eating, fucking *breathing*, and have been surviving on violence, cigarettes, and alcohol.

The alternative to the pills is being stuck in the middle of a black rage for the foreseeable future.

Rage that can't be doused by any fighting, riding, or any extended fucking sight of blood. If anything, it's been mounting, intensifying until it's the only form of oxygen I suck into my lungs day in and day out.

The only time I can breathe properly is when I stare at Bran's texts and stalk his social media like a stage-five creep. I hate that I can't hug him to sleep or kiss him. I hate that I can't look at him and cling to him like an annoying octopus. After he poured his heart out to me in the tub, the last thing I wanted was to leave him, but I had to.

I still *have* to.

My current state doesn't allow for me to see him. I don't trust myself not to hurt him. I really, *really* fucking don't.

Even now, I'm battling the urge to grab him by the fucking throat and bruise his lips in front of the whole world. He'd hate me for good this time, but who fucking cares.

The only thing that puts a halt to my plan is the presence of his less pleasant eyesore twin.

"What the fuck do you think you're doing here?" Jeremy asks on everyone's behalf.

Everyone, and I mean every single fucking person present, is alarmed by the asshole.

Everyone but his precious brother, who looks pained on Landon's behalf.

He's never looked at me like that. Has never shown me an ounce of the concern he unconditionally has for his brother.

It's an illogical thought, but I can't shove it out of my broken mind. My muscles tighten and a flood of rage douses me in one fucking go.

"I thought this was a birthday and everyone was invited." Landon speaks with a nonchalance that scratches my wavering resolve like nails on a chalkboard.

"You're not," Kill replies.

"Seems that I am now." The motherfucker has the nerve to walk to my sister. *My* fucking sister. "Happy Birthday. Aside from the gift of my attendance, I have something else for you, but I'd rather give it to you in private—"

My body moves on autopilot as I slam my fist in the cunt's face. He staggers back and blood explodes on his lip.

"Lan." Glyn leaves Kill and rushes to him. "Just…go."

"I didn't go through all the trouble of bribing incompetent security guards just to leave," he continues talking in that casual tone that will get him killed. Preferably tonight.

I step forward to finish the job and lose his brother for fucking good, because I'm suicidal like that, but Mia clutches my arm and then signs, "He's not worth it, Niko."

I'm going to kill him.

I'm going to fucking kill him.

Kill—

"Time out." He lifts a hand. "Before you proceed with your attempts at rearranging my features, allow me to clarify an important element. I happen to be in the process of courting your sister, and any attempts at ruining my face will not play in the favor of said task."

What did this asshole just say?

Did he just mention *courting*? And who? *My* sister? *My* Mia?

"I'm going to fucking kill you before you lay a hand on her." I storm toward him.

"Oh, that's already done."

Bran closes his eyes and pinches the bridge of his nose as he breathes slowly.

What the fuck…?

He's not surprised.

Why is he *not* surprised?

"What the fuck did you just say?" I ask slowly, my fucked-up brain refusing to believe the words I heard.

No. I'm refusing to believe Bran knew about this fuckery all along. He wouldn't…

Why not? He obviously cares about his brother's safety and opinion more than yours.

"I said." Lan stands toe-to-toe with me. "The touching part already happened. In fact, our rendezvous included more than touching, but I'll spare you the details since you're her brother."

"You fucking—" I raise my fist, but when I'm about to drive it into his face, Bran slides in front of him.

It's too late.

My fist slams into Bran's face.

Fuck, fuck, fuck!

The blow is so powerful that Bran falls back against his brother and Landon grabs him, then dabs at the blood at his lip.

I don't resist when hands pull me back. I don't even know whose they are as I stare at the blood gushing out of Bran's nose. His face is pained, but he's trying hard to remain unaffected.

Fuck!

What the fuck have I done? Me hitting Bran? How could I do that? Even unintentionally?

My jaw tics and every fiber inside me urges me to make sure he's okay. But I can't do that when his fucking brother is all over him.

So I direct my wrath at my sister. "Is it true?"

Her eyes double in size like whenever she's done something she's not supposed to. This, however, is drastically different from sneaking out at night or plotting trouble with Maya.

"Is what the fucker said true, Mia?" I ask again, a vein nearly popping in my neck. "Have you been sleeping with him?"

She steals a glance at Landon and then signs, "It's not what you think."

"And what does he think?" Landon releases Bran and I have to summon ungodly fucking resolve to not look at him and focus on his brother instead.

"You shut up," she signs.

"I'm happy to shut up, but only if you tell the truth and nothing but the truth."

"What is he talking about?" Kill asks with a note of tension.

Mia flashes Landon her signature hostile glare and signs, "It was just a ruse that meant nothing. It's all over now."

He grins with a note of sadism. "I disrespectfully disagree. It was more than a ruse and is far from being over. Mia and I came to a slight disagreement about priorities and my notorious penchant for anarchy. Despite my dramatic entry, I'm not here to stir up any shit. On the contrary, I came to propose a long-due truce between our clubs."

"Not even when you're buried six feet under," I snap, and this time, I can't help it. I steal a glimpse at Bran and pause when I find him looking at me.

His eyes are begging, *pleading*. For his fucking brother.

All this time, Landon has been an annoying asshole, and despite Jeremy's attempts to rile me up against him, I took Kill's side and let everything he did slide. Because like Kill, I'm in too deep with Landon's sibling, and I can't hurt him if I want to be with his brother.

However, Mia is off-fucking-limits.

I'm going to kill Landon for touching my sister. No one will stop me, not even Bran.

"I wouldn't be so quick to rule it out," Landon says, still looking at Mia. "This rare chance will work out so well for both of us if you just give it a go."

"My sister is not for fucking sale," I growl, my voice unsteady and dripping with the tension that's flooding me.

"I never suggested that. Unlike what she said, Mia came to meet me every night. There was no coercion involved in our nighttime rendezvous."

What the fuck?

I look at Mia as if an alien abducted my real sister and put an imposter in her place.

She's not the type who'd fall for Landon's fake charms. She's... Mia. My sister is better than this.

Which is why I'm proud when she signs, "Whether the truce happens or not, I'll never go back to you."

A smirk curves his lips. "Never say never."

"You're insane," she signs.

"Guilty as charged."

"You won't have me."

"I had you once."

"Won't be happening again."

"We won't know until I try."

"Stop being delusional."

"Stop fighting the inevitable."

That's fucking it.

I wedge myself between them not so gently, and Jeremy accompanies me as I glare at the motherfucker. "Leave before I fuck up your face."

"Last I checked, that's not a good starting point for a truce, no?"

Bran grabs onto his brother's arm and doesn't look at me as he says, "Let's just go."

"I won't be taking a step outside unless you give me your word about the truce." Landon stares at Jeremy. "You know this is for everyone's benefit. Cecily and Glyn included."

"Not happening." I speak with difficulty, trying not to grab Bran and shove him to my side.

"It can be for your benefit, too," Landon tells me. "In return, I will refrain from breaking your face for the damage you inflicted on my brother."

"Forget it, Lan." Bran tugs harder on his arm, his voice sounding strangled. "I'm fine."

"No, you're not." Landon cocks his head and glares at me. "I don't like it when others harm my family."

"Funny coming from you. Once I'm done with you, nothing will be left for anyone to recognize."

Bran finally looks at me and I stare back.

I'm going to fucking kill your brother. Since you already hate me, I might as well go all the way.

"Please stop," Glyn takes her brother's side and pleads with Kill. "Lan isn't the type who offers truces, so can you take it?"

"Even if we agree to the truce," my cousin says, "Mia is off the table."

"That's not for you to decide, is it?" Landon smiles, and I swear to fuck, he's the most provocative asshole on this planet. And here I thought Kill was dire.

Jeremy keeps a strong grip on my shoulder and even that can't keep me in place. "She already told you no."

"I can work with a no." Landon walks to my sister, passes her a velvet box, and has the audacity to whisper in her ear.

I push Jeremy away and shove Landon back so hard, he falls

against his siblings. Bran staggers to keep his brother upright and I curse under my breath.

Tonight is just a fucked-up fucking case of fucking fuckery! Why did he have to be here?

This is why I didn't want to fucking see him.

Fuck!!

"I'll take that as you saying yes to my offer. As for the Mia issue, I'll leave that to her. Just know that I won't take lightly to any censorship or attempts to keep me away from her. You can torture me if you fancy. I'll also leave my door open in case you want to kidnap me and exact revenge for past travesties, so let me know your plan. Or don't. I'm open to surprises." Landon glides his attention to Kill. "You and I are even, considering the whole Glyn situation."

My cousin's face hardens and he steps forward, but Glyn and Bran tug their brother back.

"I'll be out of your hair," he calls. "For some reason, it feels like I'm not welcome here. I wonder why."

"You motherfucking—"

I lunge at him, but I stop when Bran mouths, "Please."

Fucking hell.

I let Jeremy and the others pull me back as I watch the three of them going down the stairs.

Bran glances at me one last time, his shoulders crowding with tension, his eyes full of anguish.

I just found out my baby sister is getting in bed with the enemy in every sense of the word, but the part that makes me lose my fucking mind is the damn pain in Bran's eyes.

Can we talk?

We can meet briefly in the penthouse. You don't have to spend the night if you don't want to.

You looked really on edge. I just want to make sure you're okay. Can I see you?

So you're not going to apologize for punching me? Not that I'm cross with you or anything.

Okay, I am but not about the punch. I know you didn't do that on purpose, but you're definitely ignoring me on purpose.

About Lan and Mia, I didn't want to keep that a secret, but I knew you'd throw a fit if you found out, and, well... I was right, wasn't I?

If it's of any consolation, I think Lan is really serious about her. He's never been serious about anyone in his entire life. He's never had a relationship or fought for a girl's affection. Can you believe he asked me to teach him how to practice empathy just to win her over? That's the first time he's ever asked me anything and I'm loving it. We got close this week, and I'm really enjoying our time together.

I even showed him a few of the paintings I keep a secret and he said he's proud of me. Can you believe it? Lan being PROUD of me? The last time he said that was when we were young... Well, I might have played a part in how we grew apart, but anyway, he said he knows the right agent for me, and it's HIS agent. He introduced us the other day and I really like her better than the one Mum has been trying to make me sign with. She understands my vision so well, and maybe soon, I'll stop keeping those paintings a secret. I'm starting to have hopes and it's because of none other than Lan. Isn't that crazy?

Though I'm not in a particularly good mood.

Hint. It's because of you.

I kind of miss you.

Okay, that was a lie. I REALLY miss you.

Nikolai, please. Don't do this.

You're clearly reading my texts, but you can't spare me a few words? You know what? Forget it.

Those were the texts Bran sent me over the past week, and yes, I read every one of them, but I couldn't reply.

If I did, I'd get disastrously violent. My racing thoughts and fucked-up head haven't calmed down yet. For the first time ever, I've spent two weeks on a high. A whole two fucking weeks.

This is *not* the state I want to talk to him in.

But against my better judgment—which is MIA lately—I'm out-side the Elites' mansion, where I used to wait for him every morning.

I lean against my bike that's camouflaged by a bent tree and stare at the reason why I rode all the way here.

Despite the fact that I don't reply to his texts, I actually follow his every move, whether through his or his friends' social media.

An hour ago, he posted a picture of Remington clutching him in a chokehold as both of them laughed. They were fucking *laughing*.

What made it worse was the caption. *Late-night chats with Remi are the best. I'm so thankful to have you @lord-remington-astor.*

And then Remington's reply. *Cheers, mate. You know you're my fave. Don't tell my spawn.*

I wasn't thinking when I came here. Something I haven't been doing enough of.

Sometimes, I believe the best solution for this whole fuckery is to go into the Elites' mansion, kill Landon, then kidnap his brother, but something tells me that won't go over well.

As if that dilemma wasn't enough, he had to post that picture with *Remington*. In his damn bedroom.

Jesus fucking Christ.

Is that what 'Forget it' means? Has he already found a replace-ment and tossed me aside?

Not in his goddamn dreams.

My fingers are stiff as I type.

> **Me:** Come outside.

> **Bran:** Look who decided to finally acknowledge my existence.

> **Me:** Come fucking outside, Brandon.

> **Bran:** Where? Please don't tell me you're here.

> **Me:** Outside. Now.

> **Bran:** Fine. You're such a joy today.

I narrow my eyes at the phone. Of course I'm not a joy compared to that clown *Remington*.

Bran even once said, "He's just so funny." He fucking *isn't*.

My muscles are about to snap from how wound up and tight they feel. Two weeks on a high is just too long and I don't sense any signs of coming down anytime soon.

I took the pills the night I punched Bran, because I couldn't trust myself anymore. I had to admit that I was losing control. They didn't help. Unless nearly fucking drowning in the pool is considered help.

Still, I took three of them earlier so that I won't do something I'll regret. The thought of hurting him fucking terrifies me. But I don't think they're working. The urge to punch someone is greater than I can contain.

I should've stayed away.

I really shouldn't be here—

My heart rate picks up when I catch a glimpse of Bran striding hurriedly toward me. He knows the exact place where I'll be waiting.

God-fucking-damn-it. I've missed him and his sophisticated presence. The plain black shorts and the gray T-shirt do nothing to hide his fit physique.

His hair is in a bit of a mess, falling haphazardly over his forehead, making him look more human instead of his uptight side.

He comes to a halt in front of me and his expression slowly shifts from anger to...softness? Since when does he soften?

"We could've met in the penthouse. You didn't have to come here. Not that I didn't want you to be here..."

I stare at him and keep my mouth shut. I don't trust myself not to snap right now.

"Nikolai, listen." He rounds the bike and stands in front of me. "There are a lot of things I want to talk to you about. I actually spoke to my friends and Glyn and—"

"Shut the fuck up." I grab him by the throat and shove him against the tree's trunk. "I'm not here to talk."

I crash my lips to his and he releases a startled sound, but I swallow it the fuck up. He tastes of lemon, ginger, and honey.

He tastes like my imminent downfall.

I thrust my tongue against his, slurping, tugging, and biting until he moans.

He moans for me as if he's been fucking waiting for this. As if he didn't already replace me with someone else.

"Niko...wait." He wrenches his lips away.

"I'm done waiting." I chase his mouth, then claim it again. He pulls on my hair, but I feel nothing. No pain. No thoughts.

Just fucking blind possessiveness.

Twisted desire.

The need to fucking *own* him claws inside me like a beast.

I yank my lips away from his and whirl him around, then shove his face against the tree, my fingers wrapping around his nape. I tug down his shorts, revealing his ass.

"Nikolai...?"

My lips line up with his ear and I breathe so harshly, it's nearly a growl. "Tell me to stop. This is your only chance to do so. Tell me you don't want me anymore. Say it and I'll go."

"It's not that..." His choppy exhales echo in the air like my own aphrodisiac.

"If it's not that, shut your fucking mouth."

"What's wrong...?"

"Shut it." I pull out my cock that's been hard since I saw him, and spit on my hand. "No lube. This will have to do."

He releases an affirmative sound, but it ends with a grunt when I push past the tight ring of muscle.

My body that's been uncharacteristically dead for the past two weeks roars back to life when I'm sheathed inside him.

"Fuck," I growl, my teeth biting down on the hollow of his throat.

Bran turns his face to glimpse at me and I don't like it.

I don't like how he looks at me with those soft eyes as if he missed me. As if he didn't fucking *replace* me.

So I thrust harder, reach deeper, go faster.

"Niko..." he groans when I hit that spot with my piercings. "Fuck...we're in public."

"And yet you're so hard you're humping the tree. You get hot and bothered about the prospect of being caught."

"Jesus...mmfuck...I missed the way you fuck me."

"Shut the fuck up." This time, I wrap my fingers around his mouth. I don't want to hear his voice. I don't want to hear what he has to say and I don't want to get lost in him again.

I'm just proving a point. The fact that he belongs to me and only *me*. The fact that he still only wants me and will never fucking replace me.

"You're mine, Brandon. Fucking *mine*. If you think there's another option out there for you other than me, I have a news flash for you." I bite the shell of his ear and he moans, the sound muffled by my hand. "You fucking don't. Just know that I'll slaughter *anyone* you let near you and fuck you in their blood."

I squeeze his cock and jerk him fast and rough, matching the rhythm of my cock in his ass. He thrusts his hips forward then back, slamming his ass against my groin over and over until his madness mirrors mine. The slaps of flesh against flesh echo in the air as I pound him, rough and unhinged.

Fucking fuck.

He comes all over my hand, groaning and trying to say something, but my grip on his mouth doesn't allow him to.

Even after he comes, he continues to ride my cock, jerking back and forth, milking me, dragging the orgasm from somewhere deep in my fucked-up soul instead of my body.

I come deep in him and he moans, his teeth sinking into my fingers, and his body shudders beneath mine.

If I didn't know it before, then I'm sure now. I'll never enjoy fucking again if it isn't with him.

He fucking *broke* me.

Literally and figuratively.

My mind is still a goddamn mess even as I pull out of him. My cum trickles down his balls and thighs, and I want to fuck it right back inside him like I usually do, but this is not about touching.

This is about proving a fucking point.

When I remove my hand, Bran's lips reach for mine, but I step back and out of reach.

I've never seen him so hurt, so distraught as he looks right now. All the pleasure has vanished and he watches me slowly, warily, as if he's seeing my eyes for the first time.

We tuck ourselves in as he faces me.

I grab his hand and he stiffens as I remove the watch and check beneath it. There's an old scar but no new ones that I can see. Though he could be doing it somewhere hidden, like with the fucking nicks due to 'shaving.'

"I didn't…" He slowly pulls his hand free. "I haven't done it since the last time."

"Good."

He cocks his head, his face unreadable. "Can you tell me what's wrong now?"

"You better not let anyone else touch you or I swear to fuck my murder threats will become reality."

He nods, his expression serious. "We're exclusive, remember?"

"You should be the one who remembers that."

"What the hell is that supposed to mean?"

I turn around and hop on my bike.

"Wait. You're leaving? Just like that?"

"Just like that."

"Nikolai. Don't you fucking dare walk away from me."

"You've done that countless times. Why can't I?"

His expression drips with pain and he opens his mouth. I should be on my way, but I can't. Not when he has something to say.

"I'm sorry."

"What the fuck did I say about apologizing?"

"What do you want me to say or do? I'm trying to get close to you, but the harder I try, the further you slip away."

"Let me ask you." I turn sideways to face him. "If you had to choose between me and your brother. Who would you pick?"

"Neither. It's not supposed to be a choice. Besides, if you accept him with Mia, he'll have no choice but to accept you with me."

"My sister is not up for fucking negotiation."

His face falls and he swallows thickly. "Then I guess you made your choice."

"And so did you." I rev the engine.

I need to get out of here before I proceed with my very irrational idea about kidnapping him.

A voice inside me demands that, scratching and clawing at the fucking foundation of my being just to keep him close.

But if I do that, if I take him, I'll hurt him. I just know I will fucking *lose* him.

So even though I continue staring at him in the rearview mirror, standing there with his hand in his hair, I don't go back.

I need to eliminate the vermin that is Landon King.

Then I need a whole bottle of the fucking pills.

TWENTY-NINE

Brandon

> **Nikolai:** I'll make the choice for you about Landon. Consider him dealt with.

T HAT'S THE TEXT I GET AFTER ANOTHER FUCKING WEEK OF radio silence from Nikolai.

After he fucked me against the tree and then left. Without letting me kiss him. Talk to him. Nothing.

He even gave me an ultimatum while being nonnegotiable about his own sister.

Lan and I might have our problems, but he's my twin brother. The person I know the best. The person I look to whenever I'm drowning in fucking self-loathing. Watching him be his shameless, confident self gives me hope that I could be okay. If my identical twin is, then I could be as well.

No one but Lan and I understand the complexity of our relationship. Not even Mum and Dad are privy to that.

So how could Nikolai give me that ultimatum? How could he suggest that he'll 'deal' with my brother and think I'll let him?

How the fuck could he even *make* me choose?

At Mia's birthday party, I noticed he wasn't himself. He had this empty, bottomless expression, and sometimes, he'd look at me and I didn't think he was seeing me.

I've wanted to be there for him, and I've fucking tried countless times, for that matter. He's the one who's slammed the door in my face.

I can't help thinking this is revenge for all the times I kept him at arm's length. The push-and-pull game has reversed and I'm now on the receiving end.

But I've never threatened his family. I might have hidden Lan and Mia's fling, but I really thought it would blow over and it'd do more harm than good to let him know.

And yes, I might have been distant at times, but I was there when he wanted me to be.

He, on the other hand, has made it abundantly clear that he wants nothing to do with me anymore.

He doesn't communicate. Doesn't come to the penthouse. And he's completely fine with the prospect of losing me by hurting my brother.

Forget about being heartbroken. I'm fucking livid right now.

I texted Mia about her brother's plans and she gave me a code to access the Heathens' mansion.

That's where I am right now after driving like a madman.

However, when I arrive at the annexed house where Mia told me to meet her, I'm stopped by three bulky guards. Two of them are built like rocks and look at me as if I'm a cockroach.

They're standing on either side of the metal door, arms crossed in front of them, but I catch a glimpse of their guns holstered at their waists.

The one who steps forward is a younger blond man who looks no older than me, but his expression is solemn as he orders in a Russian accent, "Step back."

"I'm here to see Mia," I say in my firm voice.

"That won't be possible. Leave the property or we'll escort you out. The second option will not be pleasant."

"I won't move until I see Mia and my brother."

He steps forward, but I remain rooted in place. I have no doubt that he'll pummel me to the ground, but I don't care. At this point, all I want is to take my brother home in one piece.

"Tell Nikolai I'm here," I say when he reaches for me.

"What?"

"Tell him I want to see him and that he doesn't want to fucking test me."

"Why would Nikolai want to see *you*?" he says with a note of condescension that gets under my skin.

In his eyes, I'm Lan's identical twin and, therefore, Nikolai would hold the same level of contempt for me. But that's not true. Even Jeremy and Killian actually like me and have always differentiated me from Lan's antics.

Nikolai has, too, from the beginning. He calls me lotus flower because of it. But now, he's being a massive dick.

The guard starts to push me and I fight against him. But before he can punch me in the face, the door creaks open.

My breath hitches when Lan steps out, swaying on unsteady legs. Blood gushes from the corner of his lip and purple bruises decorate his cheeks and neck.

But the part that leaves me paralyzed is the way his left hand lies limp by his side as he holds his forearm.

No, no, no…

I wrench myself from the guard's grip and run to him. "Lan… are you okay?"

"What the fuck are you doing here, Bran?" he snaps and grabs me by the nape. "Why can't you just stop being a busybody and stay still?"

"I can't watch you being hurt and do nothing." I inspect his arm, my heart thundering loudly when I touch his wrist and he groans. "Is your…wrist okay?"

He waves me away. "Nikolai was jealous and tried to break it, but I think I got away with a sprain."

"Nikolai did?"

"He said either I leave Mia or he breaks my artist wrist."

I close my eyes briefly, but it does nothing to disperse the pain flooding through me. "You picked Mia."

It's not a question, because I know now how much he'd self-destruct for her. I've never seen him dedicated to anyone as much as he is to her.

A pained, bloody grin curls his lips. "Sure as fuck. Would do it again in a heartbeat."

He coughs and then spits a mouthful of blood on the concrete floor. I grab him by the waist and start dragging him to where I had to leave the car near the entrance.

"Let's get you to a doctor."

He grumbles a noise at the back of his throat, but he leans on me and lets me half carry him.

"I've got to say, it's refreshing to see you worried about me." He ruffles my hair.

"Stop messing around, Lan. You screwed up your wrist and all you can think about is me being worried about you?"

"It's a very important element."

"Seriously?"

"Uh-huh. It means you care."

"I always care. You're the one who doesn't."

"Fuck that. If you weren't here, I would've introduced that bunch of Heathens to my special brand of fucked up."

"And get yourself killed?"

"Will you cry at my funeral?"

"Lan! Don't joke about nonsense like that."

"But I want to know. Will you?"

I sigh as I help him into the passenger seat. "You're my twin brother."

"And?" He looks at me expectantly, like a fucking hyena who's waiting to pounce on its prey. Or maybe it's just expectation and I'm reading too much into it.

"And that means I wouldn't be the same without you. Not that you share the sentiment." I start to close the door, but he shoves his foot against it, keeping it open.

"You know, that's your problem, Bran. You always assume things about me instead of fucking *talking* to me. It's a nasty habit that needs to go." He holds my gaze with his identical one. "I wouldn't be the same without you, either, twat. You're part of me."

"Ownership again? Classic."

"It's not fucking ownership. If I *owned* you, I wouldn't give two flying fucks about you because I'd already have you in my grasp." He clutches my hand and I wince at how hard it is. "I want you to listen to me and listen carefully. You're *part* of me. That means I'm critical of you like I'm critical of myself. I see your safety as my own, sometimes even more so because you tend to think of others' comfort more than your own. I hated it when you closed yourself behind a fortress and kept me out. I *need* you to understand that."

I swallow thickly, his words demolishing a wall inside me brick by brick.

"You put me as Spare Parts in your phone when we were thirteen."

"Because you demanded your own room. You said, and I quote, 'I don't want to share space with that vermin.' I'm nothing if not petty."

I wince. That was around the time everything started to fall apart.

All I can do is nod and pull my hand from his.

He groans when he lays his wrist on his thigh, and the anger from earlier washes over me again.

"Give me a second."

"Where are you going?" he asks, but I lock him in the car so he doesn't try to follow.

Then I march back to the annex house. I catch a glimpse of Killian and Mia walking toward the main house as she signs furiously and he listens with a tight expression.

Jeremy is talking to Nikolai in front of the annex where the guards are still poised nearby.

I stride toward them, but once again, I'm stopped by the blond guy.

Nikolai lifts his head and a frown appears between his brows. His hair is tied in a ponytail and he's actually wearing a T-shirt and trousers. But then again, he wouldn't want to get my brother's fucking blood on him.

"Let him go, Ilya," he tells the blond and he reluctantly releases me.

I walk forward and I drive my fist into his face. He reels back and clutches his cheek as his darkened eyes snap to mine.

Jeremy is stunned for a second. I am, too, as I resist the urge to shake my hand. That fucking *hurts*.

It's worth it, though.

"Congratulations, Nikolai. You get your fucking wish." I point a finger at his chest. "We're over."

Jeremy stares between us with a calculative expression, as if he's linking patterns, but I honestly couldn't care less anymore.

I turn to leave, but Nikolai grabs me by the arm and his hard chest presses to my back as he growls in my ear, "In your fucking dreams, baby."

Fuck him.

I elbow him and release myself from his grip. Without looking back, I jog to where I left Lan.

Maybe it's time I put this whole thing behind me.

For good.

THIRTY

Brandon

"Y OU'RE LOSING FOCUS, SON."

I lift my head and jerk when I accidentally touch the hot pot.

"Bran!" Dad takes my hand in his and inspects my fingers.

His touch burns my cursed wrist. I feel as if his laser eyes will reach beneath the watch and see the evidence of how fucked I am.

Glyn was right. My parents love me—they *always* have. But a part of me can't help thinking it's because of the façade I put on so well. Their dutiful son, an obedient teenager, never complains and never throws a fit.

Never gets in their way. Never causes them headaches like Lan does.

A part of me believes that if they see me for who I truly am, I'll lose the Son of the Year Award faster than lightning.

That prospect scares the shit out of me.

I subtly pull my hand from Dad and plaster on a smile. "It's nothing. Just a little burn."

"You need to be careful in the kitchen. That's the first rule of cooking."

"I know. Sorry."

Dad pats my shoulder affectionately and goes back to chopping carrots, but not before he offers me his golden smile. The one Lan and I inherited. Though he's a much blonder, more muscular version of us.

Mum said he was the most popular guy in school and garnered more attention than he should have. And I can see it. Not only does he drip with the 'superior' King genes, as Grandpa Jonathan likes to call them, but he's also levelheaded and charismatic to a fault.

A select few prefer to do business with him instead of Uncle Aiden because he's much more amiable. Uncle is…well, let's say his motto is his way or the highway. Eli and Lan definitely take after him in that department.

While many have flocked to Uncle Aiden, Dad is the actual gem with his intense yet caring personality. His outward ruthlessness yet inner warmth. His firm demands and bear hugs. Dad has always been the ultimate role model and the type of man I've strived to be.

Responsible. Reliable. In control.

Too bad I'm too messed up in the head to ever be able to achieve that.

I thought with time, everything would get better, but the ink has been festering inside me and painting every beautiful color and memory in black.

And the thought of everyone seeing me at the end of that process makes me nauseous.

I'd rather bleed to death than let anyone see me like that.

"Bran?"

I blink at my dad, that last thought still coiling my stomach as I smile. "Yeah?"

"Shouldn't you be adding the spices now?"

"Oh, right." I focus on that and methodically sprinkle precise amounts of each one into the pot.

But even this activity that I used to take immense pleasure in only causes me pain now.

I can't stop thinking about the times I was cooking in the

penthouse and Nikolai was being clingy, and while I called him annoying, I actually loved having him around.

I loved the fact that he couldn't stay away from me—not even for a minute. He made it his mission to touch me all the time as if I were the magnet to his steel.

Then everything came to an end.

"You sure it's okay to be away from school all this time?" Dad asks amidst the sound of chopping. "It's been a week since you came home."

"Yeah. I told my supervising professor I'd be working on my graduation piece from here." I smile and joke, "Bored of me already?"

"Nonsense. I'd rather you move back in. You know that." He sighs. "Have kids, they said. They'll keep you company, they said. And here I am trying not to haul the three of you back home."

"You and Uncle Aiden left Grandpa, too."

"That's different. Your grandpa is a bloody dictator and a ruthless autocrat. He couldn't wait for us to sod off so he could crack on with his plan to conquer the world."

"The same grandpa who worships at Nan's feet and treats Glyn like a spoiled princess?"

"That one, yes. Your nan tamed him. Before her, he was an insufferable prick and was often cross with us. We clashed all the damn time." He shakes his head with apparent nostalgia and extends his hand.

I pass him the bowl of potatoes before he even asks for it. We're in sync like that, Dad and I.

"Really? But you guys have a good relationship now."

"That's the thing about relationships. They take work and time. Besides, admittedly, I was a little wanker as a teenager. I might have burned down his mansion and caused enough problems in school to make him a permanent visitor."

My hand pauses on stirring the broth. "No way."

"Let's say I was wild."

"I can't believe that. You, wild? Intense, yes. But *wild*?"

"Wilder than an untamed black horse. No one could restrict me. Not even your grandfather."

"Wow. It's hard to imagine you doing all that."

"Who do you think your brother gets his behavioral issues from?"

"Oh." I continue stirring, breathing in the smell of aromatic basil and oregano. "Oh! Is that why you were strict with him at one point?"

"It was like watching myself and seeing the image from Uncle's point of view. Not a pleasant feeling." He clutches my shoulders. "But I have you, so I can't complain."

He pushes past me to the cupboard and I remain frozen in place, the thoughts from earlier rushing to the surface like a hungry shark.

"Will you be ready to serve in twenty?" he asks while fetching a salad bowl.

"Yeah, I think I can make it."

"Make what?" Mum calls before I'm attacked from behind by a hug.

She's much shorter than me and I have to bend so she can kiss me on the cheek.

Mum's hair is gathered in a messy bun and some paint smudges her shirt's sleeves. Unfortunately, I came at a time when she's battling a deadline, so I haven't seen much of her and she keeps apologizing for that, but I get it. I'm also supposed to be working on something. The keyword being *supposed* to.

The thought of painting those mindless nature scenes bores me to fucking death.

"Something smells divine." She tries to sneak past Dad, but he wraps his arms around her waist and kisses her, then pushes her in the direction of the dining room.

"Go relax. We'll serve in a bit."

"I love it when my boys spoil me." She strokes his hair and fixes his collar.

While I continue stirring, I can't help watching them.

I grew up surrounded by their passionate, unconditional love and that's one of the reasons that hope was kept alive inside me—as futile as it is.

"Dad, the oven," I say and he finally releases her.

"By the way, Grace will be joining us for dinner. Can you count her in?" She stops beside me, grinning contagiously. "This is a good opportunity for you, baby. She's really considering signing you. Isn't that wonderful?"

"I already found an agent, Mum."

"Oh. Who?"

"Maxine Saul."

"Landon's agent? She's high on sculpting and wouldn't get you. Besides, Grace is a household name and much more well-known and respected. She'll get your work out there in no time. I was so lucky when she took me on."

"I don't think she appreciates my style."

"She said she does. Come on, Bran. Just listen to what she has to say. If you don't like it and still prefer to go with Maxine, I'll respect your choice."

I nod and she hugs me again before disappearing to the dining room.

"You don't have to agree to anything," Dad says. "Your mum wants you to sign with a celebrity agent because she worries about your future, especially since you've been refusing to take part in exhibitions, unlike Lan. But if you want to tell us anything, we're all ears. Maybe you don't want to continue with art. Maybe you prefer to go a different path. Whatever it is, we're here."

The tension disappears from my shoulders as I nod with a smile. Why does he always say the right words to make me relax?

When the four of us sit down for dinner, however, that tension returns in waves.

I try to swallow past the lump in my throat as they talk about Mum's upcoming exhibition and how they're expecting brilliant results.

Everyone *can't* wait for it.

"You'll be there, right, Bran?" Grace asks me with her posh, slightly snobbish upper-class accent.

Grace Bruckner is indeed a household name. She has three artists under her wing, all of whom are world-renowned and have bagged multiple awards. She's about Mum's age but couldn't be any more different.

She dresses in red most of the time. Even now, she has on a red camisole, heels, earrings, and lipstick. The only different color is her black pencil skirt.

Her platinum blonde hair falls to her shoulders in a perfect bob, and she often wears a fake smile, probably because of the Botox.

"Sure. Anything for Mum." I smile and my mother gives me heart eyes.

"Lan, too?" Grace pushes.

"You'll have to ask him. He's been...quite busy lately."

"Apparently, he has a girlfriend who's keeping him in line." Mum's words drip with glee like when I first told her about Mia and how she's possibly taming her 'wild child.'

"*In line?*" Dad scoffs. "I'll believe it when I see it."

"You have my word, Dad. I've never seen him dedicated to anyone like he is to her. He even asked me for lessons in empathy."

"That seems serious."

"Dead serious."

"How charming." Grace takes a sip of her wine. "What about you, Bran? Any girlfriend?"

Pain rips through me at that and I choose to remain silent as I stuff my face full of food.

"No one?" she insists.

"Forget it, Grace. Bran likes to keep his relationships to himself." Mum laughs. "Maybe one day we'll get to meet your special someone, hon."

Fat chance.

"So, Bran." Grace leans forward in her seat. "I'm sure Astrid told you, but I'm officially considering signing you. Can you make time for us to discuss this further? Preferably in the studio, where I can see your recent work."

"How about Glyn?" I ask.

She continues sipping her rosé wine. "Glyn is still too young and is in the process of developing her style. I'll wait a few years before I move on to her. Let's focus on you now."

"Isn't that exciting?" Mum grins at me. "We can do exhibitions together in the future."

"That's an excellent idea," Grace agrees. "In fact, depending on what I see, I think we might be able to slip a painting or two into your upcoming exhibition."

"Oh my God. You can do that?"

"It's not an easy feat, but I can make it happen for you both."

"Bran? What do you think?" She smiles so big, it makes me sick to my stomach. "Lev, hon, we need to open a bottle of champagne."

He gauges my expression. "Are you ready to take this step, son?"

"I...need to think about it." I dab my lips with the napkin and stand up on slightly unsteady feet. "I have to work on an assignment. Please enjoy the rest of your dinner."

I walk out of the dining room with a calm I don't feel. Instead of going to the studio, I take the stairs and head to my room.

As soon as I'm inside, I fall on the bed headfirst and wish I could suffocate myself with the fucking pillow.

Black ink creeps over me, pushing weight on my back until I'm panting for air.

I reach underneath the pillow and snatch my Swiss Army knife, then yank away my watch and hold the blade against my wrist.

One cut. A small one.

I just need to breathe.

I want to fucking *breathe*.

My phone vibrates and I startle. When I see the name lighting the screen, I let the knife fall to the mattress.

Nikolai.

The more the phone vibrates, the harder I breathe, scrabbling, fighting for air that doesn't exist. My trembling finger hovers over the screen like every time he calls, but like always, I don't answer.

One missed call appears on the screen.

Then, as usual, a text follows.

Nikolai: Answer the fucking phone.

I open his texts and flip onto my back to read them, inhaling deeply, holding it in my churning stomach, then puffing out the air in a long, shaky exhale.

Little by little, I can feel the ink retreating to the shadows, even if its invisible hands are still strangling my cursed wrist.

I scroll up, reading all the texts he's sent since I left the island after I made sure Lan's wrist was safe.

At that time, I needed to get away from it all and figured being with my parents was the perfect solution.

I'm not so sure anymore.

It hurts everywhere, whether I'm on the island or here.

Still, I can't help rereading his texts. They've gone from raging to pleading to raging again. He calls me twenty times a day like a damn stalker.

A couple of days ago, he stopped the texts and calls altogether, so I thought he'd given up, but he called me just now. What does that mean?

Am I supposed to feel hopeful because of it?

I exit the texts and open Instagram, then go to his profile like a junkie. He hasn't posted anything for a long time, but I scroll through the old pictures. As if I don't have every single one saved on my phone in a special folder.

A knock startles me before Mum's voice filters through. "Bran, hon, you awake?"

I throw the knife under the pillow and sit up in bed to put on my watch, then clear my throat. "Yeah. Come in."

My fingers tighten around the phone, keeping it against my chest like makeshift armor as the door opens.

Mum and Dad walk in with handfuls of snacks, popcorn, and beer.

"Film night," Dad says. "Don't think you're escaping."

I smile and slide my phone into my pocket. "Shouldn't we go to the home cinema for that?"

They abandon the contents of their arms on my desk and sit on either side of me.

"Before we do that…" Mum trails off. "I wanted to have a little chat first."

"Okay," I say warily.

"I wanted to apologize, honey. I was reflecting on my words and realized that in my attempts to get you the best deal possible, I've been pushing you, and I think that made you uncomfortable. If you prefer Maxine over Grace, go for it. I'll stand behind you every step of the way."

"Really?"

"Of course, Bran. You can tell me these things head-on. You know that, right?"

I nod.

"Do you forgive me?"

"There's nothing to forgive, Mum. Anyone in your position would think it's an honor to be represented by Grace. But I'm not at your level yet. I don't want that pressure."

"I understand. One step at a time, right?"

My smile is much more genuine this time.

"It wasn't so hard to express yourself, was it, son?" Dad asks, throwing a comforting arm on my shoulder.

"We're your parents, not your guardians or people you need to be wary around." Mum takes my hand in her smaller ones. "You don't have to think about it when you talk to us. You can tell us what's on your mind freely."

My breathing comes easier with every inhale and exhale as I summon all the courage I have and say, "Mum, Dad. I want to tell you something."

"Anything," she says and Dad gives an encouraging nod.

"So…the thing is. I…well, this is a lot more difficult to speak aloud than I thought."

"Take your time." Dad strokes my back. "Whatever it is, you're not alone, Bran."

"Thanks, Dad." I clear my throat. "Remember when a long time ago I asked you why am I not normal?"

"When you were fourteen?"

"Yeah. You asked me in what department did I not feel normal, and I just shrugged and hoped you'd let it go. That thought came to me when I saw Lan and everyone else shagging their way through school. Lan first had sex at thirteen. I didn't even consider it at that time."

"Oh, my word." Mum gasps.

"You weren't supposed to know that." I grimace. "Anyway, he told me all about it, said I'd get around to it myself, and gave me a lot of pointers. I was more bemused than interested. I didn't like the concept of sex. I didn't find it appealing in any shape or form. I thought I was a late bloomer and Lan agreed, which made sense. But even at fifteen, sixteen, seventeen, or beyond, I didn't like the idea. I didn't want to have it and didn't find anyone attractive."

"But…" Dad pauses, seeming to measure his words. "You had girlfriends."

"Yeah. I did have sex. I didn't like it, but I did it anyway to blend in."

"Oh, honey." Mum watches me with a wretched expression. "Why didn't you talk to us? We could've—"

"No. The idea of being different haunted the hell out of me. I couldn't just admit it out loud. Even to you guys. I didn't want to be seen as a freak."

"Not wanting to have sex does *not* make you a freak, Bran," Dad says firmly. "Everyone is different and that's the beauty of it. Just because you don't have the sexual drive doesn't make you any less of who you are."

"I'm starting to learn that now. I wish it was easy to express one's different sexuality without being judged for it."

"We would never judge you, hon."

"You wouldn't, but society would, Mum. Society would compare me to my sex-god twin brother and label me as the defective one. They already think that in the art circuit anyway. I didn't want to add my sexuality to it."

"Society can go fuck itself," Dad says. "What's important is *you*. As long as you're comfortable in your own skin, everyone else can fuck off. If they say anything, I'll drag them through enough courts to make them wish they'd never crossed your path."

I smile a little. "Thanks, Dad."

"Did...something change?" Mum asks in a hopeful tone.

"What makes you think that?"

"You often look at your phone and have a longing expression on your face."

"I do?"

Both of them nod and I wince. I didn't realize I was *that* obvious.

"Did you find someone who understands you?" Dad asks.

"Will you be too shocked if I say it's a man?"

Mum's lips break into a grin. "I *knew* it."

"Me, too," Dad says.

"What?" I stare between them as if they're aliens. "How...? Why...? When? I didn't even know it myself."

"Well, hon. You had your first crush on a guy."

"What?"

"My stepbrother, Jayden."

"Jay?"

"You called him a prince and said, 'Mum, he's *so* pretty,' when you first met him. You were, what? Five at the time? Lan was having fun watching girls fight over him, but you were all over Jay. That didn't last long and you eventually became friends, but I definitely saw the attraction in your little eyes."

Right. I do remember thinking he was really pretty. But then puberty came and I never thought of him in that sense. I never thought of *anyone* in that sense.

With one damning exception.

"Afterward," Mum continues. "You were more into girls, so I thought maybe you were bi, but I didn't want to broach the subject until you told me yourself. I'm happy you felt comfortable enough to tell us."

I smile at her, feeling a bit daft for being so stupidly worried about this. Then I tilt my head in the direction of my father, who's been awfully quiet.

His face is unreadable as he seems to be fighting his demons.

"Dad? Are you...okay with it?"

"Your sexuality? Naturally. This guy, however, I'm not sure yet. What's his name? Age? Parents' names?"

"Uh...so...remember Killian?"

His lips part. "Please don't tell me you're with your sister's boyfriend. Ex-boyfriend?"

"What? No. Of course not, Dad."

"Ew, Levi." Mum smacks his hand.

"Fine, okay." He releases a breath. "It can't be worse than that."

"He's his cousin."

"Oh, for fuck's sake." Dad's face literally pales and I kind of feel bad for him. He's been dealing with Lan his whole life, then he had Kill, who's also a diagnosed psychopath, and I don't think he's even processed that.

"Please tell me he's the levelheaded cousin who keeps him in check."

"To be honest, and I can't believe I'm saying this, but Killian is definitely the one who keeps Nikolai in check."

"Fuck my life." He exhales. "Astrid, Princess. I think I'm having a heart attack."

"Dad...are you okay?" I study him closely. "I'm actually not with him right now, so you don't have to worry."

"Oh, screw *that*." Mum shakes him again. "Your dad just needs to stop being a baby."

Coincidentally, Dad's expression returns to normal. "You're not together, you said?"

"Levi!" Mum scolds.

"What? I can't have this bunch of psychos corrupting my children. I'm sure you'll find someone better, son."

A sad smile curves my lips. "I don't think so, Dad."

"What happened?" Mum asks in a soft tone.

"Something concerning Mia."

"Lan's girlfriend?"

"Yeah. She's also Nikolai's younger sister and he really, and I mean *really*, hates Lan's guts. Mostly because, well, my dear brother caused him and his friends a lot of trouble."

Mum sighs with resignation. "Lan, oh, Lan."

"So did Lan beat him up?" Dad asks with a note of anticipation.

"Levi!" Mum scolds again.

"I approve of Lan protecting his siblings."

"Way to set an example for your children, hon."

"Did he?" he asks me.

"It was the other way around, and I'm mad at Nikolai for that."

"Well, didn't Lan beat up Kill once?" Mum asks.

"That's my boy." Dad nods in approval and Mum rolls her eyes.

"Still, he shouldn't have done it. I begged him not to and he didn't seem to care." I release a long sigh. "Anyway, I'm going to be fine."

"It's okay if you aren't." Dad slaps me affectionately on the back.

Mum hugs me and kisses the top of my head. Her smell and warmth engulf me as she whispers, "I'm proud of you, hon. I love you just the way you are."

I wrap my arm around her even as I think.

I wish you didn't.

Now that this admission is out in the open, I know it's only a matter of time before the rest bulldozes through my weakened defenses.

And when that happens, I doubt I'll be able to hug her again.

The following morning, after I come back from my run, I shower and go to the kitchen to prepare breakfast for my parents.

It's the least I can do after the love and understanding they showered me with last night. They're the reason I've been hanging on to that thread of hope for years. If they weren't in my life…I don't even want to think about it.

Even though Mum is on a deadline, we sure as hell went to the home cinema and watched my favorite *Poirot* episode, "The Murder of Roger Ackroyd".

Dad dozed off halfway through and Mum talked me into painting his face—something we always used to do whenever he fell asleep around us. The four of us. Dad had no chance of winning with four chaotic artists in the family.

Though only Glyn takes after Mum in being a chaotic creative. Lan and I are too consumed with perfection. Too methodical. Too... focused.

I'd actually never thought about that. Lan is a sculptor and I'm a painter, but we share the same creative energy.

Guess we've always had similar traits, no matter how much I've tried to ignore it.

Anyway, breakfast.

Dad will be up soon and Mum spent an all-nighter in the studio. I know how important this exhibition is for her. She's been working for two years on her next big thing and I want to be there for her every step of the way.

I will not, under any circumstances, distract her.

Which means I should probably go back to uni soon.

I puff out a breath of air, dread, and another queasy feeling enveloping me at the thought of what waits for me on the island.

Our butler, Nolan, walks inside, all dressed in his impeccable suit and the slightly crooked bow tie.

"I've got this, Nolan. Thanks," I tell him as I fetch eggs from the fridge.

"Sir, that's not it."

"Then what is it?"

"You have a peculiar visitor."

"This early...?"

I lift my head and I can hear the sound of my shattering heart as my eyes meet those deep-blue ones.

Nikolai is in my parents' house.

THIRTY-ONE

Nikolai

THE PAST WEEK HAS BEEN A RED MIST.

No. *Black* would be a more accurate fucking description.

With everything that imploded back home, I had to go to the States and assess the fuckery for myself. As if everything wasn't already fucked up, I also had to clash with none other than Landon—also known as the reason behind every fucked-up emotion I've been experiencing over the past couple of weeks.

The reason why Bran has been completely ignoring me.

Let's just say Landon said I shouldn't mention anything about his impromptu visit to my parents. I still hate the fucking guy and I'd rather see him burn at the stake than be with my sister, but I don't really have a choice after he saved her from certain death.

Motherfucking fucker even managed to stop raising Dad's hackles. *My. Dad.* As in the man who brought me up to be the twins' second watchdog after himself.

A lot of fuckery happened, including many familial conversations and disturbing revelations. Through it all, I couldn't be fully present, not when I'd left my fucking heart on the island. I returned as soon as I could, but it turned out Bran wasn't there all along.

I had to get information about his whereabouts through Kill and Jer because Glyn and Cecily were mad at me. Probably because of the part I played in the beating up of Landon.

Let the record show that I'd do it again in a heartbeat. Though maybe I wouldn't threaten his precious fucking wrist. Just damage his face so he no longer resembles the most beautiful man on earth.

Said man looks at me as if I'm a barbarian walking into his empire with primitive weapons and the intention of burning down his forts.

He's not mistaken.

I have to exercise self-control I don't actually have to not jump him and bruise those parted lips, tug them between my teeth, and devour them with my tongue.

We have company. Chill, Kolya. Just fucking chill. This behavior wouldn't work in your favor.

Bran straightens to his full height, his surprised expression slowly fading as he wears his control like armor.

My gaze greedily takes in the cold lines of his face, the muted blue of his eyes, the slight tic in his sharp jawline, and the unfortunate absence of my mark on his unblemished neck.

A few chaotic brown strands fall on his forehead, half damp as if he just walked out of the shower. If I inhale deep enough, I can breathe the citrus and clover into my starved lungs.

My attention falls on his white polo T-shirt and how it stretches over his planes of muscles. It rides up as he slowly shuts the fridge, revealing his smooth abs and that delicious V-line that unfortunately disappears beneath his dark-blue pants.

He smiles at the man standing beside me, who looked at me like I'm a vicious stray dog trying to bite his master. If I wasn't trying to get brownie points with Bran, I would've punched him in his standoffish face.

Violence doesn't work with Bran. Violence. Does. Not. Work.

If I keep repeating that, maybe I'll forget about my fists enough to not start a fight.

"Thank you, Nolan. I'll take it from here." He speaks in a collected voice that destroys any of my feeble attempts to remain civil.

How dare he be so unaffected when I've barely been able to breathe properly since he's been gone?

I crunched more pills than I have in my entire life just to bring myself down from the high. So that I could see him without being weirded out about the fact that I could hurt him.

Even Mom, who's Team Pills, was worried shitless about the very possibility that I'd overdose on the fuckers and hid them away from me.

"Are you sure?" Fucker Nolan gives me a judgmental once-over although I'm fully fucking dressed, even wore a damn leather jacket over my T-shirt to hide the tattoos.

He pales at my glare that must say, 'I'll fuck up your face right here and now,' then focuses back on Bran.

"Yeah. Go ahead."

Nolan gives him another uncertain look before he nods and walks away without a sound like a fucking creep.

"What the fuck are you doing here?" Bran snaps, and although his voice is firm and low, I revel at watching the cracks in his control.

That's it. Break for me, baby.

"What does it look like I'm doing?" I stride toward him, unable to resist his gravitational presence. "I came to see you since you didn't bother to answer my texts or calls."

"That was answer enough. I had no desire or intention of getting in contact with you. As I previously told you. We are done."

"As I previously told you. In your fucking dreams." My voice lowers as I stand toe-to-toe with him, caging him against the counter.

His heat penetrates my skin and melts away the ice that's been enveloping me since he's been out of my sight.

God damn.

I missed his comforting heat and that look in his eyes. Maybe the reason I've been on that high longer than usual is because I didn't have him. He has a way of grounding me, pulling me down when I go up.

Since he came into my life, I haven't gone on self-destructive sprees—except the last few weeks.

In the past, I couldn't care less about whether or not I survived the violence and the mayhem. Now is different.

Now, the thought of being without him terrifies me. Death terrifies me because it would take me away from *him*.

I'm never leaving him again. Not even if I have to inhale pills and turn into the zombie I despise for it.

Bran crosses his arms over his chest, not giving an inch as his features freeze into cold indifference, but I don't miss the clench in his jaw.

"Can't take no for an answer? Pathetic."

"Then I'm pathetic. Who fucking cares? Oh, wait. You do."

He releases cruel laughter that's so uncharacteristic of him. He's an asshole, but never mocking. Condescending, but not evil. "If you think I ever cared about you, then you're sorely mistaken. It was just *physical*, remember? Like how you fucked me against the tree and left without a look back, then proceeded to threaten my brother's whole future because of your nonsensical pride."

My molars grind together and I have to bite my tongue to keep from shouting that he's mine and he needs to deal with it.

But how dare he?

How fucking *dare* he say it was just physical?

He and I were never just *physical*, not the first time I kissed him or the last time I fucked him or anytime in-between. And he *knows* that.

He better well fucking know that and just be trying to summon the asshole energy in himself.

"Your brother's wrist is just fine," I grit out.

Now, *that* gets him pissed. And I mean fucking shaking pissed. Red blotches cover his pale skin and his eyes turn a shade darker, nearly shooting laser beams at my face.

That's it, baby. Show me the side no one else sees.

He uncrosses his arms and jams his index finger against my chest, and is it wrong that I'm loving his touch even if he's nearly boiling over with rage?

"That's not the fucking point!"

"Then what is?"

"The fact that you kidnapped him and beat him up in the first place."

"He had it coming when he messed with my fucking sister."

"You were messing with his fucking brother!"

"I never forced you."

"And you think he *forced* her? If you weren't so up your own arse, you would've seen the way she looks at him. She loves him, Nikolai. She's *in love* with him. And you might not want to believe this, but he loves her, too, in his own fucked-up way."

I bite my tongue again, this time due to the images I came back with from the States. A part of me refuses to subscribe to the very foundation of that idea, but he's right. Annoyingly so.

"Okay."

His finger falls from my chest as the anger melts at the edges, replaced by bemusement. "Okay?"

"Yeah, okay. I was home and Landon was also there, trying to woo my parents."

By the grimace on his face, he knows very well that the scenario I just described is a recipe for disaster. That's the difference between Landon and Bran. The psycho just pushes through everything and hopes for the best. My lotus flower is much more calculated and gets off on control. He'd never make a decision before he mulls it over.

I can't believe I'm thinking this, but I really wish he was a bit like his brother sometimes. Not his character—fucking revolting—but the way he lets himself loose.

"What did he do?" he asks carefully. "Did you get into a fight again?"

"No."

"You mean to tell me you were in the same room with Lan and didn't punch him?"

"I would've loved to."

"Then why didn't you? I'm pretty sure your punch-first-think-later mentality wasn't the reason you restrained yourself."

"No, it wasn't. But I knew if I hurt him again, I'd lose you, and that's not a fucking option."

His lips part and I want to bite the bottom one beneath my teeth and feast on him, swallow him whole, and fuck this morbid tension out of the both of us.

But then he opens his stupid fucking mouth. "Too bad. You already lost me."

I plant my palms on the counter on either side of him and lean into his face until he has no choice but to step back or let me kiss him.

He goes for the former, but that leaves him trapped between me and the counter.

"Want to test that, baby?" I invade his space until my lips are mere inches away from his.

"Back off," he orders in that bossy tone that gets my dick all twitchy.

"Not in this lifetime."

He jacks his forearm against my throat, nearly crushing my windpipe as his eyes shine with dangerous anger and uncontainable lust. "Don't even think about touching me."

"You're the one who's doing that. Can't keep your hands off me, baby?"

"I'm pushing you away."

"Still counts. Mmm. I missed the feel of your skin on mine."

"You're fucking crazy."

"About you. Always."

"Nikolai…"

"Yes, baby?"

He expels a long breath and I inhale it deep into my lungs. Herbal tea and honey. Of course he'll have tea first thing in the morning, my Prince Charming.

"Listen, you bloody twat." His voice is deep and firm, oozing command. "You don't get to ignore me, pretend I don't exist, then proceed to hurt my brother after I basically begged you not to and waltz back into my life as if nothing happened."

"I'm not pretending it didn't. I'm just saying I'm in your life *despite* everything that happened. And I didn't ignore you because I wanted to. I was on my high and things would've turned ugly if I came close, especially with the shit with Landon. I punched you, Bran."

"You didn't mean to."

"I still don't like it. I hate the very idea of hurting you, even unintentionally. I was haunted for weeks by the sight of the blood that gushed out of your nose. I'm so sorry. I'll never let myself do that again. That night in front of the Elites' mansion was enough proof that I had no control and was capable of hurting you. Also, I could never pretend you don't exist, motherfucker. You're everywhere like goddamn air."

His grip loosens a little, giving me more room to breathe. "You could've told me."

"Like you so readily told me about the cuts?"

A line appears between his brows and he breathes harsher, his chest rising and falling with difficulty, but he has no reply, because even his hypocritical analogy doesn't make sense.

"Now, you listen to me, motherfucker." I wrap a hand around his throat. "You don't get to hide from me and demand to know me. You don't get to bury yourself six feet deep and think you can still read me like a book. If I'm splitting myself open for you and allowing you to see parts of me no one else is privy to, you need to do the same. You owe me that fucking much."

His lips are set in a line and I expect him to refuse or flash me his surprisingly devastating anger, but he releases a sigh. "Are you really going to let go of the Landon thing?"

"I should've listened to you and exchanged you for Mia. You can say I told you so."

"No, Nikolai. I don't derive pleasure from seeing you hurt or conflicted, and I know how much you love your sister. But it's hypocritical to want Lan away from her while insisting on having me. Lan is my twin brother and he will always be a massive part of my life. You can't, under any circumstances, make me choose. I need you to understand that."

"I get it. I'm sorry."

His expression softens. "Apology accepted. You'll try not to punch him next time you see him?"

"Yeah. Not sure he'll do the same, though."

"What did you do now?"

"Me? He's the one who threatened me in my own fucking house. He said, and I quote, 'I've seen the way you look at my brother, you uncultured swine, and I'm telling you right now that if you come near him, I'll break your fucking legs.'"

Bran's face pales. "He...knows?"

"I didn't say anything. I promise."

He shakes his head, a pained expression crossing his features. "You didn't have to."

"You hate that?"

"I wouldn't say I hate it... I'm just trying to figure out why he hasn't said anything to me. Is he also waiting?"

"Waiting for what?"

"It's nothing."

"Brandon," I grit out, and he looks at me with...disappointment? Pain?

"What?" he asks in a hurt tone.

"I hate the word nothing. It's at the top of my shit list with *fine* and *sorry.*"

"Well, I hate it when you call me by my full name, too."

Fuck me.

His lower lip pushes slightly forward in a little pout and I can't help the feeling of complete adoration that floods me.

He's so goddamn cute for an asshole.

"Won't happen again, baby." I cup his nape and crash my lips to his.

Bran gasps and I swallow the sound the fuck up. My tongue pushes past his teeth, only to be met by his eager one. A growl spills from me as he clenches his fingers in my hair and switches us around so that my back hits the counter and he's the one crowding me, breathing the intense, angry passion through me.

Our mouths war as I flip him again, forcing him to gobble down the taste of my aggression that only he can tame.

God-fucking-damn-it. I missed him.

I want the madness, the pressure, the war. I want all of him *in* me. Bleeding inside me. Breaking apart *for* me.

"Don't ever do that again." He pants against my lips, his fingers pulling on my hair until it's painful. "Don't you fucking dare walk away from me or ghost me. I don't give a fuck if you're on a high or a murder spree. I couldn't care less if you hurt me. You don't come to me when you're only okay, you come to me at all times. Am I fucking understood?"

I lick his bottom lip then bite down. "You don't hide from me, either. I want you raw. Am I fucking clear?"

His hot breath whooshes out in harsh pants against my mouth. "What if you don't like what you see?"

"Not sure if you noticed it, but I like everything about you—your control-freak tendencies and nagging included."

I'm about to seal that with another kiss when I register commotion behind me.

While I don't usually stop when there's an audience, this isn't just anyone. It's my Bran.

It takes me a godly amount of effort to release him and step back.

Bran looks at me with unconcealed disappointment as he's forced to let me go. I quickly wipe his mouth with the sleeve of my jacket, but I'm afraid nothing can hide his swollen lips.

Or mine.

Christ.

I'm thinking of the best way to deal with that, but it's too late.

Bran's eyes grow in size as an older male voice booms in the air. "Morning, Princess."

"More like night," a feminine voice says, followed by a yawn.

I turn around so that I'm standing beside Bran as I watch an older version of him with blond hair wrapping an arm around the waist of a smaller woman who creepily resembles Glyn.

He smiles at her as they walk to the kitchen. "Son, are you up—"

His voice is cut off when he lifts his head and notices me standing beside his son.

When I took the first flight from the States, I hadn't had much sleep. My only thought was to get Bran back, so don't expect me to have had the foresight to realize I'd actually see his parents.

And judging by his father's hardening features, I would say it's not going well.

An idea pops into my head and I'm actually goddamn proud of how quick-witted I am.

"Hi, good morning," I say with my most welcoming smile that I only show my parents. "I'm Bran's friend from school."

His mom smiles. "Are you, by any chance, Nikolai?"

I steal a glance at Bran. Did he *mention* me?

Jesus Christ. Am I supposed to be this happy that he said my name in front of his parents?

And why is he not freaking out like whenever we're in the same public place?

If anything, his expression is peaceful.

This is starting to creep me the fuck out.

So imagine my fucking surprise when he threads his fingers through mine and smiles at his parents. "Yeah, Mum. This is Nikolai and he's more than just a friend."

THIRTY-TWO

Levi

HE CAN'T POSSIBLY BE WORSE THAN KILLIAN.
Anyone is better than Killian.
It was an exaggeration on Bran's part to emotionally prepare me.

Again, no one can be worse *than Killian.*

Those were the thoughts I had before I went to bed last night, and I woke up today in a proper fantastic mood.

Until now.

Or, more accurately, since I walked into the kitchen and saw the motherfucking gangster who's built like a fucking wall, standing beside my son.

I knew it was the little fucker Nikolai before Bran even introduced him. It doesn't take a genius to figure it out when Bran's lips were all swollen and the bastard's long hair was finger-raked.

Dear fucking God, I know you're out there somewhere and I beg you, take this arsehole and give my son a normal lover. Just once, I want fucking normal.

First I get a psycho son. Okay, fine. Love that. Best challenge of my life and pretty sure I passed it. I didn't need to have my daughter with a psycho boyfriend.

And now, it's the psycho's psycho fucking cousin.

What the fuck have I done to deserve that? Was I a mass murderer in a past life or something?

"Levi!" My wife pulls on my shirt's sleeve from her position on the table beside me. "You're staring."

"Oh, I'm sorry. I was supposed to be fucking glaring," I say loud enough for everyone to hear.

We're sitting around the dining table for breakfast. We had to order takeout from the local bakery because I'm not in the right headspace to cook anything.

And it's all because of the fucking wanker on my left, right beside my son. I narrow my eyes at the full sleeves of tattoos decorating both his arms. Motherfucking gangster. A delinquent bastard who's in no way fit to be with my well-mannered, completely selfless son.

My son who's hidden himself so as not to bother us—his own parents. His closest flesh and blood.

Why would he end up with Killian's more unruly cousin? At least that waste of space is presentable. This one looks like he was chewed up in a tattoo gun, broke the fucking thing, and got spit right out.

Don't get me wrong. I have tattoos and so does Lan, but we're not covered in them like damn mafiosos.

Astrid clears her throat and smiles at Nikolai, who had the decency to put his fork and knife down when I spoke.

Even with his hair tied back, he still gives a major creeper vibe.

Just what the fuck does Bran see in him? He looks like one of those violent wankers. Aka me when I was young. I know an adrenaline junkie when I see one.

"So how old are you, Nikolai?" my wife asks in a soft tone. "You look about Bran's age."

Bran swallows the mouthful of toast and grimaces. "He's actually four years younger."

"Shut the fridge." She gasps. "He doesn't look a day younger."

"Thanks, ma'am. That's what I've been saying." He slides his fork and knife on either side of his plate again. "Also, it's only three and a half years. I'm going to be twenty in a couple of weeks."

"Don't ma'am me. Just call me Astrid. Make yourself comfortable and treat this like your home."

"I wouldn't recommend that." I cut my toast with scrambled eggs and glare at him.

To give him credit, he doesn't hold my gaze or glare back like his fucker cousin.

He lowers his head and says, "Once again, I'm sorry for showing up without previous notice. I thought I'd see Bran and leave."

"Aw, such good manners." My wife smiles. "And don't worry, you're welcome here any time."

"I wouldn't use the word *welcome*."

"Dad," Bran mouths pleadingly and I resist the urge to roll my eyes.

There he goes defending the little fucker. I'm losing my children one by one to a bunch of wankers.

"So where did you guys meet?" my wife asks, battling against my every attempt to scare him away. Hopefully, he'll act up and Bran will realize Nikolai is not for him.

Let's cross all fingers for that very happy ending.

"It was at a…" Bran trails off. "Party."

Nikolai smirks. "Yes. A party. I was all over him in no time."

"You were *what*?" I snap.

"I mean." His smirk disappears. "I was the one who noticed him first."

"And you couldn't keep your attention to yourself?"

"Levi." Astrid pinches my thigh beneath the table.

"I'm afraid not, sir," he answers with a straight face. "It was my destiny to meet your son and I wouldn't have it any other way."

There it is. The same arrogance that courses through Killian's veins instead of blood.

Bran ducks his head and smiles as he spreads an unhealthy amount of apricot jam on some toast.

My heart kind of fucking bursts.

I haven't seen my son smile so broadly since...well, his pre-teen-age years. Puberty changed him into this overly responsible, slightly depressed man. Where Lan grew into his obnoxious, too outward self, Bran turned inward.

Last night, when he told us it was because he didn't want to come off as abnormal, it made me feel like a shitty father. I often tried to make him feel as special as his brother, but that didn't matter if he himself didn't believe in that fact.

"That's so sweet." My wife, who seems already taken by the little shit Nikolai, smiles and passes him a plate of eggs Benedict.

"He prefers a sweet breakfast, Mum." Bran slides the jam sandwich that I thought he was making for himself in front of Nikolai and even gives him a whole plate of macarons.

"He doesn't look the part," she says.

"Don't be fooled by the muscles. He has the most tragic sweet tooth I've ever had the misfortune to witness."

"Guilty as charged," Nikolai says after he finishes the toast in two bites like a barbarian. "Honestly, I work out so I can consume as many pastries as possible."

"One day, you'll go into a sugar coma," Bran says with a sigh, as if he's mentioned this countless times before.

"Worth it."

"That's the spirit." Astrid raises her glass of orange juice in his direction and he clinks his against it.

"So what do you study in uni, Nikolai?" Astrid asks.

"Business management. I'm supposed to be taking over the family business that my parents have been leading for decades."

"Oh, how exciting. You and Bran share something in common."

"Really?" he asks, too eager. "What?"

"Heirs to a family business. Though Bran clearly expressed that he'll have nothing to do with the management side."

"Eli, Lan, and Creigh will do that just fine. I prefer art."

"That's my boy." She reaches across the table and pats his hand.

"I find it hard to believe you do well at school," I comment dryly.

"I actually have a GPA of 4.15, sir. I might not look like it, but

I have an awesome memory. Though your other son likes to call me stupid."

I smile to myself, proud of Lan, but then Bran strokes Nikolai's arm. "You're not stupid. Besides, Lan finds ninety-nine percent of the human population mentally challenged, so he's the problem."

Is he consoling him right now?

Dear God, please blind my fucking eyes.

"As long as you don't think that, I couldn't care less about Landon's opinion of me."

"You guys are so sweet." Astrid has this dreamy expression all over her face that could only be described as swooning.

"We are, right?" Nikolai grins like a fucking idiot and nudges my son's shoulder. "Hear that? Even your mom thinks we're sweet."

"Stop it," he hisses under his breath, more out of embarrassment than annoyance.

I really wish it was fucking annoyance.

"So what do you like about my son?" I ask in my solemn tone, and that immediately puts a damper on the cheerful mood.

Nikolai is the only one who doesn't get the jab or the tone, or if he does, he completely ignores it. "The right question would be what I don't like about him. Which is maybe three things...actually, I take that back. I like those things sometimes as well, so they don't count."

"Is that your way of not giving me one single thing you like?"

"I'm happy to. How much time do you have, sir?"

"As much as you need."

"Okay then." He inhales deeply and speaks in one continuous breath. "I like that he's responsible, punctual, takes all of his engagements seriously, steps up for justice, and helps in every way possible. I like his cooking, his rare smiles, and how dedicated he is to running and staying healthy. I like making him laugh and, eh, watching him sleep. I like how he's fully concentrated when he's in the art studio, but most of all, I like how he let me into his life and made a place for me there. I even like the boring Agatha Christie movie adaptations now, not because they're any good, but because he's truly obsessed with that shi—I mean, *stuff*. I even like his nagging and control-freak tendencies most of the time, so yeah, there's nothing I don't like...actually, there's something. He has this habit of putting everyone else's comfort before his own, or he pretends to be fine when he's obviously not. I don't only dislike that. I hate it."

My wife has fallen into an irreparable puddle on her chair, but she's not what's making my blood run cold. It's the look in Bran's eyes as his entire body angles in Nikolai's direction.

It's awe and affection but also fear. A fear so deep, even I can see it. What is he afraid of?

He doesn't look to be scared of Nikolai, more like he's scared *for* him. But why and from what?

There's also another disturbing emotion. I recognize that look. That's how I looked when I first realized the depth of the emotions I felt for his mother.

He's *in love* with him. It's not a crush, mere admiration, or a fling. My son is fully, truly, and irrevocably in love with the gangster.

God rest my soul in fucking pieces.

"By the way." Nikolai grins at Bran. "I'm totally going to tell my dad to ask you that exact same question when you meet him. I want to hear what you have to say."

Bran smiles again and passes him a few jam-filled scones that he chomps on like a monster.

After breakfast, Astrid ushers them to the living room.

"Mum, shouldn't you rest? You spent an all-nighter in the studio."

"Nonsense. I wouldn't miss the chance to meet Nikolai for the world. I had my English Breakfast tea. I'll be fine."

"Ma'am..." he trails off when she glares at him. "*Astrid*...I'm sorry I intruded on your resting time."

"At least you're aware of that," I mutter, following close behind them.

My wife scolds me with those bright-green eyes that could make me do anything—absolutely *anything*—except for handing over my precious Bran to this wanker.

"I can leave if that's better—" His words come to a halt when Bran clutches his wrist and shakes his head.

"Absolutely not," my wife says. "You're our guest."

"Not one I approve of."

"Levi, seriously. Shouldn't you be going to work?" She hikes a hand on her hip and offers me her stern look.

"I'm calling in sick."

I'm *literally* sick to my fucking stomach over the thought of yet another one of my children leaving the nest.

Yes, they've been going to university for a few years now, and I should be used to this feeling, but I most definitely am not. Besides, a part of me thought Bran would choose to move back home and stay with us for life.

Am I saying goodbye to my dream right now?

"Anyway, Nikolai," my wife says after she shakes her head at me. "Do you want to see Bran's baby photos?"

"Hell yeah," he agrees readily like an eager child, then blurts, "I mean yes, please."

"Mum." Bran gives her an incredulous look.

"You have no idea how long I've waited to do this."

Astrid leads Nikolai to her favorite sofa that faces the garden, then goes to the cupboard to fetch all the albums she treats like treasures.

Bran falls back so that he's standing with me, a safe distance away from them.

We watch as his mother sits beside Nikolai and begins with pictures from the day she found out she was pregnant with the twins. We didn't know they were twins at that time.

I remember that day so well. The joy that washed over us at the thought of having our own family was so palpable, I can still taste it on my tongue. It feels like yesterday, but it isn't, because one of my first babies has his own life now and probably won't call or text me when he needs a pick-me-up.

As Astrid tells Nikolai the story behind every picture, he listens carefully while looking at the album on his lap with keen interest.

Fucking creep.

Bran steps closer to me, his expression sheepish as he rubs the back of his neck and then speaks low so that I'm the only one who hears him. "Do you hate him that much, Dad?"

"Oh my, what gave you that impression?"

"You kind of made it obvious and, well, you're still glaring at him."

I break my staring contest with Nikolai's skull. I figured if I glared hard enough, it'd crack and we'd be rid of the nuisance.

"I thought you said you weren't together anymore?" I ask with a raised eyebrow.

"I...thought so, too." He sighs and shakes his head. "It's impossible to stay away from him. Believe me, I've tried. *Multiple* times. Each time, it only got harder, not easier, and I really can't imagine my life without him in it anymore. I hurt him enough by denying my sexuality and him. He was patient and even agreed to see me in secret although he's openly bi. I can't hurt him anymore, that would be worse than causing pain to myself. The idea of losing him scares the shit out of me, Dad."

Bloody hell.

I see it again. That look he had earlier. This time, it's more intense as he stares at him.

He's not afraid *for* him, he's afraid of *losing* him.

The delinquent gangster motherfucker.

I knew that bastard Killian was trouble. Not only did he shove his unwanted presence into our lives, but now, there's his cousin.

Though I admit Nikolai is a lot more well-mannered than that psycho.

Bran slides his attention back to me. "All my life, I thought I was one of those people who was meant to be alone, but he changed that. Single-handedly. He chased me and made it impossible to ignore him. He's helped me become a better man—more balanced, less...agitated and lonely. He's the only one for me. So...if you don't hate him a lot, can you try to accept him? I love you and respect you a lot, Dad. You know how much your approval means to me."

"Come here, son." I half hug him. "I don't actually *hate* him. I just don't like the idea of him replacing me."

"That's impossible. No one can take your role in my life." He steps back. "You're also my only worthy kitchen mate. Nikolai can't cook to save his life."

"Pretty sure he can't do much to save his life."

"Tell me about it. He's so unorganized, it drives me bonkers. He'll be throwing everything around, leaving milk outside the fridge, and meditating underwater. He can't even tell the difference between basil, oregano, and coriander. 'They're all grass', he says. He also didn't know who Agatha Christie was until recently. He barely knows who Zeus or most historical figures are. He said the only superior one is Hannibal because he was a badass general who nearly brought down an empire, and the rest of them don't merit a place in his head. Can you believe that?"

My sigh is deep and fucking defeated. "You love him that much, huh?"

"Yeah—" He cuts himself off and his eyes widen as he swallows thickly. "I mean... I...I..."

"It's fine." I clutch his shoulder. "Take your time to come to terms with it. I know it's scary, but it'll get better."

"Thanks, Dad."

I smile. "Let's join them before your mother embarrasses you any further."

He grins in return and we walk in as Astrid says, "That's Jayden, or Jay for short."

"A relative?" Nikolai asks.

"You could say that. He's my stepsister's half-brother and was Bran's first crush." She winks at our son and he shakes his head.

"First crush you say?" Nikolai's tone turns mysterious as he looks at the picture in which Bran and Jay are wearing Minion jumpsuits, clutching each other by the shoulders and grinning with glee.

"Yeah," my wife says, completely unaware of the fire of jealousy igniting in Nikolai's gaze. "Bran went through that phase of obsessing about everything Minion and Jay was his partner in crime."

"Hmm. And where is he now?"

"In the States. He's the youngest hotshot NASA scientist. I'm so proud of him."

"Is he at the headquarters or one of the other field centers?"

"Headquarters, I believe."

"Good to know. Is he Jayden Clifford?"

"No, Adler."

"Jayden Adler. DC. Cool."

Jesus fucking Christ.

He sounds like a damn mafioso who's collecting information about a potential target.

Astrid keeps showing him other photos, but Bran definitely picked up on the energy, because he says, "Jay and I haven't really seen each other much over the years. He's a genius student and barely has time for anything but studying."

Nikolai shows a poker face for the first time today. "Did I say anything?"

"Don't even think about it," Bran says low, but I hear him.

"No idea what you're talking about."

"Nikolai," he warns.

"Yes?" He smiles and I want to punch him, but I can't, because my son loves this twat.

Nikolai hides his yawn. "Excuse me. I came straight from the States and couldn't sleep on the plane."

"Oh my word." Astrid closes the album. "Bran, you should take him to rest."

"No." Nikolai holds on to the album. "I prefer childhood pictures."

"Nonsense. They'll be waiting when you wake up, deal?"

"Deal."

"I should catch a few hours of sleep myself." She appears distraught as she tries to shake the exhaustion from her face.

Nikolai stands up and nods at me. "Thank you for letting me stay in your house, sir."

I'm about to throw out a 'No, I'm not letting you,' but the expectation on Bran's face forces me to change my mind, and I release a begrudged affirmative noise instead.

My son smiles and mouths a "Thanks" before he and the fucker go up the stairs.

He better take him to the guest room.

I'm about to remind him of that when Astrid shakes her head. "Don't even think about being a dick. You did enough damage this entire morning."

"I don't like the idea of him in our son's room."

"He's a twenty-three-year-old man, Levi. Stop treating him like a child. Besides, Nikolai is just so well-mannered."

"Have you seen the tattoos?"

"You mean how beautiful they are?"

"How many there are, Princess."

"So what? Those don't make his personality. Since when do you judge a book by its cover?"

"Since it walks into my house and steals my son."

She laughs and wraps her arm around mine then leans her head on my shoulder. "You're such a papa bear. Just be happy that Bran found someone who cares about him like Nikolai does. You heard the part he hates, right? That's exactly what we struggle with, and not only has he picked up on it, but he chose it as the only thing he dislikes. You know how closed off and inward Bran can be, so we should be celebrating the fact that he's letting someone close, not be babies about it."

I release a grumble.

"Levi, come on. Have you ever seen Bran smile so much?"

I groan. So she noticed that, too. Of course she did. And I hate to admit it, but she's definitely right. I've never seen him as happy as he was this morning.

Fucking hell.

"I know you're also glad deep down." She kisses my cheek. "You better not cause Nikolai trouble."

"So you're Team Nikolai now?"

"I'm Team Bran and he loves that man. Besides, he's a real lad."

"A *real* lad? Seriously, Princess?"

"He gets my stamp of approval." She kisses me again. "Want to sleep some more since you called in sick?"

"You know I won't say no to that."

After we go to the bedroom and Astrid slips in for a quick shower, I open my group chat with my cousin and friends.

Me: I think I'm depressed.

Aiden: Midlife crisis? Is that why you called in sick?

Me: More like theft-of-my-children crisis. No one told me they'd slip away one by one.

Xander: Tell me about it, Captain. I still can't believe my baby bee has some lizard boyfriend.

Ronan: An actual lizard? Bloody hell, Xan. What happened to baby Cecy?

Xander: He's a person, but I'd rather think of him as a lizard so he doesn't grow on me.

Me: I like that idea. Dehumanization won't allow them to grow on me. Though I really doubt it with this one. Why can't we invent a time machine so they'll stay young forever?

Cole: Don't even remind me of that, Captain. I get nightmares about the day my babies will introduce me to some fuckers.

Aiden: Pretty sure you know at least one of them, if not two.

Cole: What are you insinuating?

Aiden: You might want to sit down for this.

Cole: Sit down for what?

Aiden: One day, my Eli will marry your Ava and we'll be in-laws.

Xander: Jesus. Is that a script for a horror film?

Aiden: A reality show.

Cole: I'll kill him first, Aiden. You know that.

Aiden: Good luck trying to stop my son. We King men always get what we want.

He's right. It's not only about him, me, or Uncle. The younger generation is the same as well. Bran included.

I saw it in his eyes earlier. He wants to be with Nikolai and he'll do it no matter what it takes.

He'll be with him even if the whole world is against him.

I guess Astrid is right. It's better to be happy for him than trying to sabotage Nikolai's existence.

And he is much more well-behaved than Killian, so there's that silver lining.

"Still thinking about your precious baby?" Astrid walks out of the bathroom wrapped in a towel and steps between my legs. It doesn't matter how old we get, she'll always be the woman who does my head in. In every exciting sense of the word.

"Not anymore." I wrap my arms around her waist. "Let me help you sleep better, Princess."

"I love you so much." She kisses me, and I'm done for.

I'll think about everything else later. Now, I need to be there for the love of my life.

My wife.

My forever.

THIRTY-THREE

Brandon

"**M**AYBE THIS ISN'T A GOOD IDEA." NIKOLAI PAUSES AS soon as we cross my room's threshold.

Leather jacket in hand, he rubs his nape, causing the white T-shirt to ride up his inked abs.

His jeans hang low on his hips, stretching over his muscular thighs, giving him a lethally attractive edge. His whole look is. From the leather jacket to his hair that's unfortunately held up now.

His bicep flexes, drawing my attention to the tattoos on his full sleeves, stretching to the backs of his hands. I never thought so many tattoos could be so sexy until Nikolai.

But then again, it might be because the tattoos are *on* him.

I seem to be irrevocably drawn to everything about *him*.

If he hadn't come today, I have no doubt that I would've some-how, someway, gravitated toward him again. I would have tried to stay away and failed.

I would've pretended to have pride, then crushed it to pieces and sprinted toward him.

He's beginning to have this undeniable effect on me and that frightens me. Not because of him, but because of me.

Though *beginning* is a massive lie. He's had it for a long time, but I just refused to admit it.

Nikolai lets his arm drop to his side, putting a halt to my shameless ogling session.

"I think it's better if I stay in a guest room," he says in a careful tone. "I don't want to give your dad more reason to hate me."

I can't help the smile that tugs on my lips. He's so fucking adorable. He's been acting like this respectful gentleman in front of my parents, and I could tell he took the entire thing very seriously.

"Don't smile like that, baby. I'm barely stopping myself from jumping your fucking bones. You know I have no self-control when it comes to you."

I stand in front of him and lean over so I'm speaking against his tempting lips. "Why start now, then?"

Hot breaths expel out of his mouth and dance along my jaw, drawing goosebumps over the skin.

I swear he's about to kiss me, but then he steps back with visible difficulty. "Your dad, remember? I don't want to be on his shit list more than I already am."

Disappointment tugs on my insides, but I shake my head as I close my bedroom door. "He doesn't really hate you. He's just overprotective. If you think that was hate, you should've seen the King envoy he dispatched when Killian visited."

A splash of hope blossoms on his face. "Kill had it worse?"

"Absolutely. You're much less antagonistic than he is, so Dad was really just giving you a hard time on principle. He'll eventually warm up to you."

"Even if he doesn't, it's my mission to make him like me."

"Why would you do that?"

"Because he's your dad and you obviously care about him," he says as if it's a given, and I smile again.

I can't seem to keep control over my jaw muscles today.

"Just don't come on too strong. He's very British, so in-your-face emotions are extremely frowned upon. The same applies to both of my grandfathers, by the way."

"You're taking me to see your grandads? You must really like me, huh?"

Ah, shit. "I mean one day. If you want. We're kind of close, so I thought…forget it. And stop looking at me like that."

"Like what?" He grins like a damn idiot as he watches me closely.

"Like a gloating twat."

"I have every right to gloat, baby." He wraps an arm around my waist and presses me close to his hard chest. "I didn't think you were so into me that you told your parents about me. Now, you're even thinking about telling other members of the family."

"I'm not *so* into you."

"Baby, you came out to your parents and introduced me to them. If that's not into me, I don't know what is."

"Well, you're the one who came all the way here."

"I told them I was a friend, you could've gone with that."

"No." I stroke his cheek and he leans into my touch, rubbing his skin on my palm like an eager fucking puppy. Jesus. How can a man be so ruthlessly hot and adorable at the same time? "I don't want to hide you, Nikolai. I also told Glyn and my friends about us."

"You…did?"

"A couple of weeks back, yeah. You're not my dirty secret, and for the record, I was never ashamed of you."

I was and still am ashamed of myself.

"Baby, you need to stop saying things like that because I'm really never going to let you go now."

"Who says you have to?"

"Does this mean…we can be in a relationship?"

"I thought we already were?"

"We were?"

"It was a secret, but it wasn't only physical, either, right?"

"Abso-fucking-lutely. You really pissed me off when you said that earlier. I love spending time with you whether we're fucking or not."

"Me, too."

"So we're going public now? Actually, no question mark, we're definitely going public. I need everyone to know you're fucking mine."

I nod, even though my airway gets constricted. I swallow past it and refuse to let nausea rule my emotions anymore.

"*You* are mine, Niko." I tug on his hair. "I thought we'd established that, hmm?"

"Jesus fucking Christ. I love it when you go all possessive on me. I want to eat you the fuck up."

"Go to sleep and I might let you."

"You're kidding, right?" He wedges his legs between mine and presses his erection against my thighs. "There's no way in fuck I'll be able to sleep before I devour you, my lotus flower."

"I thought you were worried about my dad?" I smile against his lips and hiss when his thigh brushes against my hardening dick.

"We can lock the door. I really can't keep my hands off you, baby. You drive me fucking crazy. Besides, Kolya hates me and has been acting like a literal dick ever since I deprived him of you."

I burst out laughing and he has this intense look in his eyes before he dips in and bites my lower lip into his mouth. I groan when he sinks his teeth in the sensitive flesh and then swipes his tongue along the mark he left.

His mouth pulls away before I can feast on him, and I try not to look disappointed as I throw a questioning glance his way.

"Mind if I use your shower? I need to get the flight's grime off me."

"Uh, yeah, sure." I point to the far right. "It's over there. I'll try to find you some of my loose-fitting clothes."

"Be right back." I think he'll kiss me again, but he grabs my face and brushes his lips on my forehead in a soft, intimate kiss. "I missed you so fucking much, baby."

I stand rooted in place long after he disappears in the bathroom. My face is so hot, I'm surprised I don't burst into flames.

Fuck.

Unable to remain standing, I fall against the wall and press a palm to where my heart's about to jump out of my chest.

Bloody hell.

I'm so irrevocably *doomed*.

Screw this.

I tug my shirt off and strip out of my sweats and boxers on my way to the bathroom. I don't even care that I've thrown them on the ground a la Nikolai.

My feet pad along the wooden flooring and I slip inside through the ajar door, because Nikolai has never closed the bathroom door. Not once.

Unlike me, he has nothing to hide.

Unlike me, he owns everything about himself, faults and mental issues included.

And for once, I want to rip a page from his book and be as open as he is. As forward as he is. Even if it's only this time.

Steam swirls around the bathroom and I'm thankful for the fog that covers the mirror as I turn in the direction of the shower.

Nikolai's clothes are all over the floor as usual, but I don't give a fuck about that.

My breath hitches when I see him standing beneath the showerhead, facing the wall as water cascades in rivulets down the intricate ink on his back, sliding to the dips in his arse and over his muscular tattooed thighs.

He tilts his head back to rinse away the shampoo and his black hair gets glued to his neck, reaching the blades of his rippling shoulders.

My lips part as I watch his closed eyes beneath the stream, the sharp line of his jaw, and the dark shadow of his stubble.

He's, hands down, the hottest man that ever walked the earth. I just can't keep my eyes or hands off him.

I'm walking on air as I reach the glass door and pull it open.

He doesn't seem to notice as he grabs the shower gel bottle and smiles a little when he sniffs it.

I stand behind him, getting soaked in a second, slide my arms on either side of him, and grab the bottle—or start to.

He swings around fast and slams me to the door with his forearm to my throat. My dick twitches and holds an immediate standing ovation.

Christ. Why do I love it so much when he gets rough?

Nikolai's grip loosens when his eyes meet mine. "Baby? What

are you doing here…oh, fuck me. Don't tell me you're joining me in the shower?"

"Isn't that obvious?" I coax his arm away and he releases me but only because I take the shower gel from him.

"Couldn't stay away, huh?"

"No, I couldn't. I need to touch you."

His lips part and I catch a glimpse of his cock thickening. "Holy fuck. I expected your usual shut up."

"Not today." I squirt the body wash on my palm and lather it over his shoulder blades, enjoying the rippling of his muscles beneath my hands.

I quickly come to the realization that I really love washing him. Why the hell haven't I done this before?

Oh, right. Because you're broken and trying hard not to look like it.

"Jesus fucking Christ. Love it when you touch me." He groans, his palms landing on my hips, stroking and feeling me up.

It's the sweetest distraction.

"You do?"

"You must know how much of a glutton I am for your touch, baby. I'm so hard, I'm bursting to be inside you."

I smile, but it falters when I reach his pectoral muscle and find a new tattoo in the spot he left blank on purpose.

My hands freeze as I study the artistic patterns of the lotus flower and make out the elegant font beneath it that reads *Property of B. King.* He had it inked on the spot that he said was for something special.

"Fuck…" I breathe, pressure forming behind my eyes as I look up at him. "When…did you get this?"

"After that night when I came to see you outside the mansion."

"When you were on your high?"

"It wasn't an impulse, if that's what you're asking. I've been wanting to do it for some time."

My heart aches, and I want to say so many things, but all I manage is a choked, "Thanks."

He narrows his eyes, and it looks so erotic with water cascading down his face. "You're not panicking?"

"Why would I?"

"Because this means I love the fucking shit out of you, baby. I can't live without you and you're not allowed to leave me."

My lips part and I watch him with a lump in my throat and my heart thundering so loudly, I can hear it over the buzzing in my ears.

"Hello?" He waves a hand in my face. "You going to say something? You're starting to freak me out."

"I don't want to leave you," I whisper the words that feel as if they're being pulled from deep in my battered soul.

"Then don't."

He says it as if it's simple. And it *is* simple for him. I wish it was the same for me.

I wish I could be the man he deserves.

I wish I could say the words back and not be flooded with the black ink and nausea.

Since I can't, I get on my tiptoes and seal my lips to his. For the first time, my kiss is gentle, imploring, wanting to explore him, to express the burning feelings I can't say out loud.

My fingers slide in his hair and I pull him closer until our chests press together, and we kiss under the water stream.

Nikolai's arms wrap around my back to fuse us closer, but he doesn't rush it, doesn't turn it into a lustful frenzy like we're used to.

Maybe it's because he, too, knows this isn't about lust anymore. It stopped being about lust a long time ago.

For me, it was *never* about lust. I was drawn to him, which is why I wanted him. It wasn't the other way around.

We kiss for what feels like hours. We kiss until it's impossible to breathe in anything but each other's air.

My hand strokes his hair while the other slides over his shoulder, back, and waist, then I grab a handful of his arse and grind him against me.

He releases a low rumble that explodes from his lips all the way to his chest. I feel every vibration against my heated skin.

All the blood rushes to my already aching cock and it pulses with need.

Nikolai hisses when I plant one leg between his and wrap the other around his thigh. His cock brushes against mine, the pierced crown eliciting primal pleasure from deep inside me. The new angle lets him rub the length of his dick against mine, sliding, rutting until we're panting in each other's mouths.

The sucking sounds of our lips echo louder, needier, now in the midst of streaming water as I hump him with a desire so colossal, I feel like I can't survive if I don't touch him.

I reach between us and tighten my fist around our cocks, jerking us in a firm grip, squeezing the way he loves it.

All this time, I've been so attuned to what and where he likes to be touched that I've become an expert in sucking his balls dry. Literally.

It took me time compared to his experience and natural talent, but I'm nothing if not a fast learner.

His sharp intake of air gives me the incentive to go rougher until he's bucking his hips and fucking my hand.

"Jesus, fuck, baby. You know how to make a man lose his mind." He blows out a sharp exhale against my swollen lips.

I fist his hair tighter. "Not just any man. *You*."

"Not just any man," he repeats with a blinding possessiveness. "*Me*. Only fucking *me*."

"Tell me you're mine," I order and it's such a low blow when he's trapped in the cloud of lust, but I want to hear it.

"I've been yours since I met you, baby." He rubs his chest against mine. "I literally have the ink to prove it."

"Umm. Fuck. I love the tattoo."

"Yeah?"

"Uh-huh. It's my favorite of yours. I want to feast on it and you."

"Holy fucking shit. You need to stop talking dirty or I'll come here and now."

"Then come."

"Nope." He bites my lower lip. "Need." *Kiss.* "Inside." *Lick.* "You."

My head is in shambles, but I have enough clarity to grab him by the wrist and pull him behind me. I don't even bother to dry us, but he fetches his trousers and grabs his wallet, then throws it down again.

"Uh, baby? I don't want to freak you out, but we're dripping all over the place."

"Fuck it."

"Oh wow. Who are you and what have you done to my OCD lotus flower?"

"Less talking and more fucking, Niko." I push him onto my bed and straddle him, grinding my arse against his erection.

"Fucking hell, you're on a roll today. You're driving me fucking *mental*, as you say." He grins in that sexy way that leaves my heart distraught.

I kiss him because I can't *not* kiss him. I'm addicted to his taste, to the way his jaw clenches beneath my fingers, the way he growls like he can't get enough of me.

I'm addicted to him and have been through enough withdrawals for a lifetime.

From now on, he's not allowed to leave my sight.

Nikolai pulls back only to wrench out a packet from his wallet and then tosses it to the side.

I breathe heavily, brows drawn. "Since when do we use condoms?"

"Not condoms. Lube. I figured you didn't have any here."

"I didn't think you'd come over...do you go around carrying packets of lube?"

"Only when I'm going to see you."

"You're actually thinking ahead for once."

"Gotta impress you, baby."

"Consider me impressed."

"Mmm. Your husky voice is hot as fuck." He tears the packet of lube with his teeth and that sight isn't supposed to make me leak so desperately over my abs.

Playfulness and intensity dance in his dark-blue eyes as he squirts the liquid on his palm and circles my rim. I lift myself higher so he has better access. His finger thrusts inside me and I arch as he opens me up with shallow pumps of his hand before he adds a second finger.

A burst of pleasure goes through me when he teases that button of pleasure inside me, but through it all, I don't stop looking at him, watching him, drowning in that enchanting gaze.

God, I missed him.

I'm never allowing him out of my sight again.

He's mine.

Mine.

Fucking *mine*.

"You're drooling, baby. Am I that hot?"

"The hottest, if you ask me."

"Jesus fucking Christ. You're going to be the death of me today."

"Don't die." I spread some of the lube on his length. "I need your cock inside me."

"Fucking fuck. I meant to prime you properly, but I can't take this anymore." He removes his fingers and clutches my hips and positions me on top of him. "Sit on my cock. Let me watch your sexy face as you ride me."

Heat of desire explodes inside me, and I hold myself on one hand as I fist his rock-hard cock with the other and then guide him inside me. My dick twitches when the crown slips in and I bite the corner of my lip as I go all the way down.

My groan mixes with Nikolai's and I breathe harshly as his huge cock stretches me open. I close my eyes to soak in the sensation and the otherworldly feel of him in me.

"Open those beautiful eyes. Look at me."

I blink and my breathing is chopped off when I find his intense gaze devouring me whole.

Oh fuck.

I always loved the way he looks at me, how he seems so in tune with me more than I'll ever be in tune with myself.

But most of all, I love how he likes me when I couldn't care less about my own existence.

"You feel so good, baby. I can be buried inside you for eternity, you know that?"

"Mmmfuck. It feels so full." I lift myself up and then come down in shallow thrusts. "I missed your cock in me."

"Holy fucking shit. From now on, I'm going to need you to be on whatever drug you're on today."

"That's easy." I pick up the pace, riding him in a long, unhurried rhythm, then I place a palm on his chest and flick my fingers on the lotus flower tattoo. "The drug in me is you."

I can feel his cock thickening inside me as he curses. He jerks his hips up to meet my fall down, but he doesn't rush the pace and lets me fuck myself on his cock slowly, enjoying every lick of desire and every roll of my hips to take him fully.

Every scrape of his piercings and every groan of pleasure breaks me apart little by little.

He can't get deep enough or fuck me hard enough. He's wrong. I don't need drugs. I'm high on his smell, his touch, but most of all that look in his eyes.

It's not lust. It's love. He looks at me like he loves me, and that nearly makes me burst into both pleasure and tears.

He strokes his hand on my thigh and hips before he fists my cock and jerks me in the same rhythm I fuck him, slow and measured, as our eyes clash and my heart nearly spills out. If the beat beneath my fingers is of any indication, then his heart is also on the verge of exploding.

I realize with astounding clarity that I'm not fucking him. I'm making *love* to him.

He's not only touching my body. He's breaching my newly born heart and my bruised soul.

He pulls back the foreskin and teases my tip, using the precum to lube me up until the sloppy sounds echo in the air. He squeezes and teases my balls in the right places until I'm delirious.

"I love how you ride my cock, baby, but do you know what I love more?" He flashes me the most gorgeous smile. "You."

I don't even feel the wave until it submerges me. My balls tighten and the release rushes through me in powerful waves. My cum squirts all over his hand and abs as he thrusts deeper inside me, fucking me to oblivion through my orgasm.

"Fucking Christ, I love watching you come." He growls before he fills me up with his cum.

I roll my hips, riding him until his cock deflates inside me, then I lift myself up and moan when I feel his cum dripping out of me.

Both of us watch it soaking his cock and balls before I fall as a heap all over his solid chest and bury my face in the crook of his neck.

We breathe heavily as I nuzzle my nose in his wet hair and he sandwiches my legs between his.

"Sorry...fuck." I try to get up. "Am I crushing you?"

Nikolai wraps his arms around my waist and shoves me back down. "No way in fuck you're moving right now."

I chuckle against his neck. "I don't think I can, to be honest."

"Fuck right. That was the top-five fuck of my entire life."

My throat works with a swallow as the pleasure haze slowly withers away. "What are your top four?"

"In no particular order. The first time I made you come. The first time I sucked you off. First time I fucked you. The second time I fucked you after you were all jealous. The first time you got on your knees for me. That time you jumped me as soon as I stepped into the penthouse and demanded I fuck you. The time you agreed to stay. The time you woke me up with your lips around my cock."

"That's more than four and they're all about me."

"You're the best fuck of my life, baby."

I lift myself up and cross my arms on his chest so that I'm looking at his handsome face and his glorious damp hair splaying on the pillow. "You want me to believe I'm better than all the men and women you fucked your way through?"

"They were only physical. They meant nothing."

"And I do?"

"Baby, you mean fucking everything."

My heart does that violent thud again and I'd swear he can feel it against his chest, but I don't care enough to pull away from him.

I tease my fingers over his new tattoo, a sense of raging possessiveness engulfing me. "Good. Because you're my property, Niko. You have the ink to prove it."

"And you are mine," he breathes out with the same intense possessiveness.

He drags my lips to his and we kiss for what seems like an eternity. Then I lift myself enough to retrieve some wet tissues to clean us up before I prop myself back up on his chest.

Nikolai spears his hand beneath his head and watches me with that permanent grin that I'm only privy to.

It slowly disappears and a frown appears on its behalf.

"What's wrong?" I ask.

He grabs my wrist and my breathing is cut off when he removes my watch. I don't stop him, even though every fiber of my being demands I do.

My heart aches when he releases a puff of relief upon seeing I haven't indulged in my self-destructing habits.

I expect him to let me go, but he strokes his thumb over the scarred skin, and the more he touches me, the harder it is to breathe.

My fucked-up head starts fogging up and I plunge headfirst into the inky lake of my mental state.

I try to pull my hand free, but Nikolai's firm grip keeps it in place as he gauges my expression.

"Remember the part where you don't get to hide from me anymore?"

"I don't think now is a good time…"

He shakes his head and the words get stuck in my throat.

Nikolai's touch turns softer and his voice becomes more gentle. "Tell me, baby. I just want to understand and help you. If you don't speak to me, I don't know where to start."

"I'm fine—"

"What did I say about that fucking word?"

"I'm really okay now. I'm over it."

"I'm not sure if you're lying to me or yourself at this point."

"Can't you just let it go?"

"No, I can't just let it go when it's a huge part of who you are. Why can't you tell me? Do you not trust me?"

"No, no, of course I do." It's because I trust him so much that I'm scared shitless about his reaction.

He'll leave you when he knows what you've done. Everyone else will see you as the weakling you are.

I swallow past the lump in my throat as that voice hammers inside my head.

"Then why the fuck are you hiding from me?" His voice drips with frustration and I want to erase that, I want to protect him, especially from myself.

Because he shouldn't love me. I'll hurt him, even unintentionally, I know I will.

But I offer him something, just a little truth. "Remember when I told you I hate myself?"

He nods, his expression easing, and he goes completely still, as if my words are a ceremony he wouldn't dare disrupt.

"A long time ago, I did something so fucked up and I never…forgave myself for it. Every time I look in the mirror, I see that version of me, and I can't stand it. The need to crash and burn it flows inside me every second of every fucking day. That's also why I stopped drawing people, animals, or anything with eyes. I feel as if they're my own reflection from the mirror following me everywhere." I smile with difficulty. "The only reason why I never took a shower with you is because I didn't want you to witness that version of me whenever I look at the bathroom mirror. I'm sorry."

"Don't apologize." His voice softens. "Can you tell me what you did to make you feel that way?"

"One day. I just need to get my shit together to be able to talk about it. Can you wait?"

"Absolutely, and, baby?" He kisses the top of my head and his next words nearly give me a heart attack. "Even if you hate yourself, I'll love you for the both of us."

THIRTY-FOUR

Nikolai

I F A FEW WEEKS AGO SOMEONE HAD TOLD ME MY LOTUS FLOWER would be taking me on one date, let alone *three*, I would've called an ambulance.

But here we are on our third date. That's right. *Third. Outside.* With people around us. And he's not panicking.

I stare down at his hand in mine, our fingers intertwined, and I discreetly pinch my nape. That hurts. This is not a fucking dream.

We walk down a dirt path in his favorite park in London that's close to where he lives, Hampstead Heath.

He said he needed something simple after all the touristy things I made him do with me. London Eye, London Bridge—or Tower Bridge as he liked to correct me, with an extremely snobbish expression, I might add—Camden Lock, and a whole day in the food market. Yesterday, we went everywhere, from Coal Drops Yard all the way to East London and then back to central London and Covent Garden where we watched some opera show in the Royal Opera House.

Definitely *not* my thing and I sure as shit stood out even in formal wear.

But I went for Bran's sake since he loves those prim and proper things. Besides, he looked fucking mouthwatering in a suit, so I wasn't complaining. Needless to stay, I fell asleep after the first ten minutes, and he let me use his shoulder as a pillow. So I might have pretended to stay asleep for longer than needed.

Today is surprisingly not that cloudy, and the sun shines through the gigantic forest-like trees of the park. It looks half kempt and half unkempt with a few asphalt roads and others left as dirt.

It's definitely better weather than yesterday. We had to run for shelter after a sudden downpour, and Bran pulled me into a corner and kissed me shitless. While people passed by.

I nearly came in my pants then and there.

Is it normal to feel as if I hit the jackpot because he's being so open?

Ever since we fucked so slowly and lovingly four days ago, he's been exceptionally affectionate. He also took me shopping since his clothes are too small for me.

And yes, he totally introduced me to his grandads, his grandma, and his uncle and his wife after he invited them for dinner, which he cooked with his dad. The uncle, Aiden, is Levi 2.0 and even told me, "Listen, kid, you hurt my nephew and no one will know where you disappear to, got it?"

To which Levi smiled and nodded, so I told them, "I'm not fazed by threats, but I respect that, sir. I'll do my best to get your approval as long as you don't meddle between me and Bran."

Aiden raised a brow at that and Levi grumbled and walked away, but I did catch a glimpse of my lotus flower smiling.

He's smiling again now as we walk by a lake and pulls me to a wooden deck that overlooks the water. Sun reflects off the surface, turning it glittery. A few birds mingle around and this big fucking seagull squawks at me, and I swear he glares when I approach before he flies away, flapping his wings and throwing a tantrum.

Jesus.

Bran leans his forearms against the wooden railing and releases my hand to point at the vast lake. "The swans are here today, see?"

I try not to sulk like I'm twelve because he's not touching me anymore as I park my back against the old wood and prop my elbows on the railing. I glance sideways at a few swans gliding on the water amongst some ducks.

"They're not here usually?" I ask.

"They are, but they go to the other pond sometimes." He smiles and I can't help watching him.

He looks so fucking attractive in jeans, a polo shirt, and a casual jacket. His Prince Charming hair is in full stylish mode, but there's something different.

It's his expression.

It's much lighter now.

These past few days, he's been talking about himself and his family without me having to ask. He took me to his high school and to the places he used to frequent, usually with his brother or friends.

This is the last of them. Earlier, we walked up to a hidden nook that took us an hour and a half to finally reach. He said it was his secret spot and where he used to go to in order to clear his mind.

I didn't miss how he revealed it to me when no one else knows about it. He seems to be much more relaxed around me, and unlike in the past, he doesn't think twice about everything he says.

Except for when it comes to his wrist.

I try not to pry too much, especially after I promised him I'd wait, but I don't like the look in his eyes every time we step out of the shower and he stares at his reflection as if he wants to destroy it.

But at least he doesn't push me away anymore.

At least he hugs me to sleep and even gets annoyed if we pull apart during the night.

I never loved sleeping in a bed until him. And I tested it after we started falling asleep together. It doesn't work without him. I'm still unable to fall asleep if he's not there. He calms my demons in mysterious ways and I feel like I can be a lunatic and he'd still embrace me anyway.

All this time, I thought I'd rather free fall into a pit of violence and die in a crash than dedicate myself to one person. I really, *really* never considered myself monogamous. But it's been so easy with Bran.

In fact, I became possessive of him early on—since I saw Clara's claws on him—and I needed to have him all for my-fucking-self.

So imagine my fucking surprise when I realized I'm not opposed to commitment if it's to him.

Some would argue I've been the one chasing him for that purpose from the beginning. If he'd stayed in the closet for another fucking decade, I would've probably shoved myself back in again if it meant being with him.

I'm that in love with this asshole. Who hasn't been much of an asshole these past few of days.

Arms resting on the railing, he cocks his head to the side so that he's watching me. "What are you thinking about?"

"You."

A full-blown grin curves his lips. "Wow. You're *that* obsessed?"

"Yeah. It's not even funny anymore."

He bumps his shoulder against mine. "You don't have to think about me when I'm right here."

"Tell that to Kolya. He doesn't seem to listen to me anymore."

He laughs, the sound long and so happy, I feel an immense sense of pride that I'm the reason behind it.

Watching my lotus flower smile is a glamorous five-star experience that instantly makes me happy as well.

"Are you enjoying my struggle, baby?"

"It's just funny whenever you treat your dick as if it's a separate entity."

"Considering that he listens to you more than me, he very much is."

He stares at my crotch and whispers, "Behave, Kolya. I'll make it up to you later."

"Uh, baby. Kolya has a very important question. Can later be right now?"

He chuckles and teasingly hits my shoulder again. "Behave, both of you. We're in a public place."

"Fiiine."

"Stop sulking. How old are you? Five?"

"I was just thinking, we can go back to your room so I can eat you up before your dad comes back from work."

"Nikolai Sokolov." He mock gasps, pretending to be offended. "Are you only using me for sex?"

"Says the guy who woke me up with his lips around my cock at five in the fucking morning."

His smile drips with seduction. "Well, I had to convince you to go on a run with me."

"You don't have to bribe me. I'd run with you anyway."

"Does that mean I have to stop waking you up that way?"

"Like fuck you'll stop. In fact, you should use that currency some more." I pause as a gust of wind blows my hair in my face. I left it loose on purpose since Bran is *obsessed* with it. He often plays with the strands or tucks them behind my ears like right now. "Why do you love running so much?"

"It's a habit." His eyes get lost in the lake. "It started as a coping mechanism. Wake up at five, run at five thirty, shower at seven, breakfast at seven fifteen, studio at seven thirty, school at nine, friends or activities after school, shower at eight, studio at eight thirty, sleep at ten thirty. Keeping my life going according to schedule forbids me from having alone time and, therefore, getting stuck in my own head."

"Is that why you fight so much for control?"

"Yes. I love patterns, methodical decisions, and living according to a plan. They make sense and keep me in check." A small sad smile crosses his lips. "Which is why you're a massive glitch in the matrix. You're everything I can't stand and wouldn't have touched with a ten-foot pole."

"Baby, it's because we're drastically different that you couldn't stay away."

"Don't let it get to your head."

"Too late. I love how you couldn't resist my dripping charm."

"More like shameless flirting and constant pushing."

"That comes with the charm."

"You're impossible."

"You know you love it." I wink. "Besides, you let go around me, and I'm so fucking proud of that. I want you to know that you can give up control and trust that I'll never use your vulnerabilities against you."

"I know," he whispers, but the sad note in his voice throws me off, but only for a second before his face returns to normal.

I realize the topic is closed before he speaks. "What do you want to do? Any other touristy things? Maybe a pastries tour? I know a few hidden Italian and French bakeries around North West and Central London."

"I thought you hated the touristy things and even kept apologizing to many people and whispering, 'He's American, sorry.' I can't believe they nodded in understanding and had the audacity to look like they were pitying you."

"Well, you talk too loud and keep making eye contact with strangers until they nearly shrivel and die."

"I thought they were stunned by my handsomeness."

"More like appalled by your unwanted attention. We don't do that in London."

"Okay, London boy. Seems everyone is a bunch of snobs like you."

"We're not snobs. We're just big champions of respecting others' personal space and privacy."

"I don't do that with you."

"Don't I know it." He touches my arm. "Tell me. What are you in the mood for?"

"You already catered to what I want. We can do what *you* want today. Walk around the park or watch ducks all day. It doesn't matter."

"It's your first time in London. I want you to have the full experience, including the clichéd photos in front of the red phone booths."

"It's not my first time. I've come with my parents and sisters before and with Dad a couple of times to meet his godfather who lives here."

"Oh. Then why did you make it sound as if this is your first?"

I lift a shoulder. "I wanted to experience it with you. It feels like the first time. I couldn't pass up the chance when you said you'd take me on a date."

"I can't with you."

"I know I'm your favorite. Now, you tell me. What do you want to do?"

"I'll take you to those bakeries anyway. We have to satisfy the sugar monster living rent-free in your stomach. After that..." He reaches a hand back and I tense, expecting him to pull on his hair, but he just rubs his nape. "Do you mind modeling for me again?"

"Not one bit." I smile big and kiss his cheek. "I love getting naked for you."

"You love getting naked everywhere."

"Not everywhere. For *you*, baby." My voice lowers. "I can't wait to bury my cock in your ass and have you begging and writhing beneath me."

"Stop talking," he hisses under his breath but I can tell he's fighting both a smile and an erection.

Over the past few days, I hung around in his studio while only wearing shorts as he worked on his paintings.

At that time, I was contemplating the best way to smash Landon's sculptures to pieces without being canceled by Bran faster than a nineties show.

So imagine my surprise when he walked up to me with a brush and started painting all over my chest, then he slid down my shorts and kept going. Best foreplay ever.

Needless to say, I fucked him against the floor right after. Ever since then, he'd asked if I could model for him and I've jumped at the opportunity.

From the sketches I've caught glimpses of, I think he's replicating my tattoos, and that's a good sign, I think. I'd do anything in my power to help him get over not being able to paint people.

Astrid showed me a lot of his paintings from when he was younger, and it's clear he has a god's talent. He painted people with so many details and soul that it would captivate anyone—even an illiterate at art such as myself. That soul is tragically missing from the landscapes he does now.

Bran is about to say something when a little girl with dark skin and hair held up in colorful ribbons stops in front of him and gives him a daisy. "This is for you."

He smiles and lowers himself to his haunches in front of her and has the audacity to accept the flower. "Thank you. Are you lost?"

"No, Mummy is just slow."

He laughs, the sound like smooth honey.

And I'm *not* the reason behind it.

Am I thinking about pitching a little girl in the water so she'll join the fucking ducks?

Yes, yes, I am.

She must feel my glare, because she looks up and glares back. This little shit isn't scared of me while most people obviously are. Let's say that during our walks, dogs like me, but their owners definitely do not. Both dogs and humans love Bran, though.

Not that I care or anything.

Except for glaring at anyone who bats their eyelashes at him. Bran is so fucking oblivious to their attention, but he's also too polite for my liking and engages in any conversation people start. Why can't he just give the 'fuck off' vibe I'm notorious for?

Because he's such a Prince Charming, that's why. I have to work at not being murderous or entertaining kidnapping thoughts whenever I see him exchanging pleasantries with others.

This little girl is a new situation, though. Especially since she's immune to my superior glares.

She leans in to whisper something in Bran's ear, and he listens attentively before he whispers something back.

The girl releases an exasperated sigh. "But why? You're like a prince from the fairy tales."

"I am?"

"Totally."

Okay, that's *enough*.

"Hey, kid." I pull Bran up and wrap my arm around his waist. "He's *my* prince. Back off."

"Nikolai!" He elbows me. "You'll scare her. Stop it."

"Shoo." I wave her away.

"Nikolai!"

"Hmph." She hikes a hand on her hip. "When I grow up, I'm going to marry him."

"Dream on."

Bran has dug a hole in my side by now.

"Nour!" an older woman calls as she hurries toward us, panting. "What did I say about running off...?"

She stops in front of us and stares, unlike all of Bran's precious Londoners. He pulls away from me, and although it's subtle, I don't like it. But then again, many people are homophobic assholes, though I haven't encountered that here and I'm thankful, not for *my* sake, but for Bran's. I don't give a fuck what people think, he does.

Though he didn't seem to mind when he kissed me in public yesterday or the day before that.

I expect him to put distance between us, but he threads his fingers with mine.

Fuck me.

Maybe he really doesn't care anymore. The fact that he's holding my hand without feeling an ounce of shame—which he shouldn't—makes me want to kiss him.

"Look, Mummy. I found a fairy-tale prince and his servant."

"That's not his servant, Nour." She smiles apologetically. "I'm so sorry. She loves running around."

"No worries." Bran smiles. "She's adorable."

"Aw, thank you." The woman grabs her daughter's hand and starts dragging her away.

The kid has the audacity to tell Bran, "Wait for me. I'm going to come back for you when I grow up."

Her mom apologizes again as she laughs and whisks the girl off before I go ahead and dump her in the lake a la serial killer.

"Stop glaring, Nikolai."

"The nerve of that little shit." I snatch the flower she gave him and throw it down.

"Are you seriously swearing at a kid?"

"What did she whisper to you?"

"You need help, fairy-tale prince?"

"That fucking—"

"I mean, you do give off scary vibes."

"And what did you tell her?"

"That's a secret."

"What do you mean by secret? Don't tell me you're taking a fucking kid's side over mine?"

"Don't tell me you're actually *jealous* of a kid?"

"What if I am?"

"You're serious? I've never been in a real relationship before you, never been intimate with anyone until you, never liked someone despite disliking most things they do like I do with you. How can you still feel jealous?"

I try not to smile, then scrunch my nose up. "I don't know. You clearly had a *crush*. You called him a *prince*, too. Jayden Adler. NASA Headquarters. DC."

"Stop saying those details in that monotone voice. You really sound like you're putting a target on his back."

"Maybe I am."

"Nikolai!"

"Yes, baby?"

He drills me with his dark glare that I've learned runs in the family. From his grandad to his dad, uncle, and even his psycho brother. "You will not hurt Jay. He has nothing to do with this."

"You coming to his defense doesn't help his case. Pretty sure Mom knows someone powerful in DC. Hmm…"

"I'd forgotten the entire thing until Mum mentioned it again. Jay and I are just friends and he barely has time to come back to the UK anymore."

"So if he *did* have time, things would be different?"

"No. You know why?"

"Because I wouldn't allow it?"

"Because I never wanted a prince. I prefer an unhinged motherfucker."

"Hey! That's me!" I grin so wide, I can see my reflection in his bright eyes.

"Don't smile. You'll grow on me."

"Awe. I thought I was already."

"Seriously, stop grinning. I don't like sharing it with others."

"Who's the jealous one now?"

"I don't share, Niko. Am I clear?"

"One thing we have in common."

"You still didn't wipe that look off your face."

"Jesus, chill. I can't believe everyone thinks you're such a golden boy when you're, in fact, a fucking control freak."

"You have complaints, baby? You can voice them, but there's no guarantee I'll take them into account."

My lips part and I can feel my heart crawling up to my mouth and spilling on the ground at his feet.

His smile falters. "What's wrong?"

"You just called me baby."

"Oh. It—"

"Don't say it was a mistake."

"It wasn't. I want to call you that sometimes."

I clutch him by a fistful of his jacket and drag him against me. "I need to kiss you—"

The words aren't fully out of my mouth when he seals his lips to mine and sears himself in my fucking heart with the most passionate kiss. He kisses me with yearning, longing, and emotions he's still hesitating to admit.

He kisses me like he will never let go of me.

Like he'll burn for me as hot as I burn for him.

I want this moment to last forever, please and fucking thank you.

THIRTY-FIVE

Nikolai

I NEVER THOUGHT I'D SAY THIS, BUT I THINK I'M ACTUALLY GOING through an intensive sugar coma.

Over the past two days, Bran has been taking me to all these Italian, French, and Chinatown bakeries that I came out of with an armful of goodies that I consumed behind his back. While he's fine with me buying pastries, he believes in an annoying concept called portioning.

Sugar's worst enemy ever.

Anyway, I still have to finish these sickly-sweet cream buns and then I can go comatose in peace.

Unfortunately for me, we have to leave tomorrow. While Bran could stay longer and work on his project from here, I've missed two tests and I'm risking my grade drastically falling. And while I couldn't care less about that, I don't want to seem irresponsible in front of his parents.

Not to mention my own parents, who keep asking why the fuck I'm not attending school. I kind of told Dad about him, but I still didn't mention he's Landon's twin. I'd rather he meet him directly instead of getting the idea that he's like his psycho brother.

Astrid will definitely miss me, as she told me this morning. We formed a bond, and I'm telling you, that amazing woman will be my mother-in-law one day. My future father-in-law, however, likes to play hard to get. Now I know where his son got the trait from. But I think even his grumpy self will miss me.

Bran had no chance with me and neither will he.

Since Astrid and I are basically best friends now, I tried probing to find out if she knew about Bran's cuts, but I don't think so. Again, they're really great parents, so I doubt they would've left him to his own devices if they'd discovered his nasty habits.

It makes sense that they haven't. He wears a watch at all times and the most annoying part is that he has steel control over which emotions he shows. When I first got to know him, I often thought he was ice-cold, when, in fact, he was just exceptionally good at sealing everything inside.

I can tell that even his parents struggle to get him to open up. Hell, the only reason I found out about the cuts was through a coincidence, and *after* I drove him into a panic attack.

His mom and dad definitely do *not* like to push him. Which might not be the best strategy to deal with someone as closed off and inward-oriented as my lotus flower.

But that's fine. I can be the villain and push him. I have to, because I've been reading about people who cut themselves and the mental ramifications, and it's never a good idea to leave them alone.

It doesn't get better as he likes to say. It's not an addiction that he can withdraw from without addressing the reason he does it in the first place.

The general consensus in the forums full of people who cut themselves is that they need to purge the pain. One guy said that when he sees the blood pour out of him, he can finally exhale a breath of relief.

My stomach twisted at that image because I could picture Bran doing the same. In that damned closed bathroom. Battling against his demons and bleeding out.

Fucking alone.

That won't be happening anymore.

As soon as we go back to the island, we have to address the mental cancer that's eating at his head.

His presence stopped me from going on suicidal missions, so I refuse to let him self-destruct.

Maybe it's because I'm more attuned to him than should be healthy, but he hasn't been himself today. It started this morning, but after we went out, he relaxed for a bit. However, he became uptight during dinner.

Minimum words. Monosyllabic replies. A noticeable absence of the usual joking around with his dad. The worst part is that he kept his distance from me—something he hasn't done over the course of the period I've spent at his childhood home.

The only variable that changed compared to previous dinners was Astrid's agent, Grace. A middle-aged blonde woman with a fake laugh and ridiculous consumption of wine.

Astrid said they had a bit of a misunderstanding because she wanted Bran to sign with her, but he chose the agent Landon introduced him to.

I remember how happy he sounded when he talked about that over text. He was basically buzzing at how his brother recognized his talent and introduced him to *his* agent.

According to Astrid, that agent has nowhere near Grace's talent, but she respects Bran's decision even though she doesn't understand it.

After dinner, I help Bran carry the dishes to the kitchen. He turns to leave, but I grab his wrist, stopping him by the counter.

He looks up at me, appearing exhausted, probably because of staying up late and trying to wake up early. This morning, I insisted we stay in bed and not go for a run at an ungodly hour. He's done that a few times at the penthouse, and I had thought it would help him feel more relaxed today, but it's only made him more agitated.

It doesn't show in his movements or his expression, but his eyes tell a different story.

Seeing the emptiness in them is no different than having a knife plunged deep into my gut.

I stroke the back of his hand. "You okay?"

"Yeah. Why wouldn't I be?"

"You were uncomfortable in there, baby. If you don't like the woman because of the pressure or whatever, just refuse to have dinner with her anymore. I'm sure your parents will understand."

"She's Mom's agent and practically family at this point."

"Family doesn't get a free pass for everything. I don't visit with members of my family who piss me off. Namely, my homophobe uncle who told me it's okay to fuck guys as long as I marry a woman and give him Russian nephews."

His expression softens and some of that emptiness cracks and vanishes with each of his deep breaths. "I'm sorry."

"What did I say about apologizing for no reason?"

"There's a reason. I hate that you feel judged."

"I couldn't care less about him and his useless, entirely meaningless opinion. As Dad says, he can go fuck himself."

"God. I love how you give the world the middle finger without caring about anything or anyone."

"If that's what they deserve, that's exactly what they'll get."

"Did you…" he trails off. "Forget it."

"If you have something to ask me, just ask."

His hands land on my hips, his face appearing a bit fragile, vulnerable, even. "Have you thought about your future within the mafia? What your uncle said makes sense and it's not like you aren't attracted to women, so you could do it for the image—"

"Don't finish that or I'll be pissed at you. Do you think I'd get married or do shit just for the mafia's sake or an image? Is that what you really think of me?"

His throat works up and down with a gulp. "No, but don't you need to have kids?"

"I don't if I don't want to. It's my decision and none of anyone else's business."

"But wouldn't being with a guy hurt your position? I know how much you love the thrill of that life, so I'd hate to see you lose it."

"I won't. Jeremy, Vaughn, and I will rule over that empire. The two of them are the most important heirs to the Bratva and they don't give a fuck about my sexuality, so neither will anyone who wants to keep his head in place."

"Vaughn?"

"The Pakhan's son. You might have seen him at the initiation. He wore the white mask."

"Oh, right. But I've never seen him around."

"And you never will—at least, not on the island. He lives in the States and just comes around for the initiations." I cup his jaw. "Point is, don't worry your pretty head about my position. I'll fight tooth and nail for what I want. Is that understood?"

He nods.

I cock my head in the direction of the dining room. "You going to do what you want and ignore the hag?"

"After Mum's exhibition. And, Nikolai?"

"Hmm?"

"Promise me you won't talk to Grace."

"Why not?"

His palms tremble as he wraps them around my cheeks. The agitation in his voice sends my hackles rising in a fraction of a second. "Promise me. Please."

"Okay, I promise."

He expels a long breath and then brushes his lips against mine. "Thanks."

When he releases me, his movements are fluid and he even smiles. "Want to model for me?"

"Always."

"Wait for me in the studio. I just need to speak to my dad and I'll be there." He starts to go but turns around and kisses me again, hard and fast, then whispers against my lips, "I can't get enough of you, baby."

And then he leaves as if he didn't just rip my heart out and take it with him.

Fuck me.

I need to chill the fuck out before I actually kidnap him to a deserted island where I don't have to share him with anyone else.

I go to wash my hands in the bathroom and as I leave, I catch a glimpse of Grace walking down the hall in my direction.

So I know I promised Bran I wouldn't talk to her, but she's the one who stops in front of me. Technically, I'm not the one who broke the promise.

She gives me a once-over as if I'm a cockroach stuck beneath her heel, then lifts her chin with an air of simmering arrogance.

Arms crossed, her witchy long red nails tap impatiently on the arm of her black jacket. "What's your name again?"

"If you don't remember it, that could be an early sign of dementia. I suggest you call your doctor."

"You believe yourself to be funny?"

"Not intentionally."

"I just don't see it."

"Your dementia? No one does at early stages."

"I don't see how someone like *you*"—she does that condescending once-over again—"can be with a gracious man like Bran. It just doesn't add up."

"And that's any of your business because?"

"I don't like seeing him wasting his talents or time on delinquents such as yourself. You must've threatened him with something."

I lean back against the wall. "Again, I really don't see why this concerns you. Hate to say it, but you're starting to sound and look like an annoying Karen. What Bran and I do with our relationship has nothing to do with you. Pick up whatever dignity you have left and walk away."

"*Relationship?*" She laughs, the sound throaty and evil. "Relationship, you say. You're delusional, boy. Bran doesn't do those."

"He does with me."

"You think you know him better than me?" Her voice and face become stone-cold. "You're *nothing* in the grand scheme of things."

"What the hell is that supposed to mean?"

She uncrosses her arms and points a finger at me. "It means you should back off and leave him alone."

"Or what?"

"You don't want the answer to that."

"No, I do."

A wicked look passes through her beady eyes, then she flips her hair. "Give me your number. I'll send you a goodbye gift."

After I do just that to mess with her, she walks away with a sway to her hips and a flick of her hair.

Forget about Bran being uncomfortable around her. I don't like the bitch one bit. There's a sinister edge that she hides so well in public and shows so readily in private, and that in and of itself is a red flag.

Could it be that he's not only stressed due to the agent thing?

I make a note to ask him about that later.

My feet lead me to the studio, and I smile mischievously when I realize I can snoop around without Bran knowing.

He's been so secretive about what he's working on and told me to be patient, but we both know I don't have that.

I snatch his sketchpad and my lips part as I flip through dozens of sketches of me. Not my tattoos as I thought, but my actual face.

There are pages upon pages of my face from different angles with my hair mostly loose, but there are some where my hair is tied into a ponytail or a bun.

And he put so many details in my eyes. Some are glaring, others are when I stare at him while smiling, but my favorites are of the intense look in my eyes during sex.

Fuck me. He drew eyes for the first time in years and they're *mine*.

The following pages are full-body sketches, and fuck me. He's so thorough about details, from the way I arch my eyebrow to the tiny dimple at the corner of my mouth when I smile. It's like I'm staring at a mirror.

I spend what seems like half an hour going through the sketches. When I'm done, I find two more notepads stacked full of me—mostly in the nude.

My lotus flower might pretend to be a prude, but I knew he loved seeing me naked.

Note to self: From now on, walk around the penthouse in no clothes.

My grin is permanent as I flip through them, greedily storing every detail in my memory.

But then it changes.

My smile falls when I see something different.

He sketched me half naked and there's what I assume is his silhouette beside me, but he's faceless. On the next page, there's a contour of his face, but chaotic black lines fill his features. On the following page, he drew black lines so deep, they punctured the paper.

Fuck.

Please don't tell me this is how he sees himself.

My phone vibrates and I think it's him, so I put the sketchpads exactly where I found them.

After I pull out my phone, I suddenly feel parched, so I pour a glass of water from the jug he keeps on the table.

The glass remains suspended in midair as I open the text I got from a number I don't recognize.

Your goodbye gift.

I click on the video attached, and my entire body tenses.

The surveillance footage shows an extravagant living room with a plush carpet and a white sofa. A younger version of Bran, no older than fifteen or sixteen, sits in the corner, doodling in a notebook. My fingers clench the glass when I make out Grace sitting close beside him with a slim arm thrown over his shoulder. She's wearing a red satin camisole and shorts that are definitely not appropriate.

"I just don't get it." He sighs. "What does Lan have that I don't?"

"Nothing, hon," she coos and strokes his hair.

"But he gets all the girls."

"They don't matter. You're the one who's meant for greatness."

"Really?" He peeks at her, sheepish and hopeful, and my heart starts fucking racing beneath my rib cage.

"Really." Her grating fake soft voice echoes in the air. "As for the girls, they're nothing. I'm more mature and beautiful. And guess what? I find you much more charismatic than him."

"You...do?"

She kisses him and he wraps a hand around her neck to kiss her back, but it's awkward and unsure at best.

The piece of fucking shit doesn't seem to notice that as she unbuttons his shirt. "I'll make you feel like you're better than him, and one day, I'll make you his god."

He nods once, but he doesn't touch her as she kisses his neck, his chest, and then pulls down his pants. He squirms when she wraps her hand around his dick. He tries to get away when she slides her shorts down her legs and positions herself on top of him.

"I...don't like this," he whispers, and his voice is so low, I wouldn't have heard it if I didn't have the volume on high.

"Shh, hon. I promise you'll enjoy it." She jerks him a few more times. "See, you're hard already."

"Grace..." He gulps, red blotching his entire body. "I don't think I like sex...please stop..."

"Nonsense, honey. Everyone likes sex." She strokes his hair and then whispers, "You don't want to be seen as a freak compared to your brother, do you, Bran? Your mum and dad would be so disappointed."

He shakes his head once and she comes down on him in one go. He screams. And it's not from pleasure.

He screams and it sounds like a "No..."

But I can't listen to what he has to say anymore because she slaps a hand on his mouth as she moans. The muffled sounds that rip from him as he tries to wiggle away will haunt me for the rest of my fucking life.

"Mmmmno... Mmmm... Mmmm..."

A breaking sound echoes in the air and a burn spreads through my arm. I can tell I broke the glass and can feel water and blood sliding down my wrist and dripping onto the floor, but I can't look away from his face.

The confusion.

The pain.

The anger.

Animalistic growls reverberate around me and I realize they're mine. My body vibrates with rage so extreme, it fills my vision with black. Demons I didn't know existed flood my bloodstream, and pressure forms behind my eyes.

As I watch and listen, I know, I just know that I'm never coming back from this.

THIRTY-SIX

Brandon

SOME DAYS, I FEEL LIKE I'M FINE. I CAN BREATHE, *SOMEWHAT*, can move, run, talk, and smile.

I can exist and not suffer from the metaphorical bleeding in my fucked-up head.

On other days, I feel like I'm being punished for the good times. I'm being punished for feeling happy when I have no right to be.

Days where my wrist itches and my mind crumbles into a satire of burning emotions and throbbing pulses.

Days where it's hard to breathe without choking on the gooey ink that's been flooding my brain since the day I gave up control because of my screwed-up pride.

Today is one of those days.

Today started with waking up in the embrace of the most beautiful, most affectionate soul I've ever met and feeling like I got my fucking ink all over him.

I felt like I was tarnishing him, digging him deeper into the black fucked-up hole of my existence until he'd also be submerged in it.

Until he'd have no way out, like me.

That's why I didn't want him to see me. I didn't want *anyone* to see me. Because the moment they get past the perfect image to look inside, they'll find a grimy, spineless piece of fucking shit whose worst enemy is his own mind.

Nikolai woke up to me wiping the smudges from his chest and thinking I was stroking him. He smiled and I couldn't look him in the eye without falling deeper into that muddy hole in my soul.

He smiled and it was okay for a while.

Until it wasn't.

Until Grace decided to come over for dinner and I had to sit across from her again and pretend I wasn't being pulled apart by my demons. I had to swallow the food and force it down when my stomach demanded I throw it back up.

It was worse with Nikolai around. The more he watched me like he could peel off my outer layer and see all the ugly parts, the worse my nausea got.

A splitting migraine has been pounding on the back of my head and is making my vision blurry as I attempt to walk to the studio.

I barely managed to tell Dad about our arrangements to leave tomorrow before I bolted out of his office.

If I'd stayed, I would've exploded. I feel like a ticking time bomb lately, on the verge of spilling my guts and ruining everything for Mum like an ungrateful brat.

She was over the moon when Grace signed her. I was over the moon when she decided to give me private lessons instead of Lan.

For the first time, someone from the art circuit called *me* a genius instead of my holier-than-thou twin.

For the first time, I felt more *important* than him.

Lan never liked Grace or got along with her, and that made me fall deeper into her trap.

He told me not to take her classes and that he'd talk to his art teacher so he could teach us together. But I responded with things like, "It's none of your business, prick" and "Stop being so jealous," then went to her just out of spite.

It was only after I grew up that I realized two things. One, from a young age, Lan's narcissism clashed with hers and he probably saw her for what she was, even if unintentionally. The reason she didn't pick him was because she couldn't control him. He's always been so sharp and manipulative, her tactics wouldn't have worked on him.

Two, she was grooming me at the time. She said the right things, pushed the right buttons, and used my love for art and my parents to shove me right where she wanted me.

And it worked like a charm.

For her. Not me.

Even before Grace, I didn't like physical touch. I made out with a few girls, and some of them gave me the occasional blowjob, but I had to stop myself from pushing them away every time they touched me. I had to play the game and pretend it was okay.

Lan, Eli, and Remi kept saying shagging was so fantastic and I felt extremely alienated in their guy talks. So for a short period, I suspected maybe I was gay. Maybe the reason physical touch was revolting was because I played for a different team.

The thought freaked me out to no end. I remember thinking, why can't Lan be the gay twin? Why does it have to be me? He already excels at drawing everyone's attention, so why can't he at least be the different one?

But that thought didn't have any credence. I never felt attracted to my teammates who stripped in the changing room, and they had pretty fit bodies. I never ogled them even subconsciously and never saw them as anything more than teammates. However, I had to test the theory.

One night, I went for it. There was an openly gay boy at school and he often flirted with good-looking straight guys—Lan and me included. When he followed me out during a party, flirting and touching, I kissed him to see if I liked it.

I nearly threw up in his mouth.

So I thought maybe it was because he was so flamboyant and I wasn't into that. I tried it with a few other boys, but the result was the same. I felt disgusted and couldn't get past a kiss.

Turned out, I wasn't straight or bi or gay. I was simply broken like a fucking malfunctioning machine. When Lan and I were in Mum's womb, he took everything and left me with nothing. That caused me a lot of stress at the time, and I wanted to talk to Dad about it, but I couldn't bring myself to. I thought he'd be disappointed or something. He had headaches because of Lan, but he listened with a grin whenever my brother told him about his endless shagging adventures. Dad didn't agree with many of his actions, but he's always been irrevocably proud of how my brother handled himself in the outside world.

I was so jealous of Lan, so filled with envy that I started to distance myself from him. I blamed him for how *I* was broken. I hated him because *I* wasn't like him. I despised him for having *everything* while I had *nothing*.

It was colossally irrational, but there was no logic in the daft, angsty fifteen-year-old me.

My biggest mistake was voicing my displeasure about Lan to Grace. She latched on to it like a hyena and got me exactly where she wanted me.

Powerless. Hopeless. *Used.*

Since then, I've been submerged in the dot of ink on my hand that I looked at the entire time she fucked herself on me. While I screamed and begged her to stop. Like a fucking weakling.

I could've fought her or pushed her off. I was hitting puberty pretty hard and was definitely physically stronger than her. But I was too confused, too caught up in the attention she showed me, too scared and horrified about the thought of hating the idea of having sex with everyone.

The reason I cut my left hand is because it's the hand I wrapped around her nape when I kissed her that day. When I gave her the opening to violate me thoroughly.

I've often had fantasies about cutting off that hand. Chopping it to pieces. Extracting the cancerous organ that signed my mental death certificate.

The reason I posted stories with #NewDay every day is because I was proud for surviving another day, for not letting my head get the better of me and pushing me down the cliff of my sanity.

It's been over eight years, but I still can't escape the ink and the nausea that flooded me during the whole experience.

I remember that day so well. After I stumbled out of her flat, I spent it roaming the streets, walking in the rain with a dazed expression. Though I was drenched, it wasn't the physical discomfort I felt. No.

I was frozen, cold and frosty, all the way to my goddamn mind.

When I got home, I stood in my shower for two hours. But it wasn't water that rinsed me.

Black ink poured down on me, covering my eyes, nose, and ears and jamming inside my throat until I was retching on the shower floor again and again. At some point, I was dry heaving. The entire time, a strong floral perfume clogged my nostrils and my fucking throat and her red fucking nails choked me.

I didn't go to my bed. I *couldn't*.

Whenever I moved, I felt her ghost right behind me, cackling and cooing, her nails sinking into my arm.

I was terrified that she'd do it again.

So I ran to Lan's room. Ironic, really, since I was the one who demanded we have separate rooms two years prior. Lan never wanted that and he became so petty afterward.

However, when I stood in his doorway, he immediately knew something was off. He jumped from his bed and asked me what was wrong.

I whispered, "Nothing. Can you hug me?"

The moment his arms wrapped around me, I broke down. I cried in his chest for so long that I think I passed out.

My brother held me through it all, and even though he doesn't know how to soothe people, he was patting my back the entire time. He carried me to his bed and let me sleep in his arms.

He whispered, "Tell me who did this to you so I can end them."

Then he begged me for the first time in his life.

I didn't tell him the real reason. Instead, I poured my heart out about how I was struggling with art and school and attention. I also admitted out loud that I hated how I wasn't as strong-minded as he was.

That worked for a while, but I don't think he ever believed me.

Then the experimentation phase I went through bit me in the arse and some homophobes started mocking me and calling me slurs.

Lan thought the breakdown was because of that, and I saw first-hand how he targeted them and turned their lives into a nightmare. To this day, not one of them is a functioning member of society.

For a long time, Lan kept watching me, but I was already good at building façades and perfecting my image.

I stopped trying to experiment with guys and kept to girls because they made me feel like Lan. Straight. High sex drive. *Normal.*

As for Grace, I handled her soon after.

She made the mistake of sending me the footage of what happened with the caption: *Study this and you'll let your raw talent loose.*

I told her she needed to be the one who told Mum that she was discontinuing my lessons because of work or whatever excuse she could come up with. If she didn't, I would show the footage to Mum.

That was a lie. I would rather die than show that to anyone.

Grace was appalled. She thought we were in it together and that I liked her. She even told me that she felt like I'd used her.

I *used* her.

Me.

She complied, not because she thought she'd assaulted me. No. It was fear of the scandal of having sex with a minor. To this day, she believes it was consensual and has often told me we could revisit 'the good old days.'

She was out of my immediate life, but she never left it completely, not when Mum's career depended on the almighty Grace Bruckner. She worked so hard to be considered by her and I couldn't be the one who ruined that.

So I swallowed the knife with its blood and pretended everything would be fine. I did encourage her. I did kiss her back. I did feel drunk on the sense of power she offered me.

A man *can't* be raped by a woman.

That's the stigma that stayed in my head even though the nausea from that time followed me for the rest of my life.

It got worse, not better, but I had it under control. I believed my-self to be *fine*.

Until Nikolai invaded my life and forced me to see just how fun-damentally broken I am. That no matter how much I hide, I'm still naked and desolate.

The truth I hid from for years coiled from the ashes. I *betrayed* that fifteen-year-old version of me and he rose from the decay and transformed into the reflection in the mirror. He became the pool of ink and the eyes who'll never forgive me for letting him down.

Nikolai fundamentally changed me, because he crushed the lies I've been telling myself for years. I thought if I convinced myself I was normal, straight, and completely unaffected by the past, I'd eventually believe it. But that was a pipe dream.

Being with Nikolai hurts because I crave him despite hating my-self. I need him so I can mend the broken pieces I shoved to the back of my closet of skeletons.

And that's wrong.

I'm using him, and no matter how smitten he is with me, it'll eventually backfire and blow us to smithereens.

If I want to keep him, I need to fix myself.

I need to find a way to talk to the fifteen-year-old me after alien-ating, discarding, and shutting him up for so long.

My muscles tighten and my migraine pounds harder when I see the woman waiting for me down the hall.

The need to run and hide pulses inside me so strongly, my vision blurs. Still, I walk at my steady pace, forcing down the deep hatred I hold for this woman.

Just suppress it for a few more weeks.

This exhibition will boost Mum to immeasurable stardom and then she won't need Grace anymore. That's when I can tell my par-ents and Nikolai. That's when I can finally do right by him and my fifteen-year-old self.

"What do you want?" I ask with a sigh, my calm voice unrecognizable.

She smiles and I nearly gag on the smell of her perfume. "Oh,

Bran. Are you seriously going to turn down this once-in-a-lifetime opportunity because of some little misunderstanding in the past?"

"Misunderstanding?" I grit my teeth, all my demons rushing out at once, and I feel my control smashing into pieces. "Did you just call it a *misunderstanding*? You fucking assaulted me, Grace."

"I did no such thing. You clearly agreed to it. You kissed me back and led me on. So don't stand there and claim assault."

"I told you no!"

"Shh." She scans her surroundings. "What's with that tone? Why are you hissing and acting like that delinquent boy toy you brought along? You're much more elegant and sophisticated and should consider your company. That Nikolai is not good for you—"

One moment she's standing there, and the next, I'm jamming my palm against her face, banging her head against the wall with a thud. She stares at me through my fingers with wide eyes, and for the first time, I see fear.

She's scared of me. Good.

"Don't you fucking dare say his name with your rotten mouth. You don't *mention* him. You don't *talk* to him, and if you see him, you walk the other fucking way or, so help me God, I *will* kill you. Am I clear?"

She nods once, her face turning red.

The urge to crush her skull between my fingers burns bright in my pounding head, but I release her. Because how can I be with Nikolai if I'm locked up for murder?

She straightens and stares at me as if I've grown a few heads, then backs away from me, probably sensing the murderous energy oozing off me.

I lean against the wall after she's gone, but I still can't expel the fucking migraine pulsing through me. Maybe I shouldn't have come home.

No.

I breathe in.

I wouldn't exchange the past week I've spent with Nikolai for the world. Holding hands, being in public, introducing him to my family, and being showered with their acceptance. It's been the happiest week of my life.

Until now, that is.

It's going to be okay.

I've survived years. I can handle a few more weeks.

I plaster a smile on my face as I push open my studio's door. "Sorry I'm late, baby. I was held up—"

My words get stuck when I hear the sound I'll never forget, not after one night, one year, or eight of them.

"Mmmmno... Mmmm... Mmmm..."

Ink explodes from the back of my throat and I choke on it like I did that night beneath the shower. It floods my eyes, nose, and ears. It swallows my whole body until I can only see Nikolai through a black haze.

His eyes are glued to the screen of his phone as that noise echoes on and on, cracking my ears open like a sledgehammer.

I don't know how I walk to him when I can't feel my legs.

I don't know how I breathe when I'm wheezing.

Blood drips from his hand as he grips the bottom of a broken glass. On and on, his blood seeps into the black lake that's swallowing me whole.

I don't think he hears me. He definitely does *not* see me, because his beautiful eyes are now as empty as mine.

I went ahead and ruined him just like I ruined fifteen-year-old me.

It's all because of *me*.

I am the fucking problem.

Nikolai finally lifts his head, and when he looks at me, for the first time since I met him, I don't see my reflection in his eyes.

That's what happens when he *sees* me. That's what will happen when everyone else sees me.

This is why I hid. This is why I didn't even want to come out.

I knew it was only a matter of time before every other fucked-up admission followed.

I was naive to think I had time.

But I don't.

I never did.

"You…you saw…you *saw*…" My voice sounds like it's coming from underwater as my vision blurs with moisture.

"You saw…"

And now you can't look at me anymore.

"Bran—" His words are cut off when I snatch the piece of glass from his hand and jam it against my neck.

Everything happens in a haze, but all of a sudden.

I don't know how I end up on the floor, drowning in my own blood and the black ink.

There's so much ink now, choking me, pulling me to its bottomless depths. My strangled breaths come in short, chopped bursts.

Then in the middle of it, strong hands wrap around me and my head is balanced on a solid surface as moisture drips on my face.

Pressure at my neck. Blood everywhere. In my mouth. On my clothes. On his hands.

I see him through hazy red, my lids nearly closing.

"Baby, please…please…" he begs in a broken voice, and I can see the tears in his beautiful eyes.

The eyes that I turned empty.

The eyes that I destroyed.

"Please don't go, baby, please…don't leave me…please…stay with me…stay with me…you have to stay with me…" His lips are all over my forehead, my nose, my cheeks, my mouth.

He yells something toward the door, but I don't hear him over the ringing in my ears.

I reach a hand for him, wanting to touch his hair one final time.

I'm sorry.

The words are on the tip of my tongue, but no sound comes out.

My hand falls as the ink swallows me whole.

It's finally over.

THIRTY-SEVEN

Nikolai

WHEN I WAS YOUNG, I REALIZED THAT MY PERCEPTION of the world differed from that of others my age.

Violence bubbled in my veins and blinded me to reality. I saw life through red lenses and liked it. No. I fucking *loved* it.

I took pride in being different, in jumping through hoops many people wouldn't dare go near. I never felt repressed by my sexuality, my preferences, or my tendencies. In fact, I wore them like a badge and flaunted them for everyone to see.

Being bi is nothing to be ashamed of, as Mom told me a long time ago.

"*It makes you different from the majority, but you were always special, son. Always,*" Dad said.

I've always felt special, too, like I could go deep and deeper, high and higher, and nothing would stop me.

This is the first time I don't feel special.

The first time I've watched my life shatter around me as I stood in the remains, surrounded by bright blood.

It was everywhere—on his neck, his shirt, his hands, the floor, me.

Every-fucking-where.

I'm in the middle of the hospital waiting area, but I can still see it dripping on the floor as I carried Bran in my arms. I can still see his pasty-white skin and hear the haunting sound that left his throat before he closed his eyes.

He's been in surgery for seven hours. Seven fucking hours and the nurse has come through twice for blood. *Twice.*

Seven hours and I haven't moved an inch from my position in front of the OR door. A nurse had to come out here to bandage my hand, because there was no way in fuck I was moving.

Seven hours of hearing Astrid crying. Glyn and Lan flew in from the island as soon as they heard the news and arrived a couple of hours ago.

Glyn has been hugging her mom and crying. Lan and Levi are now standing beside me after they finished pacing the corridor for the millionth time. Levi drove us to the hospital like a madman while I held Bran on my lap in the back seat, keeping pressure on his neck.

The bleeding never stopped. Not even temporarily. The more time passed, the closer I was to losing him.

I'll never forget how his pulse diminished beneath my fingers, how I was begging and kissing his blue lips and asking, imploring, praying for a God I've never believed in to give him back to me.

I'll do anything if you give him back.

If he asked for my life in return, I'd spill my guts on a platter.

I don't want a life without him.

I *can't* have a life without him.

"What did I say, Dad?" Landon's eerily calm voice rips through the suffocating silence. He sounds collected, but I've never seen him agitated in my life. I've never seen the almighty Landon King tremble with rage like when I showed him that video.

I showed it to Astrid and Levi as soon as Bran was wheeled away for emergency surgery. They had to call in some hotshot surgeon who specializes in nerve repair.

My Bran kept that pain to himself for eight fucking years, to protect them—his fucking parents, siblings, and the whole world. I'm no fucking philanthropist. I shoved that video in their faces so they could see the pain that grew so big that he had to stab himself to end it.

I stood there watching him jam that piece of glass in his neck and felt the world tilt on its axis beneath my feet.

His body wasn't the only thing that hit the ground. My sanity did, too, and it's still there, floundering in the middle of his blood, choking and unable to come up for air.

Astrid fainted upon seeing that video. Levi looked like he was going to be sick, but he watched it to the very end, like me.

Landon vibrated with rage. His face was red, his fist was clenching and unclenching, and his upper lip lifted in a snarl like it is right now.

"What the fuck did I say, Dad?" he repeats in a clipped tone. "I said that you shouldn't cater to him. I said that he's a fucking iceberg who hides more than what he shows. I said that he needed to be fucking pushed, but no. You believed in *space*. You believed in treating him with kid gloves, peace, love, and fucking understanding. Look where that got us!"

"Lower your fucking voice." Levi glares at him as Astrid and Glyn sob in unison somewhere in the background.

I don't look at them. I can't.

So I focus on Landon's rage. Landon's rage speaks to mine.

"I'm not lowering my fucking voice." He shakes with the way he's winding his muscles, a vein nearly popping in his neck. "That's my twin brother. My other *half*. You don't get it, Dad. He…he's my. Other. *Half*. And I couldn't be there to stop him from trying to take his own fucking life. I couldn't be there when it got to be too much. He pushed me away and I thought he hated *me*. All this time, I failed to realize he hates *himself*."

My injured fist tightens until I feel the burn of my wounds and keep my fingers there.

Levi clutches Landon by the shoulders. "If anyone should be blamed, it's *me*. I failed him as a father. It's not your fault, Lan. You wouldn't have known."

"Of course I would. I'm his *twin* brother. What's the use of being labeled a genius if I couldn't save the one person who matters?"

"None of you would've known." I speak in a voice that sounds far away even to my ears. "He made it his mission to hide behind a façade and pretend he was okay. If—*when*—he wakes up, you will *not* play this blaming game in front of him. It'll only make him feel guilty and uncomfortable. He's already had a lifetime of that, so you better get your fucking shit together when you see him."

Levi lets his hands fall limp at his sides, a pained expression crossing his distraught features.

Landon flashes me with his psychotic glare, then jams a finger against my chest. "Why the fuck didn't you stop him? You were there. Why couldn't you fucking stop him, you useless waste of bloody space!"

"Landon!" Levi pulls him away from me. "Nikolai is the reason he's still breathing. Your brother could've done it where no one was looking and it would've been too late by the time anyone found him—"

"You're right, I couldn't. I didn't see it coming." My voice chokes. "But I don't give a fuck about you or your opinions, Landon. The only one who can be mad at me is him. Not you or anyone else."

He snarls at me, but his father manages to push him back.

No matter how much I hate the prick, he's right. If I hadn't let him snatch that piece of glass, if I hadn't broken that glass, if I hadn't hit Play on that fucking video, none of this would've happened.

But it did.

And here I am standing at Death's door, begging him not to take away my Bran.

He believes himself to be all messed up, but he's the only one who's managed to keep me rooted in the present, the one who manages to stop my thoughts from racing in different directions with unnatural patterns.

As long as he comes back, I'll murder his demons one by one until he's ready to look in the mirror again.

Until he forgives himself for something that was *not* his fault.

A middle-aged doctor with Southeast Asian features steps outside and removes his cap, his face drawn and his movements sluggish.

My heart nearly drops to the floor. Please tell me that's only because he's exhausted—

"Doctor..." Levi's voice sounds strained. "How's...my son?"

"We managed to repair the nerves and the veins. He nicked his carotid artery, but, thankfully, the first aid response was fast enough and he got here in time. He was also lucky that no damage was inflicted on his vocal cords." He smiles a little. "He's stable now, but we'll keep an eye on him in the ICU tonight."

"Oh, thank you. Thank you..." Astrid pants through her tears and I realize she and Glyn have come to stand beside us.

He says something about the psychiatric department getting in touch, but I'm not listening.

My heart thunders back to life, rising from the ashes in one sweeping motion. I have to close my eyes as a long whoosh of breath escapes me.

He's alive.

I asked—begged—him not to leave me and he listened.

He didn't leave me.

Fucking fuck.

Fuck!

I let the searing emotions blast through me, whirling into the organ that beats for him. Everyone around me breathes for the first time, with shaky exhales while prayers of thanks are murmured, but I know even they realize this is not the end.

It's the fucking beginning.

And I'm going to take the first step.

Every part of me urges me to stay and see him, hold his hand, and tell him I'll never leave, not even if he pushes me away.

But before I can do that, I need to slaughter his first demon.

I walk away from the scene without a word and dial the number I called after we got here.

He picks up after two rings. "Is he okay?"

I release a fractured exhale as I nod. "Yeah, Dad. He's okay for now."

"Thank fuck."

I exhale shakily into the phone, trying not to crack the fucking thing with how much I'm tightening my grip on it.

Soon after Bran went into surgery, I called my dad, breaking apart, hyperventilating. He told me to breathe and I asked how the fuck I was supposed to do that when the love of my fucking life was fighting death on a surgeon's table.

That's when I told him everything in a word vomit. Everything about Bran and me. Everything about how that fucking pedophile is taking him away from me and that I need her gone. Erased. Fucking eradicated.

Dad said simply, "Then we'll get it done."

He jumped on his private plane while I was talking to him and said he'd make arrangements with his godfather to find the vermin.

"Just landed, son. It'll take me approximately an hour to get to North West London."

"Give me an address, Dad. I need the fucking address."

"Listen to me, Nikolai. I know you're agitated. I can hear it in your voice, and it's okay to feel like that, but you will *not* make a reckless fucking mistake that will get you arrested. I told you if we're doing this, we're doing it my way."

I run a frustrated hand over my face. "I can't wait anymore. I need her fucking blood."

"Nikolai. Think of Brandon, okay? Think of how he'll feel if he wakes up and finds out you're being arrested for murder."

"Fuck!" I drive my fist against a wall and ignore the pain that explodes in my knuckles.

"The UK is different from the States," he continues in a collected tone. "It's smaller and more contained, so there's no room for mistakes. Tell me you understand that."

"Just get here, Dad. Please, hurry."

"I'll be there in fifty-three minutes. I'll forward you the coordinates. Let's meet there."

After he hangs up, I check the map he sends me as I stride through the hospital door.

A hand lands on my shoulder and I whip around to find Landon staring at me with harsh eyes. "Whatever you're doing, I want in."

Grace lives in this glamorous residential area in St. John's Wood that's full of fucking cameras and private security measures. That's why Dad insisted we wait until his contacts had everything under control.

When we get the okay, Dad, Landon, and I don't even have to sneak around. We walk into her building and take the elevator to her apartment.

We enter the code and stride right in.

My throat floods with disgust when we get inside her living room, where that video was taken. The sofa and the decor have changed, but it's still the same revolting place where she stole a piece of my lotus flower.

It's time she gives it back.

Landon must feel the same, because he snarls at it, his fists clenching.

A commotion reaches us from the bedroom, things being knocked over, curses sounding in the air.

Dad stands in the doorway and nods at us. "Go do your thing. I'll be here."

I nod sharply, thankful beyond words for having him as my father. Not many encourage their children's murderous ideas or their need for vengeance.

My father, Kyle Hunter, the most elite sniper you'll ever encounter, feeds my tendencies in the healthiest ways possible.

Landon and I move silently to where the sounds are coming from. Grace doesn't seem to notice us or the deep fucking hole she's dug for herself.

She's packing a suitcase, shoving clothes in with their hangers, and curses when they don't fit. A red satin robe covers her body and her makeup-free face reveals the fucking monster lurking beneath.

Landon is the one who strolls in, both hands in his pockets as he whistles. "Going somewhere, Grace?"

She jerks, knocking the giant suitcase off the bed.

Her beady brown eyes widen as she watches us, her gaze ping-ponging between us. "What…how did you get in…?"

"That's not important." Landon grabs her by a fistful of her hair and she shrieks. Good thing she's rich and can afford a soundproof apartment. "What is important, however, is what you did to my brother. *My*. Fucking. Brother!"

"I…I don't know what you're talking about. Lan, let me go. You're hurting me."

"Good. It'll hurt a lot worse in a minute, you worthless fucking bitch!"

"Lan…please…" Her voice cracks, tears pooling in her eyes.

"Too early to beg. We still haven't done anything."

"I'm sorry, I'm so sorry."

"Sorry doesn't bring back the years you took from him." I speak for the first time. "Sorry doesn't give him back the blood he fucking lost tonight!"

"I really thought he liked me as well. He kissed me." Her lips tremble. "He *always* kissed me."

"He asked you to stop. Countless times," I snarl in her face. "You shut him up and took what you wanted."

"I'm going to need you to say it out loud now, Grace." Lan tears at the hairs on her scalp. "I'm your god and I want you to confess what you fucking did."

"Lan, please."

"Fucking *say* it," I roar and pull out a gun from my waistband, then jam it against her forehead.

"I did it! I assaulted him when he was fifteen. I'm sorry, I'm so sorry, I really didn't think he hated it. Please don't kill me. I'm so sorry!"

She's full-out sobbing now, shaking, and being a fucking mess of snot and tears. If Landon wasn't holding her, she'd fall in a heap on the floor.

"Channel that energy and write it down." He shoves her onto her vanity chair and I grab the notepad and pen from her bedside table and throw them in front of her.

"W-what do you mean?" She stares at us with a lost expression.

"Write down everything you did to him," I say. "In detail. Confess your fucking sins."

"Including the grooming." Landon grabs her hand, shoves the pen between her fingers, and slams them on the paper.

She tries to shake her head, but my gun at the back of it stops her.

"Make it quick. We don't have all night."

Grace cries the entire time she writes, her hand trembling and blotches of tears smudging the words.

After she's done signing it per my order, she releases a choppy breath as if she's run a marathon. Landon reads her letter and then puts it in front of her again. "Ask him for forgiveness. Ask Mum for forgiveness for breaking her trust. Write about how you know nothing you can say can forgive what you've done, but you've been tortured for years and have never forgiven yourself for it."

She jots down the words, sniffling. After she's finished, Landon reads it again and nods in approval. Then he grabs her by the hair and drags her to her bathroom as she screams.

I follow them to find him shoving her into her gigantic bathtub and turning on the faucet full blast.

She thrashes, sending water everywhere. "What are you doing? Let me go this instant! I already did what you asked!"

"You thought that was a punishment?" I grab her left wrist while Landon takes the right one and we pull her arms apart as if she's about to be crucified.

Her feet slide in the tub as she tries to get away, but there's no escaping us.

I bring out my knife first and slash her wrist so deep, blood explodes onto my face. "That's for every drop of blood he shed over the years, for every time he looked in the mirror and hated his reflection because of you."

Landon cuts her other wrist. "This is for putting your hands on him and driving him to the fucking edge. You better wait for me in hell, bitch. I'll fucking murder you all over again."

Blood splashes on his face and fills the bathtub, turning the water red. Grace tries to thrash, her survival instinct kicking in at full force, and she screams.

She screams so loud, Dad shows up at the doorway, but he doesn't make a move. No, he just watches his son and his future son-in-law take the life of a woman and smiles.

I smile, too, viciously, as I slam my palm against her mouth, just like she did when Bran begged her to stop.

And then I peer down on her as her muffled screams turn into moans.

I peer down on her until she finally goes silent and her lifeless eyes stare at nothing.

I don't believe in justice. I believe in fucking vengeance. And this woman signed her death warrant the moment she touched my Bran.

My dad and his people will make this look like a suicide, and the note she wrote is her reason. I could've tortured her to death or made her disappear, but no, this isn't about her. It's about Bran.

I hope he feels closure if he sees that she regretted her actions and was tortured by them for years to the point that she took her own pathetic life.

One demon down. A dozen more to go.

THIRTY-EIGHT

Brandon

THE FIRST FEELING THAT SURGES THROUGH ME WHEN I BLINK my eyes open is crushing relief.

Not the burning in my neck, not the sandy feeling at the back of my throat.

As I stare at the ceiling and the four holes from which light shines down on me and hear the machines beeping, my eyes burn from the sense of relief that floods me.

When I lay in my blood and watched Nikolai cry out my name and beg me not to leave him, I regretted everything. I wanted to stay, to think that I could have a future, after all.

But it was too late.

The ink submerged me and I couldn't take being seen like that by him. I wouldn't have been able to live it down.

So I did the one thing that could end it all.

But it *didn't* end.

The second feeling comes rushing in with Mum's voice. "Bran…?"

Guilt. That's what's etched on her usually radiant face, her eyes bloodshot, her lips puffy.

The guilt she projects in waves slams against my own until I can't breathe.

"Son?" Dad is on my other side. "You came back, oh, thank fuck."

He reaches above my head to push something.

Failure. That's what Dad looks like. He feels a sense of failure. Like I did for almost a decade.

"Bran?" The broken sound belongs to Glyn. She's crying, rivulets of tears streaming down her rosy cheeks.

Her feelings of grief mix with the myriad of emotions rippling through me until I choke.

What have I done?

"Honey, can you hear us?" Mum asks.

"Yeah…" My voice is groggy and choked as I try to sit up.

The three of them help me carefully, as if I'll break if they touch me the wrong way. And I hate that I've put them through this. I hate that I'm the reason people important to me are struggling.

I single-handedly crushed them because I couldn't be strong enough.

The doctors come by to check on me and ask me a few questions. The entire time, Mum holds my right hand and Glyn my left one. Dad watches from the side, looking ten years older than his actual age.

What the fuck have I done?

As soon as the doctors leave the room, I look behind them, searching for the presence I need with me the most now.

But I don't spot a large tattooed man.

You expect him to have stayed after you showed him how much of a fuckup you are?

Mum squeezes my hand. "I'm so sorry, honey. So, so sorry."

I stare between her and Dad. "What… What are you sorry about? I'm the one who should be sorry."

"Bran, no." My father shakes his head, pain erupting in his exhausted features. "There's nothing you should be sorry about. Absolutely *nothing*, you hear me? We're the ones who need to apologize for letting you down."

"No, Dad…"

"We saw the clip." The words tumble from his lips like an ancient destructive curse. And I feel myself teetering on the verge of another breakdown.

Only, now, surprisingly, there's no black ink.

Mum sobs and that makes Glyn cry harder.

Dad strokes her shoulder. "Astrid, get it together, please."

"I'm sorry." She drags in a heavy breath and faces me on a long exhale. "I'll never forgive myself for bringing her into our lives. For not seeing the signs and even pushing you to make her your agent, for not being there for you—"

"No, Mum, no," I cut her off. "You were always there for me. *Always.* You respected my decisions and choices and never pushed me to do anything I didn't want to do. I'm the one who hid myself. I'm the one who decided not to say anything. I never...*never* blamed you, so please, don't do that. Please."

"I can't." Fresh tears flow out of her. "I just can't help thinking that if it wasn't for me—"

"Don't." I shake my head. "Don't say that, please. That's what I used to tell myself day in and day out. I used to think that if it wasn't for me, this family would be perfect. I don't want to hear you having those thoughts as well."

"Brandon, son." Dad sits beside Mum and they both grip my hand tight. "This family can't exist without you, you understand?"

"I don't want it without you," Mum says on a sob.

"Yeah, Bran." Glyn strokes my cheek, eyes glittering with unshed tears. "I can only be here because of your care and understanding. You've helped me countless times. I wouldn't have gotten here without you. So please, *please*, let us help *you* this time."

"Let us be your family," Dad says, and I can't control the tear that slides down my cheek.

All this time, I thought I was the decay of a perfect family. My ludicrous jealousy and inferiority complex toward Lan ate me alive and I let it consume me, which led me to Grace. Things took a nosedive into disaster after that.

The worse my mental state got, the harder I fought to remain afloat. The more sinister my demons became, the more insistent I was about my mantra of avoiding and pretending.

At some point, my mind turned on me and I became my own worst enemy. Through it all, I grasped at straws, fighting and struggling to keep belonging to this family I was lucky to be born into.

I thought if they saw me as a weakling, as the man who said yes then denied it and claimed to be wronged, they'd be disappointed. I thought if they saw me as someone who was not perfect by any stretch of the imagination, they'd turn their backs on me.

But as I look at their faces, at the grief mixed with relief, I know without a shadow of a doubt that was never the case.

I let dark thoughts infest my head and drag me into the black hole of self-hatred. And in doing that, I failed to see just how much I mean to these people. How the thought of losing me has left them shell-shocked and unrecognizable.

I never thought my larger-than-life father would look to be on the verge of collapsing because of me. And I want to hug him. I want to tell him how grateful I am to have him.

But first…

"What…" My words get stuck in my throat and I gulp before I look at Mum. "What about your exhibition? I ruined it, didn't I?"

"Fuck that. I don't need it or my whole career as long as I have you, Bran. I need you to know that."

I hug her then, burying my face in her neck, trembling in her hold. "Thank you, Mum."

"No, thank *you* for coming back to me, hon. Thank you…thank you…"

Dad pats my back and Glyn leans on my shoulder as she cries softly, her body shaking.

And I know, I just know I'll be fine as long as I have them.

It'll hurt.

But it won't be as painful as hiding myself from them.

It's time I properly say the words I should've shouted eight years ago.

I pull away from Mum's embrace and suck in a sharp breath. "Mum, Dad. I have something to tell you."

"Anything, son."

"I think I need help. Please help me get better."

I spent what seems like hours spilling my guts to my parents and Glyn. Everything that I couldn't say before, everything that I buried in my chest and swallowed down with air.

There was a lot of crying and hugs, but I didn't feel sad afterward, no. More like hopeful and light. As if I finally breached the surface of the inky lake I've been drowning in for eight years.

Dad said he's pressing charges of sexual assault of a minor against Grace, and Mum said she'll have her banned from the arts council that she currently presides over. She'll have her stripped of her peer title in the House of Lords and drag her through the mud.

The thought of courts and a legal process gives me a headache, but I want justice.

I want to finally give fifteen-year-old me what he always wanted—justice—and hope that one day, he'll forgive me.

He'll one day look at me in the mirror and smile. Even if only once.

I know it'll take time and a fuck ton of therapy, but I can wait. He waited for me to catch up for eight years, the least I can do is be patient as he leaves the cave I shoved him into for so long.

Earlier, I spoke to the therapist the NHS sent me and it was hard, but I blurted the words out.

I want to get better not only for myself, but also for the man I love.

The man who's nowhere to be found. Dad told me Nikolai is the reason I'm alive. He's the one who kept the pressure on my neck as if his life depended on it and carried me to the car before they drove me here.

He stayed for the entire seven hours of the operation, but apparently, he left as soon as they were told I was stable.

Thinking about the possibility that he wants nothing to do with me makes me jittery.

It's why I did what I did in the first place. The thought of him seeing me differently and hating me gave me that shove over the edge.

I stare at Glyn and she smiles as she cuts me some avocado. Dad is talking to the police. Mum is with the doctors.

But my sister refuses to leave my side.

"I don't suppose you know where my phone is?" I ask.

"Nope. But you can use mine." She unlocks it and passes it over.

"Thanks."

I type Nikolai's name and call him. The longer the phone rings in my ear, the louder my heart thumps.

My chest falls when it goes to voicemail. He doesn't check those—ever. I don't know why he even has the service.

"You mean I could remove it?" is literally what he replied when I asked him that once.

"I'm sure he'll come around." Glyn offers me an encouraging look. "I'll kick his arse if he doesn't…or maybe like send Kill because he's really scary."

I smile and give her back her phone.

The door opens and I look up, hope blossoming in my chest with a force that hurts.

But that's the thing about hope, it exists to be crushed.

It's not Nikolai who walks in.

My disappointment is short-lived, however, when my eyes clash with my identical ones. I gulp, my heart swirling in a puddle of my own humiliating feelings that I confessed to my parents not too long ago.

I wanted to ask about Lan, but I didn't dare to. A part of me is relieved that he's here. The part that held on to the fact that he does care, even if everyone said he didn't.

His face looks the most distraught I've ever seen. Lan doesn't do emotions. At all. I thought the only exception was Mia, but as I stare at his worn-out gaze and the lines of relief around his eyes, I think maybe I was wrong.

"You okay?" he asks as he stops beside me. His voice isn't right.

It's too careful. Too restrained. Definitely does not fit the Lan I knew my entire life.

I nod.

"Glyn, get out," he says.

"No." Her gaze is alarmed as she looks at me.

"It's okay," I say with a smile. "Go."

She gives me an unsure glance before she hugs me and narrows her eyes on our brother. "You better not say anything funny, Lan."

He doesn't reply or even look at her. His intense attention remains on me until the door closes behind her, his hand curling and uncurling into a fist.

"You're going to punch me for daring to hurt your identical twin?" I try to joke to break the tension.

That only manages to make a vein throb in his neck, nearly popping from the skin. "I'd kill for you, I'd shoot myself if that makes you breathe better without me shadowing you, but I'd never...*ever* hurt you, Bran."

My lips part and I stare at his tight expression and know that he means every word.

"I was kidding," I breathe out.

"Don't joke about shit like that. Your life is *not* a fucking joke. Fuck!" His chest rises and falls in heavy succession and I'm seriously scared he'll pop a vein or have a stroke.

I shift in the bed, the injury in my neck burning and itching for some reason. "Lan—"

"I'm sorry."

The words nearly split me open. It's different to hear that from Mum and Dad or even Glyn, but this is Lan. He never, *ever* apologizes. Not even when he nearly drove Mia away for good.

I thought I'd come down from the emotional high, but they rush back to the surface until my own chest is heaving.

Our harsh breaths echo in the damn hospital room that witnessed me at my lowest.

"What are you sorry for?"

"For not pursuing you that night. For thinking it was because of the rumors and letting it go at that. I'm sorry for allowing you to hate me without doing anything about it."

"I never *hated* you, Lan. I hated myself, yes, but never you." I release a mock laugh. "You were the half I looked at whenever I needed hope. Seeing you being your unapologetic, confident anarchist self made me believe I'd eventually be okay. You gave me strength, even unknowingly, so you shouldn't apologize. This isn't on you, it's on *me*. You couldn't have known when I didn't let you in. And I didn't let anyone in."

"What can I do?" he asks with a wretched expression. "What can I do to stop you from doing that again? I don't understand emotions, but you do, Bran. You do spectacularly well, and I'm asking, no, I'm *begging* you to tell me what I can do to make it better. Should I fuck off out of your life? Cut contact? Not visit Mum and Dad while you're there? Will my disappearance stop you from having that nonsensical inferiority complex?"

"That's about the worst thing you can do, Lan. I need you by my side. I always have. Pretending I didn't is what shoved me into that dark hole in the first place." I smile. "I never felt happier than when you asked me to teach you empathy. I was proud that you needed me for once."

"I always needed you, idiot. I used that as an excuse to spend time with you because you'd made it your mission to avoid me for the past eight years. I fucking *hated* that. You were supposed to be the one who understood me best, but you turned your back on me."

"I'm sorry."

"Don't apologize. Just...*stop* doing that. Give the middle finger instead. Works so much fucking better."

"If I do that, will you stop being so agitated? You're starting to creep me out."

He expels a long breath and nods once.

"Come here." I open my arms and I suspect he'll push me away since he's allergic to showing affection.

However, my brother slides right between my arms and hugs me for the first time since that night eight years ago.

He breathes shakily against my shoulder, his hands pressing me so tightly that it actually hurts. But I must be hurting him, too.

"I love you, little bro," he whispers. "I *need* you to know that. I need you to know you're the first person I loved unconditionally and always will. I might annoy you, might act like a dick to get your attention, but that's only because the thought of losing you scares the living fuck out of me."

"Love you, too, Lan." I exhale against his neck, my chest nearly bursting with emotions.

We remain like that for what seems like forever before he reluctantly pulls back. "You tell anyone what I said just now and I'll deny it till the day I die."

I laugh. "I got you, bro."

"Damn straight." His charming smile spills through, and my brother finally returns to sporting his eternal cockiness.

Honestly, I wouldn't have him any other way.

"Hey, Lan?"

"I don't like that tone. What?"

"Since we're sharing our feelings—"

"Lord, no. Please no. What is it now?"

"I think you know already since, well, you went to the States and, uh, Nikolai was there… Point is, I love him and I want to be with him. If he'll let me." I blurt out the last part so fast, I'm not sure if he hears it, and if he does, whether or not he understands a word I've said.

"Why the fuck wouldn't he let you?" He lifts his nose up with an air of arrogance. "The peasant should be honored and worship at your feet for you even looking in his direction."

"You…you're okay with it?"

"I don't like the idea of anyone taking you away, let alone that distasteful brute, but I guess I can try to tolerate him for your and Mia's sake."

"Thanks." My heart beats faster. "Despite his violent exterior, he's really a teddy bear deep down, you know. A golden retriever through and through. He's extremely affectionate and respectful and makes sure I'm comfortable and happy."

"What type of voodoo did he use on my control-freak brother? More importantly, why did it have to be *him*? You're allergic to violence and I'm pretty sure he's illiterate."

"Lan! I'll have you know he has a 4.15 GPA. Don't make fun of his intelligence again or I'll be really cross with you."

"Jesus Christ. You're *defending* him?"

"Get used to it. I won't allow you or anyone else to insult him."

"Wow. Okay. Bring down the protectiveness a notch. It's revolting."

"No. Deal with it." My good mood slowly withers as I clear my throat. "Can I use your phone to call him?"

"There's no need. He was with me and is currently waiting outside your room like a moping wanker." He stands up. "I'll fetch him for you."

Fire spreads through my chest, and for some reason, it's hard to swallow, but I nod anyway.

Even if that nagging feeling remains.

What if he doesn't want to see me? What if Lan forces him?

My brother stops at the door. "One more thing."

"Yeah?"

"Please tell me you top the motherfucker."

I let my lips curve into a smile as I shake my head. Lan's face falls and he looks like he's on the verge of a heart attack.

"Bloody fucking hell!" He throws the door open and then shouts, "Nikolai, you fucking wank, come here."

There's a bit of a commotion and I'm scared they're fighting. I stand up from the bed and grab the IV drip, but before I can move, a presence that's larger than life is shoved into my room.

Lan winks at me before he closes the door, trapping me with Nikolai.

My hand slowly falls to my side as I study him. He's in different jeans and T-shirt from the ones he wore last night, his hair is tied into a ponytail, and his face is...fuck.

Anguish and displeasure war into a tight knot. His lips are pursed, and his eyes are dark and enraged.

But at least they're not empty. I can deal with rage.

One problem.

He's not looking at me.

Not once has he looked at me since he walked in. His gaze is fixed on the floor and both hands are shoved in his pockets.

"Nikolai…?"

A harsh breath rolls out of his expanded chest, his jaw clenching and his biceps tightening, causing the tattoos to ripple.

"Are you going to look at me anytime soon or do you prefer to stay outside—"

He lifts his head and the words are cut off in my throat. The fear and rage that lingers in his eyes leave me speechless, completely taken in by him.

"How *could* you?" He strides toward me, his voice vibrating with fear instead of anger. "How could you try to leave me? Don't you know I can't live without you anymore?"

The moment he's within reach, I take his hand in mine. The feel of his skin is like a shot of dopamine right through my veins.

"I'm sorry. I thought… I thought you'd find me weak and revolting. The idea of you seeing me differently haunts me, Nikolai. I don't want to lose you."

"But you're okay with me losing *you*? I'm a shell without you, Bran." He drags my hand to him and slams it against his chest. "This thing only beats for you and *because* of you. I used to live an aimless life where adrenaline was my god, but you came along and tamed my demons. You balance me. You complete me. You're fucking *in* me. So seeing you bleeding out on the floor was no different than watching myself die. No, it was worse. I've never felt so scared for my life, but you…you're my everything. How could you do that to me? To us?"

"I'm so sorry. The last thing I want is to hurt you."

"Don't apologize. Tell me you won't do it again. Promise me."

"I promise, Niko. Never again. I'll do everything in my capacity to get better. I'll go to therapy and pick myself apart to be strong enough to deserve you. Just don't leave me, please."

"Not even if you beg for it. I love you, lotus flower, and that means I'll be by your side during all of your battles with your demons. I'll kill them for you if you let me. I'll listen to them if you want me to. But I'll never leave you, so you're stuck with me."

I stroke his cheek over the stubble and try to stop my heart from bursting into flames. "You're the one who's stuck with me. There's no one on this earth who's able to understand and love me like you do. It's why I gravitated toward you without even noticing. Falling for you was effortless and final. I thought I was unworthy of you, I fought myself to be with you, but it was pointless. I never loved myself the way I love you, baby."

That beautiful grin breaks through the pain and I can feel my heart soaring. "Does that mean you're mine now?"

"I think I always have been."

"Thank you for coming back to me, baby."

"Thank you for never giving up on me, Niko."

And then I let him feel how grateful I am by pressing my lips to his.

The first kiss of our new life together.

EPILOGUE 1

Brandon

Six months later

"STAY STILL," I CHASTISE, PUSHING NIKOLAI'S HAND OFF my waist.

He groans and his palm lands back on my hip like a rubber band. "This is fucking torture."

I flick my brush over the ridge of his pectoral muscle, careful not to get red paint on the lotus flower.

My thin strokes slowly transform into the image of his necklace, painting the bullet on his skin, then drawing the chain so it's wrapped around it in the shape of a lotus flower.

And just to mess with him, I make shallow strokes over his nipple. The sexy rumble beneath my fingers has me biting my lower lip to suppress my own noises of pleasure.

He's effortlessly the most attractive specimen to ever walk the earth, beautiful in his confidence, loud in his assertiveness, and absolutely hotheaded in his loyalty.

Every day, I wake up to his stunning face and thank all gods and religions for putting him in my path. I never believed in fate until this mountain of a man flipped my world upside down and made me love every second of it.

Our journey hasn't been easy. Far from it. But he's stood with me every step of the way.

He was there when Dad broke the news that Grace committed suicide in her bath and left a note in which she confessed what she did and asked Mum and me for forgiveness.

My mother replied to that by having her disgraced in the art circuit and permanently removed from the art council's Hall of Fame. She was also stripped of her peer title.

A part of me was happy for that outcome. At least that meant justice took place without having to drag myself into court.

Though I never really wanted her to die, I'm not mourning her, either. I mourned myself. Which is why the next difficult part was finally getting help.

Therapy is good, but it's hard. The most important part is that it's working, but I'm not deluded enough to think I could've done this on my own.

I'm lucky to have the most loving and understanding parents, friends who lift me up, an adorably supportive sister, and even Lan. My twin brother is finally my twin again after eight years of playing hide-and-seek with each other.

He'll never be mushy or emotional, but he'll always be my brother. A *part* of him, as he often reminds me. We finally have each other as 'Other Half' on our contacts.

However, the process wouldn't have been possible without the man standing in front of me. The way he held me through it all while dealing with his own issues made the entire thing worth it.

Nikolai lets me see him on his bad days. The days where he can't stay still, where he paces and chain-smokes and is unable to sleep, but that's not much different from when he's on a violent spree. And the best part, he really, *really* wears me out during those days. Physically, not emotionally. He can't keep his hands off me and pulls me into dark corners so we can do filthy things to each other.

Not that I'm complaining. I love it when he gets rough.

He says I calm his demons down, and that's the best compliment he can give me, especially since he's the main reason I'm able to battle my own demons.

Other times, when he thinks his mind gets too out of control, he takes the pills and they're…well, I don't like them. They kill the light in his eyes and turn him into a lethargic zombie who moves like a robot, talks with no intonation, and refuses to leave the house. He doesn't smile, not even at me, and looks fucking depressed.

I immediately took his dad's side on that and told him to ditch them. But Nikolai is seriously creeped out about the prospect of hurting me—which has never happened.

"Once is enough, baby," he told me with that wretched expression. "I'd never be able live with myself if I even accidentally hurt you, touched you too hard, or pushed you too much. I'd rather slash my own soul in half than do that to you."

The fear in his gaze back then broke my heart. Possibly because that was coming from Nikolai, who, according to his dad, refused the very notion of the pills early on.

But he embraced them for me.

We spoke to his doctor, and he said there's a possibility of a new medicine that's able to put the manic episodes under control without murdering his soul in the process. We're in the testing stage and he's only used them once, but I like them much better.

At least they enable him to look at me without looking through me. He's just less playful, which is something I can live with once in a while. And really, in the last six months, he's had episodes exactly four times. One was a fuck fest, the second and third were zombie-like due to the ludicrous pills, but the fourth was a mixture of both, and I'm good with that. He was also happy about it and came down from his high in the span of two days.

In the beginning, when he felt himself spiraling, he'd send me a text.

My mind is turning up in volume. I'm getting bad. Maybe you should visit your parents for a week or so. Just stay away from me, baby.

No way in hell was I doing that, but he still tried to convince me to stay away the second time. Again, didn't happen. If anything, I quit everything just to be by his side like he's always glued to mine. And I told him that. I told him a relationship is being there for each other through the bad and the good. I won't take while he gives—that's not how this works.

The third and fourth time, he learned his lesson and his texts changed in tone.

I'm getting bad. I need you, baby.

They were the most endearing texts he's ever sent and I never felt happier than when he started to depend on me and be openly vulnerable with me. It's only fair after he saw me at my lowest and picked me up. Literally and figuratively.

He sneakily slides his hand on my waist beneath my shirt. A map of goosebumps erupts where his fingers stroke the skin at a rhythmic pace.

It doesn't matter how long we've been together or how often he touches me—which is a *lot*—whenever I'm with him, my body, heart, and soul hum with uncontainable energy.

The need to touch him is constant, vibrant, and gets more intense with time.

But right now is about the worst circumstance for that.

"Nikolai," I warn.

"Yes, baby?"

"Stop acting like an impatient toddler and remove your hand."

"But it's not fair that you're touching me and I'm not touching you."

"Behave, or you won't get your prize."

"Fuck no. Kolya and I are thirsty for the prize." He rolls his hips and tugs me against him with a pull on my drawstrings.

My cock bursts to life, standing to attention when it grazes against his. I have to lift the brush in the air so I don't ruin what I've been working on for the past hour.

I slide my palette on his desk and sneak my fingers through his hair. It's longer now, brushing against his shoulders in a glorious fashion. I'm positively and irrevocably obsessed with it, so I might have forbidden him from cutting it.

He enjoys the attention a bit too much and leans into my palm as he rubs our dicks in a sensual rhythm. Despite my sweatpants and his shorts, I grow hard in an instant.

I tug on his hair. "Who's the one who asked me to sketch him new tattoos to fill in the gaps?"

"You can do that after you give me my prize."

"I'll lose my flow."

"You can sketch me up while I'm inside you, baby. I'm starving to feel your ass clenching around my cock as you beg me to fuck you harder."

"Jesus. That mouth of yours requires urgent intervention."

"You know you're aching for it. Bran Jr. demands a meeting with Kolya."

I laugh. "You seriously need to stop giving names to dicks."

"Not all dicks. Just yours and mine." He strokes his fingers along my V-line, eliciting a sharp intake of air from deep in my throat. "I can give you a prize first and choke on your cock. You love it when you fuck my mouth while pulling on my hair. You have this look of ownership all over your face when you stare down at me with those fuck-me eyes and fill my throat with your cum."

"Jesus fucking Christ."

"I'll take that as a yes." His breath fans my lips, a mixture of honey and whiskey from the drink he had earlier with his dad.

Speaking of which…

I jerk him back with immeasurable control. "Cut it out. We're heading down for dinner with your parents."

"They can wait a bit more."

"Not a chance. I don't want to make a bad impression."

"Uh, baby. Are you kidding? They're fucking in love with you. More than that tool Lan for sure."

"Still don't want to risk it."

His lips pull in an evil smirk. "You really love being labeled as the one who tamed the wild Niko by my mom and sisters, don't you?"

"What can I say? I welcome the expression."

"You're so full of shit."

"Kyle, Jeremy, Gareth, your aunt Reina, and even Kill should be added to the list of people who've used that expression."

"You look proud of that."

"It's because I am." I stroke his hair and speak an inch away from his lips. "I love having a special place in your life. It turns me on."

"I'm so going to fuck you," he growls and is about to close the barely existent space between us when a knock comes on his bedroom door.

"Niko?" His dad's voice filters through. "Are you decent or am I going to be exposed to your shenanigans?"

"Go, Dad. I'm more indecent than a hooker on Satan's lap!" he yells as I push him away with a scowl and go to open the door while adjusting my erection.

With a few breaths, I manage to feel somewhat normal. I smile at Kyle, who's in the process of shaking his head.

Ever since I graduated from uni, I've been working on my paintings while continuing to live at the penthouse with Nikolai. We were practically living together anyway. Soon after, he brought me to meet his parents for the first time, and I came to a very stunning realization.

Nikolai has the most beautiful relationship with his mum and dad. Rai calls him her little miracle. Kyle is more than just his father. He's his close friend and his confidant, and I often overhear Nikolai talking to him on the phone whenever he's in or out of his off phase.

Appearance-wise, Kyle is leaner but has a sharper look in his blue eyes. He's well-built and often wears designer suits that give him a sophisticated edge.

What I love about him, aside from being raised in the UK and, therefore, having a very British sense of humor, is how much he's one hundred percent behind all his children. In that department, he reminds me a bit of my dad, who's definitely Team Nikolai now.

He never really hated him, but after he saved me during that black day, Dad gained an immense sense of respect for my man.

At this point, only Killian is falling behind on the popularity vote in the King household.

"Oh." Kyle looks at us and releases a breath. "I thought I was intruding."

"You were." Nikolai appears beside me, pouting like a child. "Cockblocker of the Year Award goes to the almighty Kyle Hunter."

"Nikolai." I elbow him.

Kyle, however, doesn't seem fazed and even raises an eyebrow. "Seems adequate. Finally some revenge for all the cock-blocking you indulged in during your toddler years."

"I was literally a toddler. Get over it."

"And your junior years and preteen years," he counts on one hand. "Teenage years and uni years...should I keep counting?"

"I can't believe this!" Nikolai throws his hands in the air. "Hello, Petty Police? I'm reporting my dad."

"Lock me the fuck up."

"I might withdraw the charges if you just go away. Fucking now, please."

I smile at their bickering. They have the most comical relationship I've ever witnessed, and they're just great fun to be around.

"Your mom and sisters are waiting for you for dinner. You'll have to delay your plans for later." He looks at me with a soft smile. "I apologize for his unruly behavior."

"Dad!"

"What? You've had him locked in here for hours."

"More like he's had me locked up and I didn't even get my prize," he mutters like a kicked puppy.

"I'm really okay," I tell Kyle.

"Hey, Dad." He nudges him. "Do it."

"Do what?"

"That thing we talked about."

I stare between them as Kyle actually rolls his eyes. "Do I have to?"

"Come on, I've been asking you for months!"

"Fine." His eyes meet mine as he exhales. "This is ridiculous."

My ears prickle and I feel the heat rising to them. "What's going on?"

"Bran, I need to ask you a very serious question."

I straighten, all humor disappearing. "Anything."

"What do you like about my twat of a son?"

"The twat part didn't need to be there!" Nikolai pushes his dad teasingly.

"I also didn't need to ask that very silly question when you're already together."

"His dad did it. I wanted you to do it as well."

My chuckle breaks their banter and I clear my throat. "I like that he oozes confidence, too much so sometimes. I like that he's fiercely loyal, intensely protective, and loves with every fiber of his being. I like that he never fakes his actions or his emotions—what you see is literally what you get. But most of all, I like, no, I *love* that he loves me."

A shit-eating grin covers Nikolai's face and I smile back, not even embarrassed by saying all that out loud.

"That was actually very touching," Kyle says, then nudges his son with a foot. "Happy now?"

"Very. Now, go away, Dad. Seriously. Or I'll be sleeping on your goddamn bedroom floor later."

"Five minutes, Niko," he says over his shoulder. "And put a shirt on!"

"No way in hell!" he shouts back and leans over for a kiss, but I pull away and his lips land on my throat, trailing kisses and nibbling on my Adam's apple.

"Baby, please? You can't say shit like that and expect me not to fuck you."

"Not happening. Everyone downstairs will know we're having sex."

He pulls back with a small pout, muttering, "Fine," before he trudges to the bathroom, probably to wash his hands.

I know I'm supposed to go downstairs first, but I'm notoriously weak to his adorable pouts.

So I follow after him and stop when I'm behind him as he dries his hands. I meet my reflection in the mirror and swallow past the sensation crawling up my throat.

It's not nausea. It's awareness.

I can finally look at myself in the mirror without feeling the need to smash it to pieces. I still haven't been able to smile at myself like the therapist has been urging me to. It just feels weird.

Tattooed arms wrap around my waist from behind before Nikolai's chin rests on my shoulder. I didn't even notice when he changed position and slipped behind me.

"You're the most beautiful thing on earth," he whispers against my neck, peppering kisses there as he meets my gaze in the mirror. "I'm lucky you allowed me in your life." *Kiss.* "I'm lucky you love me." *Kiss.* "I'm lucky you're letting me fight your demons with you."

My heart crawls its way to my throat and I have to swallow down the burst of emotions to remain standing. What the hell did I do to deserve this man?

"I'm the one who's lucky to have you, baby." I unlock his arms from around me, turn, and face him. "I was supposed to give you this present later tonight, but you're making it impossible to hold it in."

I tug my shirt free and his grin returns. "You're going to give me my prize anyway…?"

His words trail off and his lips part when he sees the actual reason why I removed my T-shirt.

"What do you think?" I ask carefully.

His fingers ghost over the elegant sans serif font I had tattooed on my heart. Like where he got the tattoo for me.

This is the first and last tattoo I'll ever get, since I'm absolutely not a fan of pricking my skin anymore, but I had to ink him on the heart that beats because he exists.

"You had *Niko's lotus flower* tattooed on your chest?"

"Not on my chest." I take his hand in mine and press it on the skin. "My heart."

"Fuck me."

"In a good or bad way?"

"I fucking love you, baby." He kisses my lips long and hard. "I can't believe you have a tattoo."

"For you."

"For *me*," he repeats with raging possessiveness.

"Hey, Niko?"

"Hmm?"

"Remember when we met that little girl in the park and you asked me what I whispered back to her?"

"You said it was a secret," he grumbles.

"I told her I don't need help because I'm in love with you."

His lips pull in the most contagious smile. I love being the reason behind his happiness. I love that I'm the only one in the world who has this effect on him.

"Remember when you told me to tell you something in Russian?"

"You said I was cute."

"No. I said 'I can't live without you,' and we take that quite literally in Russia."

"Aw, Nikolai."

"Point is, I love the loving fuck out of you, baby."

"I love the loving fuck out of you, too."

He wraps his arms around me and lifts me up with sheer force until my feet leave the floor.

I'm laughing and trying to push him away as he spins me around and kisses my chest, my collarbone, my throat. Everywhere.

I continue laughing even as I look in the mirror.

Because for the first time, I don't see a lonely boy there. I don't even see the healing twenty-four-year-old version of me.

For the first time, I don't see the past or the present.

I see my future with the most infuriating enigma.

The most chaotic person on earth.

And the love of my fucking life.

EPILOGUE 2

Nikolai

Two years later

"BABYYYY!"

Everyone, and I mean every single person in the hall, looks back at me.

Some laugh, others stab me with their elite, snobbish expressions, and many shake their heads, including Levi and that fucker Landon.

He's most definitely in the glaring category. I swear to fuck, if it weren't for Bran and Mia getting between us, we would've ripped each other's throats out a long time ago.

Anyway, the people here don't matter. I couldn't give one single flying fuck about any judgmental, patronizing eyes, because the only person who matters faces me with a grin so wide, I nearly go into cardiac arrest.

Oh fuck.

Fuck me.

He's suited up in the most flattering, flawless tuxedo that showcases his lithe, fit body. His hair is styled in his gorgeous Prince

Charming look and his eyes are so bright, I'm positively drowning in their depths.

Sometimes I look at him and think I'm floating in an alternate reality. Sometimes, he whispers he loves me before he falls asleep in my arms, and I spend the entire night watching his face just to make sure it's true.

He's real.

We are real.

In what world did someone like me end up with someone like him?

No fucking clue, but I'll take it. All day. Any day.

There's no way in fuck I'll ever let him go. Not after our lives have become so intertwined that I can't breathe properly unless he's beside me.

It's why the past week was fucking torture. I graduated this summer and had to go back to the States for my new role in the Bratva.

As much as I wanted to delay it, Jeremy has been waiting too long for me, and I can't just leave my bro behind.

But I was rethinking the whole fucking thing the first night I slept without my lotus flower hugging me. The second night, I nearly spiraled into that black hole lurking in my mind and went back to smoking.

So yeah, I quit smoking a year and a half ago since I refuse the very notion of causing my Bran any form of health hazard namely the stupid second-hand smoke. Besides, he helped me all the way through it.

Just kidding. When it got a bit too much and I craved a smoke, he became his pragmatic stern self and announced a ban: either I touch him or a cigarette.

I quit within the week, thank you very fucking much.

My recent trip to the States felt like a redo of that time. No, it was much worse since I couldn't even see him. We spoke on the phone for hours, despite the time difference, and he didn't hang up until I actually drifted off to sleep.

I don't want to ever, and I mean *ever*, get used to the feeling of sleeping in an empty bed. I prefer the bed where he pulls my head against his chest and strokes my hair until I fall asleep. A bed where I can hug him from behind and kiss his nape as we drift off.

This past week's experience is just not happening anymore.

Bran couldn't come with me because of this award ceremony he was attending for winning some important art shit. Don't ask me what it is. It has a stupid complicated title.

All I know is that my man is a fucking genius who broke the internet with his viral videos and the art people's souls with his work.

It started as a joke when I once filmed him so concentrated on work while he was wearing just shorts and painting me. People went crazy about that, especially after they saw the final result. Since then, I've been taking sneaky videos of him all the time. And he's gotten so many fucking deals because of that.

And awards. Many of those, too. He's now as well-known in the art community as his psycho brother. Which should've been the case from the beginning, just saying.

I know Bran doesn't like attention, but there's no one in the whole fucking world who deserves it more than him. He's so dedicated, disciplined, and a ridiculous perfectionist.

He deserved that solo exhibition he had two months ago more than anyone. It was a smashing success and the best I've seen.

Not that I've seen that many—only the ones he and his mom participate in. Sometimes he drags me to Lan's exhibitions and I go just to talk shit about that psycho. Anyway, this one was special, and not only because it was his first solo. Most of his paintings were of me and my tattoos, but the center painting, the one that I begged Dad to spend over a million pounds from my trust fund on just so I could have it for myself forever, is my favorite.

I still have it as my lock screen.

It's the one painting he couldn't finish all those years ago.

The one where I'm standing and he's leaning against my shoulder. He finally managed to draw his own face, and this time, he's fucking smiling.

Never giving that painting up. Will probably have to put a request in my will to bury it with me so that when I meet Satan, I can tell him all about my lotus flower.

Speaking of whom, he abandons his company of hotshot art people who either love me for the way he depicts me or can't stand my rowdy, brutally honest, beautiful self.

As Bran walks toward me, I'm once again hit with that inability to believe he's with me. My heart is so full of him, it's about to burst. I missed him so fucking much, I have to stop myself from kissing him, because it definitely wouldn't stop there.

Something tells me the snobs wouldn't appreciate me shoving him against the wall and letting Kolya and Bran Jr. say hi to each other.

Chill, Kolya, dude. Your future parents-in-law are here.

"You made it," he breathes, his smile blinding the fuck out of me.

"Wouldn't miss it for the world."

"But there was a storm on the east coast. Please don't tell me you did something reckless to get here."

"Reckless is my middle name. But in this case, I couldn't have done anything even if I'd wanted to. We had to get the okay to fly. Took off as soon as I could." I point at the award in his hand. "I'm sorry I wasn't here for the actual ceremony."

"You're here now. That's all that matters."

"Congrats, baby!" Because I *have* to touch him, I wrap my hand around his nape and stroke the side of his neck. "I'm so proud of you and how far you've come. You did it!"

He pushes the award into my hand and forces me to grab it as he shakes his head. "*We* did it. I would've never been able to do this without you, baby."

"You were born for great things and would've been able to do this whether or not I was here."

"No, I wouldn't. You're the reason I even want those great things, remember?"

I nod and kiss the top of his head, lingering for a second to sniff his gorgeous hair. "I missed you so fucking much. Totally not flying without you by my side anymore."

He fixes my crooked bow tie, a small smile tugging on his lips.

He's always fixing me up, my lotus flower, whether physically or emotionally. He still likes to nag, too, but it's music to my ears at this point. The day he stops nagging is the day he stops caring.

"You better not leave me again," he whispers. "I couldn't sleep without you."

"What the fuck? You told me to stop being a baby every night we spoke on the phone."

"Well, I didn't want to stress you out. That doesn't mean it was any easier for me, you know."

"You're totally coming to the States with me. Or I'm staying here. Jeremy and Vaughn will kill me, but it's a price I'm willing to pay."

"I told you I'll come over. I can work from anywhere."

"Thank fuck."

He interlinks my fingers with his. "Want to get out of here?"

"Fuck yes."

I'm about to haul him away so I can kiss him, but he presses his chest to mine and devours my lips in a searing, passionate kiss.

In front of the whole world. *His* whole word.

If anyone had told me about this scene a couple of years back, I would've called them a borderline liar.

But my lotus flower can't seem to get enough of me as much as I can't get enough of him.

Before I can deepen the kiss, he pulls back, putting a halt to Kolya's diabolical plan.

So I drag him behind me, pushing through the bodies of people, desperate to get him alone.

Bran drives us to his parents' house, which we'll probably have to ourselves for a while before his parents and Glyn come back, bringing the other psychos, Landon and Kill, along.

During the entire ride, I'm kissing Bran's throat, nibbling on his Adam's apple, undoing his bow tie, and unbuttoning his shirt to leave hickeys on his collarbone.

The perfect image he loves so well shatters against my tongue and fingers as he moans my name and groans his pleasure.

My lotus flower is the most unbothered driver you'll ever find.

He never gets his feathers ruffled, never gets mad, never drives recklessly, but even he has to stop the car on the side of the road, and I haul him onto my lap so that Kolya can say hi.

The dry humping session comes to a halt, though, because he can't have us getting arrested for indecency. Despite his car having tinted windows.

The only reason I stop is because I don't want a quickie in the car. I need to feast on him properly after a week of being deprived of him.

Don't get me wrong, I loved the phone sex, the filthy texts, and the dick pics he sent occasionally—after I bombarded him with a thousand pics of Kolya weeping in agony—but the real thing is better by fucking miles.

As soon as we're inside the house, I slam my lips to his, both of us stumbling as he shoves me against the wall, his tongue demanding and warring with mine.

I reverse our positions so that he's against the wall, our bodies pressed together from the dick up.

"I missed you so much, you have no idea," he breathes against my lips. "You're never getting out of my sight again."

"Mmm. Never again, baby." I speak against his throat, trailing my tongue and lips against his throbbing pulse and the faint scar from when I nearly lost him forever.

He's come so far since then. Has gotten so much better at dealing with his emotions. Has learned to forgive himself and even smile at his image in the mirror.

That didn't stop the control-freak tendencies, though. That's a personality trait—one I love just like he secretly loves my reckless behavior sometimes.

He doesn't try to change me and embraces me the way I am. He doesn't care who I have to maim as long as I don't get hurt in the process. That's when he loses it.

I kid you not. Once, Kill threw a lighter at my head since he loves hitting me with random shit. Bran threw it back at *his* head and told him point-blank not to hit me anymore or he wouldn't stand for it.

Did I fall in love with him a bit deeper after that? Possibly.

Bran shudders and his hands wrap around me, one gripping my waist and the other pulling my hair free as he throws his head against the wall with a throaty groan.

I inhale him into my lungs and keep him there—citrus and fucking mine.

"Bed. Now." I growl against his fully marked neck, and the best part? He doesn't hide my hickeys anymore. If anything, he loves leaving some of his own, too.

"Can't have you running around and attracting unwanted attention. The world needs to know who you belong to," is what he tells me every time.

"I have to show you something first." He pants and leads me down the hall.

"Can't it wait?" I wrap my arms around him from behind, matching his steps as I kiss his neck.

It's awkward and definitely not fun to walk in this position, but Bran doesn't complain and even gives me access to his throat, moaning when I nibble on his Adam's apple.

"Baby…stop…" His voice trembles as he pushes the door open.

"You can't call me baby and ask me to stop. I'm so going to devour the fuck out of you."

"Nikolai…"

"Mmm?"

"Focus, please."

"Give me a sec…"

"Nikolai!"

"What?" I lift my head, slightly annoyed that he's stopping me when we're both burning for this.

As if that's not blasphemous enough, he pulls away and faces me. That's when I realize we're inside his stupid home studio.

Not going to lie, ever since he nearly bled out on this floor, I've been kind of traumatized and would rather not come here unless it's absolutely necessary. Good thing we live on the island, and whenever we visit his parents, he's not in the mood to work.

Now, however, he thrusts me back into this ominous place, and even Kolya's legendary libido is shrinking as images of that day play in my head.

It was a long time ago, and we've come to terms with it. I even went to therapy with him for it, but no amount of therapy will erase the feeling of 'I'm losing him' that beat into my skull as I held his unresponsive body on the floor while his life essence poured out of him in sickening red.

But now, as he stands in front of me in his rumpled suit and with his glittery smile, those images slowly disappear.

He's here.

He'll always be fucking here.

He came back for me.

For *us*.

"What did you want to show me?" I ask with a note of sarcasm. "What's so important that you chose violence, aka cock-blocking us both for it?"

He clears his throat. "I thought since now we'll be starting the next chapter of our lives and moving to a new place, we'll need a painting for it."

"I already have my favorite painting of yours." I pull out my phone and show him the lock screen. "This is going in the living room so that it's the first thing everyone sees."

A look of adoration crosses his features. "In that case, let's put this one in the bedroom, then."

He pulls on a sheet that's covering a canvas, revealing a stunning piece of work. And it's not about the sharp details or earth-shattering beauty of what his hands are capable of.

It's the scene he chose to paint. Him sitting on my lap while I'm wearing the yellow-stitch mask. And he didn't paint his own mask.

It's from the first night we met.

The night after which I couldn't purge him from my mind even if I wanted to.

His expression in the painting isn't what I saw back then. I thought he was embarrassed or humiliated, but through his own eyes, he looks intrigued, confused, and most of all, aroused.

"Wow," I breathe out, actually glad he showed me this before the fuck fest that will totally happen in a few. "This is…wow."

"You like it?"

"I fucking love it, baby. Look at all those details." I step closer to take a better look. "Definitely going in the bedroom. Don't want anyone to see that expression on your face. It's only for me."

He chuckles, the sound light and contagious.

I smile back. "Why this scene, though?"

"It's the night I developed a crush on you. I thought it came afterward, but no, I was definitely intrigued by you from the beginning. I wanted to keep that feeling alive forever through this painting."

"You did such an awesome job. Man. Now, I don't know which one I want on my lock screen. What do you think…?"

I trail off when I face my lotus flower and he's on one fucking knee. What the…?

"That scene was our beginning, as unglamorous as it was. No matter how scared I was of you and everything you presented, I wouldn't have it any other way. You're the purest, most passionate soul I've ever met. You loved me when I didn't even like myself. You held me together when I was falling apart and helped me put myself back together one piece at a time until I became the man I am today." He reaches into his jacket and pulls out a dark-blue velvet box, then opens it to show two rings. "I love you more than words can describe and I'll be honored if you choose to spend the rest of your life with me so I can give back a fraction of what you've given me. Nikolai Sokolov, would you marry me—"

The words aren't fully out of his mouth when I fall to my knees in front of him and drag his lips to mine, kissing him like a fucking madman until I'm lost in him and he's breathing my air.

He wrenches his lips back but seals his forehead to mine. "Is that a yes?"

"Fuck yes, baby. I'll marry the fuck out of you and make you my husband today if you want."

His grin nearly blinds me as he slips the ring onto my finger. The inside is engraved with a fucking lotus flower and N X B.

"Good." He lifts my hand to his mouth and kisses my knuckles over the ring.

"I'm supposed to be the one who proposes," I grumble while slipping his ring onto his finger. "I hate you for beating me to this."

"You pursued me in the beginning. I had to be the one who proposed first."

I glide my hand across his nape and pull his forehead to mine again. His fingers stroke my hair as we breathe each other in.

This is the happiest moment of my life and I want to soak in it for as long as possible.

"The rest of our lives, huh, baby?"

He nods, lips curling into the most gorgeous smile. "The rest of our lives, baby."

"I wouldn't have it with anyone but you." My mouth reaches for his and I kiss him slower this time, taking my fill of him.

I love this man with everything I have and don't have.

I love him with my sane and insane parts.

He's my lotus flower.

My Prince Charming.

The love of my life.

Mine.

THE END

You can check out the audiobooks of the couples that appeared in this book:

Killian Carson & Glyndon King: *God of Malice*

Kyle Hunter & Rai Sokolov: *Throne Duet*

Levi & Astrid King: *Cruel King*

WHAT'S NEXT?

Thank you so much for reading *God of Fury*!
If you liked it, please leave a review.
Your support means the world to me.

If you're thirsty for more discussions with other readers of the
series, you can join the Facebook group, *Rina Kent's Spoilers Room*.

Next up is the story of Eli King & Ava Nash and the last book in the
Legacy of Gods Series, *God of War*.

ALSO BY RINA KENT

For more books by the author and a reading order, please visit:
www.rinakent.com/books

ABOUT THE AUTHOR

Rina Kent is a *USA Today*, international, and #1 Amazon bestselling author of everything enemies to lovers romance.

She's known to write unapologetic anti-heroes and villains because she often fell in love with men no one roots for. Her books are sprinkled with a touch of darkness, a pinch of angst, and an unhealthy dose of intensity.

She spends her private days in London laughing like an evil mastermind about adding mayhem to her expanding universe. When she's not writing, Rina travels, hikes, and spoils cats in a pure Cat Lady fashion.

Find Rina Below:

Website: www.rinakent.com

Newsletter: www.subscribepage.com/rinakent

BookBub: www.bookbub.com/profile/rina-kent

Amazon: www.amazon.com/Rina-Kent/e/B07MM54G22

Goodreads: www.goodreads.com/author/show/18697906.Rina_Kent

Instagram: www.instagram.com/author_rina

Facebook: www.facebook.com/rinaakent

Reader Group: www.facebook.com/groups/rinakent.club

Pinterest: www.pinterest.co.uk/AuthorRina/boards

Tiktok: www.tiktok.com/@author.rinakentt

Twitter: twitter.com/AuthorRina